About t

Alys Earl is a writer, storyteller and folklorist. They have performed on the Norwich and the Medway Arts scenes, but now live in the wilds of Suffolk. Speciality subjects include trivia about the medieval period, and the kind of fairy tales that give children bad dreams. For more information, see www.alys-earl.com

By the same author:

Scars on Sound

TIME'S FOOL

TIME'S FOOL

ALYS EARL

Unbound Digital

This edition first published in 2018

Unbound

6th Floor Mutual House, 70 Conduit Street, London W1S 2GF

www.unbound.com

ISBN (eBook): 978-1-912618-85-9
ISBN (Paperback): 978-1-912618-84-2

Design by Mecob

Printed and bound in Great Britain by Clays Ltd, Elcograf S.p.A.

To Mattie, myn owne soote leman

Dear Reader,

The book you are holding came about in a rather different way to most others. It was funded directly by readers through a new website: Unbound.

Unbound is the creation of three writers. We started the company because we believed there had to be a better deal for both writers and readers. On the Unbound website, authors share the ideas for the books they want to write directly with readers. If enough of you support the book by pledging for it in advance, we produce a beautifully bound special subscribers' edition and distribute a regular edition and e-book wherever books are sold, in shops and online.

This new way of publishing is actually a very old idea (Samuel Johnson funded his dictionary this way). We're just using the internet to build each writer a network of patrons. Here, at the back of this book, you'll find the names of all the people who made it happen.

Publishing in this way means readers are no longer just passive consumers of the books they buy, and authors are free to write the books they really want. They get a much fairer return too – half the profits their books generate, rather than a tiny percentage of the cover price.

If you're not yet a subscriber, we hope that you'll want to join our publishing revolution and have your name listed in one of our books in the future. To get you started, here is a £5 discount on your first pledge. Just visit unbound.com, make your pledge and type JULIAN18 in the promo code box when you check out.

Thank you for your support,

Dan, Justin and John
Founders, Unbound

'The vampire is prone to be fascinated with an engrossing vehemence, resembling the passion of love, by particular persons. It will never desist until it has satiated its passion... But it will, in these cases, husband and protract its murderous enjoyment with the refinement of an epicure, and heighten it with the gradual approaches of an artful courtship. In these cases it seems to yearn for something like sympathy and consent.'
— Sheridan Le Fanu, *Carmilla*

1. Anthem for Doomed Youth

I am no longer young... Moreover, the walls of my castle are broken; the shadows are many, and the wind breathes cold through the broken battlements and casements. I love the shade and the shadow, and would be alone with my thoughts when I may.
– Bram Stoker, *Dracula*

Beside him, Lucy's head hit the table with a quiet thud. It occurred to Steven this might be some sort of prompt.

'What I mean,' he said, raising his voice above the pub noise, 'is that knowledge is the antithesis of fear.'

Across the table, John stared into his pint with an expression that suggested he'd sooner be elsewhere – but who cared what John wanted?

'Bring it out in the open,' Steven made a dismissive sound, 'and, okay, while there's some evidence that Le Fanu...'

Lucy started to move her head in a slow, rocking motion, sending seismic ripples through John's beer. Steven snatched up his own glass before her convulsions sent it over the edge of the table. He took a drink. Opposite him, Sophia massaged her temples.

'Where was I?'

'You were shutting up,' Lucy said, her voice muffled by her hair.

'Le Fanu!'

'Steven,' said Sophia.

He tipped his glass in her direction and tried to arrange a smile on his face. It was difficult, as he had reached the stage where his flesh felt rubbery and uncooperative, where his fingers seemed to be moving without him instructing them.

'Please shut up, Steven.'

'I will not be censored,' he said, or maybe he shouted it, because a couple at the next table turned and looked at him in a bemused fashion. 'No,' he said more quietly, 'I shall not have my rights violated in this fashion. Le Fanu is very important.'

'So's my birthday,' said Sophia.

1

'And technically, that isn't until tomorrow.'

'Do you really believe all that?' said John.

Steven tried to trace back over the last few exchanges to establish some context for this remark, but drew a blank. 'All what?'

'All this ghost story bollocks.'

'Well, yes,' said Steven. 'Yes, I should hope so. I mean, it is sort of central to my dissertation, so I should really try to, shouldn't I?'

John stared at him as though he was being obtuse which, all things considered, was unjust.

'He meant, do you believe in ghosts,' Sophia explained.

'No one believes in ghosts.' Steven leaned back against the booth. 'That was my point.'

'So why bother?' said John, 'Why would you study something that you know doesn't exist?' And he had that smirk on his face, the point-scoring one.

A flare of sobriety. Steven picked over his words and finally said, 'In what context are we taking "know" here, John?'

'Oh, come on.'

'No, really. I'm interested.'

'Steven,' Lucy warned.

'No, wait. You're suggesting that I *know* ghosts don't exist?'

'You just said,' John insisted. 'You literally just told me that ghosts are a load of crap.'

Steven smiled what he hoped was a pained and disappointed smile. One of his lecturers used a smile like that, and it was utterly crushing. 'Don't believe I did.'

'Sophia, he did, didn't he? He just said that no one believed in ghosts.'

'John, it isn't important.' Sophia put her hand on his shoulder. The diamond in her engagement ring glinted, bright.

'Yes, I said no one believed in ghosts. That doesn't mean they don't exist.'

'Don't argue semantics,' said John.

'Do you even know what that means?'

'Steven,' said Lucy.

Yes, that probably was going a little far. Humour was advisable. He put on his best Van Helsing hock-German: 'I suppose now you do not believe in corporeal transference. No? Nor in materialisation. No? Nor in astral bodies…'

'What?'

'He's quoting,' said Sophia, with the trace of a smile. *Good.*

'No? Nor in the reading of thought. No? Nor in hypnotism…' He raised his glass. No one said anything. 'Oh, come on.'

'Charcot has proved that pretty well,' said Lucy, in a monotone.

'What?' said John, again.

'My point,' said Steven, and he brought his arm round in an expansive motion, almost spilling wine down his front, 'is that there are more things in heaven and earth, Horatio.'

'So you *do* believe in ghosts.'

'Bollocks, I do. No, I believe in the *possibility* of ghosts.'

John closed his eyes as though he had truly had enough of the evening, but, as Steven had already observed, no one gave a damn about John.

'Look, it's faulty thinking to assume we can answer that question with any certitude. Yes, ghosts are improbable. They are wildly implausible. But if we pause to consider the humble bumble bee,' he said, or tried to say. His mouth would not cooperate.

'The what?'

'A closed mind,' Steven told Sophia and Lucy, 'is a tragic thing to see in one so very young.' But that stopped Sophia smiling. She closed both hands around her wineglass and said nothing.

Stop now, part of him warned.

'I've not got a closed mind,' said John. 'I'm just being realistic. Look, if ghosts were real, science would have…'

'Science?' said Steven. 'Which one, John? Biology? Sophia's the resident expert on that. What's the view on ghosts, Sophia? Or maybe you wanted to hear from an astrophysicist? Or climatologist?' He swigged his wine, smirked. 'I dunno. Maybe sports science has a perspective.'

John mouthed 'God' with a hard exhalation of breath. 'What I mean is…' he started to say.

'What you mean,' Steven interrupted, 'is that you are willing to discount anecdotal evidence on the basis of prejudice before conducting rigorous research.'

'Ha. Says the atheist,' said Lucy.

'Oh, I'm quite willing to entertain the possibility of an omnipotent God. I just want fuck all to do with him.'

'Religion,' said Sophia. 'Yes. That's a nice, safe topic. Let's talk about religion instead.'

'No,' said Steven. 'No, I'm curious about this. You see, John, my unbelief is sturdy. I will entertain the possibility of every impossible thing. But if you brought me incontrovertible evidence of ghosties or ghoulies, it would not shake me. Real or not, they are too unlikely for me to trouble myself with fearing them.' He raised his hands dismissively. After a moment, Steven realised that his glass was now above his head. He rectified this and took a drink. 'You, though,' he wagged his finger at John, 'your unbelief is brittle because it's unreasoning. You refuse even to consider that ghosts exist. You'll fumble for logical explanations, but some stuff we can't explain yet. So, at the moment "science" fails you.' Carefully, Steven put his glass down, then slammed his hands together. 'Bam, the local spiritualist church has a new recruit.'

For a moment, John looked like he was about to tell him to fuck off, but he seemed to remember the occasion and swallowed the insult. After a minute, and quite calmly, he said, 'That's rubbish.'

'Prove it.'

John took a drink and gave a scornful laugh. 'Yeah. How am I supposed to do that?'

'Scientific method.'

'Steven,' said Lucy, for the final time that evening, 'do shut up.'

'No,' said Steven. 'We can do this. It's Hallowe'en. It's the perfect time for this.'

'That's not until next week.'

'Says the girl claiming tonight's her birthday? Come on. If Christmas starts in early November, you can give me a fortnight for Hallowe'en.'

'After my birthday,' she conceded, 'you can have Hallowe'en for as long as you like.'

He nodded consent. 'Alright. So. We find a haunted house. We take a shufti. We'll see who sees a ghost.'

'Steven, you know that isn't actually scientific method, right?'

'And I have the perfect place in mind,' he said, ignoring the birthday girl.

Lucy and Sophia exchanged a look and were clearly about to drag up that one particular and unedifying experience from their early adolescence.

'Don't worry, it's well inside the city.'

'Not if it's raining,' said Lucy at the same time as Sophia said, 'I'll kill you if there are nettles.'

They were never going to let him forget their visit to that bloody keep. 'I've learned my lesson,' he said.

'You never learn anything.'

'Oh, I'm sorry. Which one of us is in line for a first?'

Lucy and Sophia made the kind of hissing noises people make when they're not sober and are pretending you've annoyed them.

'This is a stupid idea,' said John.

'Yes,' said Steven, reasonably. 'I'm drunk.'

'Right, okay,' said John in a smug sort of way.

'Okay, what?'

'As in okay, you're just joking, then.'

'When have I ever passed up an idea just because it's stupid?'

'He has form,' Lucy explained. 'Ruined castle form.'

'Oh, you aren't serious?'

'Why?' said Steven with a wicked smile. 'John, are you scared of *ghosts*?'

Hallowe'en. Sophia let the crowbar hang from her hands as she watched Steven and John try to get past the gate. They had argued all the way up the road and hadn't stopped yet. The precise words were lost to the rush of traffic, but she could capture the low, constant murmur of Steven's sarcasm, punctuated by John's retorts.

She looked back to the road and saw that there was no cadre of police cars rushing towards them, sirens blaring. *Hardly surprising.*

'Do you think they're going to give up soon?' she asked Lucy.

'Probably.' Lucy's response sounded like autopilot, especially as, after a pause, she added, 'God, actually, no, I doubt it.' They stared at the gates, rusty and solid against a thin, October sky. 'Hope so though. It's freezing out here.'

Steven took the padlock in his hands and gave it what looked like an ironic tug. Suddenly distinct, his voice came to them. 'It appears to be rather locked.'

John shoved him out of the way and pulled on the lock – a lot harder if the clanking noises were anything to go by. As this had no apparent effect, he grabbed the gate and shook it.

Sophia pushed her free hand into her pocket. Steven had come through on the house, at least. No rain, and hardly a nettle in sight. Better: the diamond panes in the windows caught the light and threw it back gold, and the old bricks were dirty red. She had once imagined she would live in a house like this, with its winding corridors and thick stonework, with oak panelling and candle sconces, spiders and secret passageways. She smiled; places like this were owned by businessmen, old families or heritage charities. Finding one like this, in Romantic abandonment, complete with overgrown garden and grisly reputation, was more than fortunate. It was a godsend.

She saw John give the gates a sound kick. He called, 'Love, I could do with that crowbar.'

She glanced at Lucy. Only Steven had objected to the crowbar, and that had been because it was John's idea. But none of them had expected this little contest of machismo to get quite so far. Lucy shrugged and strode to the rescue. 'You having trouble there, boys?'

'Rather predictably, the gate has been locked.' Steven smiled, more superior than the circumstances justified. 'John seems to be advocating criminal damage.'

John took a breath that whistled over clenched teeth. 'Do you want to get in?'

'Naturally.' Steven looked at his hands and brushed the last traces of rust from them. 'I'm simply not inclined to be placed in custody.'

Sophia gave Steven a warning glance and slipped her hands over John's shoulders, feeling him tense then relax at her touch. She bit down on the surging rage within her and plastered her best friendly look upon her face as she cuddled up close to her fiancé.

Once, Lucy had described Steven and John's behaviour as the best unwitting double act she had ever seen. Sophia had never noticed any comedy value in it. Besides, Steven's behaviour was never unwitting. 'So, can we go home now?' she asked.

'Of course not,' Steven said. 'It all becomes far too interesting.'

When he said that, all John's uncertainty vanished. *Great.*

'This is ridiculous,' she said.

'You agreed at the time,' Steven said, grinning.

She eyed the chain on the gate, the crowbar and John. She needed to convince him not to use it, not least because she suspected bolt-cutters would be a more effective tool. Lucy, though, appeared to have caught whatever energy was egging Steven on, because she announced, 'They should be easy enough to climb.'

Sophia gave a despairing whimper.

True to her word, Lucy hauled herself up the wobbling structure. At the top of the gate she paused, then cursed. 'Ripped my sodding jeans. Be careful here, yeah? These spikes are sharp.' Once on the other side, she leapt down the few remaining feet, before turning and bowing. 'Piece of cake,' she cried, and blew them a kiss.

Refusing to be outdone, John followed her. Sophia watched. It was fine for Lucy, a shade under six foot and built like an Amazon, to say it was no problem, but Sophia was neither tall nor convinced.

Still, they'd done sillier things. Yes, she needed a boost to get started, but Steven obliged, and after that she was more concerned about tearing her clothes than breaking her neck. The only hairy moment was when Steven started to climb before she was fully over, and, safely on the other side, she gave him a look to make him understand it was not appreciated.

John was already striding towards the door, crowbar in hand, but Lucy had waited. As they joined her she bowed again and gestured for them to precede her. 'Lay on, MacDuff.' The quote was accurate, but perhaps irrelevant.

'What's it meant to be haunted by?' Sophia asked.

'No,' said Steven. 'That's bad ghost hunting. Searching out the sto-

ries influences your perceptions. Makes your testimony unreliable.'
He laughed. 'Besides, everything I did manage to find out was
depressingly vague. Place has a bad reputation from, oh, the *belle
époque*, or something. Your average post-Victorian spook, I'd guess.
War dead and abandoned brides. Anyway, how else was I going to
get you two to take a look at it?'

'Sophia!' said Lucy in a falsetto imitation of a child's voice. 'Lucy!
There's a castle! I promise.'

Sophia rubbed her arms at the memory of nettle stings, badly kept
footpaths and driving rain. She squeaked along in reply, 'It's on a *map*.'

'And it's *only* two kilometres…'

'Okay,' said Steven. 'I read the key wrong. I have apologised.
Often.'

'It'll be in my best man speech,' Lucy said.

'Change of plan. Sophia, you're the best man.'

'Oh, don't think I'll let you off.'

They had stopped walking, too busy reprising old roles. 'So, what?'
Lucy asked. 'No one's lived here since 1914?'

'No idea. Do you girls expect me to do everything? Glad you came,
though, right?'

'What's a spot of breaking and entering between friends?' Sophia
said, but Steven had a point. The thin, red bricks were tarred by pollu-
tion, but seemed to glow with some inner light. The walls were pitted
by time and acidity, the lines of the building delicate. The door itself
was scarred and handsome, a huge Gothic arch that looked almost
like a church door – complete with outsize keyhole. The handle was
smoothed by time and use.

John had already tried to open it and given it a further token shove.
Now, he was hefting the crowbar with a look of purpose in his eyes.
Steven ignored him, tracing his fingers over the worn carvings of the
doorjamb. 'You know, I think this might almost be an original fea-
ture.' Then he raised his voice, but did not spare John a glance as he
informed him, 'And if you even *think* about using that damned thing
on this woodwork, I'll call the police myself.'

Lucy smirked.

'Right, so how are we meant to get in, then?' John asked.

Steven tried the handle.

'Yeah, I have actually done that.'

Steven nodded and twisted the handle beyond its initial resistance. It made two protesting, clunking noises. He set his shoulder to the door and pushed hard. It scraped the floor for a moment, then opened. 'Hinges had fallen a little. You don't visit many churches, do you, John?'

He snorted. 'Didn't think they'd have you.'

'Architectural interest,' Steven replied, striding into the hall. 'Not exactly your field, I suppose.'

Lucy touched Sophia's arm briefly, but she was too busy glaring at John to take much notice. She clenched her teeth. When he tried to put his arm around her a few seconds later, she shrugged him off and went into the house.

A moment later, John called in, 'Uh, sorry Steve. About that.'

'How kind.'

Oh, perfect.

Then, determined, she took stock of her surroundings. Away from the glow of streetlights that began to patch the night, the inside of the house was dim. The room she stood in was wide, and by the little light that bled through the windows, she could make out the rough shape of a flight of stairs. Dotted about were the pale, shrouded remains of furniture left to rot beneath dustsheets. She shivered and her annoyance seeped away.

When John touched her shoulder, she jumped. He put his lips close to her ear. 'Fucking spooky in here, isn't it?'

She considered telling him exactly what she thought of that kind of prank, but let him put his arms around her and kiss the top of her head before pulling away. Steven and Lucy loitered by the staircase, looking as if they had reluctantly decided against climbing it.

Steven turned to them. 'Well? What do you think?'

'Haunted,' Lucy affirmed. 'Can we go home now?' But she made no motion towards the door.

'Do you not want to have a look around, then?'

'You and old buildings, eh? You coming, Sophia?'

Sophia turned to John who still hung back, the crowbar dangling heavy from his hand. She tried, by glances, to communicate with him, but she could not read his face in the half-light. She considered saying that perhaps it would be best if they all went home. After all, she was the only one with any common sense.

But she did not want to leave. For years now, she had been the quiet one, the sensible one. It was her job to end this. But the only reason she would go now was if she were bored, if she thought there was no point in staying any longer.

And there was a point. In the dust, in the dusk, she felt something within her exhale, uncurl a little. She wrapped her arms around herself and stared up at the shadows that leaned in from the walls. Here, the main road was a distant whisper, accentuating the silence. A frisson crept over her. She thought of graveyards, of old yew trees, of the peace of centuries. She shook her head, but only to feel her hair brush against her neck.

Then, more decisive, she walked over to where Lucy was beginning to try a couple of internal doors. The first was locked or jammed, but the second opened without any particularly ominous creaks. Steven hesitated on the threshold for a moment to get assent from herself and Lucy before turning around to John, who hung back, increasingly indistinct in the failing light, the crowbar in one hand.

'Well?' Steven asked in an exaggerated tone.

The figure that was John shrugged. 'Look...' he said, and Sophia recognised his let's-be-realistic voice.

'Don't tell me you're having second thoughts, John. Not at *this* late stage.'

'I was just... oh, fine. Forget it. Let's find some *ghosts*.'

They trooped into the new room. It was almost dark by now, the sun having sunk over the horizon, but here the quality of the darkness was different; larger windows faced the moon and the lights of the city in the river valley. The walls were panelled, the floor bare tiles. A huge, empty hearth yawned across most of one wall. There was the smell of dust and time and mouse droppings. Here, too, pieces of furniture were jumbled and huddled against the walls, shrouded in dust-sheets. Filling the centre of the room was a table left uncovered save for the tattered lace of cobwebs and deep dust.

Sophia walked over to it and traced her fingers across the surface, then stopped, thinking things like *fingerprints*. There was an awful lot of furniture for a derelict house. She bit her tongue, not wanting to be the first to call a halt, turning to John for reassurance. But even in the minutes they had been there, it had grown darker, and she could hardly make out his features.

It would only get darker still. She could not see the far end of the room any longer. The shadows lengthened, grew thicker. She could just about make out the white, indeterminate shapes of the draped furniture, the darkness looming in from the corners. She noticed that her friends were no longer striding confidently across the floor; that they too were lingering, were quiet.

Their faces were white blurs – they could have been anyone, could have been ghosts themselves.

A car roared past on the road outside, headlights cutting an arc across the sky. She jumped. Once it had passed, the silence became more intense. She told herself to stop being silly, to put on her torch and banish her nervousness, but she had a child's fear of the light marking her out in the darkness, making the blackness around her so intense she would not be able to see what was hiding there.

A primal unease at the dark was clenching her stomach. Her shoulders tensed. She pressed closer to the edge of the table, biting her tongue once more, trying by pain to master her fear. But when John put his arm around her, she nearly screamed. She pressed against him, even though she was annoyed that he might think she needed his support. She squeezed his hand as if she were reassuring him, not herself.

A creak overhead.

There are sounds old houses make when they settle into themselves, their timbers swelling and shrinking. This was not that kind of sound. This was the sound of wood crying out under sudden, definite pressure, the sound of movement and agency. In the silence that followed, Sophia could not hear her heart; certainly she did not breathe. Seconds stretched. Something tightened in her until it was almost painful.

Then came the sound of a foot scuffing old, dusty floors. The sound of a person crossing the rooms above them, then upon the hollow wood of the stairs. It was worse when that steady tread dulled once again, for then it was in the hall, coming inexorably towards them. Sophia drew in breath until her chest was stretched and tight. The footsteps were not the timorous patter of someone who was afraid, nor the clamour of someone who had no more right to be there than themselves. They were firm, regular, slow.

Before they reached the door, she straightened her spine.

Into the paler rectangle of the door stepped a slim, long shape. Dark; it was a dark shape, dark clothes and hair, white blur of face. For a moment, they all stood frozen, unspeaking. A voice said, 'Ah. I do apologise. I was not aware I had visitors.' And it was level, cool and smooth. Utterly unafraid.

Sophia waited for John's sober apologies, for Lucy's gift of the gab, but it was her own voice that answered. 'We, uh, we thought the house was deserted. We'll leave, if you like.' Then, as though her tongue were her own again, she added, 'Sorry.'

The room filled with light. Dazzled, blinded, Sophia waited for the worst.

'There,' said the voice. 'Ancient circuitry, but it appears to be working.'

She blinked and blinked again, her eyes refusing to adjust.

'Pray, forgive the confusion,' the voice went on. It sounded young; implausibly young. 'I have recently inherited this house. My grandfather's. I was rather curious about the old place.'

'Ah. Yes,' Steven blundered in, far too late. 'We – we do apologise. We came here as a bet.' He gave an awkward, faux-sophisticated laugh. 'A dare, I suppose. The… your house is magnificent. Beautiful. It's just we thought it was abandoned, you see. Derelict, otherwise we wouldn't have—' He seemed to realise how that would sound, and interrupted himself. 'The door was unlocked. It was only the gate we, uh… There was a dare about a haunted building, you see and,' another pause, as though the whole debacle had not been his idea, 'not that I – we – believe in ghosts of course, but, well, this place has a reputation, I mean, unfounded, I'm sure, but…'

'I'm sorry,' said Lucy, stepping between Steven and the stranger. 'He's an idiot. But we are very sorry about all this.'

'No.' It was almost a whisper, almost lost in the traffic sounds and

the creaks of an old house settling. 'No, please, you are most welcome.'

'Sorry,' Steven said, appearing to get a grip upon himself. 'We…
we haven't damaged anything, I trust? The door was unlocked.'

She saw him now, the man in the doorway. He was not so very tall
as she had thought. He had a pinched, delicate face and he stood still,
very still. With a slow, considered movement, he bowed his head, as
though he were hurt or ashamed. 'It is of no matter. Please.' After a
moment of silence where the room seemed huge and cold and lit too
brightly, he came towards her with slow, deliberate steps. 'I am called
Julian.'

But the words were addressed to John; it was into John's eyes that
he looked, to John that he extended his hand. Sophia stiffened away
from her fiancé's clutching arms so as not to appear a complete wimp.

'I'm delighted to make your acquaintance,' the stranger said, all stiff
formality. *Keeping things between the boys, are we?* Sophia thought, and,
as they shook hands and John introduced himself, added to herself,
Upper class twat.

'Sorry about,' said John, like the rest of them, unable to stop apolo-
gising.

'It is of no import. Please. This house has been empty too long.' The
stranger turned to her then, with wide dark eyes and utter solemnity.
She fought the urge to laugh at him. 'And, you, my dear, are…?'

So she met his gaze fiercely, held out her hand and said, 'Sophia.'

His fingers were so cold she almost jumped, but she would not
give him that satisfaction. She was about to move her hand briskly,
to show how hard she could grip, but the stranger held her fingers so
very lightly and did not shake her hand. Instead, he bowed, bowed as
though he did it without thought, as though it were the most natural
thing in the world.

And Sophia could not breathe. Thrown, unsure, embarrassed, she
could not move.

Before his lips brushed her knuckles, he seemed to catch himself, to
recoil, and he stopped and looked up into her eyes.

There they stood, his touch not pressing, not painful, his lips an
inch from her skin. She looked into his face and read nothing there,

nothing that she could understand. Her skin grew hot and she longed to look away, but she would not allow herself to be the one who dropped her gaze.

Beside her, John shifted, but no one spoke, nobody broke the moment. It could not have been long, could only have been mere seconds, but the time yawned around her, infinite.

She clenched the muscles in her hand, afraid once more. As though that was his cue, Julian lowered his mouth. And perhaps after all that, she expected something lascivious, something gloating, but it was barely more than the touch of cool lips, so swift as to be impersonal.

Then he straightened and released her, saying, brisk and impersonal, 'Greek for wisdom, I believe?'

Sophia stood, still trapped, with no idea how to respond.

'They call me Lucy,' came a call from across the room, and there she stood, her hand thrust out before her expectantly.

'I am charmed, my dear Lucy,' said the stranger, and his voice changed again. No longer strange gravity, not a touch of the arrant toff, but something playful. He repeated the performance with rather more smoothness and *élan* than he had accorded her. Of course, Lucy gloried in it, bobbing her head, tossing her mane of hair, looking less like the cat who had got the cream than the one who'd taken the Sunday joint, and probably the goldfish, too. The atmosphere, if there had been an atmosphere, relaxed. Sophia rubbed her knuckles against the ball of her thumb and watched as Steven gave his name too before shaking the stranger's hand.

'I am very pleased to meet you, Steven.' Julian did not release his grip.

'Ah. Yes. I mean, likewise. And, um, we're very grateful you have been so understanding of… well. You've been terribly kind.'

Julian was still holding Steven's hand. 'It is nothing. I trust you will stay a while.'

No one replied to that, and Sophia hoped they were all sufficiently well brought up not to glance around at the dust and general dilapidation.

'Please,' the man made a dismissive gesture, finally releasing Steven and seeming to falter again, 'as my first guests here. Perhaps a glass of wine?'

Steven seemed about to say something but remembered to shut up before Lucy had to poke him in the ribs. As John jostled her towards the door, Sophia scrambled through her brain for a polite response.

The stranger laughed. 'Or another night, perhaps. When it is...' And he paused, as though the right word escaped him. Sophia did not suggest, *structurally sound*. '...cleaner. Please. You are all most welcome.'

'Yes,' Steven replied. 'That – that would be lovely. We're sorry we—'

'Yeah,' Lucy interrupted. 'Yeah. We should leave you in peace. Thanks for...'

'It is nothing. It has been a pleasure. Let me bring you to the gate.' He gave her a sly little smile. 'I'm sure I can manage to unlock it for you.'

Sophia winced. She suspected they deserved rather more than that one stab of sarcasm. Still, they made polite noises about not wanting to be any trouble, about really, how terribly sorry they were, and how he mustn't bother, as though it would no imposition on anyone from them to scramble over the gate again. All this, the man ignored. As he slipped the padlock from the chain, he turned and said, low and intense, 'I do hope that I might see you again. You are always welcome.'

And in that moment, Sophia knew that he spoke to her, and to her alone. She stood, staring at him, trying to think of something to say, but before she managed a reply, he said, 'Fare you well,' and let them pass.

Alone in the chill dark, the creature paced. Rosemary and honey. Honey and rosemary.

An innocent boy, so clever and beautiful and easily overcome.

And the woman. The woman who wore a perfume that plunged into him, that drew from him something which should have been long dead. The ghost of it lingered, beneath the chemical scents the

15

others had worn. He could taste her, still, in his mouth. He sucked it from his tongue. Honey. Rosemary.

Blood.

Thirst. He had left it too long, had been too assured. Images flashed in his mind, those bright, young people, skin tearing beneath his kiss, life ripped from some screaming soul, drowning in scents of honey and rosemary. Of blood.

A long shudder ran through him. *No. No.*

The creature raised hands over his face and tried to think of coldness, of sterility, of peace. He tried to think of hunger and its cruel allure, but tonight that would not aid him. Tonight he would kill.

2. Undisclosed Desires

Even pain may become a pleasure if it saves one from the shallow monotony of everyday life
– Anon, 'The Mysterious Stranger'

John pulled his arm tighter around Sophia as they walked away down the road. Now his heartbeat was getting back to normal, he noticed that he was horny. Ten minutes ago, he'd still been expecting police cars and sirens, thinking it wasn't possible they had got off that lightly. Now all he could think about was getting laid.

He leaned over and kissed the top of her head, pulling her against him. Her breasts were soft and tempting, but he didn't snog her. It was way too cold for that kind of messing about, anyway. He picked up his pace a bit. The sooner they got home, the better.

But she pulled out from his grasp, dragging her feet. He turned. She had stopped walking and had one hand against her lips, a knuckle in her mouth. He had a sudden image of her, derived from far too many films, as a shy librarian, all prim and understated until she unbuttoned the shirt, or let down her hair down…

'John?'

'Yeah, love?'

'Oh, it's nothing.'

He waited for her to catch up, then he kissed her, leaning down, hands in the small of her back, pressing his hard-on against her stomach. First she pulled away, then relaxed and put her head against his chest. His toes, his fingers started to go numb. 'Come on, let's get home.'

'Sure,' she said, but again, she dawdled. She was frowning. He wondered if she was pissed off with him.

'Sorry about, you know, this evening. I mean if I…'

'What? Oh, no. Sorry.' She frowned again, rubbing her knuckles, looking at them, not at him. 'No. No, you didn't. I was miles away.' Then Sophia laughed and started walking. 'We were bloody lucky, you know.'

He didn't want to think about that. He had never been able to handle trouble. Even when he'd been a kid and his mates had been taking the piss and giving the teachers lip, all he'd been able to do was sit there, petrified.

'I mean,' she prompted, 'it was really decent of him. To let it go like that.'

'Yeah,' he said, but it wasn't decent. If John had heard someone snooping around his place at night, he wouldn't have gone down to talk to them unless he had a gun, or was a taekwondo champion or something. People who broke into houses were psychos, burglars. A normal person didn't mess with that.

There had been something else about that guy, too, something John had not liked. 'He was weird, though, wasn't he?'

'Hmm?' She shrugged. 'Oh, Julian?'

'Yeah,' he said, feeling peeved, though he didn't know why. 'I mean, you know. Big empty house, and there he is, skulking about like the Phantom of the bloody Opera.'

She said nothing, carried on walking and staring at her hands.

He tried again, harder. 'And you know, that way he was talking, wasn't it a bit...?' He started to ham it up a little. 'I mean, weren't you worried he was going to go for our necks?' He made claws of his hands, gave an awkward laugh. 'Like "I vont to suk your blood!"' He grabbed her shoulders, waited for her to crack a grin. Anything. He breathed out hard, his breath steaming. 'You okay, love?'

'Sorry. Sorry, yeah. Just a bit cold. You know.' And she shivered, as if she needed to prove it. He put his arm round her and she shrugged it off. 'Sorry,' she said again. 'I just – I dunno. I feel bad laughing at him. I mean, we could be in really deep shit right now.'

'Nah, I know,' he said as he put his arm back around her, 'but he was fucking weird.'

'He was a little... strange.' She frowned again.

He kissed her on the cheek, and she looked up at him, surprised. Her face was wide, pale and pretty. Her perfume was rich and sweet. He felt himself smile. *Home,* he thought, *we're going home to the big double bed and the central heating.* His mind flashed back to that godawful crumbling pile. He almost pitied the poor sod for having inherited such a crummy heap. It'd be *years* before the place was anything like liveable.

Their flat was warm and clean, and he and Sophia were going to be spending the night there. Alone.

As he walked he ran his hand over her shoulder, down her back. 'What've you got on tomorrow, love?'

'Hmm? Not a lot. Bit of lab work, couple of lectures; then I should probably hit the library.'

His hands reached her hips, the curve of her arse. He slipped them under her jumper, under her shirt. Her skin was hot and it went to goose pimples at his touch. They both stopped walking and he leaned down to kiss her. 'So, it's not like you need to get up early or anything?'

'Not particularly, no. Wh...'

He kissed her, long and slow, walking his hands up her back, snagging them under the straps of her bra. He pulled her closer to him, and when they stopped kissing, held her there. 'You know I love you, right?' Said through clenched teeth, through the pain of his erection. She nodded, tried to move away, but he held her tight.

And she laughed. 'It's going to be real challenge walking like this.'

Steven lounged on his bed, drinking wine and only half watching the credits roll. All around him leered the red-eyed, bloodstained faces of the undead. They glared from posters, DVD boxes and from behind the clear plastic packaging that contained articulated toys of the kind collected by children and the obsessed. Every other available space and surface was covered with books, DVDs, videos, more books, and the occasional empty coffee cup. The film that was playing was Hammer's 1958 take on *Dracula*.

Just seeing Kensington Gore splash a coffin lid kindled in Steven a warm and familiar glee. He loved them all, the dark, suspense-filled yarns, the Technicolor gore-fests. Adored the gloating, fascinating villains, the gloriously anachronistic sets, the occasional inexplicable armadillo. Of course, he had his standards – if it were shot on a shoe-string budget that was good. If it were made before 1979, better still.

And if it had vampires in it, well, that was just perfect. The gods of his private pantheon were Lugosi, Cushing and, above all, Lee.

The *Dracula* tonight was a bit of a tradition. He had watched it every Hallowe'en since he had first seen it on a black-and-white television set during a sleepover at Lucy's house, when they'd both been awkward pre-teens back in their hometown; and late-night horror reruns still had the thrill of the illicit. The next day he had walked into town with all his saved-up pocket money and bought a copy from a second-hand video store. He had not been able to watch it for three weeks, not until his parents had gone out and left him alone in the house. It had lain in wait, almost burning a hole in the mattress under which it had been hidden. If anything, it was even better the second time around.

But tonight the sound track was muted and he looked at the cheap digital camera on his bedside table as often as at the screen.

That house tonight was supposed to have been empty.

It should have been empty for a very long time.

In the two years he had lived in Barchester he had never seen any sign it was inhabited. No one he had spoken to could remember when someone had last lived there. It was Ray, his boss, who had told him how, when he was a kid, everyone had said the place was haunted.

'So, no one has lived there for, what, twenty years?'

Ray had shrugged and continued to stick '3 for £20' stickers on some of the DVDs. 'Guess so. Wouldn't credit the ghost story, though. That's just something kids say. Tax reasons, more likely.'

And Steven had nodded, inclined to agree.

When he had checked at the library, however, he had found there was a ghost story attached to the place. Not much of one – something about mysterious deaths, a young man going mad – but enough to convince him it was ripe for a bit of exploration.

He remembered the panic at the footsteps and pulling out the camera, blindly hitting *record*. He had heard Lucy take a step towards him, had wondered if he were more afraid that this was a ghost, or the owner of the house.

In his room, he hit *play*. On the camera's tiny screen, he saw the indistinct movement of a small, dark shape in the gloom.

He remembered time stretching, how only the growl of traffic had made him sure he had not gone deaf, had not been deafened by the roaring in his ears.

They shouldn't even have been able to break in. That they had got so far was just a testament to John's excessive stubbornness. It was the sort of dare that never usually got carried out.

Still, just because he believed nothing would come of it did not mean that he had skimped on the research. He had even done a bit of snooping around the property in preparation for this evening. Yes, someone clearly looked in occasionally, but it was locked and shuttered. There had been no signs of life.

That man – Julian – should not have been there. Besides, it was *Hallowe'en*, for goodness' sake. Who cared what rubbish he fed John? Steven himself drew the line at such mystical nonsense.

He paused the clip, restarted it. Darkness, movement. A mumble of sound. Sudden light. He felt something in his stomach pulse, urgent and acidic. Not even the grainy footage could obscure that slim, dark form, and from that, it was only a step of memory to recall a Beardsley pen-sketch face. And the presence of the man, the kind one associated with martial arts experts, or an actor who could stand upstage right and never say a word and still command the entire theatre.

Steven played the footage again, trying to turn the volume up, but any sound remained as indistinct as music from a passing car.

That voice...

But the voice had been wrong, too.

It was the kind one heard in radio dramas in the role of an Oxbridge professor or an amateur sleuth; a voice actor's voice, the sound of someone a little too worn, a little too fat to land a television role. Of course it was lovely, but coming from that slim, pale, *pretty* man...

No. You do not do this.

He watched the snippet once again, and his memory rushed to supply the flawless white skin, the delicate, wanton mouth. That was the worst of it, the way his own lips, his own words had become clumsy. Steven took another mouthful of wine, as if to swallow that sense of indefinable mortification.

And fear.

Because Steven had seen other men look at Lucy in that way, with that same chill, focused desire. It had snatched his breath, left him gasping. He reached over to press *play* once again…

No.

With his index finger, he stabbed the button. *Delete.*

Yes, he thought, *I'm sure.*

He put the camera down and drained his glass. It was probable that he would never see Julian again.

On screen, in Dracula's library, Christopher Lee's portrayal of the Count bared glistening fangs. Alone in his room, Steven restored the sound, crossed his arms over his chest, and lay back to watch the film.

The creature returned as the city clocks slipped past midnight into a new day. Once, the passing hour would have caused bells to peal. He felt as though he were a bell himself, recently struck. His lips were trembling, his whole body trembling, every inch of his skin alive and aware. The silk and wool and linen of his clothes caressed him, the leather of his boots cradled his feet, the brush of hair upon his face was a kiss. Every few moments the aftertaste would hit him and a tremor of pleasure would rob him of thought. He gave a soft moan.

But would it not have been finer if there had been hands clutching his throat, a caress that became desperate pleading. It would have been better if the blood had been rich with arousal, if the skin had been slick and salt with kisses and with sweat…

No.

Police forces, careful documents, mass media had buried the days when he could slip in and out of bedchambers, in and out of lives. Had banished, too, his violent hunts, the days when bloody murder raised no more than local panic. So many pleasures lost.

On his threshold, the creature stopped, appalled. This anonymity, cold as it might be, was the path he had chosen. With blood coming slow and soft to his tongue, he need not kill. With their wrist or head cradled in his arms, he was a tender monster, a night's shadow. His victims slept on, unaware. If they slipped into death, they were lulled by dreams and he could glory in their passing and not despise himself.

The creature looked to nails that were not stained with blood, wiped lips that were immaculate and clean. So it had come. Death had lost its sweetness. Whatever pleasure he felt, whatever satiety, it was not enough.

The house smelled of his young intruders, smelled still of honey and of rosemary.

Yet it had not been her who had drawn him. No. It had been the boy.

They had woken him before the sun set, bickering along the path to his door. Tired and tried by his journey, the creature had lain among the crates and detritus where he had made his resting place, and resolved to let them have their prank and depart. It would not be long before the house's reputation made them afraid, until their boredom drove them away. In the old solar, he had lain still with his melancholy, listening, waiting.

And the voice had called him like a clarion. So exquisite, so uncertain, so convinced that it hid its uncertainty behind verbal games. And so very young.

Like the quaking of unsettled earth, the sound of it had moved him. Had the creature not always sought the company of such men? Of clever boys barely awake to world's size and indifference, of lonely boys whose fear drew them to seek his attentions? Of boys who would begin to reflect him and force him to watch his own movements in the dark mirror of their purity?

He had known, even then, that he must not succumb.

At every step across the floor, on each stair he descended, the creature had known that he must let this foolishness alone. That the price of going forward was one he knew too well, one that was too great.

Yet perhaps the dance would be different this time. Perhaps this child alone would neither mimic nor condemn, perhaps he might show a moment of compassion to salve the solitude the creature felt on rising each night.

And in his longing, he forgot the sheer weight of his curse.

Honey. Rosemary.

Blood.

But he had not harmed them. Hadn't they gone freely from his house, scarcely touched? Might he not, therefore, brush against their brightness once more before he let them go?

Never. The creature clenched his fists, sharp nails making his skin rend, tear. It had taken only one taste of her blood, one long press of that young man's hand to shatter his abstinence. That, if nothing else, should tell him to leave before friendship drew him in beyond hope of release. He must go before he began to feel, to recall.

Because that perfume, sweet and herbal over the scents of hair and sweat and sex...

No.

Or perhaps that lovely boy with his stooping height, with the freckles that sat beneath his skin as though waiting to bloom at the touch of the sun...

Standing motionless in hollow, dusty rooms, the creature raised his head, decided.

He would depart, go to some bleak and uninhabited place where he would not be haunted by young clever faces, by pounding veins. There, he would find silence, solitude and cold. Perhaps he would even find some peace.

And when the girl had died, along with her wise young friend, he could return home. He had no place in their guiltless, modern lives.

It was not too late. He would go.

Sophia lay awake and listened as something electronic clicked on and a low hum began to fill the flat. The noise invaded the quiet of the bedroom, as did the rush and growl of passing traffic or the occasional group of drunkards lurching by, laughing, singing, fighting. She closed her eyes and waited for sleep to come. It did not.

Bugger.

She tried not to watch the numbers on the alarm clock flicker upwards, tried not to roll around or steal the covers or throw them off. She had done all that. It had not helped. It never helped.

But neither did lying very still, hoping she might just catch herself unaware and doze off.

Sleep. She wanted sleep. And sex, of course.

She exhaled sharply, rolled on to her side and out from under the duvet. *Damn.*

Everything itched. Her back was slick with cold sweat. Sleep would not come now. She knew this by the fluttering in her stomach, the churning in her head.

John lay beside her. Even lit by the green glow of the alarm clock, he was handsome. He was the kind of person eyes followed, the kind the girls on her course had crushes on. The kind of person who, at school, would never have looked twice at a plain little tomboy like her.

She knew she should feel lucky, gratified.

Self-pity is not going to help. She rolled over once more, burying her face in her pillow, clenching her teeth.

Well, can you suggest something that might?

Masturbating, certainly, was no good. It either got her far too worked up to sleep, or worse, would make her so horny that she would try to wake him, suggest doing it again. If she was lucky, he would ignore her, roll over and go back to sleep, because then she would just be lying awake, rejected and self-doubting. It would be worse if he woke up because then they would have sex again, and she would end up back where she started.

This was stupid. John was kind, considerate, generous. He always asked her whether she had come. He didn't seem to mind that she acted like the world should be gratified because she had tied her hair back or bothered to wear perfume. He had noticed her – small, dark and unremarkable Sophia – even though she had been standing next to Lucy.

So what the hell is wrong with me?

It's just, her mind groped for reasoning, *it was just…*

It was just that she didn't like the way he smelled anymore. Most nights, now, he smelled of beer or cigarettes.

Sophia had never liked beer. Back when he had been a student they had been too broke to buy more than one bottle, so he had shared her wine. Before they had lived together, the nights he had spent on the lager were the ones he had spent with his mates.

Now, even on nights when he stayed sober or stayed at home, she could trace the smell of sour hops and yeast on him. It permeated his breath, his hair, his clothes. And every time she smelled it there was a little recoil in her. These days, that was enough to turn her off. She would think about her coursework, about what she was cooking that night, or even whether she'd forgotten to buy washing-up liquid. Then she would realise that he was coming and she'd got nothing out of it. Again.

Or worse, she would fake it so that he knew it was fine to come, so that it would be over quickly. Like tonight.

She hated this, hated these little betrayals, but all she needed was time. They would get past this bad patch. She loved John. She told herself again and again, *I love him.*

The problem was probably her anyway. There was just something that needed rewiring inside her mind, something that she could sort out, something she could fix. Still, when he had said, 'Love you,' and kissed her, and fallen asleep, she had felt a rush of anger, hard, deep and inexplicable.

A small, mean part of her wanted to kick him awake, share out the suffering, but she repressed it. *Think of something else.*

Hallowe'en. Steven's festival, really. She had never bothered with it, letting it vanish underneath post-birthday hangovers. So, it had been spent working at uni, hiding from the trick-or-treaters. Then the whole stupid business of the haunted house. The break-in. That strange young man: Julian.

The knuckles on her right stung and she sucked at the skin there. There was a roughness, the faintest suggestion of a scab.

Must have got a papercut. She reopened the wound with her teeth, tasted blood. *How did I get that?* Sleep hovered near her. She tried to relax, go with it, not jolt herself awake by concentrating too hard. *That must have been where he kissed me… same finger… strange. Strange manners. Kissing my hand…*

She remembered the coolness of his lips, how his fingers had held her lightly, as though he'd been balancing an egg.

Strange, the thought slipped across her mind, just as she fell into sleep, *being kissed. It's not happened in so long. No one kisses me. No one except Steven. Or John.*

3. The Hardest Way

Our shows are more than will; for still we prove
Much in our vows, but little in our love.
– William Shakespeare, *Twelfth Night*

Sophia should have been on a high. Her assignment was done and, for a little while, her time was her own. Tonight she was taking back her library books and meeting Steven and Lucy for celebratory drinks in the union bar.

Everything should have been peachy. But she had not taken the weather into account.

There had been a cold snap the previous night and now, instead of rain, there was sleet. It came gusting down on a bitter, northerly wind, gluing her hair to her face, drenching her thick, winter coat. Damp as she might be, her several layers kept all of her too warm – except for her hands and her face.

Her umbrella was thrust out into the wind and kept some of the ice water from reaching her. It did make walking difficult, though, especially as it stopped her seeing where she was going. She bundled on thinking, *Sod it. Everyone else can bloody well get out of my way.*

Every tenth pace, she twisted her shoulder bag behind her where it slapped, wet and bulky, against her arse. Every twentieth step or so she switched the hand which held the massive carrier bag of books. It was cold, miserable work and she wanted to give up.

Three things stopped her from turning back: the thought of the huge pile of library fines if she didn't get the books back tonight; the thought of the union pub at the end of it all; and the fact it was only a half-hour walk to the uni. Even with a storm like this blowing, even when it was dark and cold and she was carrying eight or nine kilos of books, it should only take thirty minutes. Sophia was damned if she was not going to do it in that time.

Pace, pace, pace, twist, pace, pace, pace, she counted in her head, and gritted her teeth. *I should just – switch and twist – have caught… the bloody... bus.* She looked like a drowned rat, her face flushed, her breath coming in gasps. The carrier bag gave a lurch.

She picked up her pace. Before leaving the flat she had thought about putting the books into one of those big jute bags but had looked at the weather and opted to stick with polythene. *Idiot.*

'Don't split,' she whispered as she strode onwards, hoping she was not going to walk into anything. 'Please. Don't split. Don't you bloody dare. It's not far. Come on. Come on. Please, God, don't split.'

But one bag handle stretched and came away, taking the entire side of the damned bag with it. An unbound sheaf of lecture notes glued themselves to the grimy pavement. Library books and note books sprawled around her.

Sophia stood for a moment just staring at it. 'Oh shitting fuck,' she said, very quietly. Then, holding the brolly as best she could, she knelt down to assess the damage.

She felt like she was about to cry. Had she been in less of a bloody-minded mood she might have done so. She took a deep breath and looked at the books again. *Right. Let's try not to lose the umbrella.*

'Sophia, my dear, you appear to be in need of some assistance.' The voice took her by surprise. She had not heard anyone approach. Still, it was just like Steven to stand by affecting a plummy accent when what she really needed was a hand.

She glanced round with an amiable, 'Shut up, you bastard,' already forming on her lips. Then froze. 'Oh, hi, Julian.' A moronic, apologetic grin spread across her face. 'Plastic-bag trouble.'

From the angle she was at, she could see his black greatcoat, his black boots and the way he was, without being asked, holding an enormous black umbrella over the pair of them. He looked annoyingly unaffected by the weather as he knelt beside her. 'I assume some help is required.' He began to pick up the books and stack them in size order, stopping to glance at the title page.

Sophia looked over at the book he held – *Neotropical Savannas and Seasonally Dry Forests*. Dear Christ. She felt a rush of envy towards Steven, who could tote his course books to the pub without looking like a complete geek. 'I'm just taking them back to the library.' She made a grab at the notes.

'You are a conservationist?'

'Biologist. It's for "Plant Systematics".' What she had meant to say was that he was being too kind, that she could honestly manage and there was no need for him to be a knight in shining armour or anything. Instead, she found herself saying, 'Normally, I'm a fauna girl, but this is... it's really interesting, actually.' Finished with the notes, she reached out to start her own stack of books, only to find that Julian was holding them all. Internally she cursed. 'Well, to me anyway.'

'And to myself. Life is a fascinating subject. Especially if one is something of an outsider to it.'

She smirked. 'Are you trying to convince me you're some sort of tragic loner?'

'A recluse, merely.' He rose, his movement was graceful and there was something arch in his tone.

She stood, too. 'Good. I don't hold with the Byronic type.'

He laughed and started walking, still holding her books. 'How could you charge me with such a thing? And on so slight an acquaintance.'

She hurried to catch up. 'I might be a biologist, but I know my Romantics and I won't stand for it.'

'I consider myself duly warned. If I feel a heroic couplet coming on, rest assured I will absent myself from your presence.'

His umbrella was large enough for two, curving down around them, making a comfortable space in the storm. She followed his example, standing straight and ignoring the wind. 'Let me guess, you were a literature student.'

'Unfortunately, no. But you, I take it, are studying?'

She hovered and half gestured for him to hand her the books. 'Yes. At the university.'

'Postgraduate, or...?'

'Undergrad. Final year. Look, thanks so much for the help, but really—'

'Please. You are walking to the university?'

'Well, yes, but—'

'And I am travelling the same way. Now, were you in possession of another bag, or indeed, if I had one about my person, I would happily spare you the embarrassment and let you proceed with as much endeavour as you felt necessary. But I do not. Without one, the only way you might continue alone would be if you had another arm concealed about your person.' He paused. Sophia shot him a sideways look. He spoke with complete gravity, but his eyebrows were a little raised. He lifted some fingers in a slight, defensive gesture and managed not to drop anything. 'But *you* are the biologist, my dear.'

'Alright. Point taken. But this is, well, not me. I can normally…'

'Of course. Believe me when I say I do try not to make a habit of leaping to the rescue of young women out alone. It can lead to all manner of complications.'

'Well, if it *is* just this once.'

'I give you my word.'

In silence, they came to the top of the hill and turned the corner, the lights of the university coming into view. She hardly knew him. The Hallowe'en episode had been filed under 'Things Steven has Talked Me Into', and she had been quite happy to leave it there. She had been certain that she would never meet Julian again and had felt no desire to change that. Walking shoulder to shoulder with him now, being indebted to him once more, she should feel awkward, even mortified.

But her only real discomfort was at the gulf between what she should feel and what she felt. *Hmm,* she reminded herself, *don't tell Steven any of that. It'll only get him talking about Sartre.* 'So, besides not studying literature, or rescuing young women in the rain, what is it you do?'

'Oh, you know how it is.'

'How what is?'

He shrugged. 'I read a lot.'

'I meant more like your job, or…?'

'Oh, that. Well, I trade wine, but it would be flattery to call that actual employment.'

'Oh.'

'Do I shock you, my dear?'

'No, no,' she answered immediately, without thought, and then, 'perhaps a little. More surprised.'

'Something no longer common nor popular, but I'm afraid I inherited money.' He smiled at her, provocative. 'I do beg your pardon, my dear. I would have avoided it, if I could have done so.'

Suddenly uncomfortable, Sophia laughed. 'No. No. God. I'm sorry.' With every other student she had bitched about fuckwits who had never worked a day of their lives, but she had never met anyone for whom that was true. Her main complaint had always been that it was not fair. But when had she ever expected life to be fair?

Besides, inheritance tended to involve the death of someone you liked.

'It must be quite nice, though, being able to do what you want instead of what you have to do.'

'It has its advantages.'

'So, you… What do you do? Read, sell wine?'

'I travel rather a lot,' he said quietly. 'But there, we are here. I'm afraid you'll have to direct me to the library.'

He was silent while she led him across campus and up the library steps. She wondered if she had offended him in some way. It was only when they reached the out-of-hours drop-off and he was handing her the first book, that he asked, 'And what about you, my dear?'

'What about me?'

'Your neotropical savannas. The flora and fauna of distant lands. Do you travel?'

'No. Not so much.' She scanned the barcode on the book, waited, put it in the slot. 'It's difficult, you know? I'd like to, but…'

'But what?'

There's no money. But there was no way she was telling him that. She scanned the next book. 'That's why I try to stay close to home; British bats, that kind of thing.'

'Bats?'

'I like bats. I'm doing my dissertation on the effect of climate change on hibernation patterns and colony numbers. I wanted something I could really observe, not just read about, you know? Something I could get out there and experience. Do a bit of fieldwork and… I'm sorry, I'm babbling.'

The books were all dropped off, the receipt printed, and Julian was standing there, smiling as though he were in no hurry at all. Behind him, the rain continued to torrent, but they were sheltered by the overhang of the library roof.

'Not at all, my dear. Pray, continue.'

Sophia knew that, according to all the rules of politeness, she ought to let him go, or at least stop and give him a turn to speak, and keep their topics to innocuous points of small talk. Moreover, she was a scientist who hung out with arts students and had come to the conclusion that her dissertation topic was both uninteresting and incomprehensible to anyone but herself. Experience had taught her that even the most simplistic overview of it was enough to bring a glazed expression to the face of any listener – even Steven or Lucy.

In literature, or history, or any other discipline, she was aware that she did not have the minutia of knowledge required to study at degree level. Nonetheless, with a modicum of intelligence and a layman's interest she had always found herself able to make intelligent conversation about Jane Austen, say, or Marxist politics. But as a scientist she had found that she had all but stopped talking about her degree, for politeness' sake.

It had rankled.

Perhaps more than she had realised, because Julian's innocuous request brought down six or eight months' worth of conversation on his unsuspecting head. She tried to gauge his reaction as she blathered on, tried to stop herself before she bored him senseless, but he gave no sign of it, even prompted her to say more, to go into more depth.

'No, I really need to let you get on. Thank you for...' She gestured vaguely at the library, the weather.

'A pleasure.'

Neither of them made a move to leave. 'I suppose I ought to... I mean, Lucy and Steven will be wondering where I am... You can come along if you like. It's nothing special, just post-essay drinks, but I'm sure Steven and Lucy would like to see you again.'

'I would not wish to intrude. However, I would be delighted to see you again at some point soon. And Jonathan as well, of course. My house should shortly be at least presentable. Perhaps you would all join me one evening?'

In Sophia's experience this kind of invitation was usually greeted with a 'yeah, sure' and relegated to some future date which seldom occurred. Instead, she said, 'Yes. Is next week good for you?'

'I believe so. Shall we say Thursday evening? About seven o'clock?'

'Sounds good. I'll run that by the others, of course, and get their answer, but I'm up for it. How should I let you know? By text or something?'

They were standing close enough that she noticed him do the smallest of double takes, noticed how blank his face became. Then he smiled once more, the smile that she had thought enigmatic a few moments earlier. Looking at him face on, it seemed more shy.

She wondered how old he was. On Hallowe'en she had guessed that he was a little older than herself and her friends – late twenties, perhaps. But he did not look it. If anything, he looked younger now than he had then. Healthier, too. She wondered if it had been the lighting, or the stress of moving which had worn him. Or maybe it had been grief.

'Of course. That would be easiest. It's just that, I am afraid, my dear, I do not – ah – recall my number at present. Hmm. The curse of a terrible memory. And everything is still in disarray at...' He paused. 'Would it be too much of an imposition to ask that you drop a note to my house? I might not be in, but I shall definitely get it. Then at least we do not rely on my own poor organisation.'

'Of course not. No, that's fine.' She considered pointing out that, with her number, he could let her know his, but reminded herself that he was moving house, that he could do without the bother. Perhaps a gentle prompt. 'But I'll give you my number. In case you need it.' She took out the library receipt and jotted it down for him. She wrote her name at the top, folded it and handed it over.

He took it in one gloved hand and put it in an inside coat pocket. 'Now, my dear, I must leave you to the tender mercies of the union pub. It was delightful to see you.'

'It's been great. Thanks again for, well, all the things. And enjoy your walk. Although,' she gave the gusts of sleet beyond their shelter a dubious look, 'are you sure you don't want to join us?'

'Tempted as I admit I am, I feel I must refuse.' He was smiling and once more his expression was arch, sly. He bowed and taking her hand, kissed it.

Looking down at his bowed head she felt something like tension, or fear. She told herself that it was shock at his actions, but she knew it was not.

He looked up and met her eyes. 'Until we meet again, Sophia?'

She realised she was smiling, and she tightened her grip on his hand, feeling bones through the cold leather of the glove. 'Until we meet again.'

A brisk walk took her from the cold into the fug and noise of the union bar. Lucy and Steven were already halfway through a bottle of wine. A third, untouched glass was sitting beside them. She sat down and began to remove several unnecessary layers of clothing. 'You will never guess who I've just seen.'

'Heath Ledger?' Lucy suggested.

'Close, but no cigar. It was our spooky benefactor.'

'What? Julian?'

'Yep.'

'You lucky bitch,' Lucy said, with no real rancour.

'Why the abuse all of a sudden?'

'Oh, come on, it's not fair. You've already *got* one. I wanted this one.'

'And I'm also quite prepared to fight my corner,' Steven added over the rim of his glass.

'God, you two are obsessed.' Sophia took a long swig of wine. 'And if I've "got one", how many have you got, Lucy?'

'A few. But this one's *different*. Oh, come on. There's something rather Darcy about him, isn't there?'

'I'd say more Willoughby,' Steven corrected. 'Far too charming.'

'Pedant. Does that mean you think we shouldn't trust him?'

'Well, I wouldn't want either of you to consider eloping with him just yet.' He flashed Lucy a wide, self-satisfied grin. 'Give me a chance first, huh?'

'Honestly, I can't take you two anywhere.' Sophia took another drink and relaxed, letting her mind wonder. *Willoughby*. 'He, at least, has the potential for redemption.'

Steven gave her a quizzical look.

'Willoughby. He's about the only one of Austen's baddies to get any sympathy.'

'Yes. Well, that's *a* view. I'd say she had more sympathy for the Crawfords.'

'No, the Crawfords are *nasty...*'

'Uh-uh,' Lucy said. 'Enough of the Austen tutorial, guys. Sophia, what's this about Julian?'

'Oh, it was nothing much. I was on my way up to meet you,' she began and, despite more interruptions than were strictly necessary, managed to relay the experience of being a helpless bimbo in the rain.

Lucy looked her in the face, sighed, and said, 'You *are* a lucky bitch.'

'What, for looking like a complete idiot in front of a stranger?'

Steven tutted. 'Perhaps, committed as you are to your so-charming fiancé,' Sophia glared at him, but he ignored her, 'you are incapable of understanding the effect such a dashing rescue would have upon the singletons among us. I confess, it's almost the stuff of wet dreams. He *is* quite the Willoughby, isn't he, Lucy?' He smirked and gave her a look that could only be described as incorrigible.

'Absolutely. Damnit, girl.'

'Guys. It was a spilled bag of books. I hardly had a dislocated ankle.'

'Well, needs must. I mean, for every heroine with a fortuitously fragile bone structure, every maiden of a fainting disposition, doubt-less there are a several dozen who must simply make do with a spilled bag of books and a reversed umbrella.'

'For the record, Steven, the umbrella is fine.'

'Pity. You should have told him it was busted. Then he would have walked you to the pub.'

'Mmm,' Lucy agreed.

'Yes. I think I can imagine it. Huddling together away from the rain, you all shyness and self-sacrifice, him all gallantry and charm.'

'Then, a crescendo of music as you step into the light.'

Sophia turned her attention to the wine.

'She still clutches the shattered remains of her umbrella as he says,' and here Lucy paused, presumably for effect, 'divest yourself of your eighteen outer layers, Sophia…'

'My God…'

'You're beautiful,' the pair of them finished in chorus.

'Alright. Okay, point taken. Can I get on with my evening now?'

'But, honestly Sophia, did his charms leave you entirely unmoved?' asked Steven. 'Do we not get our romance?'

'He's not really my type.'

'What?' said Lucy. 'Is he just too tall, too dark and too handsome for you?'

'He's shorter than you are, love.'

They gave her sceptical looks.

'Oh alright. I'm not blind, for God's sakes. Very tasty. But I'm kind of *engaged*.' She sucked the knuckles on her right hand, and worked out how she could get her revenge. 'So, from your reactions I'd assume you were completely uninterested in seeing him again.'

'What?'

'Well, he's invited us round, for drinks.'

They stared at her.

She examined her nails. 'On Thursday. Are you two coming or what?'

'What, this coming Thursday?' Steven asked, his voice quiet, his expansiveness falling away. 'Really?'

'Yep,' and she smirked. Steven would be mortified to know how transparent he could be.

''Fraid I can't, actually,' said Lucy. 'Damn. I've got a rehearsal on Thursday. First full cast. Bit important, and all that.'

'Oh, well. You know. Break a leg…'

'Thanks. Damn it.'

'Steven?'

'Hmm.' He seemed to stir himself from thought. 'Well, I suppose I could tear myself away from my current engagement of sitting on my tod. Unless you want me to be merciful and let you go alone.'

'Yeah. I suspect that John will also be coming, which would sort of scupper a romantic tête-à-tête.'

'And there I was – under the impression that Thursday was match night.'

Oh fuck.

She paused, confused. Surely she could go out and meet someone without John to hold her hand. 'Steven, I know you think John is an utter yob, but I hope you realise that he doesn't need to watch every *single* football match in order to function.' Her voice was a little sharper than she had wanted it to be. She made herself stop speaking before she said something she would regret.

Lucy came to the rescue. 'And you do know the only reason we let you talk about sport is because you're the token boy, right? So, come on. Show your ignorance. Do you even know if there is a game on Thursday?'

It was a moment before he said, 'Oh, buggered if I know,' and drained his glass.

Sophia followed suit and, seeing how little was left in the bottle, offered to buy another round in lieu of an apology.

But as she walked over to the bar, she remembered that Thursday was the night John's supervisor organised social drinks for 'team building' purposes, and while John didn't always go, next week he and 'the boys' were going to make a night of it, watching... Sophia couldn't remember what, but John had been quite excited by the idea.

When Sophia got back Steven was in full flow. He had even pulled a pen from his pocket and was punctuating his speech by jabbing it towards the object of his vitriol. His voice became clear over the hub-bub of the pub. 'But it *isn't* innocuous. I mean, if we begin to think about the psychosocial effect of having *this* as our cultural myth...'

She glanced at Lucy, who shook her head and mouthed, 'Don't worry.'

'Words fail me,' he concluded as she dumped the bottle on the table and sat down.

'What's bothering him now?'

'Disney.'

'Oh.' Sophia followed Steven's disgusted glare. A girl sitting nearby was shooting nervous glances at the madman giving her the evil eye. She was wearing a children's *The Little Mermaid* t-shirt that had been cropped to reveal a decidedly un-childlike form to its best advantage. 'And that offends you?'

Steven made a derisory noise in his throat. 'Of course it offends me, Sophia. Everything about it offends me. I mean, has she even heard of Simone de Beauvoir?'

Hopeless, she thought, and poured them all more wine.

'Actually,' Lucy teased, 'I'm willing to bet she has. I'd put, oh, twenty quid on that shirt being a deliberate anti-feminist statement. It's all premeditated, Steven.'

Steven's glare was transferred to Lucy.

Why the hell not? 'I agree. I bet she woke up this morning and asked herself, "How can I best refute the conclusions of *The Second Sex*?"'

'Just take it seriously. It's the way it gets inside your head, the way it twists the stories. Makes it safe and tidy and repressive. It disgusts me.' He jabbed his pen for emphasis, then seemed to calm down. 'Should I tell her?'

'What, that she's buying into a commercial and patriarchal ideology?' Lucy's query was offhand, and perhaps more logical than Steven's mood warranted.

'Huh? No. No, I mean, should I tell her how that story really ends? In the original?'

'I don't think she'd thank you,' Sophia said.

'Besides, if you're arguing that Disney is anti-feminist you've backed a loser with that example.'

'Huh?' Once again, Steven seemed taken aback. His irritation vanished. Sophia wondered how much of it was a pretence.

'Well, Andersen's "The Little Mermaid" is hardly the epitome of female emancipation, now, is it?'

'I suppose not. Hmm. Yes. Cut out your tongue, walk on knives and kill yourself for someone who doesn't care. Not particularly enlightened.'

'Precisely. Be a good little girl. Efface yourself. Seek self-destruction because nothing else will save you.'

'But it's not about that,' Sophia heard herself say.

'What?' Lucy demanded. 'She gives up everything, her home, her voice, her *life* and that prince doesn't even see her as human. I mean, what kind of a message is that?'

Sophia thought for some time, wondering what had made her speak, but found no arguments, no sense. Instead, there was the heavy, physical memory of a book with a blue cloth cover, of the smell of dust and damp, the lavender and cigarette scent of her grandmother's house. Years ago. Years and years. She could almost breathe it now, and with it, draw in the desperate tragedy of that tale, the way her chest had felt sore and there had been furious, wonderful tears in her eyes. *They're wrong,* she found herself thinking, *they are both wrong.*

'It's not about a message. It's about love.'

'Love?'

'No,' Steven said. 'She just gives and gives and he never even notices, let alone cares. How is that an admirable sentiment?'

'I'm not saying it's admirable, or nice, or pretty, or… or anything, really. It just is. She just loves him.'

Steven snorted in his worst way. 'I, for one, am not convinced. So, what you're saying is that she should just efface herself to the point of death just because she's in *love*?'

Sophia stared at the table, not wanting them to see the emotion on her face. 'I'm not saying *should*, I'm saying – I'm saying, who cares about should? That's the point. She *wants* so desperately, so badly that nothing else matters anymore. Sod the lot of it. Let it all burn.'

Lucy was staring at her, a nervous, probing look. 'Okay, but what about her poor sisters? What about their hair? I mean, self-sacrifice is one thing but that's vicious.'

'But that's the whole point. Look, I read this essay about it, once. It's *amour fou.*'

Now Steven was giving her the look, the one that pressed into her mind and made her snap at him. 'What essay?' he asked.

'Angela Carter, actually, so I'd have thought you'd approve of it. Anyway, it was all about passion, the way it hurts, the way it's so big and wild that it blanks out everything else. And so what if she has to walk on knives? Who cares that her sisters lose their hair for her? Who cares, even, if the prince never sees, never knows? It doesn't matter. It's not what it's about. She *loves*. She can't *be* any other way.'

Steven nodded, but when he spoke, his words were thrown like knives. 'And that's what love is, is it? That's what you think women should do?'

'Not should.' She swept her hand across her face to chase him away. 'It's just that's how it is, sometimes. That story, it's a tragedy. Unless he loves her, she'll die, and because they can't speak, because *she* can't speak, he can never see her as she really is. They only have the surface, so he can't love her.'

'But it's *not* a tragedy. That's what I could never stomach,' Lucy said. 'It's meant to have this lovely happy ending where she finds out that her selfless ways are going to get her a soul.'

'She's right, you know,' Steven butted in. 'It's just a bit of trite sentimentality to get women to toe the line.'

'I've never liked that either,' Sophia said. 'After everything else, it makes it seem like – I don't know – like her suffering doesn't really matter. That's not right. Her suffering defines her. I mean, she accepts death. She's gone through everything. That should mean something.'

'So, are you saying what she sacrificed should give her a head start on redemption, or something?'

'No. No. Not like that. It's just that dying like that – that is her redemption.' Sophia shifted in her seat, looking away. That hadn't been what she meant, precisely. But this mattered, and because it mattered, she could not find the words. 'Dying for love. That's all she needs.'

'What, and sod the immortal soul?' asked Lucy.

'I'll drink to that,' Steven said with forced cheeriness. He refilled their glasses. 'Sod the immortal soul.' They clinked and the conversation died. Thankfully. In her stomach, something knotted, tighter and tighter still.

Then, of course, because he was Steven, he had to say, 'But even if it does justify her, that's only because it's a tragedy. What if she had succeeded? Our passionate heroine prepared to yoke herself to that godawful prince for life? That has no glory, does it? Squandering her own freedom and talent just so she could spend all her days as a good little wife.' She knew the hectoring note in his voice. She tried not let it sting.

'Hell, you can talk,' Lucy replied. 'You like *Dracula*.'

He looked appalled. 'What's *Dracula* got to do with it?'

'Everything,'

Sophia drew a deep breath, and took her chance. 'Absolutely. There's poor Lucy Westenra, for a start. Just because she *dares* to awaken her own sexuality she immediately becomes this foul, voluptuous *thing* with no right to life. Nope, the boys' club decide she has to be controlled, destroyed so that the patriarchy can keep itself pure.' She took a swig of wine and gave him a hard smile. It said, *I can play this game, too.* 'I mean, that staking scene reads like a rape.'

'Well, yeah,' Lucy said, 'but that wasn't what I meant. I was talking about Mina, really. I mean she's... she's just staggering. It's like, all the big discoveries are hers and everything is totally organised by her. Every step of the way she keeps the whole big quest thing on track. Even Van Helsing respects her – all that bollocks about having a "woman heart" and a "man brain" – but what kind of a lot does she get?'

Sophia chased after that one, too. 'She's right, you know. They ignore her, cut her out of it at every opportunity. "No place for a woman..."'

'Yep,' Lucy informed him, 'if you're looking for blatant misogyny, Steven, *that's* where you're going to find it.'

He gave them a pained smile, but they weren't fighting anymore. Not really.

'Oh, don't look so sarcastic. You know we're right. They neglect her and they ignore her, and that's why she falls prey to Dracula. Because they left her behind.'

'A bit more than that,' Sophia insisted. 'I mean, all of that "you should have spent your energies closer to home". She clearly wasn't getting any from that husband of hers.'

'Poor girl. So marvellous, so brilliant, and she ends up yoked to that lifeless, sexless idiot.'

'What, to Jonathan?' Steven said with dreadful mock-innocence.

Silence.

Sophia did not realise she was glaring, did not realise that her eyes were burning and her fists were clenched until Lucy touched her hand. Slowly, slowly, she uncoiled.

'Jonathan *Harker,*' Steven corrected, and his neck was red and Sophia hoped it was with shame. He pursed his lips as though he could still not bring himself to apologise. 'You know, he's not so bad on a rereading, but I take your point.'

4. Since There's No Help

And when we meet at any time again,
Be it not seen in either of our brows
That we one jot of former love retain
– Michael Drayton, 'Since There's No Help'

The creature ran out of the city, out to where rain pelted through empty branches, unmarked, unseen. He raised his head and let the cold water wash the contours of his face. A human would have been panting, would have been sweating. A human would have felt the exuberance of the storm, or at least the adrenalin of the run.

The creature felt nothing.

Beads of ice washed over his cheekbones, his lips, down across his chin. Rain trailed down his throat, until his skin was slick with it, his clothing drenched. The tiny ice crystals clung to him, not melting. The cold did not send the blood recoiling from his skin or make him shiver in a desperate attempt at warmth. Still, his flesh thrilled to the rain, to the clean taste of water trickling between his lips. His ears were assailed by the sounds of wind rushing in the trees, or leaves, drenched and falling. On most nights these feelings would give him something akin to pleasure.

He ran his hands hard over his face. The pain was not enough. He used his nails, dragging them through the flesh, opening lines of blood upon his skin that healed and dried too quickly.

Fool.

He closed his eyes. All he had wished for this night was to walk in the rain and, feeling that chill, indifferent torrent, to listen to the silence in his mind. But now there was hunger for warmth, for abandon in another's arms. *If I could go to her, if I could hold her...* Lust rose in him, and a soft urging for blood. He stilled himself, letting the rain wash him like a baptism.

That I should meet her again, oh, that she should need my help...

She is not Eleanor; the creature clung to the thought as he might

43

cling to a last, desperate thread of sanity. She was just some girl, one of the thousands in this city. What's more, her hair was short and dark and wild. Her tight trews flaunted her shape, her skin was sun-beaten and sallow.

The only connection between the two was that perfume, lingering and herbal.

She was not Eleanor.

And yet, if Eleanor lived now, would she have worn her hair so very long? Would she not gladly have abandoned gowns for clothing more practical? And would not his Eleanor sooner have walked out alone, overburdened, and in the rain, than ask for aid?

And to imagine he could ever have refused her that assistance.

Fool.

For he had watched her huddle around her spilled books and believed he could still walk away. Yes. There she had been, in all her fragile, human beauty, all her weakness and clumsiness, all her vitality and struggle, and in his arrogance he had thought he could withstand her. And because he was so strong, so resolved, so aloof, he had thought an act of casual gallantry would be of no consequence?

But she had said his name, had turned to him with that sweet, dreadful perfume, with Eleanor's mixture of pragmatism and pride, and memory had taken him.

Memory. The creature thought it had been seared from his mind. Had he not suffered since then? Had he not lost and betrayed a thousand times? Had there not been scores of clever, innocent boys to dote upon? Nor the yielding arms of sweet-faced girls? Endless, the stream of humanity beneath his touch, and every time, he had called it love.

But like the farmer's wife nursing an orphaned lamb, he had kept an edge of hardness in his ardour, knowing these darlings would soon die, that it would most likely be by his hand. And so, somewhere dark within him, he had kept Eleanor enshrined.

Standing before Sophia, his every instinct had ordered him to fall upon his knees and confess, to tell her of the desperate gulf of his misplaced adoration, to tell her that he adored her for all the things she was, for all that she could never be. When he had been with Eleanor, it had been the simplest of things to be sincere, to speak to her honest and plain.

Instead, debonair nothings spilled over his lips. He had made amusing little games in speech, teasing around the truth. He had *flirted*, as any cynical seducer could flirt. He had spoken of everything other than how he felt, had sullied the weight of this passion with terrible trivialities. He had tried to make her laugh. *Fool. Fool, fool, fool.*

Was she another body to be won with empty words? Was she no more than that to him? His Eleanor.

No. No, for she was neither Eleanor, nor his.

Her very brightness, her hope were things owned by the day-lit world, a world of friends and universities and drinking in pubs. His attentions would only make her wither, the way that lilies wither in the snow. He could not touch her. They existed in worlds which should never intersect. If he had ever loved Eleanor, he should leave.

But that was now beyond his power.

Fool.

The water he had licked from his lips settled cold and uncomfortable in his stomach. He would pay in sickness for the simple, mortal pleasure of tasting the rain. He deserved it, and the weakness that would follow. He would not drown the nausea in blood, would allow himself no such indulgence.

But he would not leave.

No. He would court Sophia, as he had done this night, would flirt and smile, and be near as much as he could. Perhaps it was all vanity and delusion. Perhaps only a monster would resolve upon such a course, but the creature knew the word described him well.

Still, he must not forgive himself. Only the rain might do that. Earlier, he had hoped it might absolve him, might revive him, provide some connection to the world around him. Or at least, he had hoped that it would assure him that not everything he touched would cease to be, that there were some things as constant, as inevitable as rain.

He waited beneath the bare November trees and the rain washed his face. It was cold, colder than his skin. And it was of no help, no comfort. No relief.

Steven stared at his reflection in the library window until it blurred, then put his head in his hands. The blank sheet of paper stared at him like a reproach. He was not going to get any work done tonight. Not now.

He had come to the uni with the best possible intentions, full of ideas for his dissertation proposal, and he had meant, honestly meant, to get on with it. But his mind had wandered, and he found himself fretting about that conversation with Sophia, two nights ago, about what she had been trying to say. Thinking it might lay the matter to rest, he decided to look up that Angela Carter quote, the one about *amour fou*.

It had taken a while to find, but he had eventually located it, and read the essay. When he had read it, he put the book down and stared at the window for a good ten minutes. Then he had walked back to the shelf and found a copy of Carter's *The Sadeian Woman*, which he had skimmed through with a kind of morbid fascination. The two books lay beside each other – closed, but to his mind, ominous.

He did not agree with her. More than that, he was convinced she was wrong, but Carter seemed to anticipate his objections, to manoeuvre that opposition. Something in the way she wrote made any dissent seem bourgeois and sinister and he was trapped by this, trying to justify his opinions to himself. She was wrong. She *had* to be wrong. Everything she said about love, passion, sex, certainly everything she said about *amour fou* seemed to him just… incorrect.

Yes, he recoiled from her description of the orgiastic, but perhaps people did feel things that way. Not him, perhaps, but some people. And as to *amour fou*? Powerful, ecstatic and painful passion? Suffering and insanity? It was seductive, it scanned well, but it was wrong.

And it was not because he had been raised without a sense of sin. In fact, he wondered if Carter would believe that particular awareness to be so laudable with the dubious benefit of his experience. Was it any surprise that, to him, *amour fou* seemed so selfish, so self-righteous, so callous a form of pleasure? Having once read that Saint Sebastian was the unofficial patron saint of homosexuality, his only response was relief that he was not a Catholic. He could not understand why someone would want to immolate themselves for anything, especially love.

But did that make him some kind of a puritan? *Well, that would be wonderfully ironic.* He did not think relationships should be quiet, respectable, bland. His abstinence was not a moral choice.

Was it?

The way he waited, tentative, for love; was that merely the protestant work ethic? The squeamishness of the middle classes? He shrugged, uncomfortable. He would cheerfully live without the dubious pleasures she described – ecstatic and orgiastic both. Did that condemn him to live suspended in pre-pubescent innocence? Was that the only other option, the alternative to being guided by lust, to becoming either the brute or the masochist?

Steven shook his head and pushed the books away. *She must be wrong. There has to be another way.* He tried to pull himself together, to forget what he had read and make himself do some work.

And Sophia? asked a voice in his mind. *Sophia?* He did not notice the way his whole posture slumped at the thought. That she believed this stuff was beyond question. Was that why she persisted in making such stupid decisions?

It could almost be funny, connecting those morbid and suicidal passions with, well, John. He had none of Carter's lightning quality. Besides, Sophia's recent behaviour hardly fitted the picture of a she-devil able to outstrip all the demons of hell. *Amour fou* was something vigorous, self-justifying, something frightening in its intensity. What relation did that bear to walking through life on bleeding feet with a mute tongue?

No, the things which Sophia chose seemed more like puritanism to him. She was not seeking destruction; she was sacrificing herself to be the model girlfriend. And it was poisoning her. He had always thought she was too sensible to choose that path. But then, he had always thought her too sensible for any of the other options Carter offered, be it self-repeating sexuality, devouring passion, or even cold propriety. None of them were what he would choose, nor would have chosen for his friends. He had hoped that she, out all of them, could be rational – could make choices sensibly and have done with it. After all, they were all too intelligent to waste themselves on love.

And Steven stared into his suddenly alien reflection and asked himself if that were not the final option. This scholarly silence, this solitary, untouched existence, where there was only a cold, dark reflection of oneself and the silent accusations of books.

5. Things We Do for Love

…and, for the space of half a year, the gun–powder lay as harmless as sand, because no fire came near to explode it.
– Emily Brontë, *Wuthering Heights*

At the table in the lounge Sophia wondered if she should start eating or wait for John to get home. It wasn't as if the food wouldn't keep for him; it just wouldn't be as nice. She shook her head. To eat by herself would be admitting defeat. Let the lasagne dry out a bit. It was his fault for being late.

No, she reminded herself, *no, that isn't fair.*

The thing was, while Sophia normally liked company as she cooked, sometimes she would substitute music for conversation and surprise John by having dinner on the table when he walked through the door.

That had been the plan tonight. After all, she was going to Julian's tomorrow. It would be good for them to have a special dinner tonight. So, as soon as she was up, she had nipped to the shops and bought a decent bottle of wine and lots of lovely ingredients, none of which she could afford. Then, she spent several hours which should have been dedicated to exam revision baking a cake, icing it and listening to The Kinks.

She had been sliding an absolutely beautiful lasagne into the oven when her phone had beeped. It had been John: 'Hey babe, gonna b wrking a bit l8. Luv u. xxx'

That had been about five. She had turned the oven down, shrugged, and started reading. It was no big deal.

But now it was half past seven. She uncorked the wine and poured herself a glass. A large one. *Just how long is he going to be?* She took a deep breath and thought about it logically. The office closed at eight, which put a deadline on it. Unless of course, he went out drinking with his workmates. He usually did when he was working late. Sophia made a face. If he was going out with *them* he could at least have given her an ETA. Faintly, she smelled burning cheese. *Damn.*

She was hungry – she had only grabbed a snack lunch because she'd been planning an early dinner. She kicked the leg of the table and clenched her teeth. *Why didn't he tell me?*

Sophia took a deep breath.

He did tell me, and he had no idea I would need an exact time. I should have texted back and asked what 'later' meant.

But she was down to her last thirty pence of credit – the amount she liked to keep for emergencies. And he could hardly be expected to remember that. Still, she was hungry. And the food wouldn't taste so good if she needed to reheat it. She took a large gulp of wine. *Sod it. Romantic gestures be damned.*

She had just finished eating and was draining her second glass of wine when the phone beeped again. It was John. 'Jeez, that took ages. Srry. Home in 10.'

Sophia looked at the clock. It was eight exactly.

She stared down at her empty plate. *What is wrong with me?* Ten minutes ago, she had been eating the food in a self-righteous fury, jabbing her fork so hard it squeaked on the plate. Ten minutes ago, she had almost hated John. Now her own pettiness was thrown back at her. He had not been being vindictive or avoiding her. He had just been working late. And he *had* let her know.

John liked his job. Sometimes, Sophia had to remind herself of that. They were about to start training him as a supervisor, too; he had told her that would mean he needed to work late more often. And it was not disastrously late. Coming home at this time, he would have been even more grateful for the surprise.

But she had wrecked that, getting childish and trashing her own plans. Her whole body seemed to curl in on itself in shame and misery. She sat down on the sofa and waited for the sound of his key.

'Hey love,' she called as the door opened.

'Alright. Hey, sorry I'm a bit late.'

She went to him, let him fold her in his arms, clung to him. 'No problem.' She felt the prickling of tears in her eyes. *Damn.* She pressed her face into his chest, muffling her voice as she said, 'I've eaten. Sorry.'

'Oh. Right.' She could hear his disappointment.

'There's lasagne in the kitchen. Just needs warming up.'

'Lasagne? Ah, you bloody legend, Sophie.' He peeled himself away from her and made for the kitchen. As she watched him go, she was crying. She could not believe that she was crying.

'No problem,' she said, whispering, and it was no surprise that he did not hear her.

'You don't mind if I stick the telly on, do you? I want to get the rugger scores.'

'Um, no. No problem.' *Just pull yourself together.* With a smile fixed on her face, she went into the kitchen and made sure her voice was level and clear as she said, 'I picked up a bottle, love. It's on the table.'

'Aw, wicked. 'Spect I'll just have a couple of cans though.' He turned from the oven and grinned. 'Bastard of a day. Really thought we'd get it nailed by six. But Ron said the figures didn't look right, so we had to check through them all again. Anyway, Darren thinks...' He carried on talking as he rescued the food from the oven, snapped open a couple of cans of beer and consumed the lot in front of the TV; but Sophia had tuned out. She made the right kind of noises at the right points and he didn't notice.

In the past they had spoken about films.

After he had finished the food, they sat on the sofa with a drink apiece and watched a rubbish sitcom. But perhaps it was not a rubbish sitcom. John was laughing a fair bit and seemed to be enjoying it. Maybe it was actually a very good sitcom. *I'm in a fine old mood tonight.* She wondered if she was premenstrual, but, no, her period was not due for a bit yet. Perhaps she was just overtired.

The television blurred into a colourful haze. Maybe she should get one of her text books, do some revision... she yawned. Perhaps not. Maybe just one of her comfort reads – *Northanger Abbey*, *Middlemarch* or *Frankenstein*, something like that. But, she reflected, it would seem antisocial; she had to be fair to John...

... She was sitting by the seashore, watching the waves against the shingle. She loved to watch the sea, even now, when the clouds burgeoned black and

grim and low against it, when the waves yearned upwards to the pressing
sky. Powerful, it thrilled her in its majesty and she watched the waves with
deep, strange longings. There was a wind, although she could not feel it, could
not hear it batter against her ears, still it locked and twined and toyed in her
hair…

And in the logic of dreams, her lover was beside her and she knew they
were alone and stranded, caressed and circled by the waves. His hands were
around her, she knew this, and he smiled and the smile became a kiss which
pressed her lips and stole her breath and cut to her skin as if it were flying
sand, or the angry salt of the storm. His tongue reached cold and smooth,
deep into her thirsty mouth, seemed to lick down her throat until it brushed
against her heart, and it was rough, and the roughness was sweet. His hands
were on her, against every inch of her like the clothes she no longer wore.
Every nerve in her skin woke to the touch and she watched the swirling sky,
the maelstrom above her and below, and within, watched him touch her as if
her whole body were his very own, watched her lover kiss her, and she seized
at him, but there was nothing to seize…

Her body yielded itself, let him hold her, let him know her and it no longer
mattered she did not know herself. His kiss burned into her like ice. And she
saw, though she was watching the sea, though she was watching the sky, saw
as he slipped one hand between her legs in a slow and knowing stroke, and
he smiled and she was coming hard…

She woke with a moan. Every muscle was tensed and arousal roared
through her, cut off in the moment of bliss. *Damn it.*

John was looking at her and smiling, his face crumpled with tiredness and beer and contentment. The television was off. 'You've been
asleep. You tired, love?'

'Yeah. I suppose I must be.'

But she was not. Not anymore. Her whole body was awake, alive,
overwhelmed and struggling to breathe.

'Yeah, you looked pretty wiped out.'

'Was I asleep long?'

'Nah, about ten minutes or so.'

'Oh.' She tried to keep herself calm, to speak as if she had just drifted
off and nothing had happened, nothing had changed. But she was

very wet. And she was still on the brink of coming. *Some dream.* 'Felt like it was longer.'

'No. But it is pretty late. You want to go to bed?'

Hell, yeah. Then she realised he was talking about sleep. After all, he had work tomorrow. 'Sure. It's probably best.' She finished her wine, and tried not to look too disappointed. Tried not to shake. *One hell of a dream, though.*

As they got into bed she gave John a couple of come-ons, but he just smiled and kissed her, and said, 'Not tonight, love.' She masturbated for a bit, but it was no use. She closed her eyes. And as she drifted off, a sudden thought dragged her back to consciousness. Her lover by the seashore had not been John.

Late; it was very late and the streets and parks of the city were quiet. The creature hungered.

He had spent his nights clearing away the cobwebs in his home, the squalor, the dust. When the day came, he had blocked out the weak November sun and worked on.

Even before he had intended to stay, there had been the plumbing and other details of household maintenance to attend to, but now he also made a living space, restored the kitchen and bathroom, returned his own quarters to comfort – although that last, by necessity, was not a public room.

He had also bought a mobile telephone, his first. The sleek, elegant thing confounded him, but he had come to see that it would now seem more suspicious not to have one. Filling out the forms for it had brought a momentary anxiety, but one he knew was groundless. There were documents enough surrounding his official identity that such records were no threat to him. It was only a habit left over from having practised secrecy for so long.

All those preparations were necessary, expected. But there was one thing that remained to him to do, and so he had walked out into the night, seeking the right kind of victim.

Of all his methods of hunting, this he found the most distasteful. Robbed of the heedless intimacy of an embrace, it was more clearly theft and made the creature see with unwelcome clarity the way he was a parasite upon humanity. With the macabre equipment hidden beneath his greatcoat, he felt as though he were a hellish inversion of a doctor, a junkie for blood.

He waited. There was no hurry. He had the whole of the night.

The victim that the creature sought needed to be drunk, or at least drunk enough to attribute the lapse in their memories to alcohol and not some other cause, but he preferred their intoxication to be minimal. If their blood were too strongly laced, it would affect him and becoming inebriated was always unwise. His victim also needed to be alone – it was not that he could not subdue a pair, but two such lacunae might arouse suspicion. And they needed to be beautiful.

This third was not a necessity, true. But when the scent of blood tried his resolution, when it infuriated his half-starved tongue, he had always found a modicum of beauty in his victim was enough stay him. There was never enough beauty in this world.

So, the creature waited and, at last, the city rewarded him. The boy was exquisite. His chin was still soft with the down of youth, his eyes were wide, his face was circled by a cluster of cherubic curls that grew long and unkempt. His throat was soft, tender and white in the cold light of the moon. He looked scarcely sixteen but must have had means to purchase the alcohol that made him unsteady upon his feet. Perhaps he hid behind his brazenness, challenged any to believe he was as young as he seemed.

The creature felt himself smile. He slipped from his waiting place and made it so that the heels of his boots rang hard upon the pavement. As he passed the boy, he threw out, 'Excuse me, do you have a light?'

The boy turned, his face hostile, his mouth already forming a 'no'.

It was of no matter. Their eyes met and boy relaxed under the force of a carefully channelled will.

'There is nothing to fear,' the creature said, and his voice was gentle. 'Come with me.'

The creature turned and the boy followed with a sleepwalker's gait. They walked in single file and neither spoke. At last, they reached a place where there was little chance of discovery. 'Sit down.'

With heartbreaking passivity, the boy obeyed.

The creature reached up to brush the full, childish lips, the smooth, pale cheek. The boy did not flinch at the icy fingertips, did not even blink. *Such beauty.* The creature looked away. He removed the boy's coat, rolled up the sleeve of his shirt and tied a ligature about the arm. He saw the veins rise, constricted. He leaned close to the boy's ear and whispered, 'This does not hurt,' and with that, he slipped the needle into the vein. As the blood ran through the syringe, into the cold glass of the bottles, the creature rested his head against the child's shoulder and drank in the scents of tobacco and soap and sweat. His eyes were almost closed.

He longed to wake the boy from his trance, kiss his eyelids, his mouth, his hair, speak to him of sweetness and of pleasure. *Such beauty,* he thought again.

He took two pints. When he was done, he removed the needle, and bowed over the wound, pressing his mouth to it. His teeth swelled outwards at the smell of the blood, ready to rend, to devour. Instead, he worried the cut a little wider and kissed away the beading of blood that answered him.

Later, he would remember this moment. Later, when he would drink the blood again, but find it stale and cold. Later he would feel impersonal crystal against his lips and he would remember the night, the sensations. The boy's dark blond curls, his cocksure, youthful face, the way the cigarette smoke seemed to form the substance of his skin. And perhaps then, something of that would work its way into the bottled blood; perhaps it would taste less flat, less subdued. And perhaps he would feel more honest.

He untied the tourniquet and pressed with his thumb on the cut until the blood stopped coming. He replaced the boy's clothing and kissed him once more, without the teeth, upon his pale unresponsive cheek. 'You will go home now. Walk carefully and safely. You will go to bed, and you will sleep soundly until morning, and then you will awaken. You will not remember what has happened here. You will not remember me, or that you have ever met me. Do you understand?'

The boy nodded once.

'Go now.'

And as the creature watched him walk away, he wondered how the boy would feel when he awoke, unable to remember the evening's end, found himself sick, faint, exhausted, with the weakness in his limbs and the little bruised scratch upon his arm unexplained, inexplicable. Would he shrug and blame his drunkenness? Would he believe himself to be ill and so dismiss the symptoms that would trouble him for some weeks? Or would he always wonder at that little cut, that little bruise, that lost evening? Would it be somehow unlike those others surrendered to alcohol? Would it remain, an unsettled dream within his mind?

And the creature wondered – not for the first time – if hypnosis held the cure to his own mesmerism. Wondered if the secrets he had shut inside that boy's mind, in the minds of so many others, could be unlocked. And if they could, what then? Would it emerge from the centuries of darkness, the pattern of his night-time habits revealed naked and troubling to the moral, scientific stare? How, then, could he hope for concealment?

The creature filled his pockets with the bottles, felt them still warm beneath his hands, the scent of the boy still upon them. And he realised he was tired of hiding.

Lucy checked the time – half past three. She switched off her desktop and toyed with the mouse until she was certain the old clunker was really going to shut down. She hadn't been working or anything, just killing time before dinner and the rehearsal. She checked her bag, made sure it had all the right kind of things – script, keys, bottle of water and the like – and that there was nothing like heavy library books, vibrators or mouldy oranges lurking in it. *Good.* She opened her bedroom door and walked into the sitting room.

Steven was lounging on the sofa reading something obscure about Shakespeare.

His dark hair was flopping on to his forehead and he was wearing black. In Lucy's opinion, it made him look dead. But it was Thursday – late night shopping – so Steven would be working later at Patroclus Sound and Vision, the kind of independent film shop where all the staff wore black and stared at you scornfully until you mentioned an obscure director.

'Alright, honey?' she asked, knowing she'd have to ask twice because he was reading. After a suitable interval, she repeated herself.

'Fine. Wondering how some people get their PhDs, but…'

She dropped her bag on to his feet. He didn't react. 'Don't read it then.'

'Nonsense.' He blinked twice and finally looked up from the book. *Result.* 'A bad essay is infinitely more useful than a well written one.'

'Right.' She flopped into an armchair. The way that Lucy saw it, Steven just liked arguing. He seemed to seek out poorly written critical essays or instances of human idiocy. She sometimes thought he might be trying to induce a state of apoplexy; it was as good a reason as any. 'You want something to eat?'

'Perhaps. Is it the kind of thing you can burn?'

She smirked and did the voice: 'You mean, "the kind of thing *one* can burn", surely?'

'No, dear Lucy, I mean *you.*' He gave a sigh. 'There are many things that one would have great difficulty in burning. Asbestos. Flame-retardant fabrics. Salad. *You,* on the other hand…'

'If you're going to be like that, you can cook.'

'You're right. I *can* cook, can't I?'

Damn. I walked straight into that one.

'Whether I am *going* to is—'

'It's just, I'm going out in a minute and was planning on sticking a pizza in the oven…'

'Should I call the fire brigade now, or wait until you scream?'

'Well, if you don't fancy any dinner…'

'Pizza would be wonderful.'

She started to go to the kitchen but lingered. After a moment, she sat down on the floor and leaned her head against the sofa. He put down his book and draped an arm over her shoulder.

'Steven, do you dream in compound sentences?'

He laughed. 'Maybe. Sometimes.'

6. The Other

If the study to which you apply yourself has a tendency to weaken your affections, and to destroy your taste for those simple pleasures... then that study is certainly unlawful
– Mary Shelley, *Frankenstein*

Julian had given her the kind of wineglass that ballooned out into an impossibly frail orb and Sophia's fingers felt dry and timid, on the brink of shattering it. His grip on his own was gentle, assured, and she tried to mirror it. It was as though she were cradling an injured bird.

Tonight, there were no electric lights, no dust, only the mellow gleam of old wood, the flicker of innumerable candles, the fragrant crackling of the fire. That cold, haunted room where she had first met Julian seemed to have been touched by some enchantment, washing away the years and dust until it glowed with memories of itself.

They had been through the hellos and the small talk, through the compliments on the transformation the house had undergone, and now they were reaching the point where she should be feeling awkward, where the beeswax smell and the leather armchairs should be intimidating her. They were reaching the point when Julian would have to stop flirting with her, the point where she would have to stop flirting with him.

He raised his glass to her in a small toast.

She took a sip of the wine, focusing on its rich oiliness, its deep, red colour. On the heat of the fire on her shins, the snugness of the chair around her.

'You were saying you admired *Frankenstein?*'

'Well, yes. I do. But I was saying it was what decided me.' She brushed a curl of hair behind her ear, watched Julian's eyes following her fingers.

'To be a life scientist?'

'I was going to do literature. Like Steven.' The wine in her glass trembled with her hand. She had never told anyone this, not Steven, not John. 'It was the thought of it. Not reanimation, although obviously…' She mimed a manic laugh, the mad doctor. 'But it made me think about life. What it means. It's like, when they first found out about electricity, they worked out that running a current through a pair of frog's legs would make them kick. And it was one of the ideas, I mean, one of the things that gave Mary Shelley her ideas. But it was an illusion. Because alive is alive, and dead is dead.'

'A somewhat bleak conclusion.'

'Well, yeah. But that's *why*. Despite all our progress, all this stuff about genetics and everything, we're no closer. Not to that, not to what it means.' She pulled her hair over her face, brushed it away. 'Everything we think we've learned is just an empty avenue, and so people forget it. They forget about the frog, but no one forgets *Frankenstein.*'

He did not laugh at her, as she had half feared he might. 'So, you would suggest the story has more worth than the truth? That it addresses a need galvanic theory does not?'

She thought about that. 'I suppose. But then it's an illusion, that meaning. Which is fine in fiction, but in real life there is no sense. No great scheme. No romance or mystery.'

Julian smiled at her over the rim of his wineglass. 'That is your belief?'

'I guess.'

'No. I think not.'

'Oh?'

'Would you permit me to play devil's advocate?'

'If it's just this once.'

'I would say that in life there is every mystery and romance. It is fiction which tidies all that away.'

'Alright. How so?'

'In *Frankenstein*, life itself becomes a thing which can be created in laboratory conditions. Certain empirical processes and electrical paraphernalia can imbue dead tissue with life. The novel tells us that if we follow the chains of cause and effect, even the greatest mystery of nature – the source of sentience itself – will be stripped bare, left open to the gaze of every voyeur. And so, the most intimate of secrets becomes the cheap trick of a peripatetic mountebank. How could that be anything other than a fiction, my dear? It is in reality where the mystery lies, and all our efforts to explain it away are both trifling and futile.'

'So, you're saying that when fiction is at its most logical – read, *realistic* – it will always be at its most artificial?'

'I believe you were the one saying that.' His smile was sly, his voice teasing.

'I'm not sure I was.'

'Ah, but if I might be so bold, my dear, I believe that you were.'

'Oh, yeah?'

'Yes. For you are, and you remain, a life scientist. If *Frankenstein* is the inspiration of your work, it is because you believe that life is *not* something which can be cut, bottled, preserved and dried. Simply because the frog kicks its legs, you will not be fooled. No, the mystery remains – this great and varied romance called life.' He raised his glass to her once more.

She laughed. 'Well, that's very clever. Although I was taught not to trust rhetorical flourishes.'

He gave a little bow of his head. 'Forgive a vain man his pleasures, my dear, I beg you.'

'By all means.' She drank more wine and found her glass was empty.

Julian refilled it. 'I fear I drink rather slowly. Perhaps I talk too much.'

'Thanks. And, no, you don't.'

He was smiling. The whole room conspired to make a backdrop for him, shadows and wood and sparkling glass. She watched the play of firelight across the crystal and the wine and his pale skin.

Stop that.

'But you're still wrong,' she said, 'about the romance. That's something you get from stories, that the world is full of lost heirs and true love and miraculous recoveries, but it's just ecosystems and motor responses and—'

'No.' His voice was a whisper. 'Such things happen constantly. The question is their meaning.'

Unsettled, she changed the subject. 'I can't get over what you've done with the place. You have a beautiful house. It was your grand-father's?'

'It is the family home,' he said, with something like pride. 'It is very good to be back here again.'

'I thought it had been empty for a long time.'

'Yes.' To Sophia, his answer sounded sharp, a little too fast. For a second it had seemed that he had sat forwards in his chair, startled and tense, but no, he was leaning back, the picture of ease and grace. *A trick, then. A trick of the light.* 'Yes. It has been empty for many years. Since I was a child, in fact. Also, my grandfather was not... not well for much of his life. Like myself, he spent many years in London, or... elsewhere. For the last decade or so he has been in,' a pause, 'in care. The old house was packed away, left to the depredations of dust and mice.'

He laughed and it sounded false.

The creature wet his lips with the blood in his glass, tasted the burn of the brandy he had used to thin it. It did not do to break his own rules, to become too much at ease, to let his lies fall clumsy and sudden.

The drink calmed him. Again, he took a sip.

'Were you close to him? Your grandfather?'

Her compassion cut away the centuries of deceit, cut his memories back to his true grandfather, a man of three score, a merchant who had lived to see his children reared as gentry and then to watch them die. A man who had seen pestilence and revolt and claimed it had not changed him. 'He was not the kind of man that one is close to, but yes, I cared for him.'

She believed him. It would have made no difference what he said, she would have believed it. Already her lips were forming some trite sentiment, some formula he had heard each time he made himself his own heir. He could not bear it, could not bear that she should say them now.

'In the end,' the creature said, 'he had not been himself for some time. In many ways, the man I knew died years before.'

But her brow made a little frown, and it reminded him of Eleanor.

Had she not had that expression, once? Had it not meant that she was thinking, that she was concerned?

'I shouldn't have brought it up. I'm sorry if...'

'As I said, he had not been himself for some time. If I found it too painful I would not speak of him.' He could not meet her eyes. 'But perhaps it is not a topic for this evening.'

'No, no. Of course not. Sorry.'

The creature took another sip from a drink that looked like wine. He should warn her, should communicate the danger, should let her know that her host, the man she consoled, and with whom she spoke, with whom she flirted, was a mockery of human kind. But then a curl of hair strayed across her cheek, and she coiled it round her index finger, tugged it and tucked it behind her ear.

Brandy seared his mouth, his throat.

That movement, that curl tugged and slipped away. It had been Eleanor's mark, had betrayed a moment of uncertainty, a wish to hide. Or it had, until the day his hand had closed on hers, the day he himself had brushed it from her face.

He could feel the distance between them singing against his skin. She touched her cheek where the hair had been. It was the wrong colour, the wrong length, but...

His hand caressed crystal and he began to speak, not driving her away but drawing her in, seeking that private space that is found between a book's page and the eyes, between the ears and a story told. And this allowed him to speak without untruth; so the creature began to lie, not to Sophia, but to himself.

Around him, wood gleamed, old timbers creaked. So many nights, so many times his hands had cleared away the cobwebs and the grime, so many times he had returned his home to life.

Walking these halls there was the ghost of a young man, an honest man who had spent winter evenings between the curtains of his bed, talking, talking, telling tales of chivalry as he brushed back the hair of his young wife.

It had not been in this room, no. Still, when Sophia spoke, she spoke as Eleanor had done. When her passion was engaged, there came a loudness, a fluency that brought more beauty to her face, more luminescence to her eyes. In their privacy, Eleanor's whole body had moved, her hair had tumbled into her face, and always, it had been he who brushed it away.

But Sophia, Sophia's hair was cut short, and she crammed it back into a ponytail as if she did not care for it. Besides, Sophia had no home to make, no obligation to reproduce. Her life could unfold at the command of her own wit, her promise and her intensity. How they had both longed for that, how they had chased it on those nights, with their whispered tales their sole escape from expectations, from duty.

And now, Sophia leaned towards him, and she shaped words with her hands, and they were not Eleanor's hands, for all they moved in Eleanor's way.

Easy, so easy to believe. So simple to tell himself it was just wine in his cup, the wine he had once loved, the wine that he now must roll about his mouth and spit out before its corruption sickened him.

So, as the talk rolled back and forth between them, the creature deceived himself. Their subject drifted from the crude personal to the far more private joys of the reader, and for all he spoke of modernism and the Bloomsbury set, he let the firelight carry him back across centuries. She shared with him all the loves, confusions and enmities she had found between the pages, and the creature sipped from his glass, pretending that his conviction – that they were held apart by life and death – was only the after-image of a troubling dream.

Until she said, 'But then, I guess it's different for you.'

Silence.

It was not that he had not attended her, not that he had not leaned across to drink her every word, not that he had ignored her opinions, but he was caught without an answer. What had she said? *'Realist? I mean, seriously? All that stuff about nannies and servants and dinner at Oxbridge colleges? That's realism? Because that's like a fairy tale to me. It would have been then, as well, to most people. I mean, they saw themselves as on this frontier of authenticity but it feels more like, well, the Famous Five than my experience of life.'* Then she caught her straying hair again, tugged it, curled the strands behind her ear: *'But then, I guess it's different for you.'*

How to tell her? How to speak of this world that brushed against his own, but which he could not touch. He ran fingers down his cheek, mirroring on his own skin the fall of her hair.

Silence.

How different would his life have been? Long, dangerous journeys made safe and swift. Illnesses cured. One's profession, one's domicile, one's wife, no longer things tangled up with duty, with familial bond. A world where rich women put their children to their own breast, and fathers, oh, fathers would stay and watch the birth.

'No,' he said, and the monster in him made his voice arch and light, 'but perhaps it must always be so. Realism is as experience dictates. Thus, all that is beyond our experience is fantastical by definition alone. To be realistic is to remake the world in our image.'

Content. Once, he had been content.

'So, what's your image of it?'

The creature paused.

'I mean, sorry. I'm being nosy, but it's just,' and she gestured to the room, the fire, the candles with their naked little flames, 'this is all rather... *fantastical* to me. You grew up here?'

'This very house.'

'And you went to a boarding school, I guess?'

'No,' the truth came without thought, 'I did not.' He felt stale, alcoholic blood rush back into his mouth, and with it lies – distant public schools, a family house in London, university – and he forced himself to swallow it all.

He had a whole host of documents to explain himself away: anaemia, photo-sensitivity, intolerances. A legal persona of some irony, a list of conditions that lawyers and doctors would swear passed, unadulterated, along the male line. They had seemed wise, these precautions.

It would be almost as though he were telling the truth.

He could see the glass poised at her lips, her growing trouble at his delay.

Speak. He knew he must speak.

He took a sip from his glass because he could not look at her and lie. 'I – I am afraid I did not attend a school.' Blood in his throat, on his tongue. 'I am afraid, my dear, I have never enjoyed good health.'

Concern flowered on her face. He forced himself to watch, guilt clawing his skin. But the words could not be unsaid. Nor could he stop at that. 'Please, do not be... do not be troubled on my account. Often I am quite well. Simply, I must be careful what I eat, and... wary of sunlight, but it is not serious. When I was younger it was more... Even now, the relapses can be rather severe. However, it seemed better to my grandfather that I was tutored at home.'

'My God. I'm sorry.'

His reluctance to speak, his evasions, his awkwardness; he saw that these had only given his tale more truth in her eyes.

'My dear, it is of no matter. Please. If it troubles you, you must not think of it. Forget that I have spoken. I insist.'

'What? No. No, I just – I'm sorry. You didn't need to tell me all of that. It's personal and I, I was prying.' She, too, looked away and they sat in silence for some time. He wished that he could banish this mood, could make her talk once more of things intimate and impersonal.

'Is there no treatment?' she asked, at last. 'No cure?'

He forced lightness into his tone. 'No. A rare genetic condition. The sad effect of selective inbreeding. We are an old family, after all. I am well used to it by now.' The sound of a tentative knock. 'Excuse me, my dear. I believe that is your friend joining us.'

It was quarter past midnight and Sophia was asleep. They were on their fourth, perhaps fifth bottle of wine. *Lightweight,* Steven thought, and grinned across at Julian. Their host arched his brows and poured the last of the wine into Steven's glass.

When he had arrived, he had wondered what it was he was interrupting. A mood, perhaps, something in Sophia's glance, the way she did not greet him, the way she bowed her head as though to hide the way her gaze followed Julian across the room. He wondered if they had been flirting; if Julian ever did anything else.

It felt good. Good to be drunk here, good to be enticed. Showing off, yes; Steven had been showing off and Julian had matched him, witticism for verbal dexterity. Now, though, there was silence in this magnificent room, the fire on its embers and an evening that was everything Steven had once dreamt an evening could be. He was not quite sober enough to suggest that he should be making a move.

As Steven finished his drink, Julian rose from his chair and touched Sophia on the arm. His face was smooth and pale, touched with the faintest pink of wine and candlelight. 'My dear, I believe we may have kept you too late this evening.'

'Oh,' she said and rubbed her eyes. 'Umm, I think I was asleep.'

'Are we *boring* you, Sophia?' Steven said.

'No. Uh – I think I might be a little pissed.'

You don't say?

She started to pull herself to standing. Julian offered her his arm, and she took it. Steven was about to look away when she let go.

'I believe I must have been entirely remiss a host. We should return you to your home.'

At this, Steven got to his feet. He found that they were not entirely where he expected them to be and a trifle less steady than their wont. 'Yes,' he said, and sat back down. 'I suppose we should be on our way.' As he tried to stand again, Julian steadied him with the same arm he had offered to Sophia. The contact, even through his clothes, made him still less certain where his limbs were, made his heart beat frantic and high. He managed to say, 'Thank you for this evening. It's been wonderful.'

'It has been entirely my pleasure, Steven. I so rarely have opportunity for such conversations, or for such company.' He had not let go of Steven's arm. *Don't get worked up about it.* The grip was companionable, not sexual. It was the way a man might support a male friend.

Steven had never been supported like that. He decided not to pull away.

'You must both give me the honour of your company again.'

It was fortunate Sophia cut in with, 'Yes. We should meet soon,' because Steven had forgotten how to use his own voice. Julian's hand was strong on his arm.

It's no big deal. He made himself move away and start walking towards the door. Julian walked with him and still did not let go.

Steven told himself it was the drunkenness that unbalanced him. Told himself that his heart was not beating wildly, and that even if it were, it had nothing to do with the way Julian's hair was dark on his pale neck, or the way they were close enough to kiss. He had the feeling he was walking on black ice, that any step could make the world slip out from under his feet. *Oh, pull yourself together.* But he could not.

Earlier, it had been the limit of his capabilities not to start gushing about the house, getting too excited about vaulting, corbels and Gothic arches. Instead, he had paced himself, forcing back every compliment until he could make it seem smooth, mature. But as the evening had passed, it had been easy to fall into the rhythm that Julian set. Yes, he would have another glass of wine. No, Julian shouldn't worry, although if it were convenient... Well, medieval architecture had always been a passion...

Yes, another evening would be fine, because that meant there would be another evening here.

Steven knew his own pose of refinement and elegance was mostly bullshit, that he was just an inexperienced, middle-class boy. But here, he could pretend that he was not. Here, like Julian, he could make it seem that he belonged. And he wondered how long it would take before such playacting got the better of him, how long it would be before he was Julian's submissive shadow and not Steven at all.

As they had been walking to the gate, Sophia and Julian had spoken. Not only had he not been contributing, he had not even heard what had been said. With sudden annoyance, he thought, *It's Sophia who has just woken up, not me.*

'In which case, I would suggest a week today.' Julian smiled his knife-edge smile. 'Or, a week yesterday, if we are to be pedantic.'

Steven made himself think, concentrate, as Sophia gave all the signs of assent. *A Thursday? In the run-up to Christmas?* 'Oh. I'm afraid might be a little behind-handed again. I'm often forced to work late on Thursdays.' *And why are you talking like a Victorian novel?*

Julian nodded. 'Very well. Shall we say a late supper on Thursday?'

'As long as that's no trouble for you,' Sophia said.

'None, my dear. Next Thursday. Come when you will.'

He wondered if Julian knew the effect he had on a certain type of person, and whether he used it deliberately. He put out his free hand. 'It's been a pleasure, Julian. Thank you for tonight.'

It happened too fast for Steven to react. He was aware of the coolness of Julian's lips, slightly sticky from the wine. The kiss on one cheek, then the other, the smell of him: wood smoke and leather, alcohol and something fleshy, almost rancid. Behind it all, there was another scent, quiet yet overpowering. Julian's arms were firm in their embrace. Dry; it was a dry smell with a touch of spice, vanilla, dust, of silence and time. It calmed yet thrilled, a rush of anticipation, of sheer pleasure.

Books, he realised, *Julian smells of books.*

He opened his eyes to see Julian staring into them, still holding him by the shoulder. He felt as though he were falling. 'Goodnight, Steven.'

He could do no more than blush, mumble, while Julian turned to Sophia and bowed to kiss her hand. 'Until we meet again, Sophia. My friends, goodnight.'

As they reeled away, they did not speak. Steven tried not to think about Julian, tried not to see how everything Julian did was underlain with a sexual current.

He doesn't mean anything by it. He's just a flirt. But what troubled Steven was how much he had enjoyed it.

He forced his mind away once again. It had been good to see Sophia getting fired up, too, though, hadn't it? They had spent a substantial chunk of time arguing about political philosophy, something they hadn't done since the summer Sophia had harped on about the necessity for social revolution in a way that could only be managed by a sixteen-year-old who has just read Marx for the first time. Tonight, it had become so heated that Steven had brought that blighter Foucault into the matter in the hope of quashing her argument.

'Sophia, when did *you* read Foul… uh, Foc…' He paused, his French pronunciation escaping him.

She stared.

'Foucault. I mean, that French fellow. When did you read him?'

'God. Thought we'd left this one.' She had a point. After Foucault had entered the ring, the whole thing got ugly. Julian had not helped.

He had refused to get involved, but some might have construed the comments he did make as provocative, at the very least.

'I'm not starting it again, my darling Sophia. I just wanted to know.'

'Dunno. Was a long time ago. Summer after A-Levels, I think.' Then she started to giggle, unexpected and drunken. 'And it's Michel *Fou*cault.'

'I said Foucault.'

'No, you didn't. You said Fuckault.' She was still laughing.

'Alright. Whatever. Foucault, Fuckault, Fuck all... That's it. He shall henceforth be Michelle Fuck-all.' Without thinking he slung an arm over her shoulder. As ever, she was too short for it to be comfortable. 'Arise Sir Michelle Fuck-all,' he declared, raising an imaginary glass as they stumbled on their way.

The creature turned and closed the door against the night. The wood met the jamb with a dull echo. In the hallway and the room where they had sat, he extinguished the candles one by one. Then, alone in the light of the dying fire, he fought something he knew he would fail to control.

Sophia's eyes had settled themselves shut, her grip on the wine glass had loosened, her breathing had grown soft. Nothing more. In those moments, he had been nothing more than a man watching the sleep of the woman he loved. He had needed her, needed to touch her, to brush her skin the way a gardener might touch a rose without damaging its bloom.

So, he had unfolded himself from his chair, had woken her with the gentlest of caresses. Not her hair, or her lips, or her face, simply her sleeve. He had not breathed. And she had opened those warm, grey eyes and looked at him. That had been enough.

Enough to needle the beast, to stir up his old debaucher's tricks. Enough to wake the urge to captivate, ensnare, compel. Easy – it was always too easy. And because Sophia had refused his touch then, with the equanimity of a villain he had given Steven his attentions instead. Steven, that bright boy who was everything the creature had hoped for when he had thrust himself into their lives. Steven, who thrilled to his affections and began that slow fall the creature had seen so many times before.

That he could do the thing so lightly.

That, as he had kissed Sophia's hand, he could take a taste of her blood.

Another old trick, a thing of speed and subtlety. She had not noticed it, would never notice it, but he? Ah. It had burned dry along his tongue, as her perfume embraced him. A needle of pain had pierced him, pricking his body's every nerve. His teeth had stretched long, his fingers clutched the texture of her hand, her rough skin, the solidity of sinew, of bone, the sound of her breath.

Nearly, so nearly, he had seized her in his arms and kissed that sweet mouth, regardless of the bloody havoc his teeth would wreck. What then? To bruise her with inescapable caresses? To lick bright scarlet from her skin? To feel her shudder, moan? To take her throat in his mouth and bite down upon her life?

No.

He had bidden them a mild farewell. He had watched her walk away, back to her Jonathan, whose diamond she wore and in whose soft and mortal arms she would sleep, untroubled.

Surrounded by empty rooms, the creature knelt beside the chair where she had sat. He laid his head upon the leather and drank the scent of her skin, her sex, the scent of rosemary, honey, wine. His body trembled and for a moment, one moment, there was peace.

He breathed out a slow, enraptured breath. The pupils in his eyes grew huge and flat.

And he rose and left.

Sophia sat on the cold, hard bench, looking up at the sky. Even here in the city centre she could see the stars, cut crystal points in the heavy velvet of night. She breathed steadily and willed them to stop spinning. When they did, she picked out Orion by his belt, the curve of his bow, then the cluster of the Pleiades and the V of Taurus between them.

She remembered reading somewhere that Taurus was more than a star sign, that in some places it was the heavenly bull that belonged to

Ishtar, the bull which Gilgamesh killed. Another myth jumbled into her mind – the Pleiades, not sisters but friends, turned into pigs for their immoderate love of a ball game...

It was possible John's mates would still be drinking at the flat, talking football. She wouldn't put it past them, even at half one in the morning. Sophia had always hated sport. Watching Lucy play hockey was a trial, and Lucy was her best friend. Besides, she actually played the game; John and his mates would have spent the evening lounged in front of the TV, getting into the tribalism of it, the thoughtless violence which seethed just beneath the surface.

Snob. After all, she had liked John's uni mates, hadn't she? But there was something about his new friends, the way they spoke, the way they looked at her, their sheer *obsession* with televised competitions... She stood up and started to walk home. It was too cold to sit on the bench anymore. There was no point delaying – she could always make her excuses and go to bed.

As she turned her key in the door, she felt dread. There was every chance the three of them would be huddled there, still fomenting match fever, dissecting the game and conducting a character assassination of the referee.

The flat was empty and dark, smelling of smoke, Doritos and men's body sprays. John was on the sofa, watching comedy reruns and drinking a can of beer. He looked up when he heard her walk in.

'Hello darling,' she cried, and threw herself on to him. She kissed him, passionate and careless, even though he smelled of cheap hops and smoke; she nuzzled her face into his neck, kissing again and again. She expected to feel the ends of his hair tickling her lips, but then she remembered that he had cut it months ago, into this more professional style.

'Oh. Hello, gorgeous.' He sounded bemused and gratified.

She giggled and went to kiss him again, but his mouth tasted of smoke and cheese crisps. She pulled away, putting her hand against his chest, feeling his heartbeat.

'Did you have a good night, at what's-his-name's?'

'Yeah, it was nice.' Her hand slipped under the neck of his t-shirt, probed the hollow of his neck, 'Actually, I'm a bit pissed.' She put her other hand up the back of his shirt, feeling the hot, smooth skin there.

He jumped. 'Woah. Careful, love. Cold hands.'

She growled a little and withdrew. 'But was good. We talked. About books and things.'

'Well, I'm sorry if it was boring for you.'

'No. I liked it.' She slipped the previously rebuffed hand into the waistband of his trousers. 'I like books and things.'

John pulled away. 'Yeah? Well, that's because you're really smart. Come on, love, we should be getting to bed.' He began to stand.

Sophia clung to him and made grumbling noises. 'Oh, come on, John. We should spend some time.'

'Look, love, I'm glad you had a nice evening, but I've really got to get to bed. I've got work tomorrow.'

She let go and brushed down her jumper. She realised she was a lot more sober than she had been acting. 'Yeah, sure. It is quite late.'

John reached over to kiss her again, but her lecherous good humour was gone. She turned her head to the side and his lips met her cheek. Then, seeing his hurt expression, she relented and kissed him properly.

Later, with the insomnia of drunkenness making the room reel around her, she noticed there was a cut on her knuckle the size and shape of a papercut. It had split open and stained the bedclothes. As she lay still, watching the green numbers of the clock flicker upwards, it throbbed in time to her pulse.

7. Things Unsaid

'You yourself never loved; you never love!'
– Bram Stoker, *Dracula*

Steven lay across the entire length of the sofa, still wearing his pyjama bottoms and the t-shirt that showed a smiley face with fangs.

It was that time in the afternoon when a student's day hung between early and late; too early to make dinner, get drunk or start on an all-night essay spree. Too late to go into town, too late for most seminars, and, if the morning had been spent in the library, it had long since become expedient to leave there before the dust, silence and writer's block drove one to insanity.

Sophia tended to drop by at around this time, and she was curled up in the armchair across from him. She looked a damned sight worse than he felt. He had been lucky; the literature department at Barchester University took a dim view of making anyone work on a Friday, so he had been able to roll out of bed at 10am and crawl into the main body of the flat in search of water and Alka-Seltzer. He had then returned to bed clutching the book on Shakespeare and disappeared under the covers until midday.

As a biology student, Sophia had spent the day on campus. She was glaring at him, or possibly just the world in general. Lucy was lounging over the remaining armchair and, in view of Sophia's hangover, was directing most of her harangue at him. 'You never said next Thursday!'

'And why not next Thursday, my love?'

'Opening night,' she replied, then added, 'fuckwit.'

'Oh. Shit.' Sophia's voice sounded faint. Just hearing it made Steven's head wince in sympathy, 'Um. Sorry. We'll just tell him we can't do Thursday. I'd forgotten.'

'Nah, come Friday. Or Monday. There're always tickets Monday, whereas opening night gets rammed. But I wanted to meet the lovely Julian again. It's just not *fair*.'

'Oh Lucy, it sounds like a tragedy…'

She gave him an evil glare.

'I'll make the tea,' he said, and went to the kitchen.

As he came back with a teapot, a carton of milk, their respective mugs and the biscuit tin, he heard Sophia saying, 'So how are the applications going?'

'Oh, that. I missed the bloody deadline.' Lucy had, until recently, been applying for a PGCE.

'That sucks. So there's no hope?'

'Unless I get on to a GTP.' Lucy shrugged. 'For what is basically a graduate scheme, they're pretty mental with their deadlines. I had essays to do, you know? But I'm sure the Bar and Mutual are just *dying* to employ another history graduate. That should keep me going for a year or so.'

Steven wrinkled his nose as he put down the tea things. 'Darling, say you don't mean that.' The Barchester and Mutual was a building society based locally. It was also the city's biggest employer. It was a cliché that all Barchester students ended up there for at least six months. The three of them had vowed this would never happen to them.

'Well, I'll need a job, Steven. You will too. I mean, what are you planning on doing if your MA falls through?'

'I already have a job. Ray's always saying that he can take me on full-time.' He felt nauseous. He liked Patroclus, liked his boss, but... The end of the summer term seemed very close. 'Anyway, the MA isn't going to fall through, is it, Sophia?'

She said nothing.

He pressed his lips together. 'So, how are your plans going, then?'

'Oh.' She huddled tighter into her chair. 'Okay. You know how it is.'

'But you've got your application in for the MSc?' He knew Lucy well enough to detect the sharpness in her voice, to see the worry in her eyes. She had always told him to stop interfering.

'Well. You know. Busy with the dissertation, and money's the trouble, isn't it?'

'But you are still applying,' Lucy said.

It was a while before Sophia said, 'Yeah. At some point. It's not like there's any hurry.'

'No, no. Of course not.' Steven was unable to keep all the sarcasm from his voice. 'So, not this year then. What about next year?'

'I – I'm not sure. I mean, the thing is I don't think I want to do it in Barchester. The school's a bit limited outside of plant sciences and, well, I guess moving isn't all that realistic right now.'

Replies crowded into his head, none of them wise. Fortunately, Lucy said, 'Why not, honey? I mean, it's not that we won't miss you, but... Oh.'

'Yeah.'

'I think I've missed something of import,' he said, and found Lucy giving him a dirty look.

He glanced at Sophia. Her face was set, even hard. When she spoke, she spoke slowly and her tone threatened danger. 'Well. It's not so good for John, is it? And, as we're kind of engaged, I wouldn't really want to move without him, would I?'

'Dear God! I wasn't suggesting *that*. But come on. That's not a real reason. John works in *admin*. He can do that anywhere.'

'Yeah. Right. Perhaps I'd better be going.' Sophia started getting up.

Lucy got up too and gave him another of those looks. 'No, Sophia, please. Don't go.'

'Well, I'm sorry. But I think who I decide to marry is my business.' Her face was pinched, tight with anger.

Steven bit his tongue. That he had managed to piss Sophia off was nothing new. Normally, though, she'd just tell him where to shove it. 'Heck, no. No, I'm sorry, Sophia,' he said, and meant it, although he would stand by everything he had just implied. 'That wasn't nice. I didn't mean it like that. I just meant... it doesn't matter what I meant. I'm sorry. I can be a complete arse when I choose to, you know that.'

After a couple of seconds she said, 'Okay,' and shrugged and sat down again. But her face was cold and her voice remained distant.

The quarrel hung like a scar across the day. By the time she left they were chattering away again, but it was still there. There was something wrong and Sophia was not telling them about it.

Later, as the evening wore on and he tried to concentrate on his book, he found his eyes slid over the pages. It shouldn't be like this. They were friends and had been since they were children. The mugs he had not yet washed were beside him. Sophia's one was black and showed a bat flying in front of a full moon. It had once been his, but she had started using it a few months ago so he had given it to her. She had bought him a new one which said 'Go away, I'm reading'. The two mugs sat against each other, almost touching. Beside them was Lucy's own, bright and childish, a gift from him. He tried to think of not knowing this, of not sharing that history, but the idea seemed stupid. That was Sophia's mug, and his, and Lucy's. It was just one of those things.

Perhaps they had been friends for too long.

All they ever seemed to talk about these days were trivial things – biscuits, essays, jobs. Of course, he didn't expect them to tell him every little thing. But how much of his own sense of self was tied up with those vague, unspoken feelings, those solitary arguments and private embarrassments? How much was he, were any of them, concealing?

He remembered an incident from years ago, not long after the bad business with his parents, when he had been reading a book which ended with the protagonist's suicide. Annoyed, he had glanced up and announced that, although he'd been through rough patches, he could never understand why someone might want to kill themselves. And Lucy – bold, tough, fearless Lucy – very quietly said, 'I do.'

And Sophia had not said anything at all.

The creature slept through the short winter day. He did not twist or shift in his dreams as he had when he had been a mortal man. His habitual breathing ceased, and his heartbeat slowed to five, perhaps six beats a minute. His skin was pale, almost luminous in the darkness of the cellar. Fully dressed, with his hands folded on his chest, he might have been one of the statues which, in his youth, had been laid upon the tombs of the rich; carved from alabaster, not dead but sleeping. The only details missing were a sword, a little dog under his feet.

But as the light failed, he began to wake. Small, flickering movements twitched his fingers, his lips as he drew back from the deep wanderings of his dreams. When he fasted, they were troubled things, jumbled memories from the senseless hunger that had stripped him of his selfhood, which had robbed from him the greatest part of the last century. But, with stolen blood cooling heavy in his stomach, he had dreamt – he was sure that he had dreamt – of the heat of his human life.

Eyes opening, head turning upon his pillow, he could almost capture it, almost see it as plain as if it were still happening around him: *a September day, wet and dreary. Mud from the city streets seeping through his boots, the fart and straw smell of the cattle market hanging in his nostrils. Trade had been poor but he rode before his steward and felt nothing but lightness of heart. As he came to the manor, he saw the shape of her, saw her watching for him and felt as ever the stinging joy at the beauty of her face…*

So young. How had he not seen it then? The smooth skin around her lips, her eyes, the still childlike movements of her hands…

Her mantle sat awkwardly, her girdle hardly able to encircle the soft swelling of her stomach. Through the misting rain she came with the fluid gait of pregnancy, and she called his name. His real name.

He dismounted, and uncaring for the damp or for their clothes, uncaring for propriety, he seized her hands and kissed her smile, embracing the honey, rosemary scent of her, closing his eyes and…

And the moment passed.

The creature reached after it, but it was gone.

Still lying half drowsed, he chased it, forcing her face back into his mind until *she lay before him, face haggard, skin cold. Her eyes had been closed, but they were open once again, empty and glazed. There was stale blood streaking the sheets, a pricking in his throat, a hunger… a thirst…*

No.

He closed his eyes. Any memory but that one. Beneath him were crisp cotton covers, a mattress firm with springs. When she had lived, it had been a featherbed laid over a woollen mattress and they had lain *tangled together, her long braid bright against the white of her kirtle. Not asleep, but drifting, she lay on her side, back to his stomach, murmuring pleasure as his fingers traced her newly heavy breasts, the taut weight of her stomach...*

Almost, almost he jolted himself from memory with the urge, the need to pull her towards him, to hold her truly once more, one final time, if only in this half dream.

His face was buried in her shoulder. He ached with desire, pressed himself against her, felt her laugh. 'Soon, leman, once the child is born and I am churched.' He could smell all the sweat and rosemary and honey of her, kissed her neck, cradled her, ran his hands over her belly. And there, beneath his hand, that strange swimming motion of life, that contact shocking and intimate. He laughed, thinking, 'My son'...

But if he had been able to tear the kicking, growing thing from her womb, to strangle its life away...

She gasped, saying the child grew stronger every day. He moved to kiss her cheek, felt loose strands of her hair tickle his lips, saw the pink in her tender skin and he touched her mouth and began to sing the lullaby his nurse had once sung him, 'Lullay, lullay...' And there were shadows under her eyes for she had not slept well these past nights, and she reached an arm around his waist and held him. 'Lullay, lullay...'

Oh, if only he had wept, as she had lain warm against him and her eyes closed in sleep. The creature tried to pretend it had been so, that he had wept from the happiness and the love, for now he could not, even though it felt as though his old, slow heart might break.

Lucy stared at her reflection in the living-room window and steeled herself for this. She had waited at least until he had calmed down and stopped pacing the flat between futile attempts to read. Now he was crouched on one corner of the sofa, scowling at the page as if he meant business.

She did not want to do this. It was part of their agreement that she did not do this.

She walked over and sat next to him. 'Steven?'

'Uh-huh.' He did not look up.

Reaching out, Lucy closed the book. That was pretty much guaranteed to piss him off, but he deserved it. 'Steven, why?'

He extracted his thumb from between the pages and replaced it with a bookmark. He said nothing as he put the book down and she did not interrupt. At last he looked up at her, his hair unruly and unbrushed, his face tired. It felt as though she were looking into an exhaustion, a bewilderment, a hurt that went back a very long way. She remembered when she had first seen that expression in his eyes.

'Please don't tell me you're defending John.'

She forced herself to say it: 'No, love. I'm defending Sophia.'

He nodded. 'Is she just stupid, or something?'

Lucy looked away.

'I mean it. Is she? Honestly? Is she out of her mind?'

She reached over and took his hand. 'Could you not give her a bit of a break? Just when she's here – could you not let it be?'

'I try. Believe me, I do try. But *John*? Really? Do you think he's doing her any good? He's a... a Neanderthal.'

'A lot of girls think John's quite a catch, you know.'

'A lot of girls are bloody idiots.'

'Okay. But if he makes her happy...'

'But that's just it. He doesn't make her happy. All she's ever wanted to *do* was study.'

'Different people have different priorities.'

'Yes.' She could see his struggle to calm himself. When he spoke again, he was quieter. 'Yes, I know that. I'm quite prepared to be tolerant of other people's decisions and priorities.'

She raised her eyebrows.

'Fine, alright. I'm intolerant of them. I'll admit it, but then I detest most people and their pathetic bloody lives. Sophia, however, is my friend, and she is better than that.' He looked about him angrily. 'She's better than *him*.'

Lucy took a deep breath. She wasn't sure how far she should take this, how far she could safely take this. 'I know Sophia's doing things a little differently to how she always said she would, but people change. And, well, people do things that maybe aren't ideal because... because of things like love. Things like emotion. Sometimes you're prepared to sacrifice things if you care about someone enough.'

'But why is it always Sophia who has to do all the sacrificing? Emotion! Ugh. It's as bad as fucking *faith*. She should be studying, travelling, learning, but what's she going to do? Be a good little wifey in a job she hates just because John doesn't want to move?' He exhaled, furious. 'I just want to shake her, sometimes.'

Lucy thought about the future and what it might be like to be able to get into teaching, to put down roots, start a family. Have children. But that way madness lay.

'Come on, it's just because you don't like John, isn't it?'

'No. No, it isn't.'

She gave him a look.

Steven turned away. 'Really. I wish it were.'

'Then what's bothering you?'

'I'm worried about her. I know you are too. There's something, something not right there. It's not just John.'

Lucy nodded. Once, in the second year, Sophia and Steven had made a solemn – if drunken – pact that they would do postgraduate research or they would shoot one another. She remembered other things, too, like the way that Sophia had always been the easy-going one. She remembered Sophia's face earlier, sharp and tight with anger. 'No, you're right. But, well, it doesn't have to be John's fault. I mean, it's third year, honey. We all have deadlines. Maybe she's just stressed.'

'It is not stress.'

'Okay, not stress. But, anyway, the sciences are different. Maybe she finds the postgraduate scene daunting.' She wondered if she were saying these things for Sophia's sake, or for Steven's. It was not as if she believed them.

'Or maybe it's to do with the fact her boyfriend is a worthless loser?'

'Steven…'

'Okay, I'm sorry,' he said. Then, 'Actually, no. Sod it. I am *not* sorry. We're both thinking it and moreover it's *true*. John does not deserve Sophia. The sooner she realises this and ditches him, the sooner we can get back the girl we know and love. It's very simple. Why are we even having this conversation?'

'Steven…'

'No, really. Why can't she *see* that? Why aren't we doing something?'

'Steven, Steven. Okay. You're right. Christ's sake. But... it's got to be her decision. She'll work it out. We can't *make* her leave him, and, sweetie, you're not helping matters.' She squeezed his hand and made herself look into his eyes. The irritation had gone and that lost expression was back. She bit her lip. Some things needed saying. 'When you love someone, if someone attacks them then they're attacking you, too.'

He looked away. 'I know that. Don't think I don't know that. It's just... It's like she's refusing to see sense. And when I try to make her, she thinks it's only because I hate John.'

'And I wonder where she got that wild idea? You're so nice to him!'

'Fine. Alright. But I'm like that with everyone. Sophia should know that by now. And, well, just because I don't like him, it doesn't mean I'm wrong. He is bad for her. Why can't she see it?'

'She's much less likely to see it if you keep on at her like that.'

'I know. I know.' Steven put his head in his hands. 'Ugh. He just gets right under my skin. I... Sometimes, I've just got to say something or – pacifist or no – I'll lamp him one.' He looked up at her, and Lucy remembered an image from the past that was always somewhere in her mind: the rain sheeting, and Steven standing in the phone box at the corner of his parents' road, wearing his school uniform and his house slippers. Tears ran down his cheeks even though she could see he was trying not to cry.

Sometimes Lucy wanted to hit John too.

'We don't get to say who someone else is allowed to love. You should know that better than anyone.'

'I am trying to stop being such a bastard,' he said, and his voice shook.

She wanted to put her arm around him, but she knew his pride. 'I know, love. I know. Look, I'll have a word with Sophia. And, yeah, sometimes I don't much like John, either.' He looked at her, and his gratitude made her want to stop there. 'But it *is* Sophia's choice. However stupid she's being, we've got to let her go with it.' She nudged him. 'Hell, maybe what's getting her down is the way you two are always on at each other.'

Steven smiled. Not his usual clever, impervious smile, but a shadow of it. Close enough for now. 'Damn. I thought you'd finished telling me off.'

She stuck her tongue out to let him know it was okay. 'Nothing like, you idiot. We've not even *started* on the fact that you get so defensive of Sophia and you're never that concerned about me.'

'Oh, you can take care of yourself. You can spot a loser a mile away. I sometimes think you have some kind of radar for it.'

'Bollocks. I've dated some right throwbacks.'

'Well, yes, but you've always known that a gorilla – even a strategically shaved one put into a football strip – can never hold a learned discourse on Plato. Ergo, I do not concern myself.'

'Plato?'

Steven nodded. 'The general litmus test to distinguish *sapiens sapiens*.'

'Right, okay. Ignoring cultural relativity, your history's flawed. What did we use before Plato?'

'How should I know? You're the historian.'

'Yes. And my excavations through the sink in search of a clean fork this afternoon led me to the conclusion that someone didn't do the washing-up last night. Plus the strong signs of charring on the remains of food also suggest I was cooking. Which means it's your turn tonight.' She kept her voice light and playful, and grinned at him. 'Historian. I take the evidence to hand, I reach a conclusion about the past...'

'And that informs our view of the future? Hmm.' Steven did not sound convinced. And nothing had been solved. Still, when he picked up his book again the crease of worry was gone from between his eyes and that was enough to be going on with.

Sophia sat in her room.

It was not actually her room. Not really. *Her* room had been her flat in halls, a room with a string of fairy lights in the shape of rubber ducks around the walls, and a couple of the standard student posters Blu Tacked on the door. Her room had a reproduction of a Georgia O'Keeffe 'Jack-in-the-Pulpit' over the bed – a picture which was now in the lounge – and, over her desk, a print of Waterhouse's

'The Awaking of Adonis', which had been lost in the move. In her room, every inch of the regulation white walls had been covered with throws and photographs. She'd been able to wrap her room about her like a comfort blanket, from the matched statuettes of the Bonnie and Clyde teddies that had sat on top of her computer to the bedsheets that she and Lucy had dyed purple one summer afternoon.

The teddies were still in front of her, gathering dust on top of the monitor, but the bedsheets had been replaced with whatever had been cheap in the Co-op the week they'd moved in – cream with a bland pattern on them. The picture over the bed had been given to them by John's mum as a house-warming gift, and it had already been framed so it made sense to put it where there was already picture hook. The walls were magnolia and it was against their contract to use Blu Tack, so she felt she could not overdo it with posters or hangings. Besides, she would never have had enough bright things to fill the whole of the flat.

Most of the time, this did not bother her. After all, her stuff was still there, only spread out over a larger area and mingled with the flat's furniture and things that belonged to John. Most of the time, she thought of this room as her room. But now it swam about her, as impersonal and brittle as a hotel. Right now, she could do with being in her old room in halls again.

She felt sick. She tried to tell herself that it was the effects of the hangover, that it was something she had eaten, but she knew it was a lie. Slowly, she clenched both fists, and when the sensation of nails digging into her palms began to hurt, she released them. *What is wrong with me?*

She tried to think about the future and her mind shied away. But like all the things she could not face, it nagged at her. Next year, she would be twenty-two. Her entire life seemed like the briefest interval in the cosmic scheme of things, and the future which had once stretched out before her as an endless vista full of opportunity, seemed, like the school summer holidays, to diminish to a few mundane activities and some bad weather.

It was all so exhausting.

She wanted to shake herself, to snap out of it. She told herself that

she was moping. She detested moping. It was pathetic and self-indulgent. The kind of thing you did if you were too much of a coward
actually to get up and do something about whatever was bothering
you. She had to pull herself together, had to do something.

But how could you argue with life? she asked herself. *How do you argue
with reality?*

She felt something in her make a little sound of pain, and she started
to cry.

8. Two Contrary States of the Human Soul

'That is a dreadful imprisonment,' said Will, impetuously.
'No, don't think that,' said Dorothea. 'I have no longings.'
– George Eliot, *Middlemarch*

Steven pushed his hands deeper into his pockets and exhaled steam. It was almost December and, as if the weather last week had not been cold enough, there had been another cold snap. There had even been a sprinkling of snow.

The news anchors had forgotten the trouble in the Middle East, crime and the state of the economy, and started asking if there was going to be a white Christmas for the first time in however many years. This had been followed by weather forecasters informing everyone of a warm front moving across northern Europe with all the grim glee of a parent telling you that it's really sleet and it will not settle. But for Steven, Christmas – white or otherwise – did not qualify as a concern.

Something that *did* concern him was his final essay of the term and as he walked towards the stress of another Thursday nightshift at Patroclus, he tried to formulate a conclusion for it. The slush on the ground soaked through his walking boots. *They need some Scotchgard,* he reminded himself as his toes went numb. No chance of them thawing at work, but at least Julian would have a roaring fire.

Their Thursday night meetings had become something of a fixture. Lucy was adamant that she would not forgive them this – she was always busy on Thursdays. It had occurred to Steven to mention that he was always at least as busy as her and it never stopped him turning up.

Perhaps he was in love. That would have been the logical response to the situation. It would explain the desperate, uncomfortable happiness he felt when he was with Julian. The way that, seeing himself reflected in his friend's eyes, he could believe himself to be someone passionate, interesting; attractive, even.

Sometimes he felt something else, too. When Julian folded him in that fraternal embrace, or when he woke at night and realised what he had been dreaming about, he felt as though he stood at the edge of a precipice while a storm was brewing in the sky. Sometimes it felt as though he might be lost.

So he held his breath and spent sleepless nights writing essays, or reading prospectuses for postgraduate courses, to stop his mind from going to that place. But walking along, it was harder to keep such thoughts at bay. There was no book in which to bury himself, no conversation to distract him. Phrases from that Carter essay crept into his head to damn him. *Platonic mingling. No physical forms.*

'Ugh,' he said aloud. Then he glanced around in case anyone was watching him. There was no one.

Except a cat at the end of the alleyway, in the shadow of a hedge. Steven smiled, double-checked he was not being observed, and pursed his lips, making a kissy sound, calling it towards him.

The cat looked up, its eyes flashing an unearthly green. It did not move.

Steven crouched down and rubbed his fingers together. He made the squeaking sound again and whispered, 'C'mon kitty.'

But the animal only lowered its head to something on the ground. Steven stood, took a couple of steps towards it, fingers still pressed together, enticing. Until he saw the bird under its paws.

He stopped, felt his breath catch in his throat. The cat's head moved, biting. There was the sound, he was sure he could hear it, of hollow bones crunching, of brittle feathers being snapped. The cat looked up at him again, fierce in challenge.

He need only clap his hands.

But where was the virtue in that? The thing was dead. A cat couldn't be blamed for its instincts. All the same, Steven wanted to turn, to find another route to work.

No. If he did that, he'd be late and even colder than he already was. He moved forwards, treading quietly, not wanting to disturb it, not wanting to see anything more. The cat made a long, keening cry over its prey.

He tried to look away, but something about the spectacle fascinated him. Brown feathers, black-and-white fur. And a spasming wing-flutter, the last struggle of a broken life.

Steven opened his mouth, trying to find the words to shout, the resolve to chase the cat away and give whatever mercy was in his power. His mouth was dry, his hands poised, unclapping.

Lucy, he knew, would not hesitate – he had seen her do it before, pick up a twitching bird from where a cat had dropped it, carry it to a quiet place. Remembered her face pale, solemn, in the aftermath: *'I couldn't do anything to help it. I felt it die in my hands.'*

That cat lowered its mouth to the bird once more, and Steven turned his face away.

Later, at Patroclus, Chaz – a regular – leaned against the counter and said, 'Makes you sick to think about it. I dread to think what's happened to them.'

The shop was quietening down before closing, so it was only her and a pair of teenagers browsing the recent releases. Toes still damp and numb, Steven crouched behind the rack he was tidying and pulled out *War Requiem* from where it was nestling among the Ls. Quite what it was about the alphabet that confused so many of their customers he was not sure, but sorting out the resulting disorder took up a lot of his time.

This was what he thought about; not the struggling bird, not Julian, and certainly not the conversation at the counter.

'I dunno,' Ray said, 'you know what kids are. Odds are they'll turn up in a week or two with red faces, wondering what all the fuss was about.'

'Nah, but it's not like it was in our day. They've all got their mobile phones and their Myspaces. It's not like anyone's hopping on the back of a moped for a dirty weekend in Brighton anymore. And what with these murders…'

Steven did his best not to sigh. Because no one would give a damn about the missing teens were it not for *the bodies*, said in that hushed, sensationalist tone. *The bodies* were of a young homeless man and a local middle-aged woman, both of whom had been missing for a few weeks before they had been found concealed near the city centre. The coroner had returned a verdict of unlawful killing, which made them *these murders.*

So when it came to public notice that a pair of teenagers had disappeared within a fortnight of each other, the local paper had announced it with cheerful headlines such as 'Killer strikes again?'

Ray said, 'Well, let's not assume the worst. We don't know if anything bad's happened to them. Think of their parents, yeah?'

'I am thinking of their parents. If that were me, I'd want to be sure the police were doing their best.'

Because before this, everyone concerned had simply assumed the kids had run away, or been involved in some sort of accident. Now there was public pressure on the police to find them, and people were talking about how they didn't feel safe walking about at night.

Steven ran his finger along the shelf, checking everything was in order, and heard Chaz sigh. 'Well, I don't know what the world's coming to. This was always such a safe city.'

And, statistically, it's still a safer city than most. But Ray had told him not to say that to the customers. Well, he couldn't stay lurking in the middle of the alphabet indefinitely, so he stood up, arms full of misplaced DVDs.

Chaz jumped. 'Christ! Imagine you lurking there. I was wondering where you'd got to. What do you reckon about all this, Steven?'

'Sorry, Chaz, but I just need to…'

She moved out of his way, but not without giving him an appraising look. 'You changed the dress code in here, Ray? Only, he's looking very dapper tonight.'

He would rather they talked about the murders than that.

'Nothing to do with me. Someone's got a date when he gets off tonight.' Even with his gaze locked on the shelves in front of him, Steven could *hear* the smirk in Ray's voice.

'And you're keeping him till closing?'

'I haven't…' Steven tried to say, hands suddenly struggling with the slick covers of the DVDs.

'Oh, you're a wicked old beggar! Steven, you tell this old geezer to get stuffed. Honestly. It's about bloody time the boy had some fun.'

Steven used the heel of his hand to ram a DVD back on to the shelf. 'He's just a mate, we're not...'

'Oh, bless him, he's gone all pink.'

'Let him be, Chaz. Alright, well, you might as well leave that lot on the counter. Go on. Clear off.'

Steven felt something catch in his throat. He looked between Ray and Chaz.

'Yeah, I'm talking to you. Go and find your man of mystery – I reckon I can handle it from here.'

'I...' Steven paused, caught between, *thank you* and another denial.

Ray laughed, shook his head. 'Shoo.'

But as Steven was halfway through the door to the backroom, hand reaching for his coat, Ray said, 'Just a bit of advice, though? If you fancy him being more than a mate, you do have to clue the other fella in at some point.'

Steven stopped, turning, expecting more mockery, but there was no smile on Ray's face.

'It's not like that.'

'Sure it's not. But some things, you only get one shot.'

He hesitated, one hand still reaching for his coat, unsure of what to say.

'Ah, go on,' Ray waved at him, 'get lost.'

Steven nodded, and went through to the exit. All the same, he caught Chaz's quiet little tut and the way she said, 'Poor kid.'

Sophia sat in her usual chair, drinking red wine and letting the full depth of Julian's choice in music wash over her. Her eyes were half closed and she was carried on the rise and fall of violins, pulled by the almost sexual undercurrent of something she assumed was a cello. Other instruments she could not begin to classify roared and crashed about her, and over it all came the slight whispering static of the vinyl on the turntable. She smiled and opened her eyes.

Julian sat opposite her, the tips of his steepled fingers resting against his mouth. He was watching her as if waiting for her response, or approval. Neither spoke but after a few moments she nodded, then he did the same.

The alchemy of Julian's restoration spread a little further every week. For all his deflections about the house being too large for one man, how it was not really fit for habitation, he offered her and Steven each new room like a gift.

Slowly, all the trappings of place unfurled around them: engraved crystal glasses in a dozen shapes and sizes, the long, brocade curtains closing off the night outside, and, this evening, a handful of fragile shellac discs and the gramophone to go with them.

'It's something of a miracle they have survived. I remember my grandfather playing them, but they must have been his father's. Or perhaps his uncle's. Rather solemn works, I'm afraid.'

As the music crashed and soared about her, she wondered what it must be like to have a family like his, generations of them filling a place until it was warm with stories, love and life. How it must be to know of those who had gone before with so much certainty; how it must feel to call a place like this home.

Earlier, Julian had told her of an ancestor who had spent much of his life in Italy just after the Napoleonic wars had ended, who had wandered, peripatetic and Romantic, like so many other English men of the time. Of how he had sought in Catholic Europe truths which England, in her industrial age, seemed about to forget.

Julian had been gently scornful of his forbear's naiveté, but it had entranced Sophia. The idea of a doomed quest for novelty, discovery, even security, in the ruins of the Roman Empire, the splendour of the Roman Church. At one point, it occurred to her to ask how he was related to this long dead man, how he knew the annals of his family history with such detail and passion, but the moment passed.

Julian was a talented storyteller; that was all. He was romancing upon bare facts, creating a better tale from some footnote in his family mythology. And she derived too much pleasure from the narrative to interrupt, to query, to break the spell. She sat silent as her mind whirled with images: the Colosseum drowning under verdant flowers, the slow sadness of Venice in the rain. Now, as she listened to the music, she thought about travel, about the quest for morality and truth.

She had been abroad a grand total of twice.

A few years ago, there had been a school trip to Paris. Steven, Lucy and she had spent five days trailing round art galleries, eating badly made versions of 'traditional French recipes' and trying to slip off to Montmartre when no one was looking. They had failed.

The time before that, she could have been no more than five. It had been the last holiday her parents had taken together and all she could remember was standing outside a cathedral with brightly coloured roof tiles and concentrating on chasing pigeons while her mum and dad had a blazing row about some little thing. She had a feeling it had been somewhere in Germany, or Austria. Somewhere like that.

She thought of *Frankenstein*, of *Childe Harold's Pilgrimage*. 'Did your ancestor really do all that? Just like Keats and Shelley and Byron?'

She watched Julian's smile widen slightly. He gave a tiny shrug. 'I thought you had no patience for the Byronic type.'

She looked away, smiling. But when she spoke, she said, 'You know, I've never really been anywhere. Not like that. Holiday and things, they don't count. You don't really know the place, so you don't really see it. But your ancestor... I mean, that must have been something else. No wonder all the best writing from those centuries has travel in it, because.... Because it must have been amazing, just such a culture shock. To be away for so long....' Her voice trailed off. She felt Julian's eyes on her, and she tucked a strand of hair behind her ear.

'As you say. A strange place, a sense of... of such difference. As if all the world had changed and the wanderer with it. You must also see that Italy – as it was then – was a strange place for one born in England. In our climate things do not last. Winter and the rain destroy it all. Yet in Rome much remains of what once was.' His voice had become quiet, absorbing, but now he waved his hand, dismissing the effect of his words. 'Oh, of course, the same is true in many warmer climes. Greece was Byron's obsession, and that is similar. In much of North Africa the villas still have paint upon the walls from a thousand years past, but Italy – *Rome* – has a fascination and authority of its own. To the Western consciousness it means so much: the Roman Church, the Roman Empire, the Eternal City; it haunts us – whether we admit it or no. And to seek out these archetypes, that was part of the Romantic dream. But to seek wonder is to find it, regardless of the facts. It was nothing but novelty which stimulated the mind. Rome has no extraordinary worth, for if it did it would not be the visitors who sang its praises in the loudest tones. What to new eyes appears a wonder of the ancient world, a symbol for permanence and immutability is, to a local, simply an aspect of their daily skyline.' He swirled the wine in his glass and stared into the fire.

He was sometimes like this when Steven was not there, as though he felt a sadness that he did not wish to share. Perhaps it had something to do with his own travels, for he seemed to have been to most of the places his ancestor had visited. She wondered if he was ever oppressed by staid routine, if he ever felt the need to run away to somewhere his sense of wonder could be unleashed.

She shifted in her chair. 'But that doesn't mean it isn't wonderful; it's just that we forget about it, right? But why does it happen? If something is special, it should be special all the time, shouldn't it?'

He said nothing.

She felt something like panic. 'It's like if you live with anything, anything, however strange or valuable, for long enough you won't care about it anymore.' Her hands were shaking, she could not breathe. 'Is that really how it happens?' she asked, and her voice was like a plea.

And Julian looked up, looked into her eyes. 'Yes. I believe that it is.'

Night. It was outside the house, pressing on the doors and the windows. It was inside the rooms, filling them from their tiled floors to vaulted ceilings. The creature had brought it in when he had snuffed the candles after his guests had left. He could smell the wax smoke from where he sat on the old wood of the staircase, as he stared at that carved foliage, the wyvern that chased in and out of the leaves.

Brandy, too much brandy, sloshed inside his stomach, sickening. Steven had sat here, precisely in this place. But while the creature leaned back against the panelling of the wall, his face in his hands and his eyes staring without emotion, Steven had bent forwards, bewitched. His fingers had found, brushed, the age-polished wood with the tentative wonder of a man handling holy things.

In anyone else, the creature would have suspected a sensuality in such caresses, have felt his mind leap between the stroking of slick wood to the worship of smooth skin, but Steven had been entirely lost in his admiration, the smile upon his lips faint as his hands had traced the carving upwards, found other shapes lurking in the frieze. Under the spell of house, all the boy's guarded cleverness had fallen away to leave the open-heartedness of a child.

It was there, always, that he caught his dearest prey, by opening out what they hid of their innocence and stepping into it with them, by wondering at their wonder as though – by doing so – he could be like them once again. For was that wyvern not an old friend of his? Had he not dawdled on these same steps until adults had chased him out from underfoot, following those same lines and curls with his hands? Were not his initials still carved on the bannister's underside, where his fingers would sometimes rub against them?

But all of that was so long, so very long ago. The creature looked at his hands, pale and untouched by the thousand, thousand scars that should mark them. How could they remember the childhood smooth-ness of dark wood when they had grabbed throats and rooted among tendons, seeking the hidden parts of lives? How could he be so indif-ferent to the very things that moved his young friends – the swell of the cello, the bright glitter of a crystal glass?

If he could only fall on his knees before Steven and beg him for forgiveness, understanding, or even one breath of the innocence they had once shared in this place.

But if his young friend pitied him – if, compassionate, he drew the creature into the circle of his arms – what then? The creature thought of the soft, warm skin of Steven's neck, of the way his whole body trembled when the creature kissed his cheek.

The comforts, the mercies of those distant, human days were lost, buried beneath bloody centuries.

And if he could not be held like a man, feel love or wonder as a man might feel it, then there were other, darker pleasures open to him. He had denied himself for so very long, but if there were truly no hope of absolution, then there were consolations to be found in the night.

9. Sleep and his Half-Brother Death

He took sic pleasure in deer and roe,
Till he forgot his gay ladye.
Till by it came that milk–white hynde,
And then he mind on his ladye syne.
– 'Leesome Brand' (traditional ballad)

John drained the last half-inch of his pint and set the glass back on the table. He made an elaborate show of checking his watch. 'Alright, guys. I'd best be off.'

Dave made a whip-cracking noise.

John smiled and gestured at the table full of empty glasses. 'I said one drink.'

'Ah, it's only 8.30. Come on, mate. Play you at pool?'

'Nah. I should be getting home.'

'Back to the old ball and chain,' Ron sneered. As usual.

'Ha. At least I'm getting some.'

'Yeah, and that Sophie's a bit of alright, too.'

'Oh, shut your mouth. I'll see you wankers tomorrow.' Out in the night his head cleared. John shivered and stuck his hands deep into his pockets. *Jesus, it's cold.*

The walk home took too bloody long. Mondays were never fun. By the time the clocks had struggled their way round to 5.30pm he always needed a pint. Three hours was pushing it a bit, though. And he'd been doing that a lot lately. He guessed it wasn't fair on Sophia.

Between the lampposts, the night was black. He looked around, wondering if he should jump on a bus for the rest of the way, but figured he'd probably end up standing around for ages. The city centre gave him the creeps these days. They'd found the body of one of the missing teenagers when they'd dredged the canal, which made it three – probably four – murders.

John tried to avoid the news. Everything except the sport seemed to be about people killing each other. He'd rather be ignorant. Knowing that there was a gang on every corner or a murderer offing random strangers didn't actually help anyone. But Gavin, his boss, liked to bring the local paper into work and Ron and Dave had been gloating over the grisly details. He shook his head.

Sophia was another bloody worry, of course. She was an obvious target, too. Last Thursday he'd practically begged her to kip over at Steven's but she had ignored him and come home anyway. He'd lain awake until God knew what hour fretting about her. She just didn't have any *sense*.

Still, he was lucky to have her. Smart and good looking in an understated kind of way. She even cooked. And she was going to marry him. He smiled as he walked, planning.

In a couple of years – when he'd been a supervisor for a bit and they had some money put away – they'd have a big church wedding with both their families there. After that, they'd get a little place in the countryside and, when they could afford it, have a couple of kids. What was so wrong with stability?

Ron could mock and stay out as late as he liked, but he'd be trailing back to that beaten-up Victorian terrace he shared with three other blokes. As John turned the key in the door and walked into the warmth, he felt like nothing in the world could touch him. Standing in the dark, hanging up his coat, he heard Sophia call, 'Hi, love.'

She had a sexy voice, Sophia. It was sort of low and rough, but definitely a woman's voice. Husky, that was the word. It always turned him on that he got to come home to this.

'Alright gorgeous. Sorry it's a bit late.' He flicked the light on and took off his shoes. 'Me and the guys went for a pint or so.'

''S okay. Thought I'd have a glass of wine, you know? There's some food for you in the kitchen.'

'Wicked.' He went straight through, got the plate she'd left in the top oven and took a can of beer from the fridge. In the living room, she was sitting at the table with a half-empty bottle of wine beside her. He kissed the top of her head as he passed and sat down on the sofa. He flicked on the TV, turned the volume down, cracked the ring pull on his beer and ate a forkful of food. Then he let out a deep breath. 'Ah. So. How's your day been, love?'

She shrugged, 'So-so. Yours?'

'Yeah, it was okay. Good to be home, though.' He looked over at her. Her dark hair was bundled into a scruffy bun and her face was even paler than usual. Her eyes were red, like she'd been crying. 'Are you okay, love?'

He watched her push a stray bit of hair out of her eyes and smile like she was remembering something. 'Yeah. I'm fine. Just exhausted. Last essay of the term. You know how it is. I suppose I could just do with a break.'

'Yeah, couldn't we all?'

She came to sit next to him, slipping one arm round his waist, leaning back on to the sofa cushions. 'Nearly Christmas, hey?'

'Yeah.'

They sat in silence while he ate his dinner and she watched the TV. She kept fidgeting with her hair.

When he had finished eating, he put his plate on the coffee table and leaned back to watch the telly. After a moment, Sophia said, 'You've not seen Julian since Hallowe'en, have you?'

He shrugged and wondered why she was bringing that up. He was cool with her and Steven having some big friendship thing going on with the freak, but he had no desire to visit that draughty old heap again. 'Well, yeah, love. But then I've had work, you know. And Thursdays are…'

'I know. I know Thursday's your work thing but, well, I was thinking… Christmas is coming up soon, it might be nice to… to have a bit of a get-together.'

'Well, yeah, but you see him most weeks.'

'But that's always at his place, isn't it?' She ran her hand up and down his back, like she was trying to calm him down or win an argument or something. 'I thought maybe we should return the favour. I mean, I don't want it to look like we're taking advantage or anything.'

It did not sound like a good idea. Still, he didn't want to upset her, so he said, 'I don't know. It sounds like a lot of hassle, getting it organised, and that. Especially as we're both away for a bit. You said you needed a break.'

'Oh, that. No, I like cooking. It'd be nice – a little party. When are you back from your parents'? The 28th, right?'

He nodded.

'So how about we do it for New Year's?'

Spending the night with some spooky-looking random that Sophia had taken a liking to was not John's idea of a good New Year's Eve. But she was smiling at him. He had trouble refusing things when she smiled at him. 'Well, how about we go out instead? We could head down the Black Lion, or else the Dragon – they do food as well. Save you the trouble.'

She gave him the kind of look she gave him when she thought he had missed the point, and was quiet for a bit. Then she said, 'I don't know. I don't think Julian's much of a "pub person". And that would be really difficult to book, John. Plus it'll be cheaper to have a party here.'

'Party? That's three people, Sophie.'

'No, I meant a proper little gathering.'

Of course. She wouldn't try to organise anything without all three of the musketeers making an appearance.

'I mean, Lucy hasn't seen him either, so…'

'Well, yeah. Okay. *Party*.' He couldn't stop himself sounding annoyed. 'So, who else were you going to invite?'

'Well, Steven, obviously.' And he guessed she could read the expression on his face, because she added, 'And you could invite a couple of your mates to even out the numbers.'

'Yeah. Well, my mates from work aren't really the kind of people who like to do a sit-down meal.'

'Oh, I wasn't planning anything formal. Just a few drinks, some music, some food… We could all have a chat.' She started stroking his back again. 'It's not even like we have to do it on New Year's. The thirtieth is a Saturday, and we should all be back from home by then. Come on, John, it'll be nice.'

He did not believe it would be nice. Of course, Sophia could be friends with whoever she liked – but that didn't mean they had to like the same people. If it were just Lucy, he could cope, but…

What pissed John off the most about Steven was the way he assumed John was an idiot just because he hadn't read a load of pretentious books by writers who thought they were clever. Or the way he was always so fucking sarcastic about everything John said, even though it wasn't as if his self-righteousness was getting him anywhere. He worked in a video store, for God's sake. What was the point of getting a degree if the only thing you were going to do with it was retail?

But however much he hated Steven, he knew that this Julian guy was going to be worse. Now he was really fucking weird. John had never got over the way that he had come into the room, totally calm even though they could have been junkies or meth heads, or, well, anything. It was as if he had led some kind of weirdly sheltered existence and just didn't think stuff like that happened. Or else he was as bloody arrogant as Steven. *Yeah, an evening with those two. Perfect.*

Still, he couldn't say any of that without upsetting Sophia, and he got the impression that he was losing this argument. 'I don't know, love. I'm not sure if my mates will get on with your lot.'

'Well, if you'd rather it was just my friends we can do it that way.'

Yeah. He had totally lost this argument.

'Well, I mean, I barely know this guy. And, come on. This place is hardly the Ritz, is it?'

'And? It's just a couple of mates coming round for the evening.' Her voice was cheerful, affectionate, but he sensed he was pissing her off.

'Well, yeah, but I mean Julian… He's a bit, well…' *Posh.* 'I mean the kind of that place he lives… This is going to be a bit of a comedown for him, isn't it?'

'He's not like that. Yeah, he knows me and Steven are kind of broke. Big deal. Why are you so against this?'

'Because I'm going to be sat in the corner like a fucking lemon, aren't I? While you and your mates talk about all that pretentious shit.' The look on her face made him regret his tone, but, still, the point stood.

She moved to the other end of the sofa and didn't say anything. When he tried to touch her she shrugged him off. After a long while she said, quiet and hurt, 'I just wanted you to meet him. He's a good mate.' Then, softer, 'Oh, I'm sorry, John. Look, I think you'll like him. How about you come along this Thursday? Give the social a miss for once. He's always asking after you.'

He hugged her. 'I would, love, but Dave and I thought this week we could …' The frown that started to appear on her face shut him up. He sighed. 'Look, we can have this party if you really want. It might even be fun. But you and Steven can do the Thursday thing without me. It's not really my scene, you know?'

She nodded.

He relaxed back into the sofa, wondering what he'd let himself in for. But it was finished, he thought. Until she said, 'Why is it not your scene, John?' He hardly heard her, her voice was so quiet.

'Huh?'

'I mean, all me and Julian do is talk. You know. About books and things.'

'Well, yeah.'

She was quiet for a bit, and then she said, '*We* used to talk. About books and things.'

He turned to her, saw the look on her face. 'Oh, love. I'm sorry. It's not that I don't *like* talking to you. I know you like stuff like that. I just, I don't get a lot of time to read anymore. I've got work. You know?'

'I know.' She looked no better.

'Hey, but it's not the end of the world, is it? That's why you've got mates like Steven and Julian. You talk to them about stuff like that, and we can do the things that really matter, yeah?'

'Yeah.'

He kissed her on the cheek, then the lips. He tasted tears. 'Oh, Sophie. You that know I love you, right?'

'Yeah. Of course.' It was a few moments before she said, 'I love you too.'

It had been but four nights since the creature had seen Sophia.

In the large claw-footed bathtub, he stretched out and let the hardened gore soak from under his nails. Sophia's skin was as warm as the water which lapped and caressed him, and he lost himself in thinking of her beauty and the beauty of the kill.

Somewhere behind him, the boiler screamed and juddered, but

as the creature lowered his head into the water, the violent sounds became muffled and distorted – not unpleasant, only strange.

He let the water slip over his face, his eyes, washing the blood from around his mouth.

Tonight, and on Thursday, there had been an edge of cruelty to his actions which he had not indulged in for so long. No longer contented by a quick slash to the jugular, he had drawn out the death, had luxuriated in the screaming and the fear. It would have been easier to call it a frenzy, but it was one belied by the finesse, the precision with which he had inflicted the wounds.

And, as he had killed, he had thought of her. Indeed, what else might he do? The calculation in his brutality, the slow drive to prolong sensation, even his mercilessness; these were a lover's tools.

He pictured his victim's face, the first flinching of pain.

But, no. It was not that stranger he saw, but Sophia.

No. No, it was Eleanor... *Her mouth tightened in sudden pain, her brow furrowed. 'Nothing, sweet heart,' she said. 'Nothing to fear.' But her voice was a whisper, her body hunched upon itself. She could not straighten herself, she who had never shown weakness, and it was too early, the baby was not due.*

The creature tried to sit, tried to pull himself away from the thought, but it was there in him, vivid and sick. He had tried to comfort her, but *it was she who comforted him. 'Nothing, leman,' she said. 'The midwife told me that...' But she gasped, stumbled and grabbed at his arms, and the sound that parted her lips was like an animal's cry, like the deep groans of passion he had heard her make. But that had been pleasure and this was pain.*

He knew what came next: fetching the midwife, the rush to prepare the chamber, the way he had tried to seem so respectable, so reasonable in the face of it all. The need to stay by her and the way she – hand resting on her swelling belly, face red and ugly with pain sweat – had sent him away.

Hours and hours, pacing, fretting, praying. His steward, then his neighbours, then his friends trying to draw him away. The sheer length of the night.

And her scream: *high, wild, the echo of it fell against the tapestries. His steps faltered, breath caught, unable to move. He was a man, of course. He would not cry.*

How many times had he refused to cry?

The face of the midwife, her dry voice, 'It does her no good to hear you thus. It brings the child no faster. You must rest.' And he nodded, knowing he could not sleep. Something, he needed something that would bring sleep and only let him rise when his wife was safe, his child was born...

No.

No, he wouldn't think of it. Not think of the one lonely tavern he could find because all the honest folk were long abed. Not think of the strong ale he poured down his throat as if it would drown the sound of her screaming. Not think of how helpless and weak and drunk he made himself. Not think of the stranger.

The stranger, with clothes fit for court, but worn in a dive as low as this one. The stranger, whose dark yellow hair curled lank against his broad-bladed cheekbones, his wide mouth. The mouth which smiled, subtle and sly.

The face, the mouth that he struggled for six centuries to forget, was clearer, sharper in his mind than that of his lovely young wife. Even thinking it, he felt that old, hot lurch in his stomach, the bleak reeling in his mind.

Responsibility. He had been given so very much responsibility, and so very young. Around him, in the tavern that night, there had been apprentices and students abandoning their rightful posts; there had been men who worked their father's land by day but by night conversed with wenches and drank their way from one Sabbath to the next.

He and those men had been of an age.

Who could have blamed him for returning the stranger's close-lipped greeting, or nodding at him, or sitting beside him? Who could fault him for staring into small, dark eyes that reflected all the red of the fire, or the full, dark lips? Who could blame him for falling on the comfort of the words, *'Now here's a fair-faced youth.'*

Perhaps on any other night, his pride may have faced affront at that naked lechery and condescension. On any other night, he would have been disgusted by it, would have demanded to know who spoke to him thus. But on any other night he would not have been in a low tavern, helpless and drunk.

Instead... instead, the young man who the creature had once been had longed to be everything the stranger took him for, to be nothing more than a pretty boy on a debauch with nothing to trouble his mind.

His whole life, his family, his honour, the place for which all his education prepared him, hanging on that stranger's close-lipped smile. And he had fallen. While his wife had screamed and panted and tried to bring their child into the world, he had lost everything he had ever known.

In the darkened bathroom, the creature sat in water that had grown cold, and the taste of blood in his mouth sickened him.

It did not help that Sophia had only got about two hours' sleep the previous night. Despite the essay deadlines, she had dragged herself to Lucy and Steven's for their afternoon chat, even if she was blinking and rubbing her eyes a lot. Her mind kept wandering to things like graphs, figures and the mess that was her evaluation of the data; to other things, also, lines of reasoning for which she did not have the energy. She sipped her tea and wished it was something stronger, but she had another all-night stint ahead of her.

'Shit, man.' Lucy shook her head, sending strands of blonde hair flying. 'Half three tomorrow. Union pub.'

Sophia nodded, feeling the ache course up the muscles in her neck, the fogginess in her head.

'Fair enough, but then I've got work again. And we're going round to Julian's at eight.' Steven was far too chirpy.

'Oh, you two suck. It's the last day of term. Let's go clubbing.'

Julian's. Sophia shook herself. 'Well, how about we all go out Friday? Then you can come to Julian's with us.'

'No offence, sweetie, but what with this essay, and the play before that, it's been over a month since I got laid.' Lucy smiled, blunt but apologetic.

Sophia knew that the apology was directed at Steven and couldn't say why that bothered her. *Relax now. Then assignment. The baggage can wait.*

'Well,' Steven said, 'I'm sure Julian would not dream of refusing you, were you to throw yourself at him.'

'How could you suggest such a thing?' Lucy voice was shrill, the heroine in a melodrama.

Sophia winced.

'Steven, I am wounded! It's you I desire!'

In response, Steven gave her a cynical smile and raised one eyebrow.

I didn't know he could do that, she thought, as for a moment, she felt as though she were looking at somebody else.

Steven was lounging on the sofa as usual, but she realised his pose was more studiedly effete than it had been before. He was cleaner shaved than usual too, and instead of a t-shirt he wore a shirt tucked into his jeans. She shook her head, as if to chase the resemblance away, but it remained. It was not that he looked like Julian, it was as if he were mirroring him, his stance, his clothes, his gestures. She wondered if it were deliberate.

Lucy was talking again: 'To be honest, I'm in the market for a disposable heart-throb. It could make things awkward for everyone if I pounced on the lovely Julian.'

'I'm sure my entire gender is gratified that you consider it so highly.'

'Yeah, when a bloke does it, they call him a Casanova, and when I do it I'm a slut.'

'I can assure you, none of us was even thinking the word.'

'Besides,' Sophia added, 'Casanova wrote books.'

'And I've had enough of books to last *me* a lifetime. I mean, have you seen the state of my library card? I swear this essay is going to finish me.'

'Entertaining as it is to contemplate your imminent demise, perhaps we should find a more convivial topic of conversation?'

'Well, it's okay for you, isn't it? You've already handed the bloody thing in.'

Steven merely looked smug.

Lucy shrugged. 'You okay, Sophia? You look bushed.'

'Yeah. You know. Overwork. I'm starting to feel like this essay might be my last.'

'Know the feeling. Still, day after tomorrow and it's the holidays.'

'Yeah. Thank God.' Sophia sighed and stretched. 'Oh. Yeah. Incidentally. Are you two coming back in time for New Year's?'

'We might be prevailed upon so to do.'

'It does get pretty dull back home, especially if you're not hanging around, so…' Lucy said. Then she leaned forward in her chair. 'Ooh. Are you having a party?'

'Well, yeah. I mean, just a little one. But on the thirtieth. Anyway, I only want to do it if you can make it.'

'Why, exactly?' Steven asked. 'I mean, I know we're the life and soul and all that, but—'

'I want John to meet Julian properly. So, I've invited him round.'

'And that needs us there because…?'

'Steven, shut up. It sounds lovely, Sophia. Don't worry. We'll be there.'

'Thanks, Lucy. But, I should warn you, John's inviting a couple of those wankers from his work.'

'Oh, *joy*. So we're invited to raise the tone of the evening?'

Sophia bit her lip, waiting for the surge of anger, waiting to lose her temper and spoil another day. It did not come. Instead, she felt an elation fill her, high and fragile. 'Christ, I'm not asking you to talk to John's mates. It's just they'll be useful to have on hand if you and Julian get too into your pretentious bullshit.'

Steven touched his hand to his chest. 'Pretentious?' Evidently the *moi* was to remain unspoken. 'You don't seem to mind our pretensions all that much, my dear.'

'And I'm aware I'm in the minority, Steven love. This way, you and Julian can rabbit away to your hearts' content and John's mates can talk about sport or cars or… Anyway, it takes the pressure off John, Lucy and me. Balance. Planning. Savvy?'

'Frankly, I don't. It seems like a disaster waiting to happen.'

Disaster, yes. Maybe he's right. Then, *Maybe John's right, too.*

Get a grip. A year ago, she would have ignored him, or told Steven that John thought the same thing. A year ago, she would have laughed this off. She sank her teeth into her tongue, hoping the pain would make her mind behave sensibly again.

Steven was looking at her strangely. 'Now I think of it,' he said, falsely bright, 'we have the advantage! The forces of culture outnumber the enemy. We shall vanquish!'

'Agincourt?' Lucy suggested.

'Ah. Yes. Oh dear. Well, in light of that gem of strategical mastery, I must admit myself defeated.' He pulled himself to his feet and gave Sophia a wobbly bow. 'I promise a valiant battle my dear; we shall conquer or we shall die.' He clapped his hands once. 'And now I must depart. The hour for toil approaches! Ladies, adieu!' He picked up his bag and headed for the door. She and Lucy waved.

'Bye, Steven,' Lucy called. The door clicked shut. 'Weirdo.'

Sophia nodded, not quite sure what all that had been about. She stared at Lucy. *Disposable heart-throb.* She found herself wanting to ask, *'Does that work?'* but she didn't.

It was shallow to be jealous of Lucy. It was wrong. Okay, men fell over themselves to sleep with her, but that had never mattered because, always, in a corner of her mind, Sophia had felt superior.

Not that she had ever minded Lucy's attitude to sex. No. Most days, Lucy's approach amused her as something harmless, something liberated – perhaps even laudable. But the superiority had always been there because, deep down, she had refused to believe that Lucy's sex life could be as fulfilling, as enjoyable as her own. Had refused to accept the possibility that the sex outside of a committed relationship could even compare to that within one.

I do not have the energy for this. But the thought would not go away, had refused to go away for weeks. She told herself it was the essays, that students always got horny when they were supposed to be studying – but that did not explain why the ache of desire was tied so closely to emptiness, to disappointment.

A voice in her head, insidious and crude, insisted, *What's the point of marrying the man if you don't like fucking him?*

It's not that I don't like fucking him, she retorted, as she had done every night that week. *It doesn't mean that I don't like fucking him.*

Long ago, she had watched her mother plough through a string of unsatisfactory boyfriends and had realised that no one was going to drop a 'happily ever after' into her lap. A relationship could not always be in the first flush of romance and physical infatuation. A relationship took work.

Still, she could not help asking if this were the beginning of the stagnation that people said came with marriage. Could not but wonder if she would need to keep struggling against this for her entire life. If she and John would always end up like this.

Surely sex isn't that important to me?

'You're completely zoned out, aren't you, love? Are you okay?'

'Huh? Oh, yeah. Fine. You know. Tired, that's all.'

Lucy looked her up and down and pulled a face, 'Just essay, or...?'

'Bit of everything. I need a break.'

She nodded. 'Is that why you're having this party?'

'Sort of.'

'And I finally get to spend some time with the delicious Julian, then?'

'I guess so.'

Lucy smiled and the look combined lechery and mischief. 'Come on then – Steven's being oddly evasive. Give me the inside scoop. What's he like?'

'What, Julian?'

'Of course Julian.'

Sophia nodded. *Julian.* There was another thing. 'Oh, I dunno. He's nice enough.'

'Nice enough? Oh, come on. You can do better than that.'

But Sophia found that she did not want to talk about him. Found that she wanted to hug the memory of Julian's character to herself. *That's exactly why you're having this party.*

Julian, she thought again, clutching at her secrets. But the problem was not Julian.

It was John she missed. Not the new John with the short hair and the busy job, but her old, lovely John. The man she had locked herself away to chat and fumble with, the man in whose arms she had lain for hours. And because that John was not there anymore, she looked to Julian, who had nothing to do with the dull world of pay cheques and job searches. She was only drawn to him because he offered her the very things she missed the most: attention, time, conversation.

Novelty.

Yes, and if relationships were always like they were at the start, nobody would ever get out of bed. She breathed until she knew she could hit the right tone. 'Well, have you noticed how Steven's been acting lately?'

'What, all this bowing and high diction and lounging around looking consumptive?'

'Yeah, that.'

'What about it?'

'He gets that from Julian.'

It gratified her that Lucy started laughing. 'Dear Christ, we're doomed. Doomed, I tell you!'

'Tell me about it.' *You see what happens when you make a bit of effort?* 'It gets worse though. I mean,' and here she dropped her voice, 'he actually *trades wine* for a living.'

'How shocking!'

'Although, actually, I'm not being fair to him.' She looked down at her hands. There was a faint scratch across the middle finger on her right hand, and it ached. The hangnail on her thumb was torn, bleeding. She noticed dried blood caked under the nail of the index finger on the same hand. *When did I do all that?* 'It's not like it is with Steven. Julian's not – he's not a snob, or anything. He's just, it's like it doesn't occur to him that what he's doing is odd. But it's okay, because...' But she did not want to finish that thought. 'I think you'd like him, anyway,' she said, and changed the subject.

For the next half an hour they chatted, and things were almost normal again. The only unease in Sophia's mind was the knowledge that she should really be getting on with her essay. Or it was, until Lucy asked, 'So have you applied for your MSc yet?'

She said it in the same tone that she might have said, *'Do you want some lunch or something?'* and, for a moment, Sophia did not realise what was being asked.

'Well, let's see how this essay goes first, huh?'

'Obviously. But you are going to do it, right?'

She shrugged, 'I don't know. I mean, it all depends if I get the funding, doesn't it?'

'You're in sciences, honey. It shouldn't be a problem.'

'That only holds if I do the kind of thing that a business might want to pay for. And, yeah, I can really see a big pharmaceutical concern coughing up several grand so I can study bats for another year. It's about as unmarketable as literature, love – and Steven's better at his subject than me.'

'But that's no reason not to try. There's wildlife charities and stuff who might cough up. And, besides, you don't actually need to get the funding, not *need* need.'

Sophia shrugged again and started to chew the torn mess of her hangnail. She tasted blood. Lucy was right, of course. She could always get some kind of job that would cover the fees. John was already paying most of the bills. It would be possible. She looked away. 'I don't know,' she said at last. 'I mean, I'd still be broke, wouldn't I? So it wouldn't be fair. On John, I mean.'

'Why not?'

Sophia didn't expect Lucy to understand. She squirmed. 'Well, I mean, even with my loan, I can hardly help with the bills once the rent's gone out. He said I don't need to get a job this year, but it makes me feel cheap. Scrounging off him like that.'

'"Scrounging?" You're engaged, right? So, why shouldn't he support you? It's what couples do. Hell, I help Steven out half the time, and we're just mates.'

'You know that's not the same. It's not like that with John and me. There's no reason I should need someone bailing me out.'

'And have you asked John how he feels about this?'

'It doesn't matter how John feels about it. It's how I feel about it. Next year... I can't just let him pay for everything anymore. If I get the funding, well, maybe. But...' Sophia picked up her empty mug and held it in both hands, concentrating on its smooth surface, its hollowness. When she spoke again, she spoke slowly: 'I need to be fair, Lucy. I need to – to pull my weight. And I need to be realistic about this if me and John are going to get married.'

Lucy nodded. 'Mmm. And are you?'

'What?'

'Oh, God. I really need to work on that whole tact thing.' Lucy's voice was casual, infuriating. 'What I meant was, are you sure that's what you want to do?'

'Well, I would guess that it is. I mean, it's not as if I'm engaged to him or anything, is it?'

'Sophia, chill. I'm not saying you don't want to marry him. But. Well. It's not like you've signed a contract in blood, is it?'

'Yeah. And I'm taking it Steven put you up to this?'

'Well, maybe a little. But, still, the point stands. There's always an out. And, even if you want get hitched, it'll keep, you know? No need to rush into anything.'

Sophia struggled with herself, fought to keep her voice level, to keep the anger and misery at bay. 'I'm not in any hurry to tie the knot.'

'I wasn't saying you were, love. Sorry if I wound you up, but, look, have you thought about going away for a year, to do your Masters? I mean we'd miss you, and I know you love living with John, but long distance is a thing. You don't need to settle in Barchester if that's all that's stopping you.' Lucy looked her in the eye. Sophia saw challenge there. 'If he's worth it, he'd wait for you.'

'That's not fair, Lucy.'

Her friend lifted both hands, a gesture of resignation or dismissal. 'It's true, though.'

'John's happy in his job. He's settled.'

'But you don't need to be.'

'No,' she agreed, and realised her finger was digging into her hang-nail again. She knew that she should be reassured, should understand that there was no need to choose between her subject and John; there was no need to give up just yet. That now she should feel full of hope. After all, she had always claimed that studying was her dream job, her favourite thing.

Why was she not happier now?

'Look, sweetheart, I'll be honest. Steven put me up to this, but not because... You know I wouldn't do it, if that were all it was, right? But we're worried about you. We can see there's something getting you down and,' she reached over and put her hand on Sophia's arm, 'I'm here if you want to talk. You know that.'

Sophia nodded. For a moment, she did not think she was going to answer. Then she thought that she would lie, dismiss the whole thing.

'Okay,' she whispered. She looked away and spoke to the carpet. 'This goes no further, alright? Because Steven would be fucking unbearable if he found out. But yeah. You're right. I've not been, it's not been... good, lately.' She felt Lucy's hand tighten on her arm. 'I mean it's the – it's the sex. The sex hasn't been too great, recently.'

To her eternal credit, Lucy did not crack a smile.

'To be honest, the sex has been bloody awful recently. As in really fucking terrible.' The strength of her language, her dead tone, both of these surprised her.

'Oh, sweetheart. I'm sorry. Have you got any idea why it's going wrong?'

'No.'

'Has John said anything? I mean, have you two talked about it?'

'No. I – I don't know if he's even noticed. It's just me. Lately, I'm just not enjoying it.'

'And you've not mentioned it to him?'

Sophia shook her head. She heard Lucy sigh.

'Honey, look. He can't do anything about it if you don't talk to him.'

'I can't. It's difficult, you know. Bringing it up.' She shifted how she sat, shrugged, pulled the hair out of her eyes. 'I mean, I don't want it to sound like I think he's crap in bed.'

Lucy nodded, and looked as though she were about to say something. Then she seemed to think better of it. In the end, she asked, 'Do you have any idea what's causing it?'

'No. It's like, it will all be going fine and I'll be in the mood and then – then nothing. You know? I guess it's like I can't relax, or can't concentrate or...'

'Mmm.' Lucy nodded. 'Are – and please don't take this wrong, love – but are you sure the problem's with you?'

Sophia looked down at the floor. She thought about all the late nights that John was working, all the evenings spent in the pub. *But this started before all that.* 'I can't see what else could be causing it.'

Again, Lucy looked as though she had bitten back on something she had been going to say. 'Well, I mean, if that's all it is, you just need to, well, make it a bit more interesting for you. The obvious thing is to try something kinky.' Her tone was offhand, casual even.

Sophia stared at her. 'I wouldn't know where to start.'

Lucy shrugged. 'Well, there's all the usual palaver. Bondage, D/s, role play – that kind of thing.'

Sophia found herself gawping.

'It's just an idea, love,' Lucy said, and for the first time she sounded like she was going to laugh. 'It doesn't need to be anything extreme. What you need to do is just bring a bit of romance or interest back into it for you. Whatever that is. Just think about what turns you on and play it by ear, you know. Can't make it any worse, can it?'

'No. No, it can't.' And she felt stupid. For weeks this had bothered her and now that it was out in the open it seemed so petty a reason to be depressed.

Because it was not that she wanted better sex. Not really. What she wanted were the vague fantasies of adolescence, those years when sex had been something deep and elegant and terrifying: the ultimate unknown. When it had seemed like something to which she might abandon herself, something implacable and irresistible and cruel. What she wanted was danger, passion, something that held all the fear and allure of the maelstrom. Thinking about it, she felt something in her stir, even now.

But, in the context of the hygienic little bedroom back at her flat, all of this seemed a cliché of the lowest order.

And that was the problem. It was impossible. She knew it was impossible. She might capture it for a fleeting moment, might fool herself into believing in it as she reached orgasm, but afterwards the workaday world would return and she would see her dreams for what they were. Self-deception. Silliness and a lack of maturity. What she was asking for was entirely distinct from reality and cosy normality. And reality was where she was required to live her life.

She looked down at her fingers. Her thumb was bleeding and her fingertips were smeared with blood. She licked it away, comforted by the iron tang of her inner self. She knew what real life entailed, knew that she needed to get used to it.

But don't I get to keep even a little bit of magic? asked a voice in her mind. *Just one tiny dream to share?*

She straggled a hand through her hair. *No. I can't think about this today.*

10. A Stranger in a Strange Land

...you yourself, with your rose-red youth and your rose-white boyhood, you have had passions that have made you afraid, thoughts that have filled you with terror, day-dreams and sleeping dreams whose memory might stain your cheek with shame
– Oscar Wilde, *The Picture of Dorian Gray*

Julian held the door open for him as he came up the path, his slender form silhouetted by the golden light which spilled out around him. 'Steven,' he called, his voice quiet but carrying, 'I am told something of a celebration is in order.'

Steven climbed the steps to the house and said, 'Well, I don't know what mark I've got yet, so...' but was silenced by Julian's arms around him, the kiss on one cheek, then the other.

He would have given anything to know how to return the embrace without awkwardness, without clinging. To lay his lips on that pale cheek in answer without it seeming as though it meant too much to him.

'Come inside,' Julian said, arms still wrapped around his shoulders, 'and let's have no more of these academic qualms – I have every faith in you. And there's food waiting.'

He let himself be led out of the cold air, Julian's hand on his arm, Julian's smile filling his vision – the shadows around his eyes, the fall of that dark hair...

Stop it.

Sophia waited for them beside the table, a little flushed with wine, a glass of something dangling from her fingers and a slightly nervous expression. Supper at Julian's was never so much a formal meal as a collection of enticing bits to be picked at over the evening. There was always something a little unfamiliar, but as he looked at the long dishes with their crushed ice, he felt an evil grin dawning on his face.

The thing was, Sophia had a problem with molluscs. Once, on a visit to a quaint seaside café, a pot of *moules marinières* had reduced her and Lucy to hysterical laughter. It had been up to him and an increasingly flustered waitress to get them to shut up and eat, or at least leave. Later, when they had explained the joke, he had accused them both of having dirty minds.

'Help,' she mouthed while Julian poured him a drink.

Steven pursed his lips, shook his head. He turned to Julian. 'I do hope you've not been to too much trouble.'

'I am at best a mediocre cook. I thought it best to stay within my remit and prepare something simple.'

'I'm not really sure that "simple" and "oysters" are words most people would associate.' Even as he said it, Steven wanted to kick himself.

Julian handed him a glass with the kind of smile that could a leave a person dizzy. 'I believe they were once considered peasant food. Although that was rather before our time, was it not?'

He tried to nod. Honestly he did.

'I thought they were reputed to be an aphrodisiac?' Sophia's voice had a teasing edge.

Steven stared down at the melting ice and the rough shells.

'You're the biologist, my dear.'

'Bivalve molluscs. You know they're not my field.'

For want of something to do, Steven picked up an oyster and squeezed lemon on to the pale flesh. He had read that, eaten like this, they were still alive. He tried not to think about that, tried not to think about the way Julian's glance had measured Sophia, how it had been slow and sexual. Or the panicked tightness he felt in his chest when Julian looked at him like that.

Fumbling, he ate one, trying to remember how the things he had read said it should be done.

'Actually,' Sophia said, her tone adult and caressing, 'I don't think I've ever eaten an oyster before. I'm not entirely sure how it's done.'

Steven looked up. Julian was watching Sophia, not him.

'They can be rather daunting, can they not? But it is rather simple. Simply take a spoon and loosen the oyster from its shell. Season if you will, and then…' He paused with the shell raised to his lips, balanced between three fingers. His voice became low, confidential. 'Well, if you are uncertain, my dear, the trick is to swallow.'

Sophia copied him, motion for motion, and together they tilted the shells back. After a second, she gave a choked laugh. 'Jesus, that tastes of...' Then she blushed. And looked directly at Julian.

Who pressed his lips tight together, shaking with a suppressed laugh. 'Quite.'

'Well, I see why they say aphrodisiac!'

And Steven watched them, sharing a joke which he did not understand and would not ask them to explain.

Later, sitting by the fire, Steven tried to force his gaze away from Julian. *Like a school boy with a crush.* It was as though his eyes had acquired independence from his higher functions, for he found himself watching the way Julian's hands moved, the way his Adam's apple eased itself up and down the smooth white throat, the way the faint blush of his skin shone in firelight.

Steven clenched his fists. This was stupid. He was not even listening to his host's words, just the mellifluous flow of that voice, the deep allure of those tones. *For goodness' sake.* With a sudden jerk of movement, he turned his head away. And saw Sophia.

She was leaning forward in her chair, her face half flushed by the wine, her eyes alive and alight. She looked nothing like the person she had become in recent months, nothing like the Sophia from before John. This was someone else, someone he did not know. It was not that she was usually shy with people other than Lucy and himself; it was that when she was in a relationship she would scarcely speak to any man who was not her partner, or Steven himself.

And yet here was Sophia. Flirting.

Nothing is going to happen between me and Julian.

But his mind continued to stray to those long white hands, those thin lips, and he felt a stirring of blood in his groin. It was there, regardless of how much he insisted he did not want to feel those lips against his own, how much he did not want to touch that smooth, white skin; of how he certainly did not want to lose nights and days in a play of lips and hands and tongues of which he could imagine only a hazy, delicious warmth...

Nothing, he reiterated, *is going to happen.*

So once again he tried to look away, to gaze into the fire although it made him seem drunk and stupid, or at the floor, or into his glass, but that made it seem like he was brooding. He looked at Sophia, but she was flirting with Julian, and that brought his thoughts full circle.

Just pull yourself together. He closed his eyes for a moment, forced back all his thoughts and made himself listen to the conversation. He heard Sophia's voice, that same teasing purr that was so unlike her: 'I'm just saying, wasn't that the whole appeal of the Gothic? As well as the terror, it brought travelogue to the Home Counties. Sure, we all know I love *Frankenstein,* it's a wonderful book but... well, for a horror novel, Shelley expends a lot of verbiage on explaining to people who are never *going* to the Alps what the Alps are like. I get *why,* but...'

'My dear, after all you have said about this very subject, are you honestly attempting to argue that the kernel of terror central to that story is somehow secondary to the scenery?' Suddenly, the light, mocking tone Julian used to speak to Sophia was unimportant. Steven's eyes snapped open. 'That the sheer blood-curdling terror which has captured the imaginations of so many generations is an irrelevance?'

That is what happens, Steven thought, *when you leave a conversation unattended. Amateurs start messing with your subject. Do try to pay attention.*

'No. Not irrelevant. Not in *Frankenstein*, at least. But if you look at some of the other stuff, it's like the descriptions hijack the scariness. Come on, even Shelley falls prey to it. In *The Last Man*, the plot sort of runs out and all you're left with is autobiography and scenery.' She grinned at Julian, then she turned to face him. Her expression was both provoking and irreverent.

She must be stopped.

'No,' he said. 'That isn't the point of the Gothic at all. I would never have lent you that book if I knew you were going to subject it to *that* travesty of an interpretation. Julian, please forgive my friend. No, Sophia, in the true Gothic, the landscape becomes another character. What you so insightfully called "the travelogue" is vital to the tenor of the whole novel; the reader is plunged into unfamiliar environs and that makes them feel the alienation the characters experience when *they* face the inexplicable. It's a tried and true trope.' He gave Julian a quick smile and finished his drink. 'A sort of "here there be dragons".'

Julian poured him another.

Sophia rolled her eyes. 'Right. So the fact that Adrian dies in a boat has absolutely *nothing* to do with Percy Shelley, then?'

'Not as such, no. Okay, she ends her post-apocalyptic story with an evocation of personal tragedy, but that's really beside the point. It's about loneliness and impermanence, even in the so-called Eternal City. Among the ruins of the "big" Empire, the narrator contemplates the ruin of humanity. It's not just some incidental scenery, it's what makes the whole book so interesting.'

'Whatever you say, Steven.'

'Look, I wrote a bloody essay on this last term. It's art. It's symbolic – you need an unsettling location for an unsettling theme. It's what Austen sends up so well in *Northanger Abbey*. The Gothic belongs to the liminal, the untamed, the places where *our* rules no longer apply. The whole reason it's alien to the Home Counties is because if you put a monster there the whole thing becomes bathetic rather than ter-rifying.' *There,* he thought, *that ought to do it.*

But Sophia was clearly lost to decency. 'Remind me again, Steven, where does *Dracula* happen?'

Shit. 'The point in *Dracula* is…' he began, and then his knack for creative thinking under pressure – or bullshitting as Lucy called it – asserted itself. 'In *Dracula,* the terror *comes* from the wildness and the untamed. It comes from the savage past and invades the safe lit-tle world of the bourgeoisie. Of course, that's why it is a better novel than *Frankenstein* and, certainly, a more enduring cultural myth…'

'Ignore him, Julian.'

'A more enduring cultural myth because, like in a ghost story, it lets you know that nowhere is safe, that no matter how civilised you are, the bad things can always invade. The reader can never be sure they are safe. The savagery came to them. They did not go to it.'

'Really ignore him. He talked himself into a corner and now he's covering his tracks. I can't take him anywhere.'

Steven didn't see why she felt the need to embarrass him. He bit

the insides of his cheeks until they hurt. *Come on, she was just teasing.*
Think of a retort. But before he could, Julian said, 'You admire Bram
Stoker's work?'

Something about his tone made Steven look up. Julian's expression
was difficult to read, but Steven found himself thinking that the smile
which always played at the corners of his mouth was gone, that his
eyes were wider, sadder. The changes were so small, it could easily
have been his imagination. 'I think *Dracula* is a work of genius,' he
replied. 'His other books? They vary. *The Jewel of Seven Stars* has some
nice bits, but I don't like it as much. But that may be more to do
with the concept than the novel itself. It's sort of my pet interest, vam-
pirism.'

'It's not an interest. It's an obsession.' Sophia did not seem to have
registered the change in tone. 'He likes horror movies.'

Steven rounded on her, 'Well, yes. I like horror movies. Why is that
an issue? It's hardly a crime. Sorry about her, Julian. Yes, I'm interested in the Gothic, and vampires are a big part of that. It's all about
what we fear, what we forbid, what we repress and what we desire.
And, I don't know, sometimes it's fun to be a bit geeky.'

'Well, yeah, Steven, but… did it have to be *vampires*? I mean, could
you not get your kicks from *Star Trek* or *Doctor Who* like any self-
respecting nerd? Because all that *Dracula* shit? Those films? Buckets of
gore and heaving bosoms in nightdresses…'

'Sophia, your grasp of film criticism never ceases to amaze me. Even
if you were right about that – which you're not, but, anyway – even if
you were right, isn't it interesting that those are faults with the *vampire*
genre? I mean, why does that subject matter lead to those concerns?
Why has it become that metaphor?' He could hear himself getting
worked up, could see the way Sophia was looking at Julian, flirtation
and playful incredulity upon her face. This frustration, this mortification, was not like him. Not when he spoke about things like this. 'But
if you insist on viewing them as trash, then it's your loss, you know.
But I'm sorry, Julian. We got a little sidetracked. What were you asking?'

Julian looked down to his wine glass, then up again, meeting
Steven's eyes. Once again, Steven got the impression that he was not

really smiling. 'I asked if you admired Bram Stoker's work. I believe that you answered me.'

'I suppose I did. Do you dislike him?'

Julian shrugged. 'I have read *Dracula* only once. Many years ago. It made... an impression.' The gesture he made with his hands was tense, elegant, dismissive. 'But perhaps that is the hallmark of genius.'

The creature thought about how unwise, how unguarded he had been.

To speak of vampires and tempt discovery. To consume mortal food and risk sickness. Despite all the blood in his glass, despite the taste he had taken of Sophia, it had lain heavy and nauseating in his stomach all that evening, and he had drowned its pangs in blood-and-brandy.

That, too, had been a mistake. The more alcohol he consumed, the less well his body bore it. After his guests had gone on to continue their night elsewhere, he had stumbled back into the hallway, gripping his sides and sinking to a crouch as wave after wave of sickness shuddered through him. He bit his tongue, hoping the taste of his own blood might settle his digestion, but it was of no help and he gagged, vomiting thick strands of alcoholic gore on to the tiles. For too long, he retched, heaving and spitting until his stomach was empty. Then, weak, exhausted, he shuddered, his body shaking for blood, burning for blood.

Yet seldom had he fed so well. That should have aided him, given his digestion strength against the things it could not process, but tonight he had pushed his façade of humanity too far. Huddled upon the soiled tiles, his face truly pale once more, his clothes a bloodstained wreck, his body felt cold, far colder than he believed it had ever been. The knowledge that he had brought this suffering on himself only made the taste in his throat harsher, more acrid.

The creature sobbed, but beasts like him could not weep. Exhausted, he lowered his forehead to the floor. The smell of brandy assaulted his nostrils and he retched once more. Spitting blood-streaked phlegm into the mess, he wished that he could wash away the taste with water, that he could cry.

Desperate, he recalled the warmth of Sophia's hands, the way her eyes had fixed on him; the way that, once, in sickness, he had lain his head upon Eleanor's warm breast as her hands wrought eloquent reassurance through his hair.

Would that he were in her arms, enfolded by the softness of her. Would that his lips were pressed to her throat, that her pulse was beating into his mouth, that her blood was nursing him, the way a mother might nurse her child, chasing away the sickness and the cold.

He shook from cold and nausea. Alone. He deserved this. Deserved it for the way he had disregarded all the knowledge he had acquired, knowledge that kept him safe, kept him whole.

His lovely young friends. It was their influence which loosened his tongue, made him push himself so. If he continued to make these errors, the day when they turned from him in fear and revulsion would come sooner than he could bear.

He had seen the way that Sophia looked at him.

Even through the sickness, the thought woke the villain in him. He had been told many times that his face was beautiful, his body appealing, and he had learned to use those attractions. It would be better were she to revile him, for then, at least, she would be safe. Would be lost to him.

Yes, he had seen the way she looked at him.

And why should she not? asked a small, treacherous voice. His should be the name that sprang from her lips, his the hands that caressed her to ecstasy in the quiet of the night. Each moment that he saw her brought an onslaught of desperate, sexual memories of Eleanor.

It would be so easy to take her away from that brash, blond fiancé. So easy to persuade her into his cold, passionate embrace.

The desire for blood clawed in him, desperate. Undeniable.

Not yet. Not yet.

He stood. The blood coated his fingers, his lips, his hair, viscous, rancid and drying. For once he appeared as he was, a thing of horror.

He thought of *Dracula*, and laughed. A creature so similar to mankind that it had once been of them, a thing of sex and conversation, of intelligence and reason – no wonder the vampire so fascinated and repelled Steven.

The creature had long since lost his faith, but on the occasions when he prayed, it was for oblivion. There had been times – many times – when loss or injury had driven him to madness, and for brief, blessed interludes, he had been unaware. Yet always, always, he had returned to himself, unable to lay down the burden of his human mind.

He had not been born to be a monster.

It was all very well for Stoker to make his villain 'no common man', but the creature could not boast such worth. He had been no princeling, no great leader. His short human life had equipped him to be nothing more noteworthy than a provincial gentleman; he had been raised to be a landlord, a husband. A father.

So, for little under six centuries he had survived. No buried treasure for the merchant's grandson: he knew how to make enough money to fill his empty life with comforts. No remote fastness or stronghold in which to hide – he ran from city to city, continent to continent, seeking distraction, avoiding discovery, returning again and again as some distant descendant.

Of course he laughed. It was laughable.

And now, there was Sophia.

He wanted her. He had believed that, before now, he had felt desire. But those feelings he had believed mastering passions were only whims, easily refused or denied. It was of no help to tell himself that to be near her risked her life and his sanity. When he sat close to her, the restraint which prevented him from clasping her in his arms or tearing the jugular from her pale neck became the anticipatory self-denial of a lover, the kind which only increased pleasure when surrender came.

So he had become a monster and worse than a monster. He had teased and seduced, drawn her in with illusions and lies.

And Steven. He had betrayed Steven, too. For there, truly, was an offer of virtue, of love uncorrupted. Steven would have tried to comprehend him, might even have forgiven him.

Instead, the creature had drawn them into this circle of destruction and lust. He knew that he should feel remorse for what he had done to the boy, for the way he had behaved unworthily towards the kind of man he had always loved and respected the most. Yes, he had done so a thousand times before, but always in the past it had commanded the full weight of his remorse.

Now, though, he threatened any chance he had ever had at redemption, at understanding, even at survival. And he could not bring himself to care.

11. Lex Parsimoniae

...but besides this, there is a love for the marvellous, a belief in the marvellous, intertwined in all my projects, which hurries me out of the common pathways of men
– Mary Shelley, *Frankenstein*

There was a certain determination to the way Steven managed to ignore both his hangover and the way his clock was telling him he needed to leave for work in half an hour. The last essay of the term was finished. Celebratory drinks had been imbibed. That meant it was the holidays, no matter how much overtime he'd signed up to do. And because it was the holidays he was lying in bed, eating chocolate and reading *Dracula*. That, as far as Steven was concerned, was that.

Although the term 'reading' was a little inaccurate. With *Dracula*, the book itself was more in the nature of a prop used to trigger the memory. Still, he needed the smell of the paper, the weight of the battered volume in his hands, needed the crumpled softness of the yellowed pages. And he needed the chocolate, too.

Without even lifting his eyes from the page, he reached over to his bedside and took a square from a packet placed strategically close to the radiator. It disintegrated immediately upon contact with his tongue, and his mind followed Jonathan Harker through the Carpathians, along the Borgo Pass to the deliciously written terrors of Castle Dracula. *Perfect*. This was what it was all about: holidays, life, pleasure...

And, suddenly, his mind was back on Julian.

He shrugged, shifted, his single bed suddenly too hot, too narrow. He leapt from it and opened the window a crack. A drift of sharp, festive air stole into his room, insinuating its way under his t-shirt, nestling into the intimate hollows of his collarbone, wrapping around his thighs, tantalising, chill. He gazed past the crack in the curtain into the grey dawn and felt a sudden primal sorrow at the shortness of the winter days. The street outside was silent. Thin vapours of freezing fog slid over the ground, spreading with slow, cold, billows.

A space seemed to open in his mind. There was a low, thrilling sensation running through his veins and his erection burned like the sun on a midwinter's morning, distant and painfully bright. He thought of Julian's lips, his eyes, the way his hands had this same coldness. The way his friendly kiss was chill and damp upon Steven's cheek. There was an ache, an emptiness that seemed intolerable. Craving rose in him, a thirst which ran across his skin, across his scalp, pulling goose pimples and shivers from him. The world became a place of sensation and he stood imagining, remembering, his lips open and foolish to the night.

If you asked me now, the thought strayed, *refusal would be beyond me.*

Then he realised that he was cold, standing near an open window in mid-December, wearing only boxers and a t-shirt. His erection was uncomfortable, obtrusive as it pushed at the cotton which constrained it. Embarrassed, he laughed. The mist flowed over the contours of the road, seeped into the crevices and alleyways of the city, sensual and beautifully atmospheric. Steven ran a hand through his unbrushed hair and felt ridiculous. What had possessed him to stand here like a lovelorn school boy, risking hypothermia? However delightfully Gothic the scene, there was no reason for him to make a fool of himself.

He shrugged and shook his head, and considered climbing back beneath the covers. But the chill that had touched him had probably found its way under the duvet and he would not have time to make it warm again. He glanced at the clock. If he got up now, he had time for a quick shower and a proper breakfast.

After all, *Dracula* could wait.

Work was busy and unpleasant, but it did have the fortunate effect of banishing his hangover. Well, work and Alka-Seltzer. As he walked home, Steven found himself possessed of the merciless sense of vindication that can only be provided by habitual sobriety, gainful employment or industrial strength painkillers. Letting himself into the flat, he discovered Lucy and Sophia collapsed on the sofa, making noises of despair and trying to calculate quite how much alcohol they had consumed the previous night.

'Good – well – afternoon actually,' he announced, watching them wince at the volume of his voice. 'How are my two darling girls today? Feeling chirpy?'

They groaned.

'Come on, don't look so glum! It's the holidays!' He clapped his hands together, enthusiastic and jovial.

'Steven,' Lucy agonised over each syllable, 'you complete bastard. Stop it.'

Sophia nodded. She was even paler than usual – almost ghostly. Faintly green. It was her own fault. At one point she had been drinking shots because – and this was a direct quote – *'vodka doesn't get me drunk'.*

She made a faint whimpering sound. 'How come you look so rosy?'

'The effects of a firm constitution, my dear.' He slumped into a chair. 'Also of a full breakfast, a brisk walk through the frost and a morning spent serving annoying customers under fluorescent lights. Stop bitching, the pair of you.' He looked at them, at their wide, agonised pupils, at the lips that seemed almost black in their chalky faces. He decided to take pity. 'I'll make some tea.'

Lucy gave a frail nod. 'Yes.'

Sophia winced again. 'Tea good.' She gave a convincing groan. 'Shit, I feel like hell. I don't remember... much, honestly. I... did Julian give us *brandy?*'

'No, sweetheart. He gave *you* brandy. *I* knew it was a terrible idea.' Before she could answer, he said in a saintly tone, 'I'll put the kettle on, shall I?'

Tea seemed to help them. Within another half-hour they were even willing to make conversation which was not centred around the pain in their heads. A packet of biscuits revived Lucy enough for her to gesture to a copy of the local paper, which she had brought back from wherever she had spent the previous night. The words 'Ripper Killing Confirmed' were emblazoned over the front page. 'You know, Bank Street was closed this morning. Lots of police. I think they found another body.'

Steven looked away. Under normal circumstances he despised Christmas with the self-confessed cynicism of his kind. This year, he almost wished people would confine themselves to their usual crass nonsense about commerce and spirituality. Certainly, he wished the local rag would concern itself with nothing more serious than the Christmas lights being turned on, the ice rink outside the city's mall and the pantomime at the Royal Theatre. Instead, it spent much ink almost gloating over the crimes of an individual to whom it had given the moniker 'The Barchester Ripper'.

Not that you could avoid it on more mainstream news sources unless you were actually trying.

It had been bad enough when it had been a couple of bodies and a couple of disappearances. Now that all those missing had turned up dead, and there was a new victim each week, it was making him feel physically ill. The crimes themselves were horrendous enough, but to Steven's mind the ghoulish glee with which the papers filled their pages – the in-depth interviews, the photographs and tearful pleas for justice, the speculation – were far worse.

Of course it was a tragedy. It needed to be stopped, but Steven could not muster moral outrage. Worse things happened all the time, all over the world, but neither the *Barchester Herald* nor the national press could bring itself to care. It was all scaremongering, sales-focused tub-thumping, but it was being honoured with the title of civic duty. As far as Steven was concerned, his duty as a citizen stopped at feeling empathy for the families involved and leaving them alone to their grief.

'Are they any closer to finding out who's doing it?' Sophia asked.

Lucy opened the paper and read silently. 'Hmm. The police are following all leads… which I think translates as a "no".' She took a swig of tea. 'Yuck.'

'What?'

'Gone cold. And this also says there had been no attempt to hide the body. The one on Tuesday, I mean. It was just sort of dumped on the pavement. The last two were half concealed but now it's like the killer doesn't care anymore.'

'This used to be such a nice city,' Sophia said. 'You really think there was another one last night?'

Lucy shrugged.

'Shit. Maybe John's right. I shouldn't walk around that late. It's always around the same time, isn't it?'

'Yeah, they think so. Between two and three, as a preliminary estimate. His wife said he'd only popped out for ten minutes.'

'In the morning?' Steven said. 'What, pray tell, was he just "popping out" to do between two and three in the morning?'

'Come on. Show some humanity. This is really grim.'

'Yeah, no one deserves that.' Lucy read on a little bit. 'No, really. This is horrible.'

'How horrible?' As he said it, he heard how eager he sounded. *It must be contagious.*

'Well, the detective in charge of the investigation has referred to the "appalling savagery of these crimes". I mean, they're being coy, but whatever he's doing to the bodies it's… I get the idea it's pretty awful.'

'Shit,' said Sophia.

'Yeah.'

But Steven could not help but ask, 'Um, how do we know it's a he?'

'What?' There was no earthly reason for her to sound so disgusted.

'Well, come on. How do we know it's a he? It could be a woman doing all this.'

'Steven.'

'Crime is an equal opportunities employer…'

'Steven.'

'I mean, look at Elizabeth Bathory – she didn't let being a girl stop her bathing in other people's blood…'

'Oh, for God's sakes…'

'Look, this is horrible. We were *all* out at that time last night.'

'Yes, and we're all alive today,' he replied, with emphasis. They stared at him. 'I wasn't *just* being facetious. The police will have more hope of finding the killer if they don't make easy assumptions. "He" could very easily be "she".'

Lucy snorted.

'Alright, I apologise. Please, do not let me distract you from this unpleasant business nor its gruesome facts.' He lounged back into his armchair and turned away from them.

Mollified, Lucy continued, 'There are a *lot* of conspiracy theories. I mean, if you want to take a walk down crank lane, just look at the letters page. And warnings to stay safe, pleas from the police for any-one with information, and... oh, page sixteen: "Mother's Grief over Estranged Daughter". Shouldn't this be nearer the front? Here we go – emotion, heartbreak, picture of a woman clearly trying to avoid the cameras, fact they had to use dental records to identify her because of the, yuck...'

'What?'

'Well, because of the mess he – I'm sorry, Steven – the mess *the killer* made of her face.'

'God, Lucy, I'm trying to drink this.' Sophia sounded queasy.

'You asked.'

'You're right, that's disgusting,' Steven said. 'Why are we talking about this, again?'

'No, you're right.' Lucy put the paper down. 'This is really bad. Shit – they're asking for witnesses who were around where the body was found. They think she was killed nearby because of "forensic evidence" and CCTV footage, but they're not ruling out that she could have been killed elsewhere.'

'What?' Sophia asked.

'Not ruling it out?' Lucy repeated.

'Yeah. But...' Her voice was quiet, absent even. 'I mean, I'm not an expert, but the way he's been messing these people up, she'd have been fauceting. Blood everywhere.' She pinched the bridge of her nose between her thumb and forefinger, thinking. 'Let alone all over the guy's clothes.' She looked at them, every trace of her hangover gone. 'How could he have moved her there like that? Let alone get away from the scene? It doesn't make sense.'

'The whole thing's without sense, honey,' said Lucy. 'Why kill someone at all?'

'No. No. I mean... that kind of violence would leave more evidence – so if he's gone to that much effort covering his tracks, why only make a token effort to hide the body? I mean, didn't they say something about a cut throat on the news?' She shook her head. 'You can't make that kind of incision without hitting the carotid...'

Lucy stared at her. 'You speak from experience?'

'Oh, I don't know. Maybe you were right the first time. A psycho. I'm sure the police will figure it out.'

'Well, unless it's vampires,' Steven suggested, a little smile curling on his face.

Lucy chucked a cushion at him. 'Bad taste.'

'Seconded.'

'Oh, but come on, my loves, it's the first day of the holidays. Do we *have* to dwell on this kind of thing?' The pair of them shrugged, as if they felt bad about being cheerful. 'Look, now we're all feeling awful again and we should be having fun. You know what I suggest?'

'Not a horror movie.'

'Mulled wine.' It got a reaction, at least.

'I don't know how you can even *think* of booze after last night.'

'Hair of the dog? Anyway, most of the alcohol burns off when you heat it up.'

'Oh, alright,' Lucy decided. 'Only, you have to go buy the wine.'

'I hear and obey.'

Sophia looked at Lucy.

All that had kept Sophia going in the last few weeks had been the pressure of the essay, but today, weak from a bad hangover, mind aching from sleep deprivation, it was as though she heard her own voice making conversation while her real self sat back, at a distance, seeing everything too clearly yet unable to touch the people about her.

And so she watched Lucy.

Most women who looked like Lucy had the decency to rely on cosmetics, flattering clothes and romantic dreams to blur the lines between nature, artifice and inadequacy. Lucy still wore the jeans and t-shirt she had worn to the club the previous night, and her only makeup was a fading shimmer of glitter across her eyes. She looked artistically dishevelled, a poster girl for a 24-hour deodorant.

It had been a mistake to confide in her.

Lucy would never be able to understand because she would never get herself into this godawful mess in the first place. Sophia tried to remind herself that envy was a stupid emotion, one unworthy of their friendship.

She heard herself ask, 'So where did you spend last night?'

Lucy glanced around, as if to check no one was eavesdropping. Her smile was incorrigible. 'One lad. Two words. Rugby. Society.'

A sudden blurring of focus, and she was there, back in her body again. No, perhaps Lucy wouldn't understand, but she was still Lucy, and memories from sixth form still meant something.

She gave a small laugh. 'Very nice, I'm sure. Muddy legs?'

'Absolutely. Every inch the man.' Lucy cracked her knuckles and looked triumphant. Then she smirked. 'Although I doubt he could string two words together.'

'Do you think you'll see him again?'

'I dunno. If I'm desperate. He was a pretty good shag, and easy on the eyes, but,' she pulled a face, 'he was thick. I mean *really* thick. As in immensely, monumentally dense. Would you believe, he actually said,' she put on a deep voice, '"Come on, love, we don't need a condom, I'm clear." Fucking idiot,' she concluded, in her normal voice.

Sophia smiled.

But then Lucy said, 'Enough about me, love. How are things with you? Any improvement?'

'Huh?'

'With John. Have you had a word with him, or…?'

'Give me a bit of time, yeah? Come on, Lucy. What with the essay crisis and going to Julian's, I've scarcely seen him since then.'

At that, her friend gave her a look which Sophia could not interpret. Scepticism, perhaps, or sadness. 'Okay. Tell me how it goes, though.'

'Sure.'

Sophia felt sweat prickling her neck and nausea roiling in her stomach again. She ran over and over yesterday's conversation upon the same theme. What was it she had said? *I'm not in any hurry to tie the knot.*

She wondered why she had accepted John. Even in that posh restaurant, with the wine and flowers and the diamond glittering in its case; even then, she had hesitated.

And John had noticed, had told her, 'It's not like we need to get married right away or anything,' and she had realised that to say no would be as good as breaking up with him. So she had looked at the ring and its sparkle and thought that it was just a bauble; that it made no difference because she was planning to stay with him anyway.

She pressed her finger against the diamond and it was sharp.

She had been wrong. It was not like any other piece of decoration. It meant that she had committed herself to maintaining their relationship. It meant when something went wrong, she needed to patch and compromise and reconcile until it worked once again. She knew that she had given her word that she would stay with him until they were married, and that, when they were married, she would keep her word once more. She was stubborn; she knew that, too.

But was it possible to patch and repair so often that all that was left were the threads of the mending and none of the original fabric at all? By the time death parted them, would she even recognise what they had shared? Would she recognise herself?

'Lucy, I...' She spoke slowly, giving herself time to change her mind, not to say or ask these things. 'Do you – do you ever think you'll get married?'

In her fear, her need for reassurance, Sophia was watching Lucy's face closely. Had she not been, she might not have noticed that the smile was not Lucy's usual self-mocking grimace. 'Me? God no.'

'I know, not your thing. But if you wanted to. Is there anyone you might... I mean, is there anyone you would want to marry?'

'Seriously?'

'Yeah. Seriously.'

Lucy said in a voice which was nothing like her usual tone, 'Steven.' Then, after a pause, 'Only not gay.' Her eyes flicked to the door. Her smile was bitter and brittle. 'But then, if he wasn't gay, he wouldn't be Steven, would he?'

Sophia said nothing. She could think of nothing to say.

Lucy nodded. 'Yeah. So, now you know.'

Steven?

'How long have you…?'

'A while. Look, don't ask me if I'm sure. It's not going to change. The more men I meet, the more I know that none of them will ever measure up. Not to him.' Her smile became determined, hard. Sophia remembered seeing that smile the day when Lucy had dislocated her ankle. She had lain crumpled at the foot of their treehouse, crying and gasping and telling Steven that, yes, she was fine, but could one of them go and get her mum now, please?

Lucy laughed. 'I don't even remember their names. Not one of them. I've never met a man who even came close. Compared to him, all the other guys just seem like thoughtless, worthless bastards. Except John, of course.'

'I don't need you to like John,' Sophia heard herself murmur, as if it mattered anymore.

There was nothing else she could say. There were a thousand blandishments, but every one of them would be a lie.

Because – and this was the worst part – Steven had always loved Lucy. Loved her the way he loved Sophia, loved her with a transparent, childish commitment that could never be overcome, but would never develop into adult love. It was the way she thought about the pair of them, too. *Siblings.* And in nature, siblings would rarely mate.

She looked around to make sure he was not coming back. 'Have you…? Does Steven know anything about this?'

Lucy shrugged and wrapped both hands around her mug. 'Why ruin everything?' Her voice was low, toneless, trembling. 'I mean, I'm lucky, aren't I? I've been with the perfect man since we were in Reception together. I love him, my parents love him, his friends are my friends. It will last as long as I say nothing. And it's got everything but the sex. And that I can get anywhere.'

Sophia shifted, debating whether to reach across the sofa, to put an arm around her friend. Debating whether she should let out a spiel of society's myths about these things. But it was clear that Lucy did not want pity. Certainly, she would not want lies.

Lucy gave a hard little laugh. 'The worst of it… The worst of it is that he *trusts* me. When he… when he came to live with us, he as good as told me that he trusted me not to fall in love with him. And there was no way I could tell him he was years too bloody late.'

Sophia nodded. She had not been there, that night, but she had seen its aftermath. Seen Steven's vulnerability, his gratitude, his embarrassment. *Yes.* Because if Lucy asked, he would feel obliged to try. And trying would destroy him.

Sophia realised that she was crying, even though Lucy was not. She had honestly believed there were two immutable things in her world: the bond between her friends and Lucy's heedless confidence. And now she realised that to say one word out of place would ruin it all, forever. Her own problems seemed laughably small.

And Lucy was right. Why speak out? Why ruin everything?

Then, because silence was the only solace she could offer, she said nothing and she looked away.

12. The Carnivalesque

…the morning after orgy comes the hangover; 'never again', we cry. But the morning after ecstasy comes enlightenment, and the desire to do it again as soon as possible.
– Angela Carter, 'Love in a Cold Climate'

Sophia closed her eyes and stretched and tried to feign the languor that came after good sex. She let a few moments pass then opened them again. The bed was washed in a winter sunlight that was painfully brilliant, almost hard. It made her think of the cold outside, made her shiver despite the heat of the flat. Her legs, still tangled with John's, were sticky with sweat.

John was dozing. The shaggy stubble on his chin was almost as long as that on his head, and both glinted in the light. Sophia wondered if it were deliberate or if he had just stopped bothering to shave. Either way, it didn't suit him.

She tried not to sigh or shift, tried not to turn her back, because to do any of those things would wake him, and if she woke him she would have to explain.

She would have to explain anyway, but she did not want to have that conversation. Especially not now. Not with his body still lying on her, hot and leaden; not with his breath and hair and skin still smelling of fag smoke and last night's beer. As quietly as she could, she turned her head away.

She wanted to go to the bathroom and be sick. She hated everything. Hated herself, her stupid mind and her stupid body. Hated the sick feeling in her stomach, hated her discomfort.

More than any of that, she hated John, hated to look at him.

A sob built in her throat, but she held her breath and choked it into silence. *This is stupid,* she told herself, *this is so stupid.* John's fingers were still cupped around her breast. Only a handful of minutes ago he had been kissing her, telling her she was beautiful. And all she had wanted was for it be over.

Come on – her internal voice was cruel, abrasive – *this is John. Look at him. No, properly. He could have anyone he wanted. Someone who was actually pretty. If you're thinking in terms of leagues, girl…*

Stop it. Sophia clenched her teeth. John had claimed he liked her the way she was: small, dark and odd looking.

Stop it.

Because John had never used those words – he used words like gorgeous, sexy, beautiful; and so she could not believe him. Could not but help comparing herself to the women in the porn that he still sometimes watched.

You're just tired, she thought, struggling to remain calm and in control, *that's the only problem here.* Then, the sensible, grownup part of her said, *But you do need to talk to him about it.*

And a quieter, more petulant voice added, *Because I can't take much more of this.*

John did not sleep much longer. When he woke, his face looked puffy, blank. In the past she had found this endearing, as his hair had been tousled, falling on to his cheeks and forehead like strands of gold. But John wore his hair short now.

He said, 'Mmm. Morning again, gorgeous,' and ran one sweaty hand up and down her thigh. She remembered to smile. 'Shall we go and get some breakfast?'

'Yeah,' she said, although she was not hungry.

As she got out of bed and climbed into her dressing gown, her movements were so slow she felt she had been drugged. John sat on the bed, pulling his pyjama bottoms back on. When he noticed that she was watching, his face crinkled into a smile.

'John?'

'Yeah, darling?'

Embarrassment silenced her. She swallowed hard. *A lifetime of this.* 'How long is it we've been together now?' She already knew the answer. It was just under twenty months.

'About a year and half, I guess.'

'Is it really that long?' Even to her own ears, the surprise sounded false. She managed, at least, to keep her annoyance under control. 'Do you think–' but that was not what she wanted to say. She tried again: 'Anyway, I was thinking. Well, I mean, it might be interesting if we, um, tried something a bit different.' Her voice was bright and fake, like someone in an advert or a sitcom.

John didn't reply. He sat on the bed with a face as empty and unhelpful as the computer screen at 5am during an essay crisis.

The smile on Sophia's face began to ache. 'You know. In bed.'

John began to frown.

She ploughed on, 'You know, when we... make love.'

He was silent until he said, 'Oh. Sorry if you're not enjoying it.'

'It's not *that*! God! No, no. It's been great! It's just... Well, I was kind of thinking – thinking it might be fun if we, well, if we did something, you know? Something new.'

John had not stopped frowning. 'What kind of thing?'

Thoughts rushed into Sophia's mind, into the ache inside her. She thought of being captivated, of abject, terrifying surrender. Thought of a passion so terrible that the love was almost torture. She thought of a single spirit in two bodies, consuming itself with the force of its desire.

But she could not find the words. 'Oh, I don't know.'

'Like different positions or something?' John's tone was not unwilling but his words were like a blow.

'No. I didn't mean that. I meant – I meant something properly different.'

'Do you mean like costumes and handcuffs? All that kind of shit?'

Sophia opened her mouth to correct him, to tell him that was not what she had in mind, but, once more, she did not know how to explain.

'Isn't that stuff sort of tacky?'

Sophia forced herself to look at her desire with cold eyes. What was it she had wanted? Surrender? Captivation? Love like torture? And wasn't that all just another way of saying romance, playacting, escapism? And when John put it like that, it all seemed very cheap. All the great, Romantic cravings she had treasured against her heart since puberty, shown to be nothing more than the same old clichés. French maid costumes and fluffy handcuffs.

Sophia shook her head. 'Nah, not like that.' She paused, then added, 'I guess you're right. It was only idea, you know?'

She watched John smile, watched him pull on the t-shirt he had slept in, and she knew she ought to be feeling better. Knew that she should be happy now, because they had talked about it and her decision had made him happy. Instead, she felt she teetered upon a precipice that overhung an eternity of night. Something inside her was screaming.

She ignored it. 'It's not anything important. Not really,' and placed a smile upon her own face. 'Do you want some breakfast, love?'

In his mortal days, the creature had never had much patience with crowds. The smell, the claustrophobia, the heat of them had oppressed him. He had avoided the city; visits to the market had been a chore to which only duty reconciled him. This avoidance had continued for some decades after his death, for he had known it to be too full of dangers for the mass of humanity about him, too full of dangers for himself.

Yet, with time, there came to be a pleasure in it, a strange tantalisation of his senses and his hungers. Yes, provided he was not famished, there was pleasure in it, and he had fed so well of late that his skin was suffused with a slight, pink glow.

Even dressed archaically, tonight he seemed nothing more than a part of the crowd which buzzed through the chill streets and loitered beneath the gaudy brilliance of the Christmas lights. And yet passers-by would not meet his eyes, still veered away from brushing against him. He knew that if he were to stop any of their number, they would make the briefest possible conversation, would hasten away without understanding quite why they fled.

It was a primal revulsion, an instinct for self-preservation located deep within their minds. Only time would quieten that, would overlay it with the fascination of the fatal. There were very few who did not, on a first meeting, recoil from him.

Sophia was such a one.

To think of her was to crave, to be driven out to seek the heat of breath, the thunder of pulses. So he walked among the crush and press of breakable mortality, drinking in their scents, keeping his sharp nails sheathed in leather gloves, not forcing contact upon those who flinched from him. As he walked, he imagined wildness taking him, imagined running amok and drowning himself in the heavy tide of their collective lives. And as he walked, he thought of Sophia.

The memory of dark hair curled against her cheek, the way she would reach up and tuck its strands away. The way she smiled, the way her eyes regarded him. It was as though, even now, he could feel her gaze, could see the parchment of her skin and how the marks of his bites against it would seem like the rubric on the manuscripts of his youth. She would wear them so well, his wounds. Would be as beautiful as Eleanor in death.

I do not want her dead.

But he wanted her in his arms, wild with pleasure and with pain. He wanted her laughter to sound in his ears. Wanted to feel her softness. Wanted to hear her moan, wanted her, wanted, *wanted...*

And she desired him, too. Her lips urged him on, and when she spoke to him she leaned forwards, as though she were eager for his touch...

A small, cruel smile curved his lips. He wondered if her boy had realised, if he knew there was another man in his beloved's eyes. Wondered if Jonathan realised there was another who needed only to reach out his hand towards Sophia and...

The creature had his centuries of knowledge of the luxurious arts. Could he not provide her beauty with a more fitting lover? He had never known of a mortal woman who could withstand his love, who did not surrender willingly to his cold and practised touch, to the cunning tease of his sharp teeth.

Two nights ago, had she only breached the distance of the winter air dividing them, he would have had no choice but to become her lover, her slave. Had she only touched him, he would have ravished her senses with all the pleasure he could bring. Already half won by his clever words, if she felt the eloquence of his hands... what hope then for that poor, mortal boy?

And as he walked and gloated, he did not stop to examine these thoughts, to question what they meant, for he knew that to pause now would be to realise the full horror of what he had become. Better to indulge his whimsy. Better not to remember that she still wore that boy's ring. Easier not to recall that, although she did not shrink from him, somewhere in the private depths of her mind, she had made her choice between life and death.

So, instead, he thought of her invitation, the one that would take him to her very door; the one that would, at her insistence, give him triumph over the ancient taboo of threshold. He would accept, of course, for it would give him the power to come and go as he pleased.

It would be wiser if he did not risk the temptation, wiser to flee now, to leave the city before the alchemy of her blood broke the last vestige of his self-control.

Quietly, he laughed.

The police were looking for him. He had killed too often, and in the heat of the kill he had become careless and left the body where it lay. But his mind was too wound up with Sophia to care for such pitiful, broken things. And they had been glorious kills.

The glitter of the Christmas lights seemed like the shine of ecstatic memory, and he was gifted with memory as he walked by the places where he had heard bone crack, felt pulse stop, tasted blood, tasted life. He returned the impassive stare of the electronic eyes which made the hunt so much more dangerous, so much more divine, and shook his head; a parent amused by a child's folly.

For his intemperance was folly. Although in these rational times he need hardly fear the mob with crosses, torches and stakes, he could not count upon the blindness of his pursuers for too long. The corpses he left were always drained of blood. It would be noticed, had doubtless been noticed and would lead someone, at the least, to suspect. But Sophia's bright blood elated him; the taste of her, the memory made all this trivial. He would see her soon.

And Steven, also. There was another who did not flinch from him. There was beauty and wit that he had sworn – this time – he would not defile. He recalled the vain hopes that Steven's coolness of mind, his firm intelligence would be the dark mirror to the creature's hungers. That, this time, embracing such things would gift him with control, with restraint.

Such waste.

Steven's influence still held, but in that momentary presence of mind he did not pull back, did not abandon this destructive course. No, such respite only served to make the creature's amorous assaults more prolonged, more elegant. More diffuse.

He should feel shame, despair, remorse. Instead he found that he might dismiss such things. What did it matter any longer? Sophia began to desire him. He smiled, the shy, close-lipped smile of any young swain in love, and glanced up to the sky.

The lights of the city flashed and sparkled. Moments of brightness and shadow washed over the shoppers below. The creature saw it all; a scene of great and drunken beauty. The whole city seemed to pulse, the shoppers and revellers flowing through the streets like the blood in its arteries. He stood alone, an old hunter in their midst. The night span around him, filled with lust, desire, anticipation and desperate bliss. Were it in his power, he would seize the throat of this whole populace in his teeth. The midwinter's air was a poor substitute, but he drank it in and it gave him pleasure. He was buffeted by a violent elation, a sudden longing. If he could weave this moment into something that he might bring to Sophia, that he might lay at her feet...

This moment had happened before. This intoxication, this wildness of love and lust and desire, it had happened before, and he had been here. The creature glanced about him, bewildered, seeking some familiarity. The spire of the cathedral peaked in the distance, floodlit against the depthless blue of the sky. And nearby was a dark, brooding hulk of stone; a squat, square building.

He was in the old city's heart, standing near the church of Saint Bartholomew.

He knew this place. In his lifetime it had been a part of the tangle of alleyways and low taverns which he had visited only when it could not be avoided – and only once when he should have been elsewhere.

That night. Nerves and expectation. The blond-haired monster beside him. Drunk, he had been so very drunk. But his dizziness was not only from strong ale. The creature cringed to recall the terms that had been offered him, the endless possibilities, the eternities; cringed to recall the hot, shameful lust that had coursed through him as that fascinating man had stared into his face with a rapt hunger.

Cold as the night air, the man's hand brushed his cheek, tangled itself into his hair. 'Think on it. Wouldst thou sooner age and die than be ever young and strong and lissom? Wouldst thou not have every pleasure fall to thy touch?' And the stranger smiled a close–lipped smile and met his eyes. The look had been like a kiss.

And had he truly never felt, before that night, imprisoned by propriety and duty and tedium? Had he never sensed the door that hung ajar in his heart? His life had been so very mediocre. He had done the things that were expected of him. His pleasures had been commendable. Even his fantasies had been unpretentious.

But that night, ah, the glory of the wide world had shone around him like a mantle made from the fabric of heaven itself, and his heart had risen in him watching the stranger's clever lips, hearing his strange and beguiling tales, and he had wanted, wanted to rush to his wife and give her the wonder of it all.

It was then that it had seemed, with the smoke from houses and the brightness of the stars in the sky, that he would offer his beloved all that wonder, that eternity, that magic. When in truth, all he could offer her was death.

13. Saint Lucy's Eve

... and, for many a time
I have been half in love with easeful Death
– John Keats, 'Ode to a Nightingale'

Two days later Sophia wandered the city centre, aimless and bereft. The weather was cold and grey and she missed Steven and Lucy.

At this time of day she would normally be at their flat and stay there until early evening, killing the time that John spent working late or at the pub. But three days ago she had walked Steven and Lucy to the station to catch the train home. As it had pulled away, she had watched the Christmas lights flashing against the cloudless dusk and felt sudden loss. Every other year they had caught the train home together.

It was only Tuesday. Her train back to her mum's was booked for Saturday. She had come into the city because the flat was beginning to drive her crazy. Outside every newsagent the Barchester Herald announced 'Ripper Hunt Continues!' Each time she saw it her mood sank a little lower. *This used to be a nice city,* she thought, although she found she could not remember when that had been. Her mood was the kind that stretched outwards, thin and bleak, contaminating everything it touched.

She wondered what time John would come home tonight. Wondered if he was going to spend the evening with his work colleagues after yet another late finish. *Be fair:* his colleagues were also his friends. He was entitled to spend time with them. And he was on the promotion ladder. He would sometimes have to work late.

These justifications made very little difference.

Once again, she counted down the days until Thursday. *Dinner at Julian's,* she thought, *company.* And, suddenly, the urge was upon her to buy him a present, something to thank him for his kindnesses, for his friendship, for the look of surprised joy he had when he opened the door and realised that it was her waiting in the cold.

She had thought about doing this before and had decided against it for some reason. She could no longer remember why.

After that, her wanderings had a purpose as she looked at all the fancy, sparkling things that sat smugly in the department store displays labelled 'Gifts for Him'. Nothing was right. She did not know if Julian wore cologne, or the size he took in clothes. She knew that he wore some jewellery – cufflinks, a gold finger ring – but the selections she could find seemed dull, unsuited to him. Besides, she could not afford any of these things.

As she browsed through the boutiques and high street stores she tried to work out what to buy. She thought of his odd, foppish way of dressing, his pale skin, his voice. She thought of the firelight and the candlelight which he seemed to prefer, of their joyful leaps of conversation, and the strange, compelling stories he would tell.

As she thought, she came to realise that all the glossy, shiny tat which lurked behind the counters in these places had absolutely no meaning as far as Julian was concerned. The world which she inhabited for the rest of the week, which had raised her and satisfied her for twenty-one years, was irrelevant on a Thursday evening when she and Julian sat together, talking about books.

Alone.

The word slid into her mind, troubling and incongruous. Sophia shook her head as if to clear it. A book. The answer was a book. But even as she slipped into a back alley that would cut across the city to the nearest bookshop, she stopped and reconsidered. One of the pleasures of talking with Julian was that he seemed to have read all the books that she loved. *Damn,* she thought, and was surprised to notice that she was hardly annoyed at all.

The short-cut had taken her away from city centre and the chain stores into the cluster of lanes that huddled about the cathedral. Even here the festive atmosphere was oppressive. Ropes of fairy lights crisscrossed above her head, the windows of all the charity shops were hectic with fake snow. Artisan coffee shops, pawn brokers and independent stores jostled together. A couple of buskers defied the cold, playing Christmas carols and Bob Dylan songs. Sophia found herself smiling. She had always loved this part of the city.

A little distance away there seemed to be some kind of seasonal flea market. She drifted towards it, although it appeared to be predominantly junk. There were Christmas decorations and the kind of wrapping paper which is both fragile and transparent. A couple of stalls sold crafts and folk art; another made its trade in reconditioned, rustic furniture. Then she saw one that sold bric-à-brac and she stopped, if only from habit.

When she had been younger, Sophia had been a fiend for junk shops and white elephant stalls. Her room at her mum's house was crammed with all manner of antiques and curios she had known would not look right in her and John's tidy little flat. Still, she had never stopped browsing them. Last year, she had even got Steven a birthday present in one of these places – the kind of pewter tankard from which morris men and posers drink real ale. By coincidence, it had even had a large 'S' engraved upon it. She had warned him, with a smirk, that he should probably not use it because it might have lead in it. He had ignored her.

This stall looked less promising. There was a lot of uninspiring brass, some scruffy costume jewellery, a few 'vintage' toys and Victorian bottles. She was about to give up and move on when a flash of light caught her eye.

Between a rhinestone brooch and ring with peeling gilt, there was a pendant about the size of a £2 coin. It consisted of a ring of metal that was almost black from corrosion, and which had been engraved to suggest a tree branch. This encircled a small, flyblown mirror where, perched at the bottom, a model of a bird faced its own reflection. There was something carved along the top.

Intrigued, Sophia picked it up. It was heavier than she had expected. The stallholder nodded to her. 'Funny little thing, isn't it?' Her accent was pure Barchester.

'Yeah.' Sophia ran one finger along the inscription, squinting at it. 'Do you know what that says?'

'You've more chance of seeing that than I have, love.'

Sophia nodded. After a moment she was able to pick out the words and with them caught the memories of long Friday afternoons in her A-Level literature class, with the clock dragging as they waited for the last bell of the day so they could head off to the pub. And she remembered her book, dog-eared and annotated to illegibility. She remembered the arguments, which they had called debates; the way Steven had said it was facile and self-indulgent, the way Lucy had thought it far too morbid. And how she had seen in it a tender melancholy that was tinged so beautifully with bitterness.

Lying awake at night, too tired to read anymore but not quite ready to sleep, those words had circled in her mind, the cadences becoming a lullaby. She had mouthed the poem to the darkness and wished she had lived nearer the countryside, had wished she might hear the nightingale outside her window and translate her confusion of feelings into those words.

And, suddenly, she knew what it was that she was getting Julian for Christmas.

'It's Keats, "Ode to a Nightingale". How much is it?'

The woman shrugged, good-natured. 'Thirty quid.'

Sophia winced. That was more than she could afford by a good £20.

'But, for you, my love, I'd say twenty-five. I always did wonder what that said.'

'Twenty-five?'

'Afraid so. That's silver, you know.' She turned the pendant over and pointed to a nearly illegible mark upon the base. 'It's got a hallmark and everything.'

Sophia could see nothing but a faint smudge that might have been a row of numbers. She nodded, wondering how the stallholder could make that out when she could not read the poetry.

'Look, I'll throw in a chain, and we'll call it quits. You can't say fairer than that.'

Sophia paused, still staring at the heavy black pendant, the bird reflected in the mirror and the words above it. She thought about how it would look if it were silver, if she polished it until shone once more. She thought about the Romantic poets who had gone to Rome seeking truth and died there. She nodded. 'Will you hold on to it for me? I just need to pop to a cashpoint.'

Later, back at the flat, cleaning it with baking soda and a warm cloth, she realised she had never asked Julian how he felt about Keats.

Steven's room at Lucy's parents' house was filled with all the horror film memorabilia he had been unable to load into Lucy's mum's car for the drive up to Barchester. A narrow path led to his bed and the armchair at the far end of the room. It was here that he was sitting with his nose buried deep in *Dracula*.

Years ago, when he had first read the novel, it had been with a kind of greedy desperation; he had needed to know how the diabolical Count was overcome, how righteousness and morality were restored, yet been strangely disappointed when they were. In later years, he had reflected that it was this moment of ambivalence which had cost him his faith.

That Dracula was abhorrent had always been evident to him. His younger self had pictured no suave seducer but exactly what Harker described: a blood-fattened leech with hairy palms, lying glutted in his tomb after preying upon the innocent and the helpless. Yet, hidden beneath his bedclothes, reading the victory scene by torchlight, Steven had felt a sudden and compelling revulsion at the heroes' crusade.

It was not simply that, even as a monster, Dracula was magnetic. It was that the vigorous persecution by the protagonists had seemed so very ugly. Unsettled, he had teased through the plot again and again, looking for some definite morality there, one to which he could subscribe. And he had found nothing.

That desperate struggle had long since passed. These days he read it idly; a few paragraphs or perhaps a chapter at a time, dragging it out for the whole length of the holidays, a comfort blanket of text. Downstairs he could hear Lucy's family moving about, enjoying the holiday and each other's company. The room was dark, night pouring in through the window. The only source of light was the angle-poise lamp behind him. He was reading one of his favourite scenes.

It was the one where Lucy was first bitten, where she sleepwalked to the churchyard and Dracula bent over her neck like a long shadow. It always made him think of the time when the three of them had gone to Whitby and hung around Saint Mary's until it got dark, trying to soak up the ambiance of the place. Always before, what had struck him was the finely balanced terror of it, terror made only stronger by Mina's precise, schoolmarmish tones. But tonight the whole scene, with its racing clouds and bright moonlight, seemed charged with a powerful, dangerous sexuality.

Unsettled, Steven put down the book and turned to his reflection in the window.

He missed Sophia like a dull ache. Perhaps he and Lucy had always been closer, but the dynamic of their relationship did not work with Sophia gone. Certainly it did not seem like Christmas.

Lucy's family had a bohemian disregard for the festival. To his own parents it had been a staid, religious occasion. At Sophia's mum's, however, Christmas had been an excuse for merrymaking in the midst of the winter doldrums. That house had always been so brightly lit, it could have been used to guide aircrafts to a safe landing. It had always been Sophia's mum who had mixed them mulled wine and whisky macs for their Christmas Eve pre-gaming. It had always been Sophia and her mum who had laid on enough holly and tinsel and mistletoe to make sure everyone knew it was Christmas time.

In the past he had always been a little scornful of that desperate jollity. This year, he understood it. It seemed so very dark, so very cold that he had trouble locating any spark of seasonal goodwill in his own spirit.

Or perhaps he just missed Sophia.

And Julian. He missed Julian too.

He realised that it was Thursday. It no longer seemed to matter that, for the last two months, he had been telling himself he had no real feelings for his handsome friend, that it was nothing more than a bad case of lust. He felt a terrible jealousy as he realised that Sophia would be seeing Julian tonight.

Someone knocked on the bedroom door. Steven was annoyed, then guilty. After all, it was rather impolite of him to be lurking up here. He was a guest, really. Sort of. 'Yes?'

Lucy's voice: 'Can I come in?'

'Of course.'

She opened the door, and in the light from the landing her golden hair framed her face like a wild mane. At times like this it struck him that, objectively speaking, Lucy was gorgeous. Part of him still thought of her as the plump, scruffy child she had been, but like this she resembled an avenging angel. Then she slouched into the room in her hockey club hoodie and faded jeans and was just Lucy again. 'My parents are about to head off to the high school carol concert. They want to know if we're coming.'

'I'm quite happy to give it a miss.'

'Cool.' In the absence of another chair, Lucy sat down on his bed. 'Hey, how come your bed's more comfy than mine?'

In response, Steven raised one eyebrow. He felt that particular facial tick had been well worth acquiring as it reduced the need for witty riposte by about half.

Lucy laughed. 'Fair point. You okay, though, love? It's just, you've been a little' – she paused, before settling upon – 'hermetic.'

'Sorry.'

'Don't be. Your lurking has gone unnoticed by all but myself. Everything okay?'

'Yes. Yes, I'm fine. I just miss Sophia.'

'God, yeah.' Lucy shook her head, undoubtedly shedding blonde hair all over his pillows. 'Tell me about it. We are reduced. Still, she'll be here by Saturday, won't she?'

'I know.'

For a few moments, they sat in silence. Then Lucy said, 'You know, you're going to wreck your eyes reading in the dark like this.'

He shrugged in response, and she craned her neck to try and see what he was reading.

'*Dracula*? Again?'

'Yes.' Steven put the book down across his knees. He did not need to look at the cover. He knew every tear in it, every crease, the little patch of water damage from when he had carried it in a canvas bag in the rain. 'It's weird, you know. I'm not enjoying it half so much as I usually do.'

Lucy raised herself so that she was not so much lying as lounging. Her trainers kicked against the foot of his bed. 'Have you considered that it's because you've read it to death?'

Steven pulled a face.

'Just an idea…'

'No. It's not that, it's...' Then he realised he could not continue.

Tonight, when he had read of Lucy's awakening upon the cliff, his heart had pounded and the blood had rushed hot and ready to his skin. Rather than identifying with busy, concerned Mina, he had been Lucy moaning her way awake upon the clifftop, shedding the heavy bands of sleep only gradually as she surrendered entirely to sensation. He had remembered his hot, difficult dreams of recent nights, when he awoke twisted in his bedclothes with lips formed around a cry or gasp that dissipated upon the cold reality of wakening. Feelings he could not begin to understand had not only invaded his bed and his mind, but were creeping into his favourite novel, converting his own enjoyable readings into something dark, something uncomfortable.

He had never read *Dracula* as a pornographic novel.

He had never read anything as a pornographic novel. For Steven, reading was a cerebral exercise, a refuge. Of course, particularly with the Gothic, especially with vampires, he had always known that sex would be a part of it. It was about *thanatos*, the death drive. It was about the allure of the forbidden; it was about the paradox that humans will fight vampires yet still invite them into their lives.

That ambiguity, that ambivalence was why he liked it. Yes, on some level Dracula was attractive and every time he read *Dracula* one small, difficult part of his mind had turned to the vampire with a startled eroticism. But that was just skilful writing, revealing enough of humanity in Dracula, and enough of Dracula in humanity, to make destroying him an act of self-destruction as well as a necessity.

The attacks on Lucy and Mina were just that; the slight titillation that came when reading was contrasted with the horrific scenes themselves, and with the characters' obvious fear and revulsion. Steven had always read at one remove.

Because when he was reading he was inviolable.

Steven had never told his friends how he found being himself – rather than a child or a disciple to a demanding and vengeful God – so constant and wearying an effort. This was because there had always been books. Because, in the night, lying awake, he had always been able to switch on the light and open a book. In that refuge, his feelings grew quiet. From that sanctuary he could always bury the urge to call home, to tell them that they were right, that it had only been a phase and he wanted to come back.

So it had never been necessary to tell his friends about the way he woke in the night and could almost see his father's face, with its expression of hurt pride and sorrow and pain a perfect mirror for his own. Had never been necessary to tell them how sometimes his determination, his conviction, his whole sense of self wavered. Because books had always been safe in a way they could never understand. So he could not find the words to tell Lucy that all this had changed.

'It just seems different this time round. It feels as though something is giving me a new light on it, and it's one I don't much like.'

'Yeah? What kind of new light?'

The trouble with Lucy was that she had always been too insightful. He clicked his tongue against the roof his mouth and fought the urge to lie. 'Lucy, what does it feel like when you—' He stopped, started again. 'What does sex feel like?'

Lucy swung herself up to sitting and made a 'hmm' noise. 'Well, it's kind of difficult to explain, love. I mean, it varies and, well, with two blokes I'm guessing it would be quite different. So, really…'

Steven nodded, although that was not really what he had been asking.

'It's not a bad thing, though. Unless I suppose you don't want to be doing it. If you've been pressured or something. But otherwise it's fun. Really. I mean, you know when you,' she made the 'wanker' sign in the air, 'I guess it would feel a bit like that. Physically as well as… well.'

Steven nodded. Like masturbation. Something furtive and perfunctory. Not shameful, not fearful, but normal, healthy and without danger. As he had surely always known.

But a tiny part of him baulked at that. He knew that he was inexperienced, that he was prey to all kinds of virginal fantasies, but he could not help but be convinced there should be something more to it than mutual relief. He studied literature, after all, knew the grain of truth in that old cliché about sex and death. It was impossible that something which obsessed so many people could be so incidental, so harmless.

'But is that it? I mean, what if – what if there's love?'

Lucy gave short bark of amusement. 'Jesus, Steven, you're asking the wrong girl. I dunno. I don't *do* love. Not with my boyfriends anyway. You should know that.' She smiled at him, lips pressed tightly together. 'Ask Sophia. She'll tell you about the slushy stuff.'

'Oh God, no. Horrible mental image.'

'What, Sophia?'

'No, John.'

They both shuddered, then laughed. 'To be fair to Sophia,' Lucy said, 'he's not so bad, in that Hitler Youth kind of way he has about him.'

'Hitler Youth?'

'It's what I've always thought. I mean, don't you reckon sex with him would be a bit like a military manoeuvre? Imagine that leering over you...'

'I'd really rather not.'

They giggled again.

'If you tell Sophia I said that, I'll do something dire to you.'

'I hear and obey.'

For a few moments they smirked, but gradually the quiet of the house at night asserted itself. A car went by outside, its headlights sweeping slow across the ceiling. 'What I was saying before,' Steven said. 'About the emotions. It can't just be – well, is it really that simple?'

Lucy looked away from him. 'It depends, I guess. As I said, emotion's never been that big a part of it for me. I suppose there are the hormones you get, but that's just chemical engineering. You find yourself feeling all blissed out and gooey so you blurt out "I love you", or something equally dumb.' She turned back to him, her eyes pale, like vacant holes in her face. 'It can get you confused, sometimes. But it's not the same as love. Not really.'

'I was just wondering. Well, you know that I've never...' He was not entirely sure what he had been trying to say. After a handful of seconds, Lucy came and sat on the floor beside his chair.

'Yeah. I know.' She leaned her head against the armrest. Her hair brushed his hand. 'Do you think you will? One day?'

'I don't know.' He exhaled heavily. It was almost a sigh. Lucy had a way of making people tell the truth. 'I think I'm falling in love with Julian.'

'Oh.' Her tone struck him as a little strange. She twisted, her hair moving against his skin. She looked up into his eyes. 'Is he, well, do you know if he's...?'

'Gay? It seems likely that he goes both ways on that one.'

'Mmm. Something Sophia said gave me that impression.' She continued to stare into his face, her eyes moving in a slow appraisal. Eventually, she said, 'Well, why not go for it?'

Something churned in his stomach. 'I don't know.' He turned from her, watching his reflection in the window until it blurred and he could see only the darkness of the night. He tried not to think.

After a long time, he began to speak, still staring at the cold glass. 'Why is it that love, that desire, are the defining characteristics of humanity? I mean. If I loved Julian, if I *let* myself love him then it would almost be like I was letting go. Of, well, I mean – I could love him. Really. I think I could. But it *would* be letting go of myself, of the idea that I'm enough, on my own. I could love him. I *could*.' His eyes refocused, and he saw the trees lining the road outside, the houses opposite, the night sky. He blinked and saw his reflection once more. 'But I think he would want something from me that I don't want to give.' He turned away, unwilling to meet his own gaze.

Lucy was looking at him strangely. Sadly. Although for the life of him, he couldn't think why.

It was one of those glorious midwinter nights. The moon was only a few days away from full in one direction or another and was ringed by a glow of frost. It was still early, but the footpath beneath Sophia's feet was glistering and treacherous enough that she knew she should be paying more attention to where she was treading. As she walked, her bag thumping against her backside, a touch of guilt worried at her, chafing.

John did not know that she was out alone tonight.

Not that it mattered, of course. She was a grownup and hardly in need of a chaperone. Still, it bothered her that she had not quite man-

aged to get around to reminding him that Steven would not be walking with her tonight.

His misconceptions were his own stupid fault. John knew that
Steven had gone home with Lucy a few days ago. She could hardly
blame herself for his persistent assumption that Steven would be there
tonight. And, when she considered how overprotective he had been
recently, it was hardly surprising that she had not reminded him.

For some reason, he had got it into his head that, if she went to
Julian's tonight, she ran a good risk of being murdered. Or possibly
mugged or raped – he was never entirely clear on the subject. She had
tried laughing at him, tried reasoning with him, had finally told him
that, if it were that big a problem, he could give the fucking social
a miss and accompany her for a change. After that blazing row, she
had decided against mentioning the fact that Steven would not even
be accompanying her on her way home because Steven was not in
Barchester at the minute.

And that, she thought, *should be that,* because she was not, point
blank not, going to spend yet another evening moping at home on
her own due to his irrational fears.

Still, her behaviour was exactly the kind of childish and unforgiving
pettiness which undermined a healthy and functioning relationship.
She knew that, in her situation, an adult would sit down with John
and explain to him why going out was so important to her, how
much she missed company and how she felt sitting alone every
evening, waiting for him to come home. She knew if she were to say
this, then she and John would be able to reach some kind of compromise.

But she did not much feel like being a grownup. Besides, in her
current mood, that way of handling things seemed suspiciously like a
guilt-trip. She shook out her hair, which slipped from its ponytail and
streamed in the wind.

'I thought,' Julian said, later, when the edge of chill had left her skin
and the warmth of the wine was beginning to pulse in her stomach,
'that as it is midwinter's night, I should perhaps make a little conces-
sion to the pagan.'

'The pagan?'

Above the fire a large bunch of holly glistened, but other than that and the soft glow of the candles, there was no tinsel, no sparkle, nothing to suggest the festive season.

He raised his glass to her in a half toast. 'It is the longest, darkest night of the year and the sun is a small and distant thing.' The flames of the fire licked around the logs. Julian's face seemed a dark gold in the light of it. Red embers glowed. He was smiling, his usual close-lipped, teasing smile. 'Imagine how it must have been, in the times before electric light and heating. Villages cut off from one another as the snow drifted and the wind howled at the doors. The animals housed nearby, or inside, for there were still wolves and bears roaming the last stands of the wildwood. People sending their frail little prayers up to heaven for safety, and health, and for the harvest to outlast the cold, dark days that seemed without end. How precious those little circles of firelight must have seemed. And in the darkness beyond not only wild animals, hunger, sickness, disease, but all the fiends and beasts of the underworld, lurking, waiting to take their very souls.'

A shiver of pleasurable fear ran up Sophia's spine. She took a long sip of her wine. 'I don't need to imagine. It feels like the perfect time to tell ghost stories.'

He raised his hands. 'I am afraid I know none.'

Sophia paused. If not ghost stories, what it was he had been leading towards? 'Then I suppose we'd need Steven here. He tells brilliant ghost stories. It must be all that horror nonsense that he reads.' Then she remembered. 'Oh, Christ. You do know that Steven can't make it, right? He – well, he asked me to tell you, but it sort of slipped my mind.'

She had meant to tell him the moment she came through the door, but he had smiled and kissed her hand, and they had found themselves talking about the pictures he had hung in the hallway. A few were portraits, with strange moments of family resemblance shining through the formal, idealised forms – and examining them had chased away all her other thoughts.

Julian smiled at her, wider than his wont, showing his strangely shaped teeth. 'He had a sent me a – a *text* that said something to that effect. Evidently he has a most elevated idea of your powers of recollection.'

'Probably for the best.' She looked away to hide her blush, her smile. 'So, no ghost stories. Why do you say pagan, then?'

As he resumed his flow, she could feel him looking at her. She lifted her head from her abashed posture and stared straight back.

'I meant simply that, besieged by darkness, in the middle of winter's cold and fear, it is as though something occurs. People carve out a little piece of light, friendship and revelry to stave away the cold and the dark. It is an ancient, primal need. Perhaps all beings need that moment of warmth in the very darkness of the year. Even in the darkness of the soul.' Julian began to swirl the wine in his glass. The red tide of it lapped against the crystal and Sophia saw that it was as bright as blood. 'I believe it is so. One thing we all have in common – the need to draw close, to celebrate, to exchange gifts when all else is lost, when all is bleak and cold.'

Caught on his words, her lips parted and she felt herself nod.

'Tell me, Sophia, my dear, have you ever drunk honey wine?'

Unable to find her voice, she nodded again. Then managed to say, 'No. You mean mead, don't you? No, I never have.'

'Yes, mead. It has been thought to carry the very essence of the sun. And its colour, it is almost reminiscent of the sheen of gold. Certainly it is steeped in mythology. Sweet, strong and precious, it has been used as a symbol of so very much. Of inspiration, of love, of fertility. It is…' Julian looked about him, as if, for a moment, lost for words. 'It is very rich. Very powerful. Perhaps it is even considered the stuff of life itself. In the Nordic traditions, it is said that a mead was brewed from the blood of a god. Once, many years ago, I was most fond of mead.' He paused, and when he spoke again, his tone had changed. 'Alas, a pleasure I can no longer indulge. But it is traditional at this time of year, when things are at their darkest. Perhaps, my dear, you would do me the honour of accepting a glass?'

'Yes. Yes, of course.'

Julian left her and when he returned he carried another of his heavy, crystal glasses. It was half full of a liquid the colour of pale, clear amber. He placed it in her hands without brushing her fingers at all.

As she sipped, she could taste the intensity of the honey flavour, but it did not cloy or overpower. Beneath the sweetness, there was a dry richness which stole the moisture from her throat and made her realise that she would need to drink slowly unless she wanted to end up very drunk indeed. She lowered the glass and said, 'Thank you.'

He made a gesture of dismissal with his hands.

She remembered the necklace and, with her free hand, fumbled in her bag for the little parcel. 'Actually, I've got a something for you as well. It's – it's nothing much. Just, you know, something that I found.'

He shook his head, looking younger than ever, lost and vulnerable. 'Sophia, my dear, the mead was simply a toast. A tradition – a drink to the light, a tribute to beauty and inspiration and to yourself, of course. I only regret I could not join you. You need not have.' And as she watched, his demeanour changed. 'But there,' he laughed, fire-light glinting from the white points of his teeth, 'by all rights, I meant to give this you later, but…' He reached into the inside pocket of his jacket and brought out a small package.

'Oh, you shouldn't have.'

'Nor should you.'

She laughed, too. 'Sorry for jumping the gun.'

'Quite forgivable.'

As she took his parcel she was surprised it was not warmer. After all, it been inside his jacket, pressed against his chest. *But then it's a cold house.*

Underneath the paper was a small jewellery box in black velvet. Inside this were a pair of gold earrings in the shape of bats. Tiny and delicate, they were no fanged Gothic monsters but fat-bodied Peruvian bats, the bringers of luck and prosperity. Sophia did not wear much jewellery, but she would have worn these.

Except Sophia did not have pierced ears.

It was an easy enough mistake to make. Most women her age had surrendered to the needle, and it was hardly the kind of thing that came up in conversation. Certainly it had slipped John's mind on occasion. Even Lucy had bought her earrings. There was no explanation for slow sinking of disappointment that brought a hot ache to her eyes.

She stared at them. Steven could keep his geographically inaccurate Transylvanian beasties; the thing that most horror movies chose to ignore was that bats were cute. It was not too late to change her mind. The only reason she had never been pierced was a stubborn desire to be different. Lucy had always told her it did not hurt.

Then she thought of what Steven would say when he found out *why*.

'Thank you,' she told Julian. He had made no move to open his own present but was staring at it. As she spoke he looked up. Sophia fought to keep her voice level. 'They're lovely. Really beautiful. I hope you didn't spend too much on them.'

He shrugged, seeming distracted. 'I'm glad that you like them. I believed that they would please you, perhaps. I do not know. If they do so, then that is enough.'

Sophia made sure that she was smiling. 'No. No, they're wonderful. Perfect. Thank you.'

She looked down at the box. The bats winked and glittered as her eyes clouded. There was a hollowness in her chest that was choking her. It took her a moment to understand what she felt.

Your own fault. She reached out the tip of one finger and brushed it against a bat. *So very pretty.* Then, through a hole in the velvet covered board, she saw the kink of gold wire. There was something wrong about its curve, its length. With difficulty, she eased the earring away from the box.

Attached to the bat was a long gold wire shaped to slip around the back of her ear. Invisible, it would hold the earring in place in a way that would make it seem almost, although not quite, as though her ears had been pierced.

Her hand clenched around the box and she closed her eyes to hide the painful joy that started rising through her. 'Perfect,' she said again, and her voice was a whisper.

But Julian continued to sit, his face pale, smooth, impossible to read. He had finally unwrapped her present, the box was open in his hand and he stared at the pendant within it. Anxious, almost guilty, she put the earring back into its box. 'I thought you might… I mean, I didn't know if you…'

He shook his head. He did not smile, or touch the gift. He did not look up. For a moment neither of them spoke, and Sophia watched, feeling something that was almost fear. Then, quietly, as though he was uncertain, he began to speak: 'The voice I hear this passing night was heard in ancient days by emperor and clown.'

'Ode to a Nightingale.' He was reciting 'Ode to a Nightingale'.

And Sophia found that her own lips were moving, as she said in time with him, 'Perhaps the self-same song that found a path though the sad heart of Ruth, when, sick for home, she stood in tears amid the alien corn…' They stopped, and their eyes met as though for the first time.

Julian shook his head again. '*Immortal Bird,*' he murmured. His voice was wondering, sincere. 'Where on earth did you find this?'

The room around them was quiet, the only sounds the soft crackle of a fire that was falling to embers, the occasional drip of wax. Sophia realised that her breathing was shallow, tight. For no reason at all, she felt afraid. She gave a false, arch laugh. 'A girl has her secrets.'

'Of course, my dear. I should not pry.' And with a reverence that looked too much like worship, he lifted the necklace from its box and placed it around his neck.

14. To Cease Upon the Midnight with No Pain

He would never again tempt by a prayer any terrible power. If the picture was to alter, it was to alter. That was all. Why enquire too closely into it?
– Oscar Wilde, *The Picture of Dorian Gray*

The creature looked at the pendant hanging against the blue velvet of its case. *How had she known? How was it that she had known?* The silver was so bright it seared his eyes. The inscription felt as if burned into his mind. *Immortal Bird! No hungry generations tread thee down.*

With a slowness that was painful of itself, he reached into the box and wrapped his fingers about it. Silver. Even to the chain. It gnawed into his hands, sent slick sickness creeping along his arms. Once around his neck, he could feel it through the thick layers of his clothes. It was as though he lived again the hard and driving nausea of the turning, lived again that weakness and slow fever. He had thought ingesting mortal food had sickened him, but this? In his mouth, his teeth ached.

He lifted the pendant between two fingers and admired the careful artistry of the bird. He swallowed hard, forcing the harshness of blood and brandy back down his throat. The mirror winked at him.

Silver. And a mirror. It might almost be a joke. Stroking one finger along the bird, he ignored the way his teeth and nerves screamed their disgust. A flash of his reflection greeted him – that superstition, at least, was untrue – and he saw his lips, thin, red, without expression. He twisted them to a smile. Memory of the poem clamoured in his mind: *Thou wast not born for death, immortal Bird!*

'It's delightful,' he told Sophia, and closed his hand about the pendant as though it were precious to him. As his hand began to numb, he let it fall, heavy and draining against his heart.

She smiled, took another sip of her mead. The creature felt the room reel, felt his chest tighten, for all he did not need to breathe. In his too frequent wanderings he had often found his way to the Eternal City's blackening dusk, had paid his tribute to the bard of youthful death. In the stillness of the Protestant cemetery, had he been able to do so, he would have wept.

No more. The silver burned. *To cease,* he thought, remembering the messy crisis of his own death, *upon the midnight with no pain.*

He watched Sophia, saw the emotion and sincerity bright upon her face, felt the deep, tender communion between them. *And what now?*

Thirst troubled him. He could hear her heartbeat, the wet, enticing swish of blood. The silver made him helpless, weak. He recalled the evening he had first arisen, streaked with the filth of his body's death. He had been thirsty then; worse, he had been starved and shaking with the appetites of a monster, but no strength, no predator's teeth. An image from his memories, his dreams: *Eleanor laid out upon the bed, dead for several days.*

He could smell the blood on her over the decay, the ordure of his own body. The cold of the chamber had kept her from rot. Beyond the door, which he had barricaded in his madness, there was a pounding, as though someone were pacing, as he had paced those few short days before.

Perhaps all of it – the fever, the wildness, the physical pain – had been nothing more than grief.

Then, he recognised the pounding for what it was, the steady beating heart of someone on guard beyond the door. And knowing, somehow, what that meant, he had thrown himself on the ruined corpse of his wife and…

No. It did not matter what he had done, simply that for all these centuries that had been the peak of folly, the extremity of loss, of pain, of love.

And what now? He suppressed his trembling, sipped at the blood in his glass. The taste of brandy burned. *What now?*

Take off the necklace, said a sole voice in his mind, advising caution.

The creature looked into Sophia's eyes.

Her smile was tender, her face flushed. Her whole body leaned towards him, half eager, half ashamed.

Truly, he deserved to be damned.

He had not simply courted her, but had set out with the intention of watching her gaze on him in this way. He had said it was but a monster's need for gratification; said it was the man in him, lonely and in pain.

Lies. In his mind, he had lied to himself.

What now?

To withdraw? To leave her slighted, hurt, bewildered? There was almost humour in the thought; had that not been his resolution? Had that not been his first intended course?

Already his limbs ached. In his veins, his slow blood seemed sluggish, weary. He remembered Eleanor, how it had begun, how it had been nothing, had been almost incidental. Their marriage had been a duty made a joy by the growth of their love.

That innocence he had squandered. He was no longer worthy of such simple, honourable bliss.

What self-deceit to claim that he could drive her to the place between madness and pleasure, to say that she would fall under the artistry of lips, of teeth, of hands; to say that she would leave her Jonathan for that lure. No.

The creature had made himself believe that he could love her as a man might love her, had built a fiction for himself that, when she loved him truly, he would have pardon for his past mistakes.

Silver. It pressed into his chest like a brand.

Redemption was not bought so easily.

All he had to offer were hollow tricks. Midnight pleasures, they would wring cries from her, leave her dead and ravished by sensation too strong to bear, but it was not love. He could wound her, corrupt her, make her like himself, but he could not offer animal warmth, nor anything that did not stain.

Take off the silver. Go back to how you were. Be sorrowful, be alone.

But in his mind, there was another voice, one which took counsel from the swishing of her pulse. While he had knotted himself around that lie of knight-errantry, that voice had led him out, hunting beneath the sky. *No hope*, it taunted to the beating of her heart, *no hope, no place, no love. Begin,* it said, *begin with her.*

The creature watched her drink her mead, his outer self all vain chatter. As he spoke, he thought of her, of the honey and the rosemary, the soft press of flesh in his arms. That face would change, that affection curdle if she had even a glimpse of the nature at his heart. She would cry out, her voice low and throbbing, her neck stretched away, and his teeth would tear the skin.

And as he spoke, he wore the silver, a mark of his abasement and his pride.

Long past midnight. Sophia's thoughts were softened by the buzz produced by rich food and far too much alcohol. At last it felt like Christmas and as she walked she kept slipping into little self-conscious dances. The streets were still icy and above her the clouds raced over the moonless sky, covering and revealing stars. She was freezing despite the coat, the jumper, the copious amount of booze. All of her was freezing, except the place on her right hand that Julian had kissed.

It still made her blush, still thrilled and embarrassed her in equal measure. She knew she should be used to it by now, knew she did not want to be used to it. Her crush was miles out of control. She started to hum as she shuffled and pattered her way home. *Step, step, slide. Da-da, da-da-da daah.*

She wondered if Julian danced. It had been ages since she had been out on the town with a dance partner and she missed it, missed the way the rhythm and the music took control, the way she moved without thought. John always got embarrassed when she dragged him to join her. She touched a hand to the pocket where she had put her Christmas present and smiled. Maybe Julian did dance.

'I won't dance,' she muttered as she pranced along the pavement. 'Don't ask me, I won't dance; please don't ask me, I won't dance...' And, not remembering what came next, she picked up a different tempo and executed something that might pass for a complicated manoeuvre. 'You should see me dance the polka, you should see me cover the...' Trying to spin, she skidded on the ice and began to giggle.

It was probably a good thing she had refused Julian's offer to walk her home. It seemed that she was making something of an idiot of herself. Still, she would have enjoyed dancing with him. He liked classical music and probably knew all those old-fashioned dances – polkas, waltzes, gavottes and foxtrots.

Secretly, Sophia had always wanted to dance like that.

Ever since she had been small she had nurtured a fantasy of dancing with her prince, of a candlelit ballroom where everything was stately, elegant, where she could be someone unknown to her daytime self.

Nonsense, of course. She knew that ballroom dancing had never been sedate or intimate, and even the anachronism of privacy by candlelight would never have changed her nature; she would only trip on her skirts and end up swearing. Still, it was nice to think about.

As was Julian. It was easy to understand why the idea of dancing with him tangled itself up in that old daydream. There was something about him that made him seem a more natural part of the image than herself. For a start, there was his melancholy.

The word disturbed her. But, yes, she had noticed it, beneath the cynicism, the playfulness; a loneliness that was terrible.

He had told her next to nothing about his childhood, but she could guess. Never exposed to the wild bustle of adventure, never engulfed by institutional education, growing up in darkness, reared by an elderly relative… She wondered how few friends he must have had. Wondered just how alone he must always have been.

Perhaps that was why he was always so pleased to see her.

Sophia stopped. She felt a little sick and her bladder began to press uncomfortably. Then came the guilt. John would be worried about her.

John was being stupid, of course. There was no particular reason why she should get attacked and murdered while walking home, but he was worried nonetheless. She walked faster. It was cruel to keep him waiting just because she was in a mood with him.

She wished she could stop doing that, being in a mood with him. Wished that taking a few deep breaths would make her reasonable, would make her want to be reasonable. She wished all the things she had stopped herself from saying weren't lodged somewhere in her throat; wished that she still wanted to examine them and diffuse them.

But no. Every time she thought of John she hugged them closer to herself, a mass of tiny annoyances and angry retorts that were waiting for a time when she could haul them out and hurl them at him. In the back of her head, a sane, grownup voice berated her, telling her that she was being childish, pathetic. But it did not stop her snarling over her grievances, did not stop something in her spitting back, *And what's so great about being a grownup?*

It was nearly the spring term. After that it was a matter of handing in her dissertation, taking her finals, and everything that followed. She had experience of office jobs; eight hours a day spent with people she would never have met in the ordinary course of her life. Getting drunk to numb the emptiness, months swallowed in living for the evenings but being too tired to enjoy them, her life measured out weekend by weekend, holiday by holiday. But there had always been uni to come back to. She thought about her future, about the forty or more years between her and retirement, and she wanted to chuck it all in. *Why not?* the drunkenness whispered. *Pack it in. Live a life of adventure and mystery. Why the hell not?*

Sophia shook her head.

Too many things. Responsibility, accountability would always find her out. Suicide was the only permanent escape. Whatever she might fantasise about Julian, however much she compared him to John, she knew being with someone different would not spare her from the graft of a relationship. Sophia knew she had to be realistic.

So when she got home and found John on the sofa in his dressing gown, pointedly waiting up for her, she was weepy and irritable. And as she resigned herself to another row and the tedious apologies tomorrow evening, she felt her little knot of grievance pull tighter, felt the tiredness seep even deeper into her bones. And as she quarrelled and cried and eventually slept, she knew that this was the real world and that there was no other place for her.

But none of this stopped her dreaming of Julian, again, that night.

John looked at Sophia's sleeping back. She was snoring quietly and hogging the duvet. He clicked his tongue against the roof of his mouth, wanting some kind of sign that she was not completely oblivious to his presence.

After all, it's alright for her. Sophia was on holiday, wasn't she? No one was relying on her. So, of course, it was absolutely fine for her to go out, get plastered, then come back and fall into some kind of alcohol-induced coma. John, on the other hand, had to get to work tomorrow.

John would never, *never* hit a girl, but tonight his fists had balled in anger and he had wanted, wanted…

He had asked her over and over to give tonight a miss, told her he'd be sick with worry, but she clearly thought she was invincible. He just about managed to stop himself from thinking that it would have served her right if something had happened.

She's okay. That's the main thing, right? But then she'd swanned in at half past two, drunk and clumsy with it.

And they'd had another fight.

Sometimes it seemed like all they'd done in the last fortnight was bitch and snipe. Something had got into her, put her on the warpath and made her so fucking stubborn that he wanted to scream. *Like a bloody kid,* he thought, and then he felt guilty for thinking it. She missed her mates, which probably explained it. She wanted to be hanging out with Lucy and Steven, chatting about whatever obscure crap the three of them liked talking about. *Still, would it have killed her to give tonight a miss? Just this week, to stay in, where she was safe?*

But there was no telling girls like Sophia anything. It wasn't that John had anything against feminism, and it was great that she was confident and all of that, but this whole tomboy just-as-tough bullshit was taking it too far. Even without the serial killer – which should be enough to make anyone jumpy – the fact was the streets were full of muggers and rapists. It just wasn't safe for a girl like Sophia to be wandering around on her own.

And all she would say was, 'It's my city. Why the hell should I be afraid? If I'm scared, then they've won.' She got it from Lucy. And, of course, it was only good for a fight to point out that Lucy was taller than him and could probably give anyone a run for their money, whereas Sophia was a bare five feet.

So his only option had been to sit around scared out of his mind, until whichever hour she deigned to come home. All because she was so eager to meet up with that weirdo from Hallowe'en that she had stopped thinking about her own bloody safety.

Julian, thought John. *That was another thing.*

Sophia had got her heart set on this stupid New Year's get-together and John knew, just *knew*, it was a disaster waiting to happen. Nothing he could say seemed to be able to shake it from her head. It was one of those things about Sophia. Most of the time, she was chilled, but every now and then she would get an idea into her head and there was no shifting it. He knew by now that the only way to deal with her when she got like that was to give in and wait for the fad to pass.

Only this time it was such a bad idea. It wasn't that he didn't want her to have her friends round – it was her flat too, after all. It wasn't even that he didn't get on with her mates, because spending time with them seemed to be an inevitable part of the couple thing. It was the fact it had to be such a big deal. *I mean, a dinner party?*

No one at work would forgive him for making them spend a whole evening with Steven, and he didn't even want to *think* about what that Julian bloke was going to be like. Still, he'd invited Dave and, because he couldn't think of anyone else, Ron, expecting them to make excuses. They had both accepted with cringe-worthy haste, which was probably his own stupid fault for banging on about how good a cook Sophia was.

John knew there was no way out of it now. The most sensible thing to do would have been to keep his big mouth shut until the entire disaster was well and truly over. But when Sophia got him riled, he always ended up dragging it up and the more he griped, the keener she seemed to get.

He remembered her voice, the way she'd almost been shouting, 'Why the hell are you so against the idea? Is it really so much to ask?' Then she had given him an angry, drunken look and stormed off to bed.

And now he couldn't sleep.

Part of him wanted to make it up to her, to say he was stupid and that it was all his fault. Part of him wanted to reach out and stroke her back until she woke up, wanted take all this silly bitterness away. But he was not going to. Sophia had known how worried he was. He had told her again and again that he didn't like her going out alone, what with the murders and everything. She had known he had work tomorrow, that he couldn't afford too late a night. She just hadn't cared enough to do anything about it.

John huddled down deeper into the blankets, turned his back to her. *Better to leave it to the morning, when you're not so angry, not so tired. It'll be better in the morning.* And he closed his eyes, and tried to sleep. *After all, it's Sophie, and somehow it always comes out alright.*

'Hypocrite,' the creature whispered to himself. 'Hypocrite.' He pressed his teeth together, letting his anger show. He was wearing black, black which eased itself into the darkness; black, which did not show the stains. He lifted a loop of silver chain upon one finger, knowing he deserved the shudder of weakness it sent through him.

Years, decades, centuries of pretending there was some kind of difference between himself and all the other murderers. Posturing. That was all it had ever been, a pose of remorse. He had fancied himself some kind of anti-hero, tormented by passions he could not control. All those beautiful, clever boys, all those passionate, lustful girls. And why? The answer almost amused him. *Why?*

Because he had enjoyed it. It had distracted him, deadened the pain. Again and again, he had created things to mourn in order to indulge in the luxury of remorse. The creature wondered if he had regretted a single thing he had done since drinking the blood of the thing that had turned him. Certainly all his self-punishments, his denials and starvations had been nothing more than an act, a game of repentance and reparation. *Even the silver.*

He dropped the chain in disgust.

What does it matter?

Once, just once, the creature wanted to see the full truth of himself mirrored in another's eyes, to know himself through their fear and hatred. He wanted someone to struggle in his arms, to spit at him, revile him.

It would be best if that person were Sophia.

But always, in her presence he would revert to the lie of courtesy and adoration. The creature closed his eyes and felt the urge for blood. And he wondered if he had done a single honest thing in his life.

By the dying fire, he saw the words carved in the silver. *Immortal Bird! No hungry generations tread you down.*

They seemed a reproach.

On the city streets he was calmer, but that did not signify much. He still almost shook with the energy that screamed through him. He felt a sickness that had nothing to do with brandy or the silver that still lay beside the fire. Strength came back to his limbs. *A monster,* he thought, but the word seemed empty.

Life seethed in the night. Over his head, city sparrows and diseased pigeons shifted in their filthy roosts. Mice and rats scuttled and scurried as he walked, noiseless, past them. The scent of Sophia rang in his head, the taste of her blood sparked upon his tongue. Hunger roared in him. It was the hour when the clubs spilled out their patrons, streaked with sweat and the stickiness of spilled drinks. It was his hour, his hunting hour.

The creature crept through dark alleys. He ached, craved for something that would blot out the madness in his mind; some violence, some respite that would hammer through him, hammer silence into his heart. His pale hands clenched, unclenched their claws.

He heard the cat before he saw her. She was white, her pupils flat discs in amber eyes, her body a serpentine ghost among the shadows. As he approached, her back arched and she hissed.

Childhood superstition flashed through the creature's head: *a white cat for a death.* He began to laugh, a soft, mocking sound that showed the points of his own white teeth. Slowly, slowly, her hackles lowered and she sauntered over to him with the insolent curiosity of her kind. Meeting his eyes, she hesitated, her tail still bowed behind her. The creature dropped to one knee. 'Puss, puss.'

The myths claimed all animals would treat his kind with fear. It was not true. He had always felt an affinity with cats. When he hunted, his eyes were like theirs, the pupils reflective, hard and fathomless black. His teeth, also, owed more to feline fangs than the clumsy incisors of a primate grin. In many ways, their kinds were equal. Perhaps that was why cats did not run from him.

With rough, kneading strides, she clambered over his bent legs, twined round his ankles. The creature ran fingers through the white fur of her chin, felt her hollow throat, her quick pulse. 'There's a good tib.' He was teased by the scent of her blood. She began to purr, deep and throaty. The creature slipped his hand to her back, felt the frailty of her spine. The murderous innocence curled in her flesh.

He drew his hand away.

The white cat butted her head against his chest, pushing back her ears, drawing away the sides of her mouth as she purred and rubbed against him. There was a glimpse of yellow, elegant tooth. Without a sound, he stood and walked away.

There was no pity in his heart when he found the man. *Monster,* he thought again, with strange, bitter triumph. *Yes.*

He followed his mark. The man was handsome, stocky, perhaps in his late thirties. His hair was short around a dark face. His breath puffed at the cold of the night, although he did not hunch. There was an edge of fear-sweat about him beneath the smell of food, quickly cooked. His whole skin seemed grimed with it – that and the scent of tobacco. The man did not know he was being watched, but still, he hurried on his way.

Of course. There was killer in the city.

The creature smiled and pursued.

His prey soon realised that he was being stalked. He began to move with short jerks, fixing his eyes on his hands, the pavement, anywhere but the dead space of night behind him. It did not take long for his pace to quicken, for him to begin the brief, shamed glances over his shoulder. The third or fourth time that his prey craned backwards, the creature allowed himself to be observed, allowed his footsteps to ring on the night-time streets. He knew how he appeared, a shadow that could be neither discerned nor evaluated. His prey began a desperate stride, crossed the street. The creature followed and tasted surging fear.

Following, following, the creature closed the distance between them, step by unmistakable step. The next time the victim turned, he broke into a foolish half-run.

After that, it was soon over. The man darted and dodged, but only lost his own sense of direction, crossing streets, taking turnings without thought. It was not difficult to herd him. The creature did not run but strode, implacable, his footsteps ringing clear, beating out the last minutes of that poor man's life. He could see the sweat on his victim's brow, smell the adrenalin of him, hear the deafening, liquid thunder of his pulse. The creature watched as his prey stopped short, seeing the blank walls of the buildings on each side of him. A dead end. A single, dull streetlamp lit the scene. Facing the wall, his prey gave out a low, desperate sob.

With slow, loud steps, the creature came to him. The man's body was tensed for flight, for pain. The creature watched him, overcome by the beauty of his hard muscles, the sweet frailty of his terror and expectation. It was almost with tenderness that the creature ran a hand over the damp skin of his victim's face. The flesh felt hot, impossibly soft. He pushed it a little harder and heard the man moan in fear or pain. It was a childish sound.

The creature smiled, showing his teeth, and stroked his hand down to the throat.

It was then the man began to fight, the animal taking command, making the arms and legs flail, scrabble and punch. Pain slapped through the creature's heightened nerves, delicious, exquisite. He recoiled, allowed a treacherous hope to slither into the man's mind. But even as his prey's sight cleared, his eyes widened at the thought of life prolonged, the creature gripped the man with his full strength and pulled that hot, struggling body against his own. For a moment, the fists continued to beat, the muscles to strain and every point on the creature's body was seized with expectation and pain. For one ecstatic moment the creature felt life, and he laughed, pushing his nails into that flesh.

The body went limp in his arms.

'Oh God,' the man sobbed, 'don't hurt me. Please, oh please…'

Disappointment was the first feeling, then disgust, for he had hoped for more of a fight. Then there kindled his tenderness. And with the tenderness came the thought of Sophia, for what else should he connect with such warm and human feeling? The male smell of sweat and musk was an assault so he ceased to mark it. He thought only of the warmth in his arms, of the heavy beat of life. He remembered holding Eleanor, how even his dull, mortal senses had felt the beat of her pulse against his lips when he had kissed her throat. Remembered how she had cried out at the brush of his hands, and how Sophia's skin might run red with his kisses, her body shake with it, how she might die in his arms, in love's extremity.

He loosened his grip.

The man's face twisted upwards. It was wet with tears. The eyes were wide and horrified.

'Not hurt you?' The creature's voice was a gentleness, a caress marred by the smile upon his lips, the sharp teeth in his mouth. With one fingertip, he brushed the wetness of his prey's cheek and licked the moisture away.

He threw the man from him. Among the general impact of a body on the courtyard's concrete, he heard the quiet snap of something small. It took a moment for the screaming to begin. The creature closed his eyes as the sound flowed through him. His teeth pressed urgent against his lips, his tongue was parched. The wail of his victim died to a timorous, wounded sob. The creature moved towards him.

It took no more than half an hour.

The broken thing sprawled beneath him was no longer a man, only torn sinew and deep, empty gashes. The blood which had pumped hot into his mouth seeped its way across the ground, sticky and contaminated with the dust and detritus of the streets. In the orange glow of the streetlight, it seemed black. The ribs poked upwards, white and stark against the darkness of the chest cavity. Only the face remained, with its eloquence of fear.

It would be unwise to linger. The place had been chosen carefully, but his victim had screamed and that might have drawn pursuit. Then he would need to fight.

Still, he remained kneeling by the ruined cadaver. Tears sat, half shed, upon the cheeks. The lacerations, the contusions, the snapped bone and savaged muscle, all these things wrung their way through him. There were still shreds of flesh beneath his fingernails, trails of gore upon his chin. The creature reached into the shards of the rib cage and pulled out the mangled ruin of the heart. He shook his head and let the meat fall, but even as he did, he licked the blood from his fingers without thought.

Then the sickness took him. It was not to do with the blood, nor the silver, nor the alcohol. He could not weep. Perhaps it would have been easier had he been able to weep. A cry left him, low and keening in the night, and he vowed that this, now, would be the last. Everything in his past lay ruined; there had been no virtue nor honour there, but it would change, and it must change. No matter how desperate he became, he could no longer support the appetites of this monster within him.

But he could not deny that his hunger was in abeyance; that, even as he turned away from his own enjoyment of the screams, winces and the despair of the man beneath his hands, he felt the shame of his pleasure and pleasure in his shame. He knew that there would be no respite until he could enclose Sophia in his arms, close her white throat between his teeth.

The creature put his face into his hands as a slow, dry sob racked his chest and he lowered his forehead to the hard and frosted ground.

15. To a Noble End

A man may do many foolish things, he may even be a little wicked now and then, provided it is in nothing dishonourable
– Anon, 'The Mysterious Stranger'

Lucy dropped her bags and flopped on to the bed. As she lay, she checked if her stomach was bloated outwards; after all, it had been Christmas and she felt like she'd eaten a lethal quantity of chocolate in the last week. All other necessary festive traditions had been honoured – the annual matchstick poker tournament, the Christmas Eve piss-up in one of their old haunts, and the trek across town to drop off a card at Steven's parents' house. As usual, there had been no reply. Steven had handled that quite well this year.

She was shattered. Perhaps it was her own fault for booking such an eye-achingly early train journey, but it had meant that even three delays, two changes and a replacement bus service had not stopped them arriving home in good time for Sophia's party. She even had time for a quick nap.

And she found that she could not sleep.

Last year, after the bag-laden and freezing walk from the station, Steven had collapsed on the sofa, claiming he had no intention of moving until spring. Today he had unpacked immediately and gone to have a shower. On Christmas Eve, Lucy had noticed the pretty gold earrings Sophia had been wearing; Sophia, who did not have pierced ears; Sophia who rarely wore any jewellery. When asked about them, Sophia had come over self-conscious. Lucy had not been surprised to learn that they were a gift. From Julian.

What's he playing at? More importantly, why did he decide to involve Sophia and Steven? And, even as she tried to stop herself, she added, *Especially Steven.*

Come on, you knew it was going to happen one day. But it was not just because Steven was taken with him – or at least, she hoped it was not just that. As she lay still, Lucy tried to remember Hallowe'en, tried to remember if something about Julian had unsettled her then, if she had known he was up to no good.

Maybe. Maybe I never did like him. And she knew that this was not a reliable testimony.

But she thought again of Sophia wearing earrings, of Steven's questions and confessions. Since Hallowe'en, everything the two of them did seemed to have realigned, refocussed upon their mysterious stranger. She could see their infatuations, even if they remained oblivious. It was too sudden, too total for it to be quite right.

And it excluded her.

Was that the bulk of it? Would she have forgiven Julian for making Steven fall in love with him if she could be allowed to get a little infatuated as well? But Julian *had* invited her; she had just refused to go. Again, she could not but wonder if she had mistrusted him from the start.

That was why it was important to go along tonight. If Julian were serious about one of her friends, Lucy would be able to let it go. Even if that friend were Steven. And, of course, she would be on hand to comfort and reassure whichever of them got their feelings hurt. She could cope with that, if that was all that was happening.

But Lucy suspected that was not all, that Julian was not serious, or at least not in a way that would make either Sophia or Steven happy. If that were the case, she knew she would need to console both of them.

And if it's worse than that?

She shook her head. *Sure. Something worse than him being a confirmed flirt and breaking my friends' hearts.*

The thoughts still cried for attention: *what if he's a pimp? A rapist? A murderer?*

Don't be ridiculous.

A memory from Hallowe'en, the way that Julian had watched Steven; the lust, the hunger. The way that, kissing Sophia's hand, he had stopped and stared. The way her own muscles had tensed, ready to scream, hit, run. The way that, afterwards, she had laughed it off.

Just like she was doing now.

Because – so what? Maybe he fancies both of them. They're good–looking people. Maybe I should just tell him to make up his mind before anyone gets hurt.

So Lucy checked her watch and decided that, as Steven was hogging the shower, she should get everything else sorted if they wanted to get to Sophia's on time. She unpacked her bags, opted for jeans over a skirt, and managed to convince herself that she was looking forwards to the evening.

Almost.

Heavy clouds threatened snow, but it had not yet fallen. The wind was low, the cold intense. It stole under the creature's coat, probed, insinuated its way around the cut-throat slash of his scarf. All along the streets, freezing fog piled and billowed. Its caress over his cheekbones was damp and sly.

He did not suffer from the cold, knew it only as an ache in his bones, a thrill upon his skin as his body sank slowly to the chill of the night. His heart beat low and sluggish in his chest. His face was still, impassive; even hard. His breath did not steam in the air.

He could not trust himself.

One invitation was all he required. One invitation and he might slip into his beloved's home the way an infection slips into a body in passion's final moments.

He could not trust himself.

The creature knew the game he was playing. Hadn't he flustered over what he would wear tonight? Chosen red and black because it *suited* him? As he had fastened his cufflinks, hadn't he caught himself admiring his image in the glass? It had been some years since he had acted so much the dandy.

He looked scarcely older than the night he had left his wife in childbed. Even his paleness, the rings around his eyes, might have come from a trifling illness, a drunken night. Had one of the contemporaries of his mortal life been able to see him, had they been able to overlook the style of his clothes, the length of his hair, he believed they might have mistaken him for that honest and besotted young man.

The creature could not trust himself.

Not that he was incapable of self-restraint. The custom of hospitality held him nearly as closely as threshold's bonds. He would not turn wild, lose control of himself. Still, after tonight, he might go to Sophia whenever he willed. Might he not, then, linger by her bedside, might he not guard her while she slept? And in the dark, might he not whisper to her, might he not open her veins and let the current of her life slide over his lips, his tongue…?

Such foolish thoughts.

For underlying them was still the fond deceit that he meant her no harm. Too weak. He was too weak. All his fears, his childlike preening, were nothing but distractions from the thought of her proximity, from the feeling of her pulse against his lips.

The devil could take the consequences. Guilt, self-loathing – they could wait; they would be there anyway, marring his enjoyment, gainsaying, mocking his failures of resolve. Things would fall out in one direction or another. The creature no longer believed he had any power to alter them.

With calm decision he approached her modern apartment and knocked upon the door.

Sophia answered it.

Her clothes were grimed with flour and cooking grease, her hair inexpertly tied with stray, dark tendrils curling against her neck. There was a glister of sweat on her, and along with salt and sex, honey and rosemary, she smelled of other herbs, of onions, pepper and thin, watery blood. Her hands were stained and damp.

She had never looked so beautiful.

Just as Eleanor had been when her hands were stained and scented with lanolin, herbs or earth; when she had woken in the morning with hair tangled on her face; then she had been her most lovely. More, she had been possessed of a power which had made her beauty sing in every line of muscle, of flesh.

It was sexual; the creature appreciated that now.

He clenched his teeth. It was well that the threshold restrained him.

'Julian, hi.' She pushed the door open wider. Golden light spilled towards him.

'Sophia, my dear,' the words were forced, strained, 'it is always a pleasure.'

A moment passed. He sensed her awkwardness, the expectation that he would step inside, the way she bit her lip, embarrassed, confused.

'Please. Come in. God, you must be freezing out there.'

The barrier fell away. With triumph, he stepped into the warmth.

And his vision recoiled in a burst of pain.

It was as though some judgement were passed upon him, until he blinked and his sight returned. The lights; so plentiful, so bright. The house, so very warm.

A mortal man, dressed as he was dressed, would have been stifled. He fumbled with the buttons on his greatcoat. He had been in modern buildings before, was acquainted with high wattage bulbs and central heating. *You should have expected this.*

But he had been too busy conflating Sophia with his dead wife, too taken with the memory of her in his own candlelit home. *Fool.* The room in which they stood was cluttered, small. Sophia was very near to him. Her scent was overpowering. Noises assailed him; not the creaks and moans of an old house settling upon itself, not vermin's busy scuffle, but the buzz of the road, the city, the hum of electrical things, the noise of neighbouring dwellings. From all directions there came a pervasive, inchoate babble of music and speech.

The creature focused on the sounds. *Wirelesses,* he thought. *No, radios. And televisions, or computers, or ... Just noise. It is nothing of import.* Sophia's scent wrapped around him, making his thoughts difficult to control. His teeth pressed in painful longing against his gums. He suspected he had been smiling like an imbecile.

'You look incredible,' Sophia whispered, low, enticing. He felt her gaze as though it were a caress. He wondered if she knew her words were masked by the insensate, electronic noises. Wondered if she would have said such things had her Jonathan been able to hear.

His smile widened at the thought. 'As do you, my dear.'

Sophia laughed.

The creature took her hand and kissed it.

As his lips brushed her fingers, there was a tension in the muscles of her arm. Not resistance, but reluctance, perhaps. Or arousal. The familiarity of her blood soothed his senses.

A precaution, perhaps as wise one. Yet in the context of her sunlit life, this action seemed unpardonable, obscene. As if in mitigation, he held out the bottle he had brought. 'I thought that this might be appreciated.' *Wine for blood.* The thought recalled the sacrament.

'Oh, thank you. You shouldn't have.' Sophia gave a wide, unguarded smile.

He felt the muscles of his mouth ache to return it. He sank one fang into his cheek, satisfying himself with his usual mild expression.

'Oh, it's so good to see you!' she said, and embraced him, her lips brushing his cheek as she whispered, 'I'm so glad you could come.'

He froze.

When she pulled away, she did not meet his eyes. 'I'm still kind of cooking, so you won't mind too much if I deposit you in the lounge for a bit? Steven and Lucy shouldn't be too much longer.'

The creature could not move. The ghost of the warmth she had left against him began to seep its way through the thick fabric of his clothes. He knew it would never reach his skin. He did not to breathe, did not drink in her scent as though it were blood. 'Of course not, my dear.' *Manners. Manners.* 'But might I not be of some assistance?'

Sophia shrugged, her body flowing an eloquent dismissal. 'Don't worry about it. I'm just assembling things. I won't... I won't be long. Besides,' she raised her head and her voice dropped to that quiet, thrilling murmur, 'tonight's my treat.' And she blushed.

He felt his fingers curl, twitch towards her. It was almost as though he could feel the heat pouring from her skin. To put his hand against her face, to touch that redness against his fingertips...

The creature forced his hands to stay flat, his arms to remain by his sides. 'If you insist, my dear.' It was a struggle to keep the desperation from his voice.

'I do. Right. Sitting room. Um. Should probably warn you – John's invited a couple of his mates tonight. They're kind of, well... they're not really... Yeah, anyway. Sorry about them. I'll be done in a minute.'

'Are you certain you would not rather I assisted you?'

The creature watched her hesitate.

Then, 'No, I'll only be a moment. Just try not to mind them.'

'I shall endeavour, my dear.'

She led him into the main room. It was not large. The walls were dull magnolia, the lights too bright, the air too warm. Despite the clutter, there was a hard cleanliness – no dust to soften the air, no quiet scent of books, no wood smoke, no old leather. Instead, he could smell cleaning chemicals and the plastic fibres of the carpet, all of which were overlaid by the jangling, competing reek of the boys' colognes.

Ah. The young men. They slumped on a low, mock-leather sofa, staring raptly at an impossibly large television. Their jaws were almost slack, their eyes vacant. Worst, they seemed oblivious to Sophia. Only one – and not, he noticed, Jonathan – glanced up and gave her something approaching a smile. His low opinion was confirmed when she ignored it.

Indeed, she ignored all of them, simply crossed the room and turned off the television. Then, with similar equanimity, she switched on some manner of music player. The sound of light guitars hummed and clashed with that which pounded in the kitchen.

Sophia's comely, blond fiancé looked up and said, 'Jesus, Sophie, we were watching that.'

'Tough. Julian's here now, so let's try to be civilised.' She turned back to where he stood, and some of that bright, merciless quality left her. He reminded himself that he should find Sophia's conflict with her young man rather less amusing.

'Now, Julian, you know John, of course. And these other two are Ron and Dave.' Her gesture was vague. The creature thought it likely she could not tell them apart. 'Do make yourself comfortable, Julian. I shan't be long. I'll only be in the kitchen.'

The three men remained seated; Jonathan continued to watch the blank television screen with what seemed to be a sense of loss. Another had switched his gaze to the glowing cube of his mobile telephone, thumbs tapping a rapid rhythm against its tiny keys. The third, the one who had smiled, looked up at the creature with a distant, puzzled expression. The creature forced himself to recall that Sophia's annoyance gave him no licence.

'Good evening.' The creature addressed himself to Jonathan.

At that, the boy looked up. 'Hi.' His voice was sulky, low. The creature could almost sense his annoyance, which encompassed Sophia, the light, inoffensive music, the fragrance of food and the creature himself. And despite his own illusion of humanity, despite the taboos which hospitality placed upon his behaviour, the creature felt the desire to tear out the boy's still beating heart and crush it.

Tread carefully. He rearranged what he could of his countenance, made an effort to appear gracious.

To his surprise, so did Jonathan. The boy took a deep breath and said with unconvincing cheeriness, 'Yeah. Julian. Nice to see you again.' He stood and offered the creature his hand. Everything about the gesture was casual.

Under the clear lights of his own home, the boy seemed less appealing. He had lost whatever dash of the fugitive his behaviour on Hallowe'en had lent him. Presumably in some effort to appear mature, he had allowed several days of beard to grow upon his chin. It was a mistake. It grew like white down, rendering his jaw weak, his face soft edged and foolish.

The creature quashed these thoughts. *You are a guest.* He attempted to ameliorate the stiffness in his arm, his tone. 'Jonathan. The pleasure is entirely mine.'

The boy's hand was warm, clammy, strong. There was no trace of that fear he had sensed on Hallowe'en; Jonathan met his eyes with something like defiance. The creature returned the stare and the grip, keeping the pressure below the threshold of pain. The boy's jaw tightened but he did not recoil, just as, while flinching, he had not pulled away from the temperature of the creature's hand. Eventually, Jonathan broke the contact and kept the edge of forced politeness in his voice. 'This is Dave. That's Ron.'

'Charmed,' he said and managed to bite down upon the *I'm sure.*

At that, one of the others rose, the one who had seemed absorbed in his telephone. *Ron.* The boy was rather taller than himself, and broader by far. The creature felt himself being evaluated.

The creature knew the type, men who feared that which they did not understand and snarled at that which they feared. This was not bravery; the boy would not pick this fight unless the odds were more clearly in his favour. That was why the creature was being measured.

'Alright,' Ron said, his tone flat, aggressive. It was not a question.

The creature put out his hand and smiled with cold disdain. He pressed that warm, fragile flesh with rather more strength than was advisable, and met the challenge of those dull eyes. It did not take long for Ron to drop his hand, or look away. He felt a moment of satisfaction.

That was gratuitous.

The criticism was immediate, was enough to shame him. It was with rather more courtesy that he held out his hand to the other boy.

'Nice one, mate.' Dave did not rise and gripped his hand but briefly. He smiled from where he sat but did not meet the creature's eyes. There was no challenge there, only amiable, wilful ignorance. The creature bowed his head a little, as though giving a motion of respect.

He could not see what any of these three had in common with Sophia. Looking at the details of her home, he could find no further clues. The whole room seemed filled with a kind of frantic impermanence, a self-laudatory modernity. All around him, plastic was made up to look like wood and wood was lacquered into artificiality. Much of it, although still new, was beginning to fray. There was too much light. The only touch of personality was in the voluptuous lines of a Georgia O'Keeffe, and that could only be seen if one turned one's back to the television.

The creature wondered how she could feel any comfort in this shrine to mediocrity.

But then his own home had once been little better; he and Eleanor had been a very middling sort of people, no doubt with pretentions that those around them found ridiculous. Besides, Sophia had chosen this world, had lived her whole life in such rooms. He could not criticise them without criticising her, and it was foolishness to imagine she would abandon them for the haunted chambers he could offer her.

From the kitchen he could hear the clatter of pans, the bass and tenor of other music, could smell animal blood, vegetables and herbs. Everything in him ached to go to her, to forget the drear modern world in which she lived.

He restrained himself. Sophia had asked him to remain here.

Although no one offered him a seat, he settled into one of the empty armchairs. The young men remained on the sofa. It was clear his presence unsettled them, although perhaps no more so than the absence of noise from the television. From a speaker near his chair, a singer complained, *I can't get no satisfaction...* Beneath the music, silence stretched.

'So, Julian. How have you been keeping?' Jonathan's voice sounded laboured.

'Most satisfactory. I trust you have been well?'

'Yeah, yeah. I've been fine.' The boy's eyes flashed left and right, never settling upon the creature's own. 'Sorry about the... the Thursday stuff. I mean it's been a bit busy at work. Overtime and that. You know how it is.'

'Sophia did say something of the kind. You need not apologise to me.'

The conversation died.

Beneath the music ran the constant pounding of their blood. He turned his attention to his fingernails, to the last trace of Sophia's taste upon his tongue.

A guest. You are a guest. To occupy his mind he concentrated on the reflexes of mortality, remembered to breathe, to maintain small movements. Blinking was easy, for the lights were too wanton for his night-time eyes.

The others began to talk about one or other aspect of the arcana of their existence. It took the creature a moment to recognise the topic. Sport.

Even in his own lifetime, he had taken little interest in such recreations; enough for propriety, no more. After his death, he had lost even that. In the centuries of his disregard, the whole medium had changed; no longer blood sports nor solitary games of skill, the focus seemed to be on team occupations and endless rules governing what he had known as bloody riots.

As they spoke, therefore, the creature gave communications of polite disdain; a mild glance, a brief smile. For the most part, they ignored him. Every so often, Dave threw out a query. Each time, the

creature was forced to admit that he did not follow, did not know…
Only a very careful observer would have heard the scorn in his voice.

Conversation shifted to personalities, television shows, popular
music. The creature tried to prevent his eyes from straying too often
to the kitchen, to Sophia. Instead, he maintained each careful denial;
he did not know, had not seen… He watched the unease grow upon
their faces and began, almost, to pity them.

At their next futile attempt, he made an effort to put them at their
ease. 'I'm afraid not. I am that most antisocial of beings, a person who
does not watch television.' He gave them a small, ironic smile, inviting them to laugh at his expense.

The one called Dave stared at him in amicable bewilderment. 'No
shit? You serious, mate?'

The creature pressed his lips together. 'Perfectly.'

He heard John make a sound which, to ears less acute, would have
passed for a cough.

He felt a strange, furious wish that it had been these three who had
visited him on Hallowe'en and that he might have been able to pass
them by and never know them. 'I'm afraid I have never even possessed
such a device.'

'Jesus,' Dave murmured.

Ron was staring at him with hostility and suspicion. 'So why don't
you get one, then?'

'I lack the inclination.'

The boy flinched, looked away.

The creature ran his tongue under one tooth, filling his mouth with
his own blood. The taste calmed him. 'To be honest, as I have never
possessed one, I'm rather blind to the attraction of them. I content
myself with the company of literature.' He gave them a smile that was
free from neither predation nor warmth. 'Or people, of course.'

That would have made Sophia laugh, or Steven.

Nothing.

Ron glared down at his feet, the incipient violence held at bay
only by caution. The creature could sense the suspicion of the other
two, suspicion that was beginning to border upon fear. The creature

almost wished that they would reach a decision, make some manner of attack, if only to break the tedium.

He forced his lips to remain a neutral line, refusing to provoke them further. The music played on, oblivious, and beneath that, he could hear the quiet beating of their hearts, the breathing of their bodies. His tongue had healed, so he dragged it across his teeth again. The fresh welling of blood was little comfort. John and Dave continued to stare. He knew it was his responsibility to break the mood, to say something that would confirm their bad opinion.

The creature sat without moving. It occurred to him that he was being cruel.

When the knock came at the door, he was the only one who did not jump. *Steven.* The name comforted him enough that he gave a little smile, a self-conscious laugh. He made a gesture of dismissal which broke his own stillness, and buried the small, unconscious knowledge of him that had taken root in the three boys' minds.

In the kitchen, Sophia was cooking. Or rather, she was trying to cook and was running at least twenty minutes late. This was her own fault – she had got carried away, making side dishes, condiments, dessert, even home-baked bread. Worse, she was filthy. Her hair was wrenched back into a scruffy bun, her face was flushed. Her t-shirt and jeans had a light dusting of flour and were streaked with egg white, chocolate and the odd splash of oil.

She wanted to have been changed before anyone turned up. She knew that she should have let John answer the door, because even though he was refusing to wear anything nicer than jeans and football shirt, he was at least presentable. She on the other hand looked like scullery maid.

Whereas Julian looked as though he had stepped off the set of a period drama.

Damn. Sophia stirred peppercorn sauce and thought, *Why the hell did I imagine this would be a good idea?*

It wasn't that Julian was overdressed; she had expected that. It was that the flat was cluttered and shabby and that tonight was going to be an unmitigated disaster. She turned to where the steaks were waiting to be cooked and ground salt and pepper over them. From the lounge she could hear the total absence of conversation. The word 'doomed' echoed through her skull. Glancing round the kitchen, she decided that everything was done. Or at least done enough. She washed her hands and as an afterthought splashed her face. *Time to change. Enough time for a quick shower?*

A knock at door. 'Shit.' Then, *At least it's probably Steven and Lucy.* She more or less ran down the hall.

'About bloody time,' she greeted them, and ushered them inside. She had no qualms about hugging Lucy, who was in jeans and t-shirt, whereas Steven was wearing something that was very nearly a suit. He looked almost dashing.

'Charming. Abuse brought to the very doorstep now, is it?'

'I'm feeding you. I don't need to be polite.'

'Fine. I shan't give you this, then.' His free hand was clutching a bottle of red wine. The knuckles that had been holding it were raw with the cold. The idiot wasn't wearing a coat.

'Yes, you should. As an apology for being late.' She kissed his cheek, then Lucy's. 'I needed you here.'

'You panic too much,' Lucy said. 'And, yeah, sorry.'

'We caught the bus, and that turned an arduous ten-minute walk into a brief and enjoyable fifteen-minute ride, preceded by a delight-ful twenty-minute wait in the freezing bloody cold.'

Lucy sighed. 'Shut up, Steven.'

'I'm just relaying the facts.' His voice was level, reasonable and impossibly smug. 'As you said, the bus was so much quicker.'

'Yes. And you're not wearing heels.'

'And that's reason enough to bring our hostess to the very brink of nervous breakdown?'

'Shut up, Steven?'

'Such wit...'

'Such bullshit,' Sophia said. 'Look, I don't care why you're late. Julian's in there with John and the thicko twins, probably facing death by boredom. We need back-up. You two qualify as the cavalry, alright? So you go in there and rescue our man while I go and get changed. Clear?'

There was a brief silence. Lucy nodded as though she understood, but said, 'Wilco, skipper. But how about I keep you company? You look like you need some support.'

Sophia watched as a large grin spread across Steven's face. She gave Lucy a somewhat desperate look.

'Honey,' Lucy explained, 'I'm not in the mood to be nice to idiots. I'm freezing. And, well, if those two are that much of a problem, why did you invite them?'

'I don't know,' Steven's smile was now of dangerous proportions, 'a couple of rude mechanicals... Comic relief, perhaps?'

Sophia closed her eyes. 'They're just here to keep John happy.' *Deckchairs,* she thought, *Titanic.*

'Well, then, how about *I* go and keep Julian happy?' He was almost licking his lips.

'Oh, God, Steven. Please.'

'What? Our fair guest is in need of rescue. I'm the cavalry, aren't I? So where is the problem, my dear?' He arranged his face into a saintly expression.

Sophia shook her head. She knew that look. 'Oh dear God, no. Please. Don't start a fight, Steven.'

'Once more unto the breach, dear friends,' his voice floated back to them as he walked into the lounge, 'once more.'

Or close up the wall with our English dead. 'Oh shit,' she slumped against the wall, 'this is going to be a complete debacle.' She wondered if suicide would hurt an awful lot.

Lucy took her shoulder and began to steer her towards the bedroom. 'Come on. Buck up. It's not so bad.'

'Not so bad?' Sophia whimpered and began to drag her feet along the hall. 'Ugh. John said this was a bad idea and Steven said... Oh God. He's going to get himself beaten up again. ' She did not so much open the bedroom door as throw herself against it.

'No, come on. He's just the entertainment for the evening. He knows where the line is.'

'Yeah. And sometimes it entertains him to cross it.' Sophia stood by her desk and stared at the bed, where the dress she had decided to wear tonight was lying, sinuous and dusky grey. She didn't have the heart to touch it. After a couple of minutes, Lucy gave her a little shove.

'Come on, love. It'll be fun.'

'Fun?'

'Sure, we can be like the peacekeeping corps.'

Sophia nodded and crossed the room. Making sure Lucy's back was turned, she shrugged herself out of her t-shirt and jeans before struggling into her tights and slipping the dress over her head. The silky fabric snagged on her hand, where she'd got yet another papercut. Christ, she was a mess.

Lucy, who had been fiddling with the bears on top of the computer, turned around and gave a theatrical sigh. 'You look fine.'

Picking up her hairbrush, Sophia made a noncommittal sound.

'Come on, Sophia, it's not like you to be afraid.'

'Uh-huh?' With her hair smoothed, she supposed she looked a little better. She put on her bat earrings, dabbed on a little more perfume and pulled a face at her reflection.

'Hurry up, stop fretting. Stiffen the sinews, commune up the blood, all of that.' When she did not respond, Lucy waggled the Bonnie bear at her. 'How bad can it be?'

Sophia blinked once, nodded. 'Agincourt? Oh, what the hell. Cry God for Harry, England and Saint George!'

16. In Love and War

Then imitate the action of the tiger;
Stiffen the sinews and commune up the blood,
Disguise fair nature with hard–favour'd rage
– William Shakespeare, *Henry V*

Contrary to his expectations, Steven was finding the evening rather pleasant. Removed from Julian's old house, his infatuation seemed less dangerous, less contradictory. What did it matter, after all, if he had developed a crush? He had to grow up at some point.

So, instead of agonising, he relaxed; enjoyed the company and the wine, enjoyed talking about Proust and Sheridan Le Fanu, and the problems with the recent film adaptations of a series of popular novels. He tried not interrogate how much of his good mood was due to the way that Julian had looked at him when he walked into the room, or the way that Lucy had spectacularly refused to monopolise Julian's attention. Had he feared that? Knowing too well how she could take control, not only of the conversation, but of the attention that any men present had to offer, was he relieved that she seemed more amused by Julian than interested in him? That she had spent most of the evening talking with one of John's friends about some obscure television programme?

Sophia was a different matter. When she wasn't cooking or fetching people drinks, she stayed very close to the pair of them, listening. When she spoke it was usually to Julian. Entirely to Julian, in fact.

Steven tried not to let his jealousy get the better of him.

After all, it was clear that Sophia had gone to a lot of effort to make the evening work. She dashed about, running in and out of the kitchen, topping up glasses, asking about allergies and food preferences. Besides, she had been right about John's friends not spoiling things for Julian and himself; they seemed content to ignore him. Steven was more than happy to return the compliment.

The only person who did not appear to be enjoying himself was John, who vacillated between forced joviality and monosyllabic sullenness. He kept shooting Sophia black looks. She ignored him. Steven – who had been trying to be on his best behaviour in that regard – discovered that he could make the odd snide comment without her seeming to mind. He suspected the reason behind this alteration in Sophia's attitude.

But there were to be no regrets tonight. It was the holidays; the wine was plentiful and the food wonderful. Not that he would ever tell her this, but Sophia was a better cook than he would ever be, and tonight she had surpassed herself. He did not even regret imitating Julian and asking for his steak seared.

Which was probably a good thing. Something in the way in which Sophia had organised the table meant that only Lucy separated him from John. This meant that he was able to hear John's response to his request: a distinct and scornful, 'Ugh.' Had this comment been directed at Julian, or even at both of them, he might have let it pass. As it was, before even tasting his blue steak, he had been forced into a diatribe against anyone who defiled the poor animal by having its meat cooked any more than rare.

It had not taken telepathy to know that, at that point, Lucy had been thinking, *Medium, Steven?* But, bless her, she had not said a thing. Even Sophia had not taken him up on it.

Indeed, later, she had said to Julian, 'It's terrible, I know, but I've never been quite brave enough to try that. I think it's because I cook and, well, I can't help but think that, no, that's just not long enough to be safe.' And she had laughed, looking away from him. 'So sorry if it's a bit overdone.'

Julian had said, 'It is perfect, my dear. See?' And without asking her permission, he had cut a slither of meat and, with his fingers, laid it upon her tongue.

Sophia had leaned back in her chair to chew and swallow it. Sitting on the other side of Julian, Steven had been unable to see the expression on her face, although he suspected it of being indecent. 'Mmm,' she had said in a languorous voice. 'Oh, that is rather nice. I'll have to remember that.'

For the rest of the meal, Julian kept offering her morsels of his own food, which she took directly from his fork. Still, most of Julian's conversation was with him, not Sophia. And he was not going to let it spoil his evening.

Outside, John leaned against the wall and watched his breath steam in the air. He rammed his hands deeper into his pockets and shook his head at the roll-up Dave was offering him. Sophia would hate it if she found out he was smoking, even though it was just socially. Not that he had any reason to be nice to her tonight.

No one could pretend the evening had been fun.

Dave lit up and, in the flare of the lighter, John could see a little sideways smile on his face. 'That Lucy's a bit of something, ain't she?'

'She's alright.'

'Nah, mate. It's okay for you. But she's...' He pulled the cig away from his lips and whistled through his teeth. 'I wouldn't say no, if you catch my drift?'

'I'm thinking you made that pretty obvious.'

Dave shrugged and scratched his head. 'Yeah, well. Much good may it do me. I'm telling you, that Steven doesn't know he's born.'

That one took a moment to sink in. He managed to stop the 'huh?' halfway to his lips. 'Wrong call, mate.'

'You're joking.'

'No chance. I mean, yeah, it's all a bit fucked up, but they're not together. Just friends.'

Next to them, Ron blew out a plume of smoke. 'No such thing.'

'Yeah. Don't they like live together or something?'

'Well yeah, but,' he paused, smirked, 'he's not that way inclined, shall we say?'

'What? He's a batty boy?'

'Figures,' Ron said.

'Yeah, I guess,' Dave agreed. 'I mean, it doesn't always work like that, does it?' No one answered. 'Anyway. Whatever. Bit of a twat, isn't he?'

'Yeah.' John didn't feel like lying. 'If you ask me, he's a right bloody arsehole. Still, *Sophie* likes him, so I've got to be nice, haven't I?'

'More fool you.'

'So…' Dave sounded like he'd just realised something. 'If Steven's a fag then does that mean Lucy's single?'

'Well, yeah. Kinda. But I wouldn't want to risk it, mate. You'll wind up pussy-whipped.'

'Almost worth it.' Dave laughed. He took a long drag and shook his head. 'Still. Dunno what that lad's thinking. Not worth being gay when there's that kind of thing on offer.'

'I told you, mate. She's a ball cruncher.'

For a while, no one said anything. The other two smoked and John stared at the ground. Then Ron said, 'So that Steve's gay then?' His voice had an edge to it.

'Yeah.'

'So, what then? He pillow-biting for that other one?'

John didn't follow, so he didn't say anything.

'You know, whassiface. The goth.'

Goth. Yeah, that makes sense. 'I dunno.' Inside his trainers, his toes were beginning to go numb. He stamped his feet, shrugged. 'Maybe. I don't think so.'

'How d'you know him, then?' Ron asked. It didn't sound like a casual question.

'What, Julian?' John shrugged again. He'd not mentioned the Hallowe'en thing at work because he knew they would probably think it was bloody stupid. They were right. It had been bloody stupid. 'Oh, you know. He's just a mate. Of theirs.'

Maybe he was being paranoid, but he was sure Ron and Dave exchanged a look.

Dave puffed on his cigarette and took over. 'You mean, like, a mate of Sophie's?'

'Yeah. Yeah, one of her friends.'

'Right,' said Dave. 'Okay.'

Ron glanced at him.

Dave looked down. He shuffled his feet. He rubbed the bridge of his nose. 'Look, mate, are you sure that he and Steve aren't… you know?'

'How the hell should I know? Got nothing to do with me.'

Dave pinched the bridge of his nose again. 'Nah, I'm sure you're right mate. It's probably nothing.'

Ron gave Dave another look. John knew he wasn't imagining it this time.

'What the fuck are you two talking about?'

'Look, forget it. It's nothing.'

In his experience, when a conversation took a turn like this, it was never nothing. 'Seriously, you two. Am I going to have to deck you, or something? What's going on?'

'I told you, mate, it's probably nothing.'

'Only…' Ron began.

'Only nothing, alright? John, forget it, mate – okay?'

John remembered his management training. *Try assertive,* he thought, *not aggressive.* 'I'm going to go in if the pair of you keep this up.'

Ron seemed happy enough to talk. 'It's just… Well, you certain that Julian's not a fag?'

'How should I know?'

''Cause if he's not, he's trying it on with your Sophie. That's all.'

John felt very cold.

He heard Ron say, 'I just thought we should tell you. I mean. That's what mates are for, innit?'

'Yeah.' The conversation seemed to be happening to other people, a long way away.

'Only it's probably nothing,' Dave's voice kept on, 'I mean, you know. We could be wrong.'

'Yeah.'

And he knew. All along, he had known. Even on Hallowe'en, when he had been scared shitless that this weirdo in black was going to call the police, John had known that was exactly what Julian was doing. Trying it on.

He could hear Julian's voice, mocking, *'Sophia did say something of the kind. You need not apologise to me.'*

He must think I'm a bloody idiot.

Because there was flirting and there was… there was that business with the steak, the way that bastard had fed it to her, had licked blood and oil from his fingertips. Remembering it made him want to scream, a roar of primal anger and disgust.

And Sophia... Sophia should have laughed in his face. It was so corny, so controlling, so fucking arrogant. But she hadn't. That was the worst of it. She had smiled, simpered, blushed every time she noticed his eyes were on her, which was to say all the fucking time. She had let this guy take over the whole conversation, whereas she never let John get a word in edgeways, and all the while she had been wearing that shy little grin that made her look so damned beautiful. Oh, and she had laughed, but not at Julian – not like he bloody well deserved but...

Sure, Sophia had a weird sense of humour – but nothing Julian said was funny. Still, Sophia had kept on laughing, with her eyes fixed on Julian, and all the while, his eyes had not moved from her.

No wonder I've had a crap night.

He tried to pull himself together, failed.

Sophia had always told him that there was no one else, that she never noticed other guys. He'd known she was lying – checking out the alternatives was only natural, only human. But he hadn't thought she'd go for any of them; that she had more taste than to fall for a phoney, skinny rich kid in a dinner jacket.

John swallowed hard.

Dave was looking at him. 'You alright, mate?'

'Yeah. I mean, you're probably right. It's nothing.'

'Yeah. I mean, she's your Sophie, isn't she? It's not like she'd... Yeah. We shouldn't have said anything, mate.'

Ron's face was blank, closed. 'Of course. You know her best.'

John made himself laugh. 'Yeah. Totally. There's nothing going on there. Come on, lads. Don't you think that Lucy's more his type?'

And Dave laughed, a nervous, embarrassed laugh, and said, 'Hell, mate, I'd say she's more anybody's type.' Then he had stopped, and added, 'No offence or anything.'

No one except Lucy was in the mood for dessert, although all four of them stayed at the table with her, drinking and talking, until she had finished her battle with the chocolate mousse. After that, Sophia managed to decant them to the other end of the sitting room where Julian sat in an armchair and Steven and Lucy collapsed on the sofa.

By habit, Sophia moved to curl herself into the chair which lurked in the corner of the room, the only comfy seat that faced away from the television. Halfway there, she forced herself to stop. That was the seat Julian was sitting in. She had already known that. For a moment she hovered, before perching on one arm of the sofa. Lucy grinned up at her and resumed her attempt to persuade everyone to come out clubbing. At the edge of her vision she could see Steven's long legs stretching out across the room.

Sophia took a sip of her wine and closed her eyes. Beside her, Lucy's voice rattled on, interspersed with Steven's sarcasm. She could smell the clean, citrus notes of Lucy's conditioner. For a moment she could not tell if it was wine or blackcurrant squash in her glass, or whether they were on holiday from school or university.

She concentrated on the taste in her mouth, on the tannins and berry notes, the sourness of the alcohol. *You're twenty-one,* she reminded herself. *You're in your own flat.* She could not quite make herself believe it. Sophia opened her eyes.

Julian sat across the room from her, folded elegantly into her usual armchair. He gave her his small, ironic smile.

'We're not going clubbing, Lucy,' she said, her voice louder, clearer than she had expected it to be. 'Sorry, love. We'll go out tomorrow or something.'

Lucy shrugged, 'Fair dos. Your loss.'

And Lucy left it there – not in the kind of half-sulk someone else might fall into, but with cheerful resignation at the stupidity of her friends. Within half a minute, she and Steven were bickering once more, this time about the other's trashy taste in films.

She and Julian shared a look of amused disinterest. Earlier in the evening he and Steven had both been on top form, and had seemed to be competing for the title of 'Barchester's most well-read man'. This new argument progressed along more familiar lines and Sophia tuned it out. It was a pity that Julian was at the other side of the room, that she could not easily talk to him across her friends. She gave him the occasional smile and apologetic gesture.

When Steven stood, murmured an excuse and slipped out of the room, she was brought back to reality. She shook her head and went to take a mouthful of wine. There was only a slight red stain at the bottom of her glass. 'Huh, some hostess I am. Would anyone like a top-up?'

Without waiting for a reply, she slipped off the arm of the sofa and grabbed the bottle from the coffee table. When she had almost reached Julian, she said, 'Oh, actually, I've got quite a nice bottle of vodka in the freezer, if anyone wants to try it.'

'Hell yeah,' Lucy said. 'I'm getting a bit bored of wine. Break out the hard stuff.'

'Julian?'

She was nearer his chair than she had thought. There was still a half-inch of wine at the bottom of the glass he balanced between his splayed fingers. 'But of course.'

'I'll just…'

'Nah, you relax,' Lucy said. 'I'm nearer anyway. Shot glasses in the middle cupboard, yeah?'

'Yeah, at least, I hope it's okay vodka,' she told Julian, her voice suddenly low. 'I mean….'

'I trust your judgement.' He stood as he spoke, the movement fluid. His hand reached towards her. 'Allow me to put that down for you.'

Of course. She was still holding the wine bottle. As he took it from her, their fingers brushed. His skin was cold. She felt sudden vertigo. She could hear Lucy in the kitchen, banging about, cursing the ice that made the freezer stick. She did not quite dare move as Julian leaned to one side to set the bottle beside the television. When he straightened again she realised how close he was standing.

She whispered, 'Thanks.'

If she looked up she could just see his mouth, see the smile that was no longer one of cocksure irony.

'You are wearing your earrings.' His voice was quiet, intense.

She raised her head further, craning her neck to see his pale, sharp face, his wide hazel eyes. 'How do they look?' She could see the line of each individual eyelash. Could see the purple that seemed to shimmer beneath the skin in the hollows around his eyes. As her neck ached, she dropped her gaze again. His lips. She closed her eyes.

One of his hands smoothed a curl of her hair back, laid it behind her ear. She sensed his cold fingers, less than an inch from her cheek. The weight of her earring was lifted, dropped. Every movement was slow, careful. He did not brush her face at all. Did not touch her skin.

Her heart bruised her lungs, her diaphragm. Her limbs felt heavy, numb. It was as though every part of her from the waist down had melted into clear, warm water. Only the pressure in her chest told her that she had not been breathing for some little time. She gasped a mouthful of air through lips which had fallen open of their own accord.

'Perfect, my dear.' Julian's voice was little more than a whisper. He leaned down towards her, his face now inches from her own. His lips were clever, dark and thin. Behind them his teeth were little points of white. His hand was still near her face, almost touching the curled weight of her hair.

More than she had ever wanted anything, she wanted to touch him, wanted to kiss his mouth, to tangle her fingers in that long, dark hair. Her hand barely moved towards his, before longing and terror and rapture had arrested her. She did not know if she would ever move again, or whether that mattered very much. Her breath came short and shallow. It was as though vistas were opening before her, like remembering to fly.

But John . . .

She breathed out, dizzy, overcome, and began to move her hand away from his. She took half a step backwards and looked up into his face. There was something like pain there.

And at that moment, Sophia heard John come back into the flat and turned in time to see the anger, the hurt, the disgust on his face. *I didn't do anything!* blasted through her mind in a desperate screech of self-excuse, but she stopped herself from saying it.

Instead, she arranged her face into a smile and went to John, putting her arms around his neck, and saying, 'Hey darling.' Every movement, every word, felt as though it were pushing against the weight of the world.

John's muscles were tensed beneath her hands, his teeth were clenched. She could see that he was about to say something.

But then Lucy barged in from the kitchen with an icy bottle in one hand and a stack of glasses in the other. 'Jesus, girl, you keep your shot glasses bloody well hidden. I had to stand on a chair. I don't know how a midget like you would ever find them.' Then she saw John, and seemed to sense something of the tension in the room. 'Ah, John. I got a glass for you. You want a shot?'

Later, of course, the whole damned thing got ugly. Fortunately, John managed to bite back on whatever it was he felt like saying, and instead informed everyone that Ron and Dave had taken off after having a cigarette. For a couple of awkward, polite hours, the five of them drank vodka and chatted.

Sophia just about managed to keep it together. She was fairly certain that neither Steven nor Lucy noticed anything. *And Julian?*

She did not want to think about what Julian had noticed. Churning away in her mind was a whole mess of things, and it was best not to bring them to the surface. Best to keep them locked down into silly words like 'crush' and 'fancy', and dismiss it. Best not to think about the urge, the need, to press herself into his arms until she could sense no boundary between them.

It was probably a good thing that he had left before Steven and Lucy.

You are with John: that was all she would let herself think as Julian kissed her hand and took his leave. The words circled, miserable and desperate. Yes. She was with John. They had built a life together, made promises. She had told him that she loved him. *You*, she insisted, *are with John*. But, as Julian's lips brushed her hand, she did not think anything at all.

We were happy, once. But it was hard to think of the good things in the prelude to the fight, as John sat, toying with his empty vodka glass, cold waves of anger pouring from him. Still, she had said nothing, had bantered with Steven and Lucy until they left, had even laughed as Lucy announced that, if they were going to be dull, she'd go clubbing without them. Yes, Sophia had smiled as they hugged and kissed goodbye, and arranged to meet the next day.

And after they had left, she closed the door to the street and felt a coldness settle in the pit of her stomach. She took slow steps to the living room.

The problem, a small, treacherous part of her mind opined, *is the timing.*

She halted, one foot on the carpet, one hand pushing open the door. She knew that voice. It had been there all along, a constant, mocking undercurrent to all her resolutions towards John. It was not a pleasant voice.

It was not a voice that lied.

Because before tonight she would have been able to call on wounded innocence. She could have told him that, in the best of faith, yes, she found Julian attractive and that, no, that attraction changed nothing. But now the territory had changed. Smoothing this over, now, was going to require some level of deception.

Deceive? Surely that's not the point at all?

She pushed open the door and continued forwards.

John was on the sofa. His look was not a glare but a stream of anger, resentment and hurt pride. Sophia looked at the chair where Julian had sat, before settling on the arm of the sofa across from him. For a long minute, neither of them spoke.

'You didn't tell me that Steve couldn't make it last Thursday,' came John's first shot.

'Well, I thought you might have figured that out for yourself.'

'What?' From the look on his face he had been expecting something else.

'You knew he'd gone back home with Lucy,' Sophia said, unsure of the point of this line of reasoning. 'You knew.' And then, because she was tired and fed up, her voice was sharper than she might have chosen when she said, 'I'm sorry, but what's this got to do with anything?'

John gave a scornful snort. 'I thought you might have figured that out for yourself.'

The words felt like something hard, striking her chest. She forced herself to try and understand, even though a part of her knew and already felt like flying off the handle, screaming in his face. 'No, John. I haven't.'

'Huh. Seems pretty obvious to me.'

'You're drunk, John. Could we not talk about this in the morning?'

'No, we're going to talk about it now. Right?' She heard him take a breath.

She steeled herself.

'What's going on between you and Julian?'

'Nothing.' And then, because she did not sound particularly convincing, she said it again, 'Nothing. There's nothing going on.'

'Of course. So that's exactly why it just *happened* to slip your mind to mention that Steven wasn't about for your last little tête-à-tête?' John was louder now, sarcastic, getting into his stride.

'John, I *asked* you to come with me.'

'Well, yeah. But I didn't think you'd be going alone if I didn't.'

A cold, a hard fury. 'What? Are you suggesting that would have made some kind of difference?'

'Well – well, yeah. I mean...'

'So, I'm suddenly not allowed to meet up with a friend for dinner without a fucking chaperone?' Her voice rose as she spoke and she forced it back down. John's silence she read as assent. 'Or is it just Julian? I mean, am I allowed to see *Steven*? You've never had a problem with that. Or do you think I've been screwing *him*, too?'

'I know there's nothing going on with Steve.'

'Yeah? You sure about that, John? You don't want to reconsider? Evidently I'm some kind of nymphomaniac, so you clearly don't *trust* me with my male friends...'

'Look, it's not like that. I mean, Sophie, love, I know it's not like that with Steve. I know there's nothing...'

'And why the hell not? Why shouldn't there be...' And then she stopped, feeling the hard slap of shock and hurt. 'It's because he's gay, isn't it?' She heard herself laughing, a sound without mirth, almost hysterical. 'Jesus. It is, isn't it? He's "safe". That's what you meant.'

'Sophie...'

'Well?'

John did not answer.

'Fuck. You really don't trust me at all, do you?'

Silence.

After too long, John said, 'Sophie, come on. It's not like that.'

'No? Then what is it like?'

He reached out a hand to her. She felt herself flinch. 'I love you, Soph. And – and I don't like the way he acts with you. And you're so beautiful and gorgeous and...'

She felt a tight, furious sickness build in the back of her throat. 'Don't you patronise me, John. What? Are you worried he might just *steal* me?' She glared into his eyes until he looked away. She brandished her left hand at him, the engagement ring winking on the fourth finger. 'Do you not think that *this* means anything to me? Well, fuck you, John.' And she considered tearing the ring from her finger, throwing it into his face, but she knew she could not. Not like this. So she just clenched her teeth and stood up, and turned to leave.

John grabbed her arm. 'Please. Shit. Sophie. Love...'

When she turned back to him, the look of pain and affection on his face was almost enough to calm her. Almost. 'Don't call me that. I fucking hate it.'

'What? Would you rather I called you *my dear*?'

Cold rage. 'What do you want me to do, John? Say that I fancy him? Tell you the idea of fucking him turns me on?' She looked into eyes bleary with late nights and alcohol. She felt no mercy. 'Oh yeah, because it does, you know. He's one nice looking man, isn't he? Yeah? You want me to say that I like the fact he has time for me? That he listens to me? That he makes an effort to get on with my friends? No? Is that not what you want to hear, John? Really? Well, how about this? How about the fact that I'm engaged to *you*, huh? How about I'd give this relationship a fucking chance before jumping someone I've only just met?' She turned away to hide the fact that she was crying. 'And for the record, my name is Sophia. I'm going to bed.'

Awake and tearful in the dark, with a mouthful of bile and a hard, desperate anger still clenching her stomach, Sophia thought of the things she had said. It was as though she could still feel the shapes of the words against her teeth. Nothing could call them back now.

Perhaps it was for the best. After all, she had not been lying.

And that – that was the real pain. Because deep, deep underneath her little structures of anger and aggression and self-defence, she was still thinking about that moment when she had stood next to Julian; still thinking of her whole body tense and excited, expecting. That was where the hurt was, and with that, there was guilt. John did not trust her, and Sophia was not sure if she was worthy of his trust.

After John had come to bed and lain away from her, stiff and furious, not speaking, not touching her, she could not help running through the last two months, desperately searching for proof. She had crossed no real lines. But, all along, her behaviour had been tinged with deceit, had been full of little indiscretions, little betrayals. Now, awake in the dark, she could not help but question her motives.

What would she have said if John had not walked in at that point? How would she have answered if John had asked what had happened between her and Julian – *happened,* not what was 'going on'? Perhaps she would have told him everything. Perhaps they would have talked it through, cleared it up. Perhaps she would have promised to be more honest in future.

But John had made her angry and the anger had swallowed up her remorse. She had always taken it for granted that he trusted her. Clearly, she had been wrong.

So she lay awake with her face pressed into her wet pillow, her fists clenched and her hair sticking to her cheeks. And as she lay, she wondered if the tearing in her chest was really her heart breaking, or if it was just something else. Just some other pain. And despite all this, she could not help but feel the throbbing point on her hand where Julian had placed his kiss.

A few, small flakes of snow were beginning to fall, but as they landed they did not settle on the ground. They settled upon the creature's eyelashes, though, and his lips, resting white and crystalline until the relative warmth of the night melted them. The sickness from the little of the human food he had eaten began to abate, but he knew that to silence it he would need blood.

After midwinter, in the confidence of repletion, he had sworn that there would be no more.

His mind blazed with memories of Sophia, her hair falling softly on to a face flushed with wine and warmth and desire. He knew how close he had walked to danger, how she had been so near that he had felt the soft beat of her pulse through the air that separated his fingers and her flesh. How his control had wavered as he had watched her mouth open, and how he had nearly buried his whole soul into that kiss, or else his teeth into her throat.

But instead, he had watched that glowing rise of tenderness kindle in her eyes, had felt the slow movement of her hand towards his own. He had wavered, but he had not...

Still, perhaps it was better she had not touched him.

Even that thought made him laugh, made him shake his head in the cold air with his mouth wide open, revealing a white curve of teeth that could never be mistaken for human. Why should he not laugh? His whole body sang with it, every nerve scintillating pleasure at the memory, the anticipation. For tonight he felt the true reality of love and had seen that love mirrored in the eyes of the person he adored.

The night air tasted divine, the cold was exquisite, every shift and caress of fabric against his skin tantalising. Memories: her easy, sexual grace, her dark, smoky hair. Eyes, grey eyes which bound him more tightly than any mesmerism in his power. The bead of blood, welling up to kiss the tip of his tongue. That thrilling, dreadful hunger. The creature did not need to hunt tonight. He *wanted* to do so.

What was another broken vow?

So he hummed to himself, the melody of one of Sophia's light, modern records. For the most part, the creature had allowed modern popular music to pass him by, and he had always told himself that this was because it was a break from tradition, that it was unlike anything he had known before. But tonight he had known himself for a liar. Such music had always been there, and with it the preoccupation with easily gratified sexual desire – with love, with trifling pleasures and pains. His preference for the slow, the loud, the grandiose, was not so much a symptom of his age, but his self-indulgence.

Self-indulgence. He rode the wave of his closeness to Sophia and it seemed a fine joke. His endless self-reproaches no more authentic, no less a pose than his manner, his dress. Awakening from his madness, remorse had seemed the proper thing to feel, so he had felt it. And he had enjoyed the feeling.

As he would enjoy the hunt tonight.

The creature grinned once again, careless of his fangs. *Three of the clock on a Saturday night and all is well, and all the bright young things spill out of their clubs and stumble home. Even in this sleepless century.* It was a fine time to hunt, the time when he would prowl the city for his supplies of bottled blood. Still, in recent weeks, the solitary wanderers had become rare. Walkers huddled in inebriated twos and threes, not looking into the eyes of those that they passed. Taxis were more common than they had been.

These were the signs of a city that had grown afraid of the night. In the usual course of things, the creature would have taken these as signs that it was time to move on once more. But he would not leave.

After all, there would always be a few who would walk alone. Most were common enough, such as those who were so oblivious that they did not see the risk, the very drunk or the proud. But as he settled on his prey, as he began to follow the trail of solitary footsteps and of scent, he began to wonder if, tonight, he had been dealt a rarer prize.

Most who fell to him in fearful times were guided by ignorance, by foolishness. Few were truly brave – so very few that the creature had long believed they were growing scarcer as the years passed. Tonight, though, he was to be blessed. Tonight his prey was unafraid of the night and the terrors it might hold.

A young woman. He heard her humming, her voice level and bold. She stumbled only a little, and that more from tiredness than inebriation. Her scent was the muddled fragrance of the dance floor, smoke, spilled beer, clean sweat and body sprays – confused, layered, alive. He thought of her, a moment of light in this winter time, this climate of fear.

A hesitation. Such bright, brilliant lives should not fall prey to him. For she would fight, this girl, and it seemed obscene that her final struggle should prove so futile. If she must be killed, surely it were better that her murderer was a being she had some hope of bettering.

Yet tonight he had stood beside Sophia, he had almost touched her cheek. Did that not deserve some tribute? Did that not require some victim of great worth? What was sweeter, more vital than a struggle born of defiance, of the need to live?

The creature smiled softly, his teeth hard and anxious against his gums. His stance changed.

Following her, he took streets and alleys, courtyards and rooftops. He did not attempt to frighten her, did not indulge in tricks of foot-steps and shadowy pursuers. He would not sully this, would not give her such disrespect. All that delayed him was opportunity – the place must be safe, must be unobserved. But the creature knew the city well. It did not take him long.

His heart stirred from its sluggish pace in anticipation of the blood. Saliva was sweet in his mouth. He thought of Sophia, how lovely she had looked.

He stepped out in front of his prey.

The woman jumped back, startled but not afraid. Then she laughed and the familiarity of the sound was terrible.

'Julian? Shit! You scared the life out of me.' But her voice shook only with shocked laughter. Her long, blonde hair was a straggled cloud, her eyes were alight.

He should turn back. A voice in his mind screamed that he should turn back.

The creature shook his head. She was drunk, though less drunk than he would have expected her to be, less drunk than she had been when he had taken his leave of Sophia. She seemed oblivious to her danger.

'It is, it *is* Julian, right?' She took half a step towards him, eyes peer-ing desperately to try and make out the details of his face.

Of course, the creature thought, *it is dark. She cannot see.*

She hesitated. The creature raised his hand, took one, slow pace towards her, as if he had not heard her, did not know her at all.

The animal in her snapped alert. She did not turn, but glanced over her shoulder and then began to back away, her eyes fixed upon him. In a movement so fast she could not have followed it, the creature was beside her, catching her wrist in a grip as hard as winter death.

Her eyes burned with pain, with fierce anger, with a desperate need to live. She struggled, but the creature was stronger than she, much stronger. He watched the movement in her throat as she swallowed the reaction of panic and shock.

'Shit,' Lucy said, her voice quiet, then again, louder, as if remembering herself, 'Shit! Help! Fire! Fire!'

Even in this quiet part of the city, even in the dead of night, her voice was loud enough to rouse someone who might hear her, and all the while she fought, twisting her arm to pull it away, scrabbling with her feet against his shins, his boots, clawing him, jabbing his eyes with her nails and striking him with the heel of her free hand, lashing at his throat, his face, his solar plexus. The creature turned to spare his face her worst assaults, fended off her teeth, her arm. But many of her blows connected, and they hammered into his heightened nerves.

At last, the creature faced the fight he desired. A mortal man might have relented, found his grip broken, but he was not a mortal man, and the rents she made in his skin closed almost immediately. He wished only that she would be still.

To that end, he twisted her arm fast, too fast, snapping the bone, dragging her towards him. At the pain of it, her face paled, her consciousness fled. He caught her as she fell and touched her beautiful face, her cheeks smooth, the bruises already flowering. Perhaps it would have been kinder to place her in a trance, to kill her with her bewitched complicity, but that would have dishonoured her desire, her right, to resist him. Would have dishonoured her bravery, her blood.

He kissed her cheek, a brush of his lips.

He would not ask her forgiveness, would not do her that disservice. But he would not turn bestial, would not wreck her poor body. In death, at least, she would have dignity. In his arms, Lucy lay, cradled, inert. The lines of her mouth were still pressed hard together, troubled. There were scraps of his skin beneath her nails. He shook his head and misery burned beneath his desperate craving for blood.

And he did not even attempt to tell himself that this was no more a betrayal of Sophia than all the other deaths, not even as he pressed her into his hard embrace and tore her flesh with long, sharp teeth.

17. I Had No Human Fears

'There are darknesses in life, and there are lights. You are one of the lights. You will have a happy life and a good life'
– Bram Stoker, *Dracula*

John was on the sofa when his mobile rang.

He had woken up with a bastard hangover. Sophia had gone out before he was awake and wherever she was, she had left no note and had turned her phone off. Not seeing the point of getting dressed, he had crashed on the sofa with aching eyes while the chirpy images of Saturday lunchtime TV jumbled in front of him.

By the time the phone rang, he did not feel much better. Still, he managed to use his telephone voice: 'John Halsall speaking.'

The line was silent.

'Hello?'

There was a pause, then a man's voice he did not recognise said, 'John. Is Sophia about?'

'Uh, no. Who's calling?'

'It's me, John.' This time, he thought it did sound a bit familiar.

He wondered if it was one of his work mates trying to wind him up.

'I mean – I mean, it's Steven.'

That's not right. John took the phone away from his ear and looked at it. The number was a local landline, not one he knew. The voice wasn't annoying enough for Steven's, and there was none of that camp superiority to it.

'You still there?' The voice came out from the phone, catching in the speaker's throat, making him think of splintered wood, the way it snags.

'Yeah.' He put the phone back to his ear. 'Yeah.'

'John, I need to know. Is Sophia about?'

'No. Sorry.'

'Right. Okay.' The man on the other end did not sound okay. John heard him take a breath. 'It's Lucy. She... I had to...' John heard a quiet sob, heard it being swallowed. When the voice started again it was high and tight, and John knew that whoever-it-was was crying. 'They found her body this morning. In the city centre. I... I need to let Sophia know.'

John did not breathe. Did not say anything. Then he exhaled, feeling his body slump with the shock of it. 'If this is some kind of sick... Shit. Oh, shit. Steve. Are you...?'

'I'm fine.' The person laughed, and it was hysterical and shaky, but it was Steven's laugh. 'Yeah. I'm totally fine, John. Can you just... Can you let Sophia know, yeah? Get her to... maybe call me?'

'Sure. What... what happened? Is there anything I can...'

'Please.' There was another pause, and when the voice spoke again it sounded like Steven, level and controlled. Bleak, hopeless. 'Please don't, John. I – look, I need to go. Okay?'

'Okay.'

Then there was a click and the line went dead.

The police left. Steven sat down on the sofa and felt nothing. He had done what was necessary. Done his duty by the law and by the world. Now, there was nothing at all.

After he had let them in, and they had told him about how she had been found and how it looked like murder, one of them had asked, 'Do you mind if we ask you a few questions, Steven?'

Numb, he had answered, 'No. No, not at all.'

So they had stood in the kitchen as they went through it with him. He had known her since childhood. They had lived together for six years. Or nearly six years. No, they were not romantically involved. One of the detectives – the man – had nodded a lot. Had made notes. Both of them had kept saying that they understood it was hard for him.

It had not been hard. His replies had been automatic. Yes, he told them, he had seen her last night. When? At around midnight. Where? At a mutual friend's. She had gone out clubbing after they had left.

'On her own?'

'Yes, I think so.'

'Was that her usual behaviour?'

'Sometimes,' he had said. Then he had looked around, asked if he might sit down. One of them had said that of course he could, but he had forgotten to do so.

The male detective had said that anything he could tell them might help; that it could help them bring her killer to justice. Steven had nodded blindly until he had realised they expected some kind of reply.

'Okay,' he had said. And then, in case that wasn't enough, 'What do you need to know?'

No, she had not been acting strangely. She had not seemed anxious, or afraid. Not mentioned any new friends, new boyfriends. Had she travelled anywhere? Yes, they had gone back to her parents' house. Together. For Christmas.

Again, no, they were not romantically involved. And, no, he could think of nobody who might want to hurt her.

They had asked if he had contact details for her next of kin.

'That's not local, is it?' the woman had asked.

'No.'

So they had called the local force, who would go round and tell Lucy's parents – and he had asked if they minded him not listening to the call. If he could stay in the kitchen. Which he had done, slumped against the wall, trying to block the quiet babble of their voices.

It seemed as though it took an eternity.

When they returned, they said that – with the parents' consent – it would help if he could identify the body. Had told him that they understood if he would rather not, but that the sooner it was done, the sooner they could go about the real work, finding out who had killed her.

Steven had nodded without really knowing why.

They had waited. In the end, there was a phone call and then they left.

In the morgue, his boots had squeaked on the lino floors and static had jolted him every time he touched his hand to metal. Lucy was laid upon her back, her eyes glassy, her right arm broken. The sheet was pulled high, almost to her chin, but could not quite hide the way her throat was one raw, hollow wound.

He had tried not to be sick.

When they had asked, he had said, 'Yes, that's her,' but he had not believed it. Had known that the corpse, with its broken bones and mottled bruises, could not really be Lucy, could only be a badly painted dummy, the prop from a cheap horror movie. And that made him an actor, with his downcast eyes and dead voice giving an unconvincing portrayal of shocked disbelief. Or perhaps it was Lucy, with eye makeup smeared over her cheeks in some poor taste snuff-movie imitation. She had always had a gruesome sense of humour.

As if it would mean something, a detective had pointed out the blood caked underneath her nails. 'She took a chunk out of him, alright. We'll be able to test it for DNA. She'll have left marks on him, too.'

Steven had continued to stare at the hole in Lucy's throat.

The police had lead him away. Once back inside the flat, he had asked if he could call Sophia – a mutual friend – if he could call her and let her...

He had taken a couple of long, deep breaths. 'We were meant to be meeting her this afternoon.'

The woman had given him a look of conventional sympathy. 'Of course. You should probably let her know we'll need to speak to her, too. And anyone else who saw her last night.'

Steven had nodded.

'Look, Steven, at a first glance – and obviously, we can't be certain about anything this early – but this looks as though it's one of a series of killings. Of course, we will follow all the leads whether it is or not, but I should warn you, there is going to be a lot of publicity. This will be in the press. Perhaps you and your friend – Sophia? – perhaps you both need to prepare for that.'

And she had given him a look that he did not understand, but he had nodded all the same. 'Do you need to call anyone else?' they had asked. 'Do you want us to arrange someone to stay with you?' He had shaken his head. They had left soon after that.

When he tried to phone Sophia, her mobile was switched off. He left it a long time before calling John. Then he put down the phone and stood there for five minutes or more, not knowing what to do.

He felt no emotion, none at all. His face felt as if it would never smile again.

After a while, he called Patroclus to let them know he would not be in for a few days. When Ray asked him what was wrong he said, 'A bereavement.' Then, without thinking: 'A bereavement in the family.'

He was not sure what happened after that. The next thing he knew, he was sitting on the sofa and his mind was empty. His consciousness ran around itself like a fingernail circling the inside of a china vase, grating and void. Hollow. He held his head in his hands. He remembered opening the door to see two police officers – a man and a woman – and the professional condolence written across their faces. He had known then that something was wrong, that they always sent a PC and a WPC with bad news. Even then, there had been a roaring in his ears. Even then, he had steeled himself for the worst.

And this was far worse than that.

He felt nothing.

He should have known. He should have noticed that her door was closed, should have guessed she was not just shattered, or hung over, or shacked up with one of her random guys. Steven clenched his fists. He should have known. It did not matter that he did not believe in psychic transference, or telepathic sympathy. This was Lucy. He should have known.

But instead, he had put on the radio and got up, made a cup of tea and had some breakfast. Instead, he had buried his nose in a book and ignored the background babble of *The Archers*. He had not even twigged when he heard the knock at the door, even though it was New Year's Eve, and a Sunday, and they were expecting no visitors. He had even made her a cup of tea. It was still on the kitchen counter, where he had left it in case she woke up before it was stone cold.

Dull pain began to spread in his chest. *That was feeling,* he thought. *Surely that's a good thing.*

Later, the phone rang. It was Lucy's parents. They said they wanted to thank him, check up on him, make sure he was coping okay. They asked if Sophia was with him. He told them he had not been able to contact her.

He started crying. He was not sure if he would ever stop. They talked, even though there was nothing to talk about. Mostly, it was Lucy's mum, her voice tight, sometimes cracking to a harsh sob. Then, Steven would hear the scrape of a tissue against the mouthpiece of the phone. Talking did not help, was not comfortable, but he did not want to put down the phone, did not want to lose this one moment of contact in the isolation of his grief. He asked if they wanted him to come back home, if he could be of any help.

'We need to come to Barchester anyway. We have to collect the... oh God. For the... the funeral.' There was the sound of sobbing. 'I'm so sorry, Stevie.'

And Steven held the phone hard against his ear, his whole body tense and sick at the gulf within him, because Lucy's mum was the only person who ever called him Stevie, and she had not called him that in years.

After he hung up he stood by the phone, still crying, convulsive, involuntary, silent. Later, he stopped and just stood, shaking and helpless. The tears had not helped. He was no less alone. And still, he could not make himself think her name, could not believe that she was not just around the corner, or in her room, or out with Sophia.

When the sky had drawn towards darkness and he was still alone, some basic routine asserted itself and drove him to the kitchen, to deal with the dishes he had left in the sink that morning. He picked up a mug and slopped the cold tea down the drain. It was then that he realised. This was Lucy's mug.

He nearly dropped it. Lucy's mug. Sentimental and childish, he had given it to her when they were both thirteen years old. It was hers, as much a part of his image of her as her blonde hair, her tree-climbing, the way she laughed at action films. He had watched her pack it for university, seen her keep it safe through the thieving chaos of living in halls, witnessed the preferential treatment she gave it, the way she never let it get chipped or broken, nor allowed it to grow undignified mould on a forgotten corner of her desk. He remembered a thousand cups of tea or coffee or hot chocolate, or, occasionally, wine.

His hand tightened on it, his knuckles turning pale. Lucy's mug. Now it was gone.

No – the correction was sober, hopeless – *now she is gone.*

Steven sat down on the kitchen floor and cried for a very long time.

When Sophia had left that morning, she had not meant to return. She had meant to pull every feeling, every moment, every thought, out of the mess in her head and examine them. She had told herself that, by the end of the day, she would know. That it would be over between herself and John.

When she turned into her street, it was dark. Her gloveless hands were raw and white. Her fingers fumbled with her key and, by the time she had it in the lock, John had opened the door. *Great*, she thought as she prepared herself for the fight, *I suppose this serves me right.*

Then she saw that the anger she had expected on his face was not there, that there was a frantic, transparent concern. And relief. She noticed that his fingernails were chewed bloody and that his hair was not brushed and was free from wax. For a few seconds, she thought she saw the man she had believed she loved.

'Sophia,' he said, 'love.' For a moment, he looked as though he were going to hug her, then he took a step back. 'I think... I think you should maybe come through to the sitting room.'

She followed him. She took off her scarf.

'Have you—' Again, he paused. 'Has Steven managed to get in touch?'

Some of the implications of those words began to link together in her mind. She took off her coat. 'What? John, what's happened?'

'Shit.' He looked as though he was about to cry. 'I think... Look, why don't you sit down?'

She felt the muscles in her legs tighten, her diaphragm begin to ache. There was a slow pulse of blood in her ears. The coat dropped from her fingers. 'What is it?'

He came over to her, took her hands. The warmth of his skin burned and he gripped so hard, it seemed he were squeezing the very bones of her. 'I don't want to be the one to...' Another pause. 'This morning, they... they found Lucy's body.'

Sophia shook her head. Her tongue felt thick, dry in her mouth.

'I really think you should sit down, love.'

'And?'

He stared at her, his eyes fearful, hollow.

'No,' she said, and, 'what else?' Then, when he did not answer she asked again, 'What else? What happened? What else do they know?' It surprised her that she was still standing, that her voice was still at her command because it was shattered by gasps, and was high, and the words made no sense to her.

John reached a hand to her arm. 'That's all Steven said.'

Her throat hurt; her breath started to make a low, painful sound.

'I really think you should sit down, love.'

'Steven called you?'

John nodded.

'Why didn't he call me?'

John's face seemed to widen, flatten. 'He... he tried, love.' He looked around, looked at everything in the room except her. 'Your phone was switched off.'

'Oh.' She noticed she was shaking. 'Yes. That makes sense. Of course. And they went to Steven because of the flat. That... That... Oh Christ.'

Her knees went from under her.

The creature slept, Lucy's blood heavy in his stomach.

And, dreaming, he woke *not as he would awaken now, but slower, confused. Mortal. Awaking as a mortal. There was a strange, foul taste in his mouth: beer and sleep and something he could not place. His pulse felt quick, frantic, his head aching in time to every wild heartbeat. The light was dazzling. Winter sun burned into his eyes, he closed them...*

And, dreaming, the creature fought the impulse that would make him open them again. Then he remembered Lucy's face, bruised and still in death.

...The ground he lay upon was wet: mud and urine. He opened his eyes again. An alleyway. His clothes sodden with the filth of it. There was a pain in his shoulder.

He sat.

Roaring in his ears. The world spinning, fading. His vision failed. Slow, how slowly sense returned. He reached his hand to the burning ache upon his neck and his fingers came away smeared with blood. How had…?

The taste, the pain, the weakness. Had he forgotten? Forgotten?

The night before came back, confused: the tavern, the midwife and Eleanor… Eleanor. To his feet. The world swimming, the faintness. He almost stumbled, almost fell.

And when his vision returned, he no longer felt weak. See, he reasoned, how thought of his lady gave him strength. How his love boiled with immense vitality in his stomach, his brain. *Running was no issue to him, not today.*

Inside the city walls, somehow. Troubled recollection coming in flashes. How he had got past the gate? His head ached from the beer. All about, the huddled houses were coming awake, the slow trade of commerce going and coming from the city gates, and all stopped to stare at the mad young man, the young man streaked with blood and mud and other filth, who pelted headlong through crowded alleyways. Their gawking glanced from him; he did not need to breathe. A strength, a tirelessness in his limbs belied the swimming nausea in his head. He would return home, and Eleanor would have borne him a son…

Wanting to flinch, to waken, the creature stirred. If only he had not run. It would have been easier to bear had he not run… *and he would hear the report and, when the midwife said he might, he would dandle the baby on his knee and give Eleanor the good news. Would tell her that they were to have eternal life, love without death… And as he drew near he recalled that, of course, the manor would be a bustle of women. Recalled that he would have been missed; that his steward, his neighbours would have been seeking him.* But that, *he thought as he reached the door,* that, and only that, would be the reason for the going and coming, for the grave look upon his steward's face. *And as he stopped, he trembled, not from exhaustion…*

Half-waking, he moaned, tried to pull away from this dream. *Lucy* rang in his mind, sullen and heavy as a bell, driving him back into the vision.

His steward would not meet his eye.

His pulse was a thunder, his ears echoing like songs. He knew, already he knew.

'You have been blessed with a son.'

Nothing. It meant nothing, that joyful news, that news for which he had hoped for so many months. He felt his vision blur.

'And my good wife?' But he did not wait for the reply.

Breathe. He could not breathe.

Into the house. He forced a way into the house, staggering. Through the great hall, upstairs to the solar, every step a great effort, up to where she was, where she would be. His steward ran after him, trying to catch his arm and he knew that he should stop, should ask to see his son, should tell the midwife it was not her fault, should... So many things that he should do.

She was on the bed, the canopy open over her.

Woman's business, was it? No place for a man.

And now it was those same women who moved around her, readying her for burial.

'Out.' His voice was a yell, strange to his own ringing ears. He gasped for air. The shock was clear on their faces, this breach of hospitality, this wildness, grief beyond all measure. 'Out!'

He slammed the door behind them. Already shaking, he made his way to the bed...

Not this. The creature pulled away, twisted, stirred. Not this...

Eleanor lay upon the bed, face haggard, skin cold. Her eyes were open, glassy, without life. The women had scarcely begun their work upon the... upon the...

There was blood, stale blood, soaking into the nether-sheet and the blanket. He could smell it, overpowering. It sickened him. Yes, sickness, he felt sickness and something, something else...

Her skin was soft still, but cold. So cold.

'Eleanor.' His voice, his own voice, hardly heard. The chill of her burned his fingers, ran through him spreading, bone deep, terrible...

Would he die too? Cold. Cold in needles and splinters. Such cold. He began to shake, he started to sob, to bury his face in the dark hair spooling out over pale sheets. Rosemary and honey. Blood... blood.

The scream started silent in his chest and swelled until it broke from his mouth. The solar, the canopy upon the bed... A lick of pain strangled his throat. Grief... He believed it to be grief...

Time, shattered.

Weeping, weeping until he was dry as straw in the sun. Always, more tears. Always more heat, more burning cold, lurching from one to the next. A pain tunnelled behind his eyes, and there was only pain, grief, sweat on his skin. He watched Eleanor die. Watched the stranger's smiling face. Felt the sharp agony of a kiss. Words pounding a priest's voice, familiar but senseless, alien, insincere, and again, later, in Latin, the rite of exorcism...

He forgot that he had locked the door, barricaded himself, hauling everything in the room, all the hangings, all the furniture, everything – everything except the bed. He hauled it all and he barred the door, not asking how he found the strength.

Gums nothing but ache, limbs nothing but fire and a desperate rawness in his throat. Howling, the madman howled his grief, tore rents in his own skin, screamed and bit at his tongue, punched at the walls and the floor.

Exhausted, world spinning, nauseous, he clutched her hand. Images burst out at him, moments of lucidity... the bluish pallor of her face. The canopy torn down, torn apart, wasted. The grey of the morning sky beyond the window. Weakness at the light.

He staggered, seemed to watch himself stagger. Tightness in his chest, hard floor yielding to his weight. A tiredness beyond any tiredness.

Heart straining, fast, faster than ever, ringing in his mind. Desperate, harder, painful. Throat dry... so dry... World pulsing frantic, and then slower, and then slower, and then not at all.

Warm blackness. Eleanor. Eleanor. Blackness.

And his eyes opened...

... His eyes opened and expected to see the chamber of the solar, to make gradual sense of the rancid, irresistible smell around him. To wonder why his clothes were streaked with his own filth, why his thirst was immense and what, quite what, that delectable, wet rushing pounding sound might be. For a moment, he expected to feel his gums sore and his teeth wobbling. For a moment, the creature prepared to live again that run of sordid centuries.

Then he thought, *It would be better to die. It would be better to lie and wait for the sunlight and the hunger to finish this.*

But instead all he knew was coolness, softness and satiety. He remembered where he lay, on that same bed in the cellar's cool damp.

And when he looked down, he saw that his hands that were streaked with blood.

18. What Hope?

Blessed are those who hunger and thirst for righteousness, for they will be filled. Blessed are the merciful, for they will be shown mercy. Blessed are the pure in heart, for they will see God.
– Matthew 5:6-8

Two weeks. For two weeks Sophia just wanted the funeral to happen, for it to be over. But first there was the inquest, and that was held up by the bank holiday, and what would normally have taken days took a fortnight.

It would have been no better without the delay. When Lucy's parents had travelled up to collect the body, Steven had gone home with them. They had offered her a lift as well, but she had refused and told them she would rather be with John for a little while.

The air of the flat, the streets of Barchester, were thick with Lucy's ghost, but home would have been worse. It was not that she wanted to be with John, she just wanted to avoid Steven. When Steven was not there, she could pretend that Lucy was with him, or studying, or rehearsing, or playing hockey.

When they were alone together, there was an absence between them, and she could not fill it with her loss, with her bewilderment, her disbelief, because that was Steven's right. Because Steven had been at the morgue, had identified Lucy's corpse and he had not even been able to call her because she had wanted to be alone.

Now he wandered through life with blind eyes and slack lips. Perhaps he blamed her. If he did, it was his right.

It was in the all newspapers, on the television, in the news. Journalists loitered outside Steven's flat. There was a photograph he had taken of Lucy some months ago, which, in those two weeks, she saw so often it seemed public property – the face of a stranger, a celebrity, a Jane Doe. She stayed away from the press. In the papers all the comments of loss, of sorrow, were from people Sophia had hardly known.

Still, she read every article she could find; heard that the police were optimistic about the DNA, that the results were inconclusive, that they were following every possible lead, confident of making an arrest within days. She thought about what Steven had described to her in his expressionless voice: the broken arm, the torn-out throat, the absence of blood. She tried to understand what Steven would have felt, staring at Lucy's broken body.

There were no more murders. The coverage drifted away.

There was nothing she wanted to do, nothing she wanted to talk about.

And John was wonderful. He didn't go to the pub, didn't work late; he called her during his lunch break, made her cups of tea. He watched his sports quietly, and hardly at all. Sophia found that she could not care. There was no energy left for anger, no time for quarrels, no resources to deal with anything but the emptiness in her chest that seemed to grow bigger and more numbing with every passing day. When he was at work, she wandered from room to room of the flat, wondering what it was that she was thinking.

Term started. The university prided itself on pastoral care and she had meetings with her head of school and the chaplaincy, who told her to take her time, not to come rushing back, to wait until she was ready.

She ignored them.

Sensitively worded emails were sent, letting everyone know that the flag would be flown at half mast, and why. Others announced a memorial service to be held after the funeral, for those who could not attend that event. The hockey squad and the drama society wore black armbands. Everyone gave her sad-eyed looks. 'Are you...? You're Lucy's friend, aren't you? I was so sorry to hear...'

She did not want to leave flowers at the spot where the body was found, did not want to hear Lucy's conquests and acquaintances tell everyone what a great person she had been. She did not want to mourn collectively, as part of a multitude, even as part of a pair. She wanted to be alone.

But alone was worse.

It seemed disrespectful to read, to study, to watch TV. Disrespectful to cook, to chat. Disrespectful to fuck John just so that she felt a few moments of human warmth, so that she knew that it was not her own body that had died. She started skipping uni, spending whole days in bed. It was not like her. She knew that it was not like her.

She cried a lot. She called her mum. She tried to read.

It didn't stop Lucy being dead.

It didn't stop Lucy becoming a statistic, the last in a slew of unsolved killings. Sophia read, again and again, the coroner's report. Even though it pushed the raw, painful lump deeper into her throat, she forced herself to picture it: the sheer animal struggle, the sweat, the fear. Lucy clawing, punching, kicking – anything. And the attacker, that blind hatred, that impossible strength. The snap of bone. Blood loss, severe trauma.

Sickened, that was how it made her feel. Still, she focused upon it. Anything to keep Lucy as a separate entity, apart from the mass of victims. Anything to keep her friend to herself, to keep the pain fresh in her mind.

She knew John hated her doing this, and would catch the look of confusion, concern, disgust upon his face. She could not tell him why she needed to use those cold, those clinical words. Could not tell him even a fraction of what it was she felt, or thought. His own shock was too obtrusive, his own grief too intense.

Her dreams were twisted, claustrophobic nightmares from which she woke, sweating and forgetful and on the verge of screaming. When John asked her what was wrong, she could never remember what it was that had frightened her so badly. In the day, she sometimes walked around the city, simply for something to do, but the quaint, narrow streets she had loved now seemed hostile, precarious, unsafe. Life had become inexplicable, frail, the world so much more danger-ous and cold.

Back in their home town, Steven barely left his room in Lucy's par-ents' house.

He tried to read, but his old favourites had lost their comfort, their glamour shattered when he saw that, behind all the stage props, the fog and the castles, what they were really about was death.

Even *Dracula* failed him. The novel was little more than a barrage of death. Besides, as soon as Mina took up the narrative, Lucy's name appeared on every third page. He could not bear to see it there; could not bear the knowledge that, even in fiction, Lucy would die.

He had put the book down, and not picked it up again.

He took down, too, the film posters that still papered his room, because all that he could see, among the bloodstained faces, was Lucy, the bruises upon her, the cold light of the morgue.

Lucy's parents asked him to give the eulogy at the funeral. It helped, a little, having something to write. Hour after hour, day after day, he struggled with it. Late at night, he turned his tongue over possible patterns of words, trying to catch the truth, the essence of what was lost. He fought himself, concentrating on Lucy young and exuberant; Lucy, drunk and dancing; Lucy, flushed from a hockey fixture, or smeared in pancake and greasepaint; trying to summarise, to explain. Trying to ward off that final image: Lucy broken, cold.

Almost, he succeeded.

On the day, he stood at a podium in front of a room packed full of Lucy's family and acquaintances, and looked at his notes, then at the front row, where Sophia sat between Lucy's parents and John. He held his jaw stiff so that his voice did not tremble. 'Lucy always said that she never wanted "Amazing Grace" sung at her funeral, and that if we so much as tried it, she'd find a way to come back and kill us all.'

He watched as Sophia laughed, remembering that day, and saw the laugh turn into a sob. His own throat prickled hot, tight. He managed to say, 'I'm sure I'm not alone when I say I'm tempted to try it. Just to see her again.'

After that it was almost easy. Easy to tell people why Lucy had been special, why she deserved to be loved, and mourned, and missed. As he spoke, his voice grew louder, too loud for a funeral, and what had been a eulogy became a shout of defiance against the person who had killed her and against the world as a whole. He told them about her interests, her popularity, her talents, her compassion, and all the while, circling in his head was the thought, *You are not going to forget. Not one of you. Not her. No one here is going to forget her.*

When he had finished, Steven clenched his teeth and walked back to his seat. His eyes burning, his cheeks hot, he believed what he felt was fury, was defiance in the face of death.

As he sat, Lucy's dad gripped his shoulder, a comfort, brief and restrained. He realised that, all the time he had been speaking, he had wept.

Then came the wake. He spent most of it standing in a corner, watching Sophia talk quietly with Lucy's parents, watching John hover near them. The room heaved with students and well-wishers. Sometimes, people came up to him. His responses were automatic, unconscious. Afterwards, he did not remember them.

Towards the end, though, he was approached by a girl he recognised from Lucy's drama group, a pleasant-faced girl he had never disliked. She told him that he had given a beautiful eulogy and that, up in heaven, watching over them, Lucy would have been proud.

He had felt anger, cold and unfamiliar. 'Lucy was an atheist,' he said. Then he turned and walked away. But there was nowhere that he wanted to go.

That evening he thought about Barchester, about the publicity of the murder, the endless, mindless platitudes. He thought about his course, about his dissertation – Gothic literature…

From his armchair he could see the emptiness of his bed and he remembered the Christmas holidays, reading *Dracula*…

He closed his eyes. The chair supporting him, the smell of the room, the impression of space; they were all the same. At once, she seemed so close he believed that, if he looked, he would see her lying on his bed, her hair a cloud of blonde around her beautiful face. He could almost feel the pressure of her head resting against his knee. Almost hear her voice, compassionate, amused.

Then, bruises, her arm broken, her throat torn right down to the hollow, white sinew.

His eyes opened to an empty room.

It was impossible to pick up the pieces of a life where talking to one of her best friends was awkward and the other was not there at all.

John clung to her, but only emotionally. He seemed to think that she did not want physical intimacy. He did not try to talk her into sex, or kiss her on the mouth, did not touch her breasts or press against her when he was feeling horny.

Still, he clung. And he was always touching her – her arm, her hair – always giving her mild, comforting, sexless hugs. When he came home from work he would rush to her, would grasp her in his arms and then… nothing. Once, long before Lucy had died, such desperate embraces would inevitably have led to a quickie on the sitting-room floor. Now it seemed that all he needed from her was to know that she was still there, still alive.

She did not often feel alive. His touch made her feel like the shell of a woman, soft flesh with nothing real underneath. But she could not tell him to go away because then there would be nobody in bed beside her when she woke. There would be nobody to expect in the evening. Nobody.

So, when John held her and apologised again and again, telling her that he had done what he could, that he had tried to get out of it, really, but that it was unavoidable and he *had* to do some overtime tomorrow night, Sophia stood, frozen. Over and again, he said that he did not want to leave her alone, not after… and then his voice trailed away, and he traced his clammy fingers across her cheek in a tender, pitying arc.

Flinching, she gave him her bravest smile, told him that she was sure she would be fine, that she could manage for a few extra hours. She even did her best to laugh, said that she was not some kind of invalid, that it would be okay; she would see him when he got home. John pulled her towards him, gripped her tightly and breathed hot and damp on her neck. He stroked her hair, and he did not tell her that she was brave, or wonderful or kind, but she knew that it was what he was thinking.

That night, though, the dreams were awful. Frenetic fever dreams, all confused running; nameless fears, all gasped breath and nervousness. Flashes when Lucy was there, and everything was okay, and then, always, that sickening lurch where she realised she was dreaming and that she could not wake. Then it would start again.

Nightmares. She had been having them for months, scattering through her insomnia, fearful, disturbing. Since Lucy had died, she had been having them every night. Sometimes, now, it seemed to her that sleep was the enemy and she would lie awake shaking and terrified, trying not to let her eyes close.

When John's alarm woke her, she made no attempt to ignore it. Instead, she got up with him, drank a cup of tea while he ate his breakfast, kissed him goodbye when he left for work. They did not speak, not really. Then he was gone, and there was only the vast emptiness of the day.

By nine o'clock, the sheer weight of the time she would spend alone felt as though it would crush her.

Still Sophia did not surrender. She pulled herself together, forced herself be sensible, grownup about it. She ate breakfast. After that, she listened to the radio until it sickened her, then she wandered into town. That only made it worse. She thought she might try to go to university and find someone to talk to. Then she thought of the look of sympathy on the face of anyone who knew her.

At home, alone, Sophia slumped into her armchair and thought of the mobile lying at the bottom of her bag. Her mother would be at work. She almost called Steven.

She stood, then sat, then stood again and walked across the room to the sofa.

By four o'clock, her eyes could not settle upon her books, the radio had become background drivel and all that was on television were children's shows, their unfamiliarity, their coloured gaiety, making her recoil. It would be worse if they were shows she knew, ones she remembered watching, and mocking, with Lucy, with Steven.

She turned off the television and continued to stare at the black screen. It occurred to her that were she to spend any more time alone, she would begin to lose her mind. *John*: her mind called the word, a plea for company. But it was a hollow, desperate plea.

She thought again of her phone. But it had never been Steven she called when she was troubled, nor Steven in whom she confided her worries or her cares. *Lucy*. Sophia almost laughed. *Do I not know anyone else?*

There were the girls she knew from her lab, but their talk would be about soaps she did not watch or music she did not like. And they would pity her. Panic began to rise in her chest, pressing against her lungs, making her breath come broken, short.

When she had first heard the news, she had cried. She had sobbed and ground her teeth, slapped her fists against her chest, her arms. Had sunk to the floor, catatonic, nauseated. But that had passed, and now that she was no longer flying apart, now that she was in control once more, she had believed the worst of the grief was over.

It felt as though something had been shattered irreparably inside her. Steven, John, even her mother had been broken by this. Everyone at university had been affected by its fallout. It – no – *Lucy* had marked them. She needed to talk to someone who had not lost Lucy the way that she had lost Lucy. Needed someone who was outside the wasteland that had once been youth and inexperience.

When her breathing steadied, Sophia stood.

She slipped a coat on over her t-shirt. Before she left, she wrote a note for John, explaining that she had gone out, that she would be back later. Then she started to walk across the city.

19. Contrition, Compassion and Steadfast Longing

'I was only going to say that heaven did not seem to be my home; and I broke my heart with weeping to come back to earth'
– Emily Brontë, *Wuthering Heights*

The shadows were long when Sophia reached his house, the air dusky and chill. For a moment, she faltered. The night they had first met – the same quality of light, the same pattern of shadows. She remembered the crowbar, Lucy climbing the gate…

Tonight, it opened with a single touch of her hand.

She had not spoken to Julian, had sent him only a guarded text message to let him know the news, and to say that the police might have questions for him. His reply had been careful, sensitive.

The pathway was still neglected, still crowded with dead growth. She remembered Lucy and Steven, the ease with which they had spoken then. She raised her hand to knock, but hesitated.

Why was she here?

Because she wanted him; wanted the smile upon his face, the warmth, the surprise. Wanted to bury her face in his shoulder, to feel the contours of his collarbone against her cheek. It was that she wanted to pull him to her, wanted him to run his fingers through her hair while she sobbed out the bullshit of the last month. Wanted his voice telling her that she would survive, wanted the simple fact of him holding her to keep her safe.

When Julian opened the door, he stepped towards her, his arms outstretched as though for an embrace.

She did not fall into his arms.

He held out a hand and she took it. 'My dear.'

'Hi. Sorry to bug you like this. Can I come in?'

He bowed and pressed his lips against her hand. That she barely noticed the kiss seemed only to confirm how vulnerable she was feeling. 'You are always welcome, Sophia. Please.' He withdrew into the hall.

But not before she saw the lines traced on his face. Not before she saw his eyes ringed with shadows, skin ashen, dead white and etched with crows-feet. Even his hair seemed touched with grey. His movements were laboured, as though it took all his strength to remain upright.

Sophia took a half-step into the hall, remembering what he had said about his illness. She paused, unsure whether she should apologise for disturbing him and return straight home, but he smiled and motioned for her to follow him into the house, into the room where they had always sat together. It was dark, empty. The fire was not lit. He excused himself.

When he returned he laid the fire, lit the candles and did not trying to engage her in small talk. He did not mention Lucy or say that he was sorry for her loss. Most of all, he did not ask her how she was with the kind of solicitude that showed he was prepared for an answer other than 'fine'.

In fact, he said nothing besides, 'Please, do take a seat. I shall not be long.'

And as she watched him work, she realised that everyone she had spoken to had treated her not as Sophia, but as Lucy's grieving friend. She sat in the cold, snug leather of the armchair as the first tongues of fire began to lick over the logs, and felt something in her exhale, uncurl.

Still, she could feel it, the almost physical force of his compassion. When he had finished, when he came and sat near her, he watched her with such tenderness that, had he said anything, she would have left.

But Julian did not speak.

After some time, she said, 'I'm sorry to bother you.'

'Not at all. I am glad to see you. Very glad.'

Sophia found herself thinking of the moment in the flat, before John had come in, when Julian had almost been touching her hand.

'Perhaps you wish to talk?'

'I thought – I thought maybe it would be good to see you. John was working late. And I just couldn't spend any more time on my own.'

'I have not seen you since…' It surprised her to hear the roughness in his voice, to hear him, however briefly, lost for words.

'I'm sorry that…'

'No. I cannot imagine your loss. I knew little enough of her, but I can see how greatly she will be missed.' He held her gaze with an intensity that was almost frightening. '*Never* feel you should apologise to me.' Then his face became soft, handsome, worn once more. 'Is there anything that I can do for you, my dear?'

She tried to smile. 'Just company, please? Someone to talk to. If that's okay?'

'Your company is always a pleasure,' and, with a touch of his old archness, 'but I meant more immediately.'

She found that her lips had twisted, that she was smiling and that it took no effort at all. 'I could do with a drink.'

'Anything specific?'

She had not been drinking much, either; had not wanted to give in to the swirling maelstrom of emotion which alcohol could create. 'Whisky.'

'With soda?'

'Straight.'

Julian inclined his head, 'I believe I may join you.' He rose and flashed her a small, sharp smile. She saw the white of his teeth. A bolt of sensation seemed to strike her in her throat, burn its way down to between her legs. She looked away until she knew he had left the room.

The heat of the fire warmed her through her jeans. She drew her arms about her, thinking of the last time that she had sat there. She tugged the bat earrings, feeling the weight of the wires around her earlobes. Everything here seemed to welcome her; the heat, the light, the smells of candlewax and wood smoke. The stiff leather of the armchair relaxed around her body. A sudden image came into her mind of the room, dark, forlorn and lifeless for all of the weeks that she had been away, bound up in dust and silence, waiting for her return.

Don't be so morbid.

It occurred to her that Julian had been gone rather longer than usual.

When he did return he handed her a heavy tumbler whose crystal winked and flashed. She sipped, allowing the dry taste of peat to evaporate on her tongue, and a sensation that was beyond taste to burn its way down her throat and wrap around her heart. She let out a long, deep breath.

Julian was watching her.

Then, he began to talk. At first, he was gentle, doing nothing more than prompting her in safe topics, asking her about her course, or John, or the books that she had read. He did not mention Steven, nor Lucy; did not thank her for the party. Her answers were broken, graceless, but Julian behaved as though he had noticed no change at all. For all of that, she was grateful.

She sipped at the whisky, drinking slowly, and when it was gone, she stared into the sparkling depths of her glass.

'It's hard,' she said into the silence that had fallen between them. 'It's as though I can't, just can't imagine a world, an anything without Lucy. It's as though it's impossible.'

He watched her as she spoke, turning his own glass in a slow circle so that the edges caught the firelight. He was silent for a time, then he nodded. 'Yes.'

Sophia felt a sob rise in her throat, hard and urgent. 'You – you've lost someone, too. No. Stupid of me. Your grandfather, of course, I'm....'

His eyes were liquid hazel and they fixed upon her. She found that she could not look away. 'Not my grandfather. That was... not unexpected. This, no. This was many years ago, now.'

'Who?' She could not stop the question, could not stop herself leaning forward in her chair, reaching towards him.

Julian smiled, but the smile was soft, tragic. 'A young woman. Eleanor. My wife.'

Sophia felt herself start in shock and sympathy.

'She died young.' Every word was measured, crystalline, distinct.

'You loved her.' Sophia felt a moment of pain as she said those words, but brushed it aside.

'More than life.' He looked away. While still pale, he seemed less drawn than he had done earlier in the evening. She wondered if talking were helping him, too. 'Losing her... it robbed me of myself.'

Sophia found that she did not want to meet his gaze; that she was afraid she might find a loneliness, a grief too strong to bear. But she made herself look, and all she saw was Julian.

'Does it ever heal? With time?'

'No.' His fingers, pale, shaking, about his glass. 'Sometimes, it can be ignored, but no. Not even with time.'

For a long time, Sophia stared. Then, she leaned across the space between them and put her hands over one of his. They sat, unspeaking.

There was a map of tragedy in his thin, sensual lips, in the lost expression of his eyes. His grief was a pain to her, one distinct from her own sorrow. She wanted him, not John, to hold her in the coldness of the night. She wanted him by her side as she faced the uncertainties of the future.

She gripped his hand a little more tightly and felt it shake. He seemed about to grasp at her, about to pull away. Time passed.

In the end, he slipped his hand from under hers, gave her his usual half-smile. 'I apologise, my dear.'

Sophia shook her head. 'No. No, thank you.'

'Would you like another drink? Unless, of course, you wish...'

'Another drink would be great. If that's okay.'

Later, Sophia watched him swirl his glass – his long, slightly pointed nails, the legs of the whisky as it ran over the crystal – and said, 'I'm sorry if I've been a bit flaky this evening.'

'Not at all, my dear. And I am sorry that I interrupted your grief with mine. I should not have mentioned it.'

'No. No, you should. I'm glad you did. It's just... life just seems too fragile right now. I mean, Lucy...' As she said the name she paused, expecting to stumble upon it, expecting to feel pain. She did, but it was not as bad as it had been. 'Well, Lucy was the most alive person I knew. And if she can... I mean, if someone can, well, then, it happens to all of us, doesn't it?'

Julian stopped moving the glass. He did not look at her.

'Life's short. It's just so short. I could die tomorrow. Hell, I could die tonight. What's the point?' She wrapped both her hands around her glass, crossing her knuckles, pinching them together. 'Really, why bother? I've led such a dull bloody life – and then I'll just *die*.'

He said nothing.

'God, though, it could be worse. I could get married to John, live in some suburb, waste away until something puts me out of my misery. Fucking hell. If that's how I'm going to do things, it should have been me, not Lucy, you know?'

She looked down at the tiles on the floor, at their dull sheen in the firelight. She could almost sense his tension, his reproach.

'I'm sorry – again. It's been getting to me. I've been feeling like this so much and it's... I don't know. It's been making me think. About things. About choices.'

Julian did not interrupt her and still she did not look at him.

'It's been making me think, is all. Life is what we make it, isn't it?' She looked up into Julian's face.

His expression was blank – no irony, no compassion. His eyes were fixed upon her.

'Jesus, I'm sorry. I'm being morbid. It's just I think that maybe, that what I'm doing... with John... it's not right. And it feels, maybe, that I'm letting it all drift away from me because of that.' Her voice lay quietly in the back of her throat, little more than a halting whisper. A strand of hair had fallen in front of her eyes. She brushed it away. 'Because of a mistake.'

The words that came next, that needed to come next, had to be forced from her mouth: 'But that's not fate, is it? I could do it another way, couldn't I? I could try something else. Like being with you, I mean. How about that?'

She risked another look at his face.

For a second, she was sure that something like anger, something huge and fierce and frightening burned across Julian's face. But in less time than she took to register it, it had gone. She watched him swallow, watched him clench his teeth. His expression was frozen, shocked.

Then his lips softened, and he licked them; first one, then the other.

There was something terrible in his eyes. Sophia realised she had no idea what it was that he was feeling. She watched his hands clench and unclench. Watched him tremble. His jaw did not relax.

'Sophia.' He swallowed again and very slowly put his whisky glass down beside him. He pulled his upper lip into his mouth, bit upon it so hard she could see all trace of its redness disappear. After what seemed a long time, his trembling stopped.

'I would be lying if I – if I denied that.' Julian shook his head. He began again, 'My dear, the strength of my feelings for you is…' He closed his eyes, turned his head away. 'Now is not the time. You and I – we know so little of each other…'

She found sudden, angry strength. 'Don't give me *that*.'

Julian flinched. 'Sophia. You know that I care for you. I… Please, my dear, your Jonathan – surely, surely he cares for you too? And you are engaged.' He closed his mouth, his jaw clenched, as though he could not quite bear to continue. 'It is not, would not be *fair*, if I… were I to…' He shook his head, a small gesture, almost sad. 'No.'

'No?'

'No. My dear, you are grieving still. Your loss has been terrible. Now is not the time. It would not be right for you to make these decisions now. It would not be fair of me to let you. To take advantage.' With slow, almost fearful movements he rose and crossed the short space between them. 'You scarcely know me, Sophia. I could not… I could not in all conscience act now.'

She reached towards him and grasped his hand once more. Her pride, at least, stopped her from putting her plea into words, but she knew that it was obvious, was in the burning behind her eyes, the pressure of her fingers. She wanted to run to somewhere quiet and private and never have to face him again. At the least, she wished that she could look away, but his eyes had trapped her. His free hand reached up to her cheek, his cool fingers a light touch beside her lips.

'Forgive me, my dear.'

Her heart lashed with rejection.

She shook her head as much as she might without moving away from his touch. 'Okay. It's not… I'll be okay. Could you just hold me? For a moment? And then I'll…' Something like another refusal began to dawn upon his face. She felt herself shake. Had it been anyone else, she would have pulled away. 'Please?'

Julian lifted her to her feet and wrapped her in his arms without saying another word.

The creature sank his teeth into his lips. Through her clothing he could feel her heartbeat. He could smell her blood, her hair, her perfume and the whisky on her breath; could smell the arousal she felt at his embrace. *Do not breathe,* he ordered himself as he held his body stiff beneath the clutch of her arms.

At least, at the very least, he had been wise enough to renew his stock of garnered blood, had been wise enough not to fast entirely. And every time he had left her presence he had drunk as much as he could of that cold, stale gore, trying, aching desperately to maintain his control.

Her whole body was luscious, brimming with sexuality, plump with blood. And she wanted him. That knowledge scalded with its imperative. He wanted to press her beneath his hands, spread her body into trembling ecstasy with his cold fingers, his sharp kisses. To caress, to lick away even the concept of a memory of her grief, to open her chest and kiss the hot, red intimacy of her heart.

One of his hands strayed into her hair, stroking. Against his will, against his better judgement, he drank in the scent of her, as though that alone would give him nourishment.

It had not been like this when he had held Eleanor. Then his face had been hot with joyous tears, his heart burning with a pure love. There had been joy, arousal, gratitude. For that, he ached; to hold her as he had once held Eleanor, without reserve, without perverse desire, or fear. Without even the knowledge that there might be anything to fear.

But the strength in his arms could crush her, and the love that had once stirred in his heart was sullied, mingled with the predator's hunger, the debaucher's lust. She had come to *him* for solace...

He pulled her against him, pressing her soft, human body against the unyielding stiffness of his cold, damned corpse.

In the end she shifted from the grip of his arms. He let her go.

The tears had left red streaks upon her face. The liquid of them made her eyes shine, made them seem deeper and darker than ever before. Her warm hands clung to his shoulders for moment. She looked up, embarrassed, ashamed, even. 'Thank you.'

The creature raised his hand to her face once more, touched her cheek where the tears were still hot and stinging. She did not flinch at the chill of his fingers. 'My dear.' He expected her, then, to move from him.

But she did not. For long seconds, she did not move, until he was afraid that he had placed a spell upon her with his eyes, had robbed her will with the simple force of his desire. There she stood for moments which dragged to an eternity, her lips a little apart, her breath shallow, difficult to perceive. The scent of her assailed him, the curves of her body were warm, scant inches from him. The sound of her pulse thundered in his ears...

The creature snatched his hand from her cheek, pulled away. He watched her start, saw the look of hurt upon her face and it was all that he could do not to fall at her feet and spew out the truth of things.

It was then he knew that it was over; no longer could he veil himself in lies and half-truths. If she were to ask him outright, he would have no choice but to bow to her will.

But she did not ask. Nor, as he had half feared, did she leave. Instead, she returned to her chair and, after a few minutes of silence and evasion, she spoke to him of things of little consequence.

It was easy, always too easy to speak with her of nothings, to flirt and flatter and converse. But when her interest was roused, Sophia spoke with her whole being. Around poetry she wrapped her tongue in a lingering kiss; towards art she gazed with the intensity of a lover. It was hard to listen to her and not fuel his hunger, his desire. Was hard not to spring upon her and press her in a kiss that would leave her lips raw, her throat bloody and torn.

When, after a while, she told him that she should leave, the creature offered to walk her home. Even as he spoke the foolish words, he cursed his clumsy tongue. Even as he asked, he expected her to refuse, as she had refused before.

She surprised him.

He wondered if it were not that her bravery had been shaken by the murder of her friend. The suspicion hung in his mind, tainting the pleasure of her company. But he feared for her and he ached for her, although he knew that the greatest danger she faced was from himself.

And his need seemed mirrored in her willingness to be escorted by him; he could feel her eyes following him, lingering on his long, pale throat, his thin lips, his elegant hands. He had long since believed himself immune to the attention his appearance drew, but had he been a mortal man, his pulse would have raced, his skin prickled with the tantalising awareness of her gaze.

She huddled and shivered as she walked, breathing through her teeth, tucking her bare hands into the sleeves of her coat in theatrical response to night. She was an inept seductress, her ruse as shallow as her sideways glances were shy.

He forced himself to refrain.

But when he did not offer to take her arm, did not fold himself about her, he could see the hurt, the rejection in the sudden embarrassment of her movements, in her abrupt, false laughter. 'Don't you ever feel cold, Julian?'

'A little.' The truth of it was that he always felt a little cold, but that was not what she had meant.

In silence, they continued to walk to her flat.

When they reached the door, she turned. 'Right. Thank you. You know. And, sorry if I got a little…'

He shook his head. 'It was a pleasure to see you again, Sophia.' All the warmth, the passion that he possessed poured into those words, although he knew it would have been better had he remained stiff, withdrawn.

He watched her relax, watched a half-smile creep on to her lips. 'I'd better go. Unless you want to come in for coffee, or something.'

Almost he accepted, but he caught the treacherous words before they reached his tongue. 'I should allow you to return to your evening, my dear.'

'Okay.' She put her key into the lock, lingering at the door. He felt her body yearning towards him. 'I'll see you soon. If that's alright?'

'Of course.' He could not help that the words came out like the

sleek purr of a well-fed tom cat, just as he could not help the way that
his feet edged closer to hers.

'Well, goodnight then.' She turned the key in the lock, pushed the
door ajar. A current of warm air, a stream of golden light poured out
towards them, but she did not step into it.

Once more, he trembled as he forced himself not to snatch her into
his arms, not to pull her away from life, safety, sanity. Hunger rushed
through him, a torrent, a flood. He was not entirely sure that he could
resist.

Then the creature saw her young man framed in the light of
the door, his face showing soft concern before hardening to rage.
'Sophia,' Jonathan said.

The incandescent desire which lit her skin and her eyes, which had
burned in her for the whole of their long walk, became veiled. Her
whole body slumped. 'Oh. John. Sorry it's late. Julian offered to walk
me home.'

'Right,' said the boy. The creature could hear the struggle he had to
keep his voice under control. 'Well, you're okay, so...' He turned his
eyes to the creature, a quick flash of jealousy and resentment.

As that look touched him, the creature sank his teeth into his
cheeks, ripping the flesh, steadying his own rage.

At length, Jonathan said, 'Thanks. For doing that.'

'Not at all.' The creature was forced to remind himself that he had
told Sophia she had a debt of duty, of emotion, to this boy. That it
was not right, not wise, to act the part of a rival in love. 'Sophia, my
dear. Goodnight.'

He took her hand and bowed to kiss it. Earlier that night, half-
starved and tortured with remorse, he had found himself able to
refrain from making his wonted incision upon her hand. But he felt
the way her fingers tensed and heated to his touch, felt her pulse
quicken and her gaze upon him. He willed himself to resist, to deny
himself once more.

The blood touched the tip of his tongue. Wild hunger tore through
him, imperative and deadly. Lust scalded.

He bowed once more, and walked away.

John stood in the hall of the flat and felt a bruising pain spread in his chest. It felt as if someone had punched him. As if Sophia had punched him.

If it hadn't hurt so much, if he was not so relieved, he knew he would feel that he had been played for a fool. Instead there was only shock. When he had come home to the empty house he had thought the worst. It stopped mattering that the killer hadn't done anything in the last few weeks, that people thought they were safe again; it all stopped mattering because Sophia had not been there and she had not been answering her phone. In the end he found it, wedged right at the bottom of a bag of books, on silent. After that there had been nothing he could do except wait, hope, even pray that she was alright.

Then she had turned up, practically hanging on that guy's arm. And she had looked happy for the first time since... since he had told her the news, since long before that. Seeing her safe, thank God, and smiling, and with Julian...

Then, as she had looked at him, all that happiness seemed to drain away.

As she stepped into the flat, John put his arms around her. 'You been out long?' he asked, even though he already knew the answer.

She put her head on his shoulder. There was the smell of something strong and alcoholic on her breath. 'A bit. Sorry.' She slid out of his grip. 'I got lonely. Were you worried?'

'Yeah. Yeah, you could say that.'

'Oh. Sorry. I left a note.'

'Shit, Sophia. I know. I found the note. But, I mean, for Christ's sakes, it didn't say where you'd gone, when you'd be back...'

'I sort of thought I'd get home before you.' Her voice wobbled and her mouth pouted.

John grabbed her into another hug, pulling her to him, holding her tight. 'Could you not have taken your phone?'

'I forgot it.' And she twisted, pulling away from him again. 'Don't be angry, John.'

'I'm not bloody angry, love. Look, I'm just on edge, you know? When you weren't picking up, I...'

That seemed to wake her up. 'Oh, hell. No, I'm sorry.' For one

moment, her eyes were bright, her face full of life. 'I should have…
I don't know. I wasn't thinking straight. I needed company, you
know?'

'Right.' He had not wanted to work tonight, had tried to get out of
it. John realised that he hated that rich kid friend of hers, now.

'Don't take it like that, John. I just – I thought I could do it, and I
couldn't. Julian was about, that's all.'

'Sure.' His voice did not sound convincing, not even to himself.
For the first time in weeks she was back to something like normal,
and they were rowing already. He took a long breath, made sure he
sounded gentle, kind. He took hold of her arm again. 'No, come on.
Let's forget it for tonight, yeah? Let's go to bed.'

She nodded. 'Sure thing.'

But he lay awake that night, knowing that she was lying next to
him unable to sleep. And a little, angry corner of his mind prompted
him, wondering if she was thinking of Julian.

Images of her flooded his mind. The taste of her clung to his lips and
his throat, and he recalled the sheen of sweat that the fire's heat had
brought to her face, recalled her tears, the sound of her voice. To
know that she was in the world and that, even if he could not go to
her, that there were thousands of strangers in the city, all full of hot,
fresh blood…

His tongue was parched, his throat raw with thirst. The creature
paced, distracted, trying to calm the torrent within him.

Not tonight.

He forced himself to consider all the pure and logical reasons why
his actions during the past few months had indulged his monstrosity
too much. Had Sophia even suspected the way he had revelled in the
crisp air and hot blood, the frost and the fear, she would never have
come to love him. Every word of her declaration, everything that he
had read in her looks and her movements that night was based upon a
sham. He would never be worthy of her; to think that her words had
changed anything was a gross self-deception.

Yet the conviction remained. Were he to kill tonight it would
compound his untruths with a betrayal that was somehow worse than

the murder of her friend. He felt the ache to go to her, to confess, to fall on his knees before her and present the truth of his half-life before her hatred and scorn. But he had played his part too well. Her rational, modern mind would never believe that admission of guilt; she would think him mad, or mad herself, or else the victim of some cruel joke. Kneeling by her chair, the creature closed his hands into fists, and pressed the knuckles into his cheeks, hard enough to bruise.

The lies came so easily. When the police had come to question him, as Sophia had told him they might, and as they had done before, it had not even occurred to him to speak the truth. His face had already healed, the strips of skin gouged away by Lucy's nails no more than the faintest scars, and he had played the part of shocked and distant sorrow. *Naturally, he would do anything he could to help...*

Beside the fire was the empty glass from which Sophia had drunk. He crawled to it and wrapped his hands around it, fingers lying where her fingers had rested. The slick surface of the crystal still held the faintest trace of her scent, the memory of her lips, her skin. In lieu of a kiss, he placed his mouth where hers had touched the rim of the glass. The smell of whisky rose up to him, cloying in his nostrils, turning his stomach and crying out to be drowned in still more blood.

Beneath his fingers, the glass was at once heavy and frail. Bohemian crystal, it was cut as sharply, as precisely, as the memories etched into his mind. It was one of dozens of such things, which crammed the cupboards of this place with the singing elegance of fine glass. A century before he had bought and hoarded all manner of genteel trinkets; one of his endless distractions as he attempted to bury the ennui of his existence in beauty or decadence. In all those years, he had used them but seldom, the careful grace of his hands preserving their lovely frailty intact.

The irony that, in those decades, he had broken so many lives, did not escape him.

Around him, the silence of the house grew oppressive. Long inaction and deceit had cleaved his tongue to the roof of his mouth. Pressing hard in his throat was the weight of his crimes. In his lifetime, it had been the custom to go to a priest, to spill out the sins committed and to take penance for them. He recalled that deep searching of conscience. But where now would such a confession begin? With his lust for the one who had turned him? With his pride in desiring immortality?

It had been many years since he had lost his faith.

By any standards, he was lost to redemption.

Wanton and needless, he had taken life. He had flattered himself, been foolish and vain. But it was not his past actions which condemned him. In his life, the formula had been *sin no more.*

He ran his nails over the surface of the glass, coaxing a grating, unbearable note from the crystal. He remembered Sophia, thought of tracing his clever hands over her curves, across the fine whiteness of her skin. He sucked the memory of the taste of her blood from his tongue and felt a moan catch in his throat.

To feed...

With a cry that was almost a sob, he tightened his hand upon the glass, crushing it to shards. Fragments, so sharp they could scarcely be felt, sliced into his skin. He sank once more to his knees, his body struggling to repair itself around the slivers buried in his flesh. The pain began, became excruciating. *Sophia,* he thought, and, in the red light of the dying fire, he sucked at the torn flesh of his own hand.

20. Saint Valentine's Day

'…think me not cruel because I obey the irresistible law of my strength and weakness; if your dear heart is wounded, my wild heart bleeds with yours. In the rapture of my enormous humiliation I live in your warm life, and you shall die – die, sweetly die – into mine. I cannot help it'
– Sheridan Le Fanu, *Carmilla*

January dragged out its last handful of days, and then there was a new month. The weather got warmer, then colder again; the evenings grew lighter. Ignoring the weather's caprice, Sophia would make her way across the city alone to visit Julian at least once a week. Steven had finally returned to Barchester, but he did not ask to join her, nor did she invite him.

Julian did not allude to her confession, and she didn't broach the subject again. Still, the tenor of their conversation changed. It became strangely easy to unpick old scars, to show the raw and broken tissue that lay beneath. So she told him how she could not really remember what her father had looked like; how, in the few photos her mother had kept, what she saw was a stranger's face. Told him of the way they had parted, that casual wave across the courtroom because she had not understood that she would never see him again.

She spoke about Lucy and Steven too; of a youth spent wedged between a tomboy and a bookworm, of torn jeans and make-believe, playground scuffles and made-up codes, and the strange, hybrid board games they had invented. And she told him of her loneliness, of how, when she had arrived at the school at the start of year one, Steven and Lucy had already been friends. Told him how, sometimes, she had felt like the outsider in their group.

Easy; and if it was easy to talk, she preferred to listen. Julian had tales of cities, of London, of Paris, of Berlin, and stories about wine, of cold-spiced nights spent walking between the vines. He would tell her, too, of Venice, of grey mists, grey alleyways, grey seas. At times, he mentioned lovers and friends but he never spoke again about his wife. It occurred to her, at times, to wonder how old he might be, to question the odd, enchanted quality of his life.

Yet she did not, for – if not enchanted – what else were those other nights when they barely spoke, when they sat hand in hand as the hours passed? Sometimes he would raise his fingertips and brush her hair from her face, would touch her lips, her cheek.

She felt guilty, of course. For all that it was hardly serious infidelity, for all that she had done nothing wrong, nothing *really* wrong – still, she felt guilt. But she did not stop, and not once did she move away from Julian's hand.

Other things changed, too. Her grief eased to a low fierce ache, and she no longer found that the platitudes of life brought her to angry, impotent tears. She was sleeping better, the nightmares less frequent, less intense. Some nights, especially the nights when she had seen Julian, there were other dreams, dreams where her whole body felt cradled and caressed while she sank deep into warm, black water, or else rose on billows of white, heavy mist. The sense of passivity they inspired almost frightened her.

And with these dreams, sleep became compelling, necessary; a drug. Even after ten, eleven, sometimes twelve hours she would wake and still feel tired. In the gloom of winter's last weeks she blamed it on the weather, the lack of light, the fact she had been sleeping badly for months. But despite that, her mood improved; she began to go to uni again, began to feel better, more optimistic. It became less difficult to spend time with Steven.

She and John, though, did not talk much. Sometimes, when he kissed her, told her that he loved her, she felt her stomach squirm. It would have been worse, of course, had she still believed that John trusted her. As it was, he did not mention Julian's name and did not ask her where she had been, or with whom. Yet it was clear he knew.

When John was not with her, it was difficult to care. Sometimes, in the stillness of the night, she would find herself seized with an urgent, undeniable desire. She would masturbate, and she would think of Julian and, as she did, a little cut she'd got upon her wrist seemed to blaze as hot as a blush. Soon, just to chafe that cut upon her sleeve or a table edge was enough to make her breath come short, to bring a wave of warmth between her legs. In idle moments, she would scratch at it, keeping it open, not wanting it to heal.

As February wore on, more and more often, she would come to herself from thoughts of hazily imagined lust and indulgence, aware that she was wet. Always, at the back of her mind, there was a strangely erotic dizziness, a feeling of disconnection. As in puberty, the world around her became edged with a wild, dangerous sexuality.

At night, after an evening with Julian, after the talk and silence, the restrained little caresses, she would lie listening to John's slow breathing and wait for the delicious languor of her dreams. Unspecified desire would swell within her, stirring between her legs with its liquid heat, and she'd remember his voice, the cool pressure of his fingertips, the faint scent which hung around him, as spiced and quiet as the air in a library.

And her fingers would stray between her legs.

The creature sat in the chair where she had been, drinking in her scent, and delaying, always delaying.

He had not killed since Lucy. Instead, once more he prowled the streets, snatching barely bloodied kisses from the veins of the drunk or entranced, or those whom circumstance had left vulnerable to his kind. Bottles of blood he had gleaned from those sources filled the shelves of the refrigerator; other empty bottles littered the surfaces of the kitchen.

And there was another indulgence to sustain him.

That first night, it had been the barest nothing; a pinprick, a mosquito bite. As he had done it, he had known that it was wrong, but he had never intended to compound that treachery by causing her further harm. After all, that little had slaked his thirst, and he had no more than scratched her.

But he had returned. And, after that, he had returned again. Still, his tenuous discipline of mind had not broken for all that each night he went to her and bled her more deeply.

From across the city, she seemed to call to him. He could almost feel the sweet welling of her blood, almost hear the soft moan – between pleasure and pain – which parted her lips as his teeth found their mark in her flesh.

It no longer mattered that, each night, she slept alongside her fiancé. She had told the creature her feelings. The boy meant nothing, now.

Still, he hated Jonathan with an idle, distant disdain; hated his triviality of mind, the way he did not give Sophia the things she needed. But that hatred only flared to virulence when he recalled that it was those very flaws which had served to drive Sophia into his arms.

It was too late. Every touch, every ardent look of hers simply confirmed the thing he knew. She desired him. Was he not acting only on the spur of that desire?

Hypocrite.

He had withheld his affection on the understanding that it would, in some way, protect her; had rejected her because to do otherwise was a betrayal. As he had done it, he had felt some growing glow of self-pride.

Was it possible that he still styled himself an honourable man?

He longed for Steven, for freedom from these confused hungers. Longed for peaceful innocence against which he could play out his villainy, for more straightforward pleasures than the heat of Sophia's shy, lascivious glances. But were he to rush to Steven, he knew that he would seduce the child with cunning and lecherous words, would engulf another wise and beautiful boy in the weary torrent of his immortality.

He stared across the room where, months ago, they had first met, and the creature wished that he could counsel his past self to defy his lusts, defy the pain and longing wrapped up in Sophia's perfume, and focus instead upon the cool and intelligent words of her young friend. But with Steven, things would still, eventually, have come to such an end. If Steven had not turned upon him first.

He should have left them both alone. The creature had known that, even then.

The scent of Sophia surrounded him. *That perfume...* it was still the one that Eleanor had worn. Yet when he tried to recall his wife, it was Sophia that he saw – Sophia with her short, swinging hair and her tight, modern clothes. He began to shake, his whole cold body trembling. *Restraint. Tonight, I must show restraint.* He pushed his teeth slowly though his tongue, piercing the thick, fat muscle. Pain licked through him as his mouth filled with his own blood. *It must stop.*

Or, tonight, at least. I must not...

He was standing beside her bed. She lay, calm and asleep upon her side, her hair spreading across the pillows like smoke, her smoke-grey eyes pressed closed. He inhaled, tasting the scent of her sleeping body. The heaviness of wine rancid upon her breath, her perfume, her sweat, the oil in her hair. So beautiful.

And pale. So very pale.

The creature knelt beside the bed, staring into her face, half fearing, half hoping to see revulsion, refusal, but there was only peace. It even seemed as though the memory of a smile lingered on her lips. Her breathing was somnolent, low and regular, washing over the steady beating of her heart. The creature watched her, shutting out the city's grating clamour, the obtrusive breathing of her fiancé's rest. The creature's eyes traced the blue shadows on her face, the fine lines of her jaw, her nose. His fingers ached to caress that skin, but he knew he must not. One of her hands emerged from the blankets, wrist extended, fingers uncoiled, relaxed.

Always the same hand.

The darkness strengthened his eyes and he could see the pulsing arteries beneath the skin, the little scratch his nightly attentions had left. He bent his head to the hand, as if to kiss it. The fingers were damp and smelled of sex.

He almost choked. Until that moment, even kneeling beside her with the teeth in his mouth long and urgent, he had hoped he would find the strength to leave. Every muscle in his body was tense, coiled, as he burned towards her, needing to run his tongue over every inch of her skin, to taste and caress her body, to subdue it with pleasure, destroy it with ecstasy...

Jaw clenched, fists curled, the creature closed his eyes and waited for the violence to subside. Then, calmer, he wrapped his fingers about her palm and, with infinite gentleness, raised the wrist to his lips. His teeth grew long in his mouth as he kissed, a tearing, exquisite agony. He waited. Then, with tenderness, he reopened the wound.

Sophia stirred in her sleep; she moaned, her body arched. Blood welled. With the point of his tongue, he licked it away, worrying the incision open. Soon it came with steady beading, each drop upon his palate a blessing, a moment of completion, of overwhelming bliss.

His body tingled and thrilled aware. He fought himself, keeping back the urge to rend, to glut himself. With restraint like a lover's, he concentrated, kissing away each beat of her heart.

He took too much. Took more than he had intended and far more than wisdom would dictate. But it had been many months since the creature had listened to wisdom. As he pulled away, he found that he could not look into her face. He pressed the little cut closed with his thumb, seeing that his kiss tonight had made it wider, deeper, more ugly. Sophia's breathing was no longer calm, was a rasp in his ears. For a long moment, the creature pressed his eyes closed. Then he left.

Walking through wind and rain with her blood still burning in him, he remembered. Not the countless times that he had pushed his teeth through quivering skin, but a single moment, near enough six centuries gone. Standing against the wall in a stinking alley, the hands of his seducer on his face, his neck, pulling his clothing aside. Cold lips hesitating a quarter of an inch above his skin. Expectation, pleasure. Then pain, a strange, terrible agony that was somehow not pain at all. He could almost feel it now, the press of the stranger's body as he clasped at the cloth of the stranger's clothes, as he breathed in that man's strange, dusty musk...

A climax, a peak, an orgasm of agony.

He had pretended he had forgotten, just as he had convinced himself that he did not wish to know why he had been abandoned.

But always, when he sank his teeth into his prey, the memory was there, a silent comparison. Was that what his victims felt? Was that what Sophia had felt, what had made her cry out, what made her sleep with smile upon her lips?

And if, deep in slumber, some part of her welcomed his murderous caresses, the creature wondered if that did not excuse him in some small measure.

And he knew that it did not.

Sophia woke exhausted, with swollen glands. When she sat up in bed to say goodbye to John, her vision blurred to an ache of grey, and over everything she could hear her pulse hammering in her throat, the buzz of nausea in her ears. She forced herself to breathe steadily until she could see again, but her mouth tasted metallic, and the first pang of fear bit through her blissful languor.

She told herself that it was just a touch of flu which had brought on the tightness in her throat, the weakness in her limbs. Trying to get up, to move about the house and go to uni, she realised that even sitting upright was more than she would be able to manage that day. She emailed her seminar leaders, telling them she was ill and, suspecting anaemia, booked a doctor's appointment.

The duty doctor had said that there was a lot of this going around, but it tended to pass; that it was probably caused by a virus of some kind. Then he took her pulse and her blood pressure and booked her in for a blood test in a few days' time if it didn't clear up first. When she admitted to having felt faint for about a month, the doctor nodded and suggested taking iron supplements and staying hydrated. Sophia tried to listen, but the whole time she felt she might fall sideways off her chair. As her ears had rung and her eyes strained, her thoughts were elsewhere. With Julian.

At home later that day, she curled up under the bedclothes and thought of him some more.

She did not go back for the blood test, even as the symptoms continued their slide into the severe, because hadn't the doctor said it would clear up on its own? She fell behind with her uni work. A lot of her time was spent in bed, dreaming of the dreams she had dreamt the previous night, drowning in smooth black water while everything that kept her afloat was pulled away.

She tried not to let John or Steven or the doctors see how ill she had become. When they asked her what was wrong, she said it was just a bit of SAD, or a cold. She told herself this, too.

She did not mind, though, if Julian knew. She saw him as often as she might.

After all, what did it matter? What did anything matter except the throbbing between her legs, the mist in her mind?

In the wreck of his room in the small hours of the morning, Steven hunched over the library book, forcing his mind to understand the dry, precise text. Everything around him was bleak and comfortless. The film posters were gone, the books loaded into boxes which he could not quite bring himself to discard. His desk sat barren, his book-shelves depleted and the walls were marked with the traces of Blu Tack he had not been able to remove. The only elements of personality were a photograph of himself, Sophia and Lucy in their secondary school days, and an old home-taped VHS, labelled in red mock-calligraphy 'Horror of Dracula Undead'. This he would have hidden along with everything else, but Lucy's parents had found it, buried in an old stacking box under her bed, and given it to him.

Steven had almost forgotten about this 'film'. If he concentrated, he could just about summon up memories of his eleven-year-old self wearing an old pair of his father's glasses and struggling as he lugged Lucy's parents' camcorder in one hand and the spectacular nine-page script in the other. He had been the writer and director and had played the lead role of Van Helsing. Lucy, he seemed to recall, had taken the part of the eponymous Count, while Sophia had played a series of screaming, nightdress-clad girls drenched in fake gore. He remembered being very enthusiastic about it, very proud. As they had filmed it, they had convinced themselves it would be a masterpiece, a cult classic that would get them huge, Hollywood fame before they were fifteen. He didn't know what had possessed Lucy to keep hold of it.

The other reminders of that obsession caused him too much pain. On returning to Barchester, he had gone to speak to his tutor about changing the topic of his dissertation and about his rekindled interest in critical theory. He had attempted to make it sound like a natural progression from his original idea, and, as he had watched her nod, he had tried to convince himself that she was not just agreeing because she knew about Lucy.

Still, removed from the Gothic and its constant reminders of mortality, it became easier to lose himself in a book. Easier to forget quite how empty the flat had become. There had been a handful of days when he had considered moving out and renting somewhere smaller, but that would have meant admitting that Lucy was gone.

He missed Sophia. He had expected, as they mourned, that they would use each other as props, would cling to the only other person who could possibly understand. Instead, she had retreated into some kind of pained reserve that made him fear that something had changed in her, that he would never be close to her again. Steven was aware that, in recent weeks, she had been seeing a lot of Julian.

He yawned but he did not quite dare put the book away, because then he would hear the silence of the flat around him. He wished there were some other distraction, but all he seemed to be able to do was to read, or grieve, or worry.

The worry was about Sophia. Again. Not only was she withdrawn, she was also ill. No matter what else had happened in the past, no matter what had been troubling her, Sophia's health had always been visible in her skin, in her eyes. Now it seemed as though she were listening to a strange, compelling music that he could not hear; that she was staring through him into another place altogether. And she was pale. Not pale the way that she had always been pale, not pale through winter and misery and sleepless nights, but a ghastly, fragile pallor.

He had even considered asking John if he knew what was wrong, but Steven no longer knew what was happening between Sophia and John. It seemed so long ago that he had fretted over her love life.

Steven blinked hard and rubbed his eyes, trying to find his place on the page. After a few moments of searching, he saw that he didn't recognise any of the words in front of him. Scanning back to the chapter's beginning, he realised his eyes had just been gliding over the text. Steven exhaled and put the book to one side. It was too late. He couldn't concentrate. There was a buzzing in the back of his head and he knew, if he listened, it would be made up of unfamiliar words and compound sentences.

He needed company. For weeks now, he had been avoiding everyone except Sophia. He missed having someone to whom he could talk. He missed Julian. And with that came a lurch of guilt. Too often his mind went back to that party at Sophia's flat and the way in which he had been so taken up with his new friend that he had scarcely spoken to Lucy.

Every mistake in his life seemed caught up in that moment, every cowardice and shame. If he had just cared slightly more, if he had only refused to let her take that final walk through the night-time streets, if he had been beside her, then...

Then what?

He was no fighter, would have been no match for such violence. Lucy had always been the brave one – had been so carelessly, so energetically *good*. He could not imagine her this apathetic in grief.

But Lucy was dead.

He closed his eyes and was troubled by an image of Julian's hands upon his skin, Julian's lips upon his lips. He felt himself get hard. What had once seemed bewitching sexuality was now only restful, alluring. What peace would there be if, for however short a time, he could silence his mind?

Without Lucy, without Sophia, was there anything in his old life that he would wish to save?

Steven knew precisely why Sophia never mentioned her visits to their friend.

Steven opened his eyes, remembering the curve of Julian's cheekbones, the pale shadows of his throat. He swallowed the sour taste that had risen in his mouth. Sophia. It was Sophia who had run to Julian and the comfort that he could offer, while Steven had secluded himself with his books. Not his old, lurid plots and phantasmagoria, but precise thoughts, things that had never been touched, things that rose again from the page as clean as the last time that he had left them.

Picking up the tome once again, he tried to read.

March, the weather picking up, bright and wet. The dizziness did not go away, but it fell back a little, a background haze to her thoughts. Sophia told herself that she had known it would get better on its own, in the end.

So she forced herself to get out of bed on the bitter mornings, to make her way to uni.

Getting back into the lab cleared her mind. She drifted less often, was able to talk to people; able, even, to smile.

For the first time in a long while, she visited Steven because she actually wanted to see him. In his flat, they sat across from each other, drinking coffee and sitting in the armchairs that flanked the empty sofa. They edged about, tentative with each other, and in less than half an hour, the atmosphere was so laden with unspoken loss that Sophia felt it hammering on her mind, throttling her voice.

At first, she did the thing that she had done for months: coiled in upon herself, shut down and shut up. They looked into their mugs, into the bitter brown liquid rather than each other's eyes. Bruised, she was about to make her excuses, about to leave.

Then she realised that, in all the time she had been there, neither of them had looked at the absence upon the sofa once.

Sophia turned full face to the empty seats and said into the silence, 'Christ, I miss her.'

Steven looked up, eyes wide, surprised. 'Yes. I miss her too.'

They stared at each other, and Sophia saw her loneliness reflected in his face.

'It's been awful,' Steven said, 'these last two months.'

And then he began to talk about loss and loneliness and anger, and Sophia sat, listening, and did not feel the unconscious simmering resentment that this was about letting Steven's memories and grief supersede her own. When he had finished speaking he looked calmer, with that the same strange, exhausted calm Sophia felt spreading in her own heart.

They hugged. Honestly, properly hugged each other. And when Steven asked how she had been, she found herself telling him about her mystery illness, how it bothered her, even though the doctors had suggested it was just a possible side effect of being female and young. She had not expected his relief, his compassion. She had not realised that he had noticed.

Suddenly tearful, Sophia clung to Steven's bony chest and shook her head at her own pointless secrecy. 'Come on, why don't you come over tomorrow night? It's been an age since we got pissed together.'

And the pain that she felt as she said those words was mirrored upon his face.

But Steven nodded. 'Yeah, sure. Why not?'

So, the next night, they sunk glass after glass of red and it was a little like old times. When they were properly drunk, Steven pulled a battered home VHS from his bag and asked her if she remembered it.

'No,' she said, as some rather ominous memories began to stir. Then, because they were getting silly with their talk about the past, she added, 'It looks awful. Shall we watch it?'

And Steven said, 'Okay.'

John, embarrassed but considerate, perched at the edge of the sofa as she and Steven snorted at Steven's wonky camera footage and her own innumerable, giggly screams. Buckets of homemade fake gore were splashed about, and Sophia had a flashback to the fuss her mum had made when she saw what they'd done to the bathtub. When Steven's Van Helsing – a melding of Peter Cushing and *Just William* – explained the necessity of 'stamping out this frightful iniquity for all eternity', the older, drunker version choked on his wine, and pleaded guilty to youthful abuse of a thesaurus.

And through the whole, short, mortifying experience, was Lucy. Plump, ten-year-old Lucy hamming it up in corner-shop vampire makeup, and Sophia found that she could remember – and that remembering no longer hurt. And she found that she was crying.

When the film had finished, they got completely smashed. They talked about the past and about Lucy, and told stories that they thought the other had forgotten.

The box of wine she had bought did not last as long as they needed it to, so they made a start on the vodka. As he got drunker, Steven seemed more like his old self, became more expansive, more mocking. The newly tolerant John refused to rise to it. Still, when he gave her a mild kiss and went to bed long before she wanted to, a voice in her head asked if it were not because Steven's improved mood was beginning to wear on John's patient, gentle manner.

It had been far too long since she had heard that voice.

By the small hours of the morning, the pair of them were blasted. They had talked and sung and told the odd off-colour joke. And they had remembered Lucy; most of all they had remembered Lucy. *It's a wake,* Sophia realised. Not the timid, post-funeral mumbling and hovering, but a debauch in the grand old style, breaking down all restraints of propriety and celebrating life; and mourning death under the liberating kiss of intoxication. Yes, it was messy and undignified and irresponsible, but, *My God,* she thought, *it's necessary.*

Because, after they had watched 'Horror of Dracula Undead' yet again and had drunk the vodka down to the last bare inch, by the time the room was not so much spinning as reeling, Sophia felt better than she had done in a long time. The future was not perfect – nothing was *better* – but she could survive it.

When it rolled around to three in the morning and Steven had been lying on the floor for the last forty minutes, calling occasionally for more booze, Sophia decided it was time for her to be responsible once more. 'You know,' she said, from where she was collapsed upon the sofa, 'I don't think I should stay up much longer. Absolutely, fucking pissed.'

'I agree entirely and implicitly. I should get up.'

She watched him try. It took him several attempts to find his feet and even then he swayed. The whole thing seemed desperately amusing.

But as she giggled, he shook his head and added, 'Forced to say: do not really want to go back to the flat.' He stumbled, nearly fell over. 'Also, possibly touched too tiddled to walk.'

She found herself nodding with all the decisiveness of a drunk. 'No. You should stay here. John won't mind a bit.'

The effort it took to lurch around the flat, finding him a spare duvet and a pillow, cleared a little of the intoxication. 'I wish Lucy were here,' she said, dumping the sheets on the sofa and sitting on them.

Steven staggered over and landed on top of her. 'Me too.'

'Yes.' Then she was holding Steven's hand and gripping it until her fingers hurt.

'Thank you. For letting me stay tonight.'

'No problem. I know how it is.'

And Steven gave her a fierce, desperate hug. 'I know you do. I know you do.'

21. The Lost Art of Conversation

'There are few people whom I really love, and still fewer of whom I think well. The more I see of the world, the more I am dissatisfied with it'
– Jane Austen, *Pride and Prejudice*

The creature's hands clenched and unclenched, the edges of his nails tearing into the skin of his palms. Hunger was suffocating. He kept, before his eyes, the image of Sophia's haggard face, her slow, uncertain movements, the general absence that had replaced her vitality, and forced himself to recall the way her voice had faltered as she had said, 'They told me it's nothing, and I know, I mean, I *know* they're right. But it feels... it feels like my life is being drained away.'

Since that evening, he had ceased his night-time visits, had taken only the little pinprick as he kissed her hand.

This, too, was futile. Each night he had gone out prowling the streets and taken blood from six, seven, even eight entranced victims. And each night he told himself that next time it would be easier, and each night, it was not.

Scarce more than a week...

Last night, he had left one of his victims so drained that she had sunk to the ground, prone and unconscious, her pulse the faintest of flickers. That woman had been his fourth victim of the night. Staring at her poor, pale form, he had known that he should feel replete. As it was, he had been less surprised by his failure than by the fact she was breathing at all.

He had taken her curled, wounded body and left it where it might be found, hoping that the damp night air would not finish what he had begun. Then he had continued to hunt.

It could not last. Despite the certainty with which he had first made this resolution, he had always known it could not last.

But he had believed he would have been able to endure a fortnight. After all, he had spent six centuries without Sophia's blood to sustain him, able to keep his hunger under control.

Those six centuries meant nothing.

That he was mad was without question. At times, the creature wondered if he would wake from this dream of love and irresolution as he had woken from his other madnesses. If his only knowledge of it would be recollections which hovered out of his reach, ever present and troubling.

Yet how could he effect such an awakening? Could *this* simply burn itself from his system? Would he, as then, awaken adrift and bewildered in a strange century and be able to pick up the threads of his old, mortal façade?

No.

The only possible end was of his own making, if he were to carry out that final betrayal and kill Sophia. Or, perhaps, if time and mortality struck that blow.

No.

For even were she to die, as his Eleanor had died, he would simply be more forlorn, more hopeless and more bound than he had ever been. He no longer even wished to be free.

So he paced, beginning his path in the damp blackness of the cellars, past the bottles of wine which were his livelihood, and the bed where he slept out the days. Up he walked, through the downstairs rooms which he used and the upper floors which were still all dust and neglect. His tread was slow and measured and it covered the floor of every room in his house, even the one where he and his Eleanor had died.

As he walked, his mind circled the chant, *Tonight. I will not go to her tonight. Tonight, I shall overcome.* And he paced through the darkness and the silence, trying to negate the emptiness of the night, the loneliness, the long hours; pacing out his hunger.

But when he had finished, the night still remained. With deliberate slowness, then, he went to the kitchen and drank glass after glass of bottled blood. It was cold, the taste was rancid, and soon he was glutted.

And as it had been in Lent or when the season was lean, when he would eat plain pottage until he could swallow no more and still feel a wild craving for the savour of meat, salt and spice, he hungered. And he continued to drink, drink until his stores were dry, until his skin took on a pink glow, until he sickened. And even then, even with his cheeks blushed and his heart racing, even with his lips smeared carmine, he ached for Sophia's blood, Sophia's skin, Sophia's scent.

He sank to the floor with his hands clenched to fists, and pressed his teeth so hard together that they ached.

And in the end, he rose and walked out into the night.

At first, she thought that it was a dream, something brought on by the alcohol. After all, she had been drifting, throat parched, whole body heavy in the slight fever of passing drunkenness. She had pressed her eyes closed, because if they were open the green glow of the alarm clock spun. She still felt the swaying but was unsure if it was the first giddy fingers of sleep or just a by-product of the vodka.

So when she realised that she was being watched, she decided that she was asleep. Her eyelids flickered as she toyed with the desire to see who it was in the corner of the room, but something between antic-ipation and fear held her still. Time slowed to a trickle as her breath grew shallow and the nausea, the whirling intoxication, began to sub-side. The figure was at the other side of the room, too far away to be anything but a shadow. She could feel its gaze as though its hands were laid upon her, holding her to the bed. A tiny part of her brain told her to struggle, but the effort seemed too great.

She sensed, rather than heard, the figure come towards her.

Her skin prickled cold and hot at once.

For most of her life, Sophia's senses had been disconnected from her dreaming self; her dreams were pictures, emotions, impressions, only sporadically accompanied by sounds. She felt a twinge of surprise as she realised that she could smell the figure who knelt beside her. It crept into her nostrils, a faint, familiar scent of dust overlaid by some-thing unpleasant, fleshy, almost rancid. Once again, she considered opening her eyes.

Something cold brushed along the upside of her arm, and it was tender. It came to rest over her wrist, light and chill. She struggled against the bewitchment of her apathy, trying to clear the drunk-enness from her mind. The cold touch encircled her wrist, turning her hand palm upwards, stroking the tendons and the arteries that lay beneath her skin. She felt a pressure, like the thumb of someone who was taking her pulse.

A hand, she realised, *it's a hand.* A bolt of fear shocked through her as she knew she was not dreaming. And the hand was still wrapped about her wrist.

She snapped her arm towards her chest, dragged herself backwards across the bed, tumbling into John's sleeping body. She opened her eyes. And stared straight into Julian's.

For a moment, a trick of the light made them seem red, but then she saw that they were all pupil, as reflective and black as a cat's in the darkness. He hissed, half-recoiled from her, his hand still stretching out towards her own. In the green glow of the alarm clock she could see into his mouth, could see the delicate curving fangs, all sharp incisors and long canines. Fear and sickness clawed in her throat. She scrabbled back against the headboard of the bed. He hesitated, still in his half-crouch beside her, his hand still reaching towards her. She saw his face…

'Fucking shit,' she breathed.

And that seemed to break the paralysis. Julian closed his mouth and shrank back into the darkness. Sophia gulped air into her lungs and shouted, 'Fuck. Fuck! Steven!' Then, louder, again and again, 'Help. Steven! Help!'

Consciousness came to Steven in a burst, his heart already pounding, the fear rushing liquid and sickening down his throat. For a while he did not know where he was, what it was that he was hearing, but it did not stop him stumbling from the sofa. It was not until he had lurched along the hall that fragments of memory shot into his mind, and he remembered that he had been drunk, that he was sleeping at Sophia's. None of it mattered. His only thought was the yelling in his mind: *Please, no. Not you. Not you as well.*

He had never, *never* heard Sophia sound like this.

His eyes were gritted with sleep, his dark hair matted and twisted, his mouth foul and dry and he did not stop to think as he slammed open the bedroom door and slapped his palm against the light switch. For a moment he was blind in the sudden glare. Then he saw.

Fixed in the flat, yellow light, there were three figures frozen in a tableau: a woman, two men. Horror and shock and violation.

I know this scene.

Steven blinked, trying to make it go away, trying to shake the world back to its proper shape, back to reality, to sense. *The moonlight was so bright that through the thick yellow blind the room was light enough to see. On the bed beside the window lay Jonathan Harker...* The words trotted on, familiar, sickening. Pushed half upright, John was staring out, eyes wide and lips pale. Beside him was Sophia, huddled – *kneeling on the near edge of the bed facing outwards...*

No. No. Her knees were drawn up to her chest, one fist resting against her collarbone as she clutched the duvet to her throat. Her face was white, very white, with high spots of red on her cheeks. Her mouth hung slightly open, stopped halfway through a scream, and she stared out in hatred, in terror, in fury. And there was a man in the middle of the room – *a tall, thin man, clad in black.*

Dracula, he found himself think. *The Count.*

Julian.

He could not mistake that long sweep of dark hair, those old-fashioned clothes. Steven slumped back against the wall, too tired, far too tired, and drunk as well. He began to laugh, high and thin, hysterical even. Yet he knew that, whatever was happening here, it was not funny.

The figure turned. Steven was not surprised to see the fangs in the mouth, the small, sharp points that had always been hidden by the lips. *Of course,* he thought, *what else would it be?* And his laughter continued to send spasms through his body, humourless and involuntary. Julian's usually immaculate clothes were disordered, his pale skin flushed, and there was a cold, unhealthy look to him. And, again, the teeth... *Well, of course,* Steven's mind repeated.

He propped himself against the wall, drawing in shaky, gasping breaths. All that time, Julian's eyes were on him. Nobody spoke.

Something. He knew that he should do something, but he was caught, all of them were caught like actors without a script.

How?

Steven tried to form the words, to look at Julian, to wring some reason from the scene, but there was none.

Sophia curled upon the bed, one hand cradling her wrist, stroking along the sinews with her thumb, pressing hard.

At last, after far too long, she spoke. And all she said was, 'You.'

'Yes.' Julian replied, his voice low.

Steven watched the slackness of her mouth, the way her thumb jabbed at that spot on her wrist, jabbed and jabbed. Her gaze did not falter. 'You've been – you've been doing this? To me?'

Hunched, Julian seemed small – smaller than Steven had ever imagined him to be. Without elegance or poise, he looked a young, young man with no hope left to him. And still so very beautiful.

This is wrong. Steven knew how he should feel, knew his part in this, in scenes like these. He should feel like an avenging angel, should be wielding a crucifix in one hand, a sharpened stake in the other. And Julian should be storming, gnashing his teeth like the villain in a melodrama. But there was none of that. No.

Instead, there was only Julian's quiet, empty voice saying, 'Yes, my dear,' and Sophia sobbing low.

In the books, Steven knew he would be charging forward, a soldier of righteousness, but he had no weapon and no faith. 'But...' The words died in his throat, ludicrous, improbable. 'Are you...? You're a vampire, aren't you?'

Julian lifted his head. Wide hazel eyes. No expression. 'When I was alive, we did not use that word.'

Something in Steven buckled. Nausea, drunkenness, exhaustion. He leaned hard against the wall.

'What. The. Fuck.' Coming when it did, John's voice seemed very loud. He had dragged himself to sitting, and stared at each of them in turn, demanding, almost begging for someone to explain. After a moment he repeated, 'What the *fuck?*'

This isn't... but Steven could not even finish the thought. He stared at Julian, and tried to understand how he had not seen it, how he had not known. *Because it isn't possible. Because it isn't real.*

'No,' he said to Julian, 'you're not. That's not...'

For a moment, it seemed as though Julian were about to reach out to him, about to place his hands on Steven's arms as he always did, as though he were about to wash the whole thing away in that embrace.

Steven felt his fists clench, his chest shaking with a sob.

'I was born in the fifteenth year of the second Richard's reign. And we did not use that word.' Silence. A white face without expression. A body that was too still to be human.

Sophia said, 'So it was you, wasn't it?'

'Yes.' And the tiredness in that voice was frightening.

Sophia nodded and did not look away. Steven did not understand.

'What?' John demanded. 'What was him?'

Still Sophia did not drop her gaze from Julian. 'The murders.'

Steven staggered, swallowing the vomit that rushed into his throat. He forced words past the knot in his chest, hearing them echo strangled, foreign, even insane: 'No. I… That's not… You… The…' He was gasping air, fighting for words, for breath, for some coherence in his mind. 'No. Lucy. You. It was you who…'

'Yes,' he heard the vampire say, 'it was.'

'No, no, no. That's not….'

'I could lie to you, if you would prefer that, Steven.'

And he stared into the vampire's lovely, expressionless face and he thought, *Yes. Yes. Lie to me.*

Then rage.

If there had been any weapon to hand, he would have seized it. He wanted something that could sear every trace and memory of this creature from his life and from his mind. But nothing, nothing in the world could do that.

Slumped against the wall, Steven choked on his sobs. 'You're a monster, you're a—'

'Yes.'

'What do you mean, "yes"? You kill people. I mean, you kill *people*.'

The vampire closed its eyes, pressed its thin, red lips tight. 'Yes,' it said.

'God, why? Why would you do that?'

The vampire raised one pale hand. 'It is what I am.'

'Fuck that. You don't have to. No one *has* to do that.'

And the vampire raised its head, looked into his eyes. 'Perhaps I do not.'

Six centuries, Steven thought, *six centuries of murder, and you do not die.* He shook his head, not wanting to face this, wanting to run now, but he could not leave. 'But,' his mouth started to move without his mind engaging, 'if you don't have to, if you don't need to... And Lucy. Why did you...?'

'Shut up now, Steven.' Sophia's voice was gentle. She was sitting at the head of the bed now. Beside her, John's face was wet, red and shining, but her eyes were dry and fixed upon the vampire. 'Julian. I need you to explain.'

The vampire's head was bowed, its body curled in on itself. It did not move.

'Julian?' Sophia said again.

'Your blood. Your blood. It is...' A silence. 'I am...'

Steven's chest gave a low, throbbing ache and he neither knew, nor wanted to know, what it might be.

'I trusted you.'

'Yes.'

'And you, and you've been coming here, and—'

'Yes.'

'And the fainting. That was—'

'Yes.'

Steven looked at Sophia and saw her mouth set in a thin, hard line, the steel fury burning against her composure. John was watching her too, his mouth slack and open.

'You killed Lucy.'

The vampire nodded, as if he could no longer speak.

'I trusted you. I thought...' And Steven watched as Sophia began to cry. John reached out to touch her arm, but she threw him off. It seemed at once as though she were not mere feet away, but somehow impossibly remote. 'You were killing me. God. Is this what you do? You lie and you...'

'I—'

'And all that crap. About how sorry you were, and your wife dying and… Was it all just lies? I mean, was she just someone else you killed?'

'No. With… with Eleanor I was not this thing I am now. Sophia, I have never wanted to lie to you, I…'

'But you're fine to murder me? Well?' She did not pause, did not give him time to respond. 'Because that's what you're doing, you know?'

'I never meant you harm. Any of you.'

'Didn't stop you, though, did it?'

Silence.

'Why, Julian? Why do any of this?'

At this, the vampire straightened a little, turned to face her, moved towards her half a step. 'I believe you know why, Sophia.'

She did not flinch. For a little while, neither of them spoke.

'Did you choose to become this? To be a…' When she reached that word, she stumbled, did not say it.

'I was very young, and I was very drunk. I have regretted it, since then. But I still live, so perhaps I do not regret it enough.'

Sophia rubbed her wrist with her thumb, as if she were not aware of the movement. It was an odd, uncomfortably private gesture.

Once more, Steven looked away.

When Sophia next spoke, her voice was low, so low that Steven thought he had misheard her: 'Do you not – did you not think of asking my permission?'

The vampire's voice was equally soft. 'You would have said no.'

'What?'

'You would have said no.'

'I had a right to say no.'

There was a long silence. Too long.

Steven looked up to see the vampire standing like a man facing the firing squad, his head high, his spine stiff.

'You, you…' Sophia's voice shook; her eyes shone brighter than Steven had ever seen them. 'Don't you realise? It's like *rape* if you don't ask me.'

And the vampire stumbled backwards as though physically hurt.

Sophia sat bolt upright upon the bed, face streaked by tears. Violated, furious, hurt as she was, there was something about her that was forceful, almost terrifying. Her expression was fixed, merciless. She did not drop her gaze and stared full into the vampire's face with the weight of her accusation.

Steven half-expected a hail of excuses, of pleas, of any kind of feeble self-defence, but the vampire only looked at the floor, all self-possession gone, shattered. 'There is nothing I can say. No excuse. I have… I have done you wrong. Do you wish me to leave?'

'Yes.'

The vampire bowed. 'I will not come near you again.' He inclined his head to the confused figure sitting beside her. 'Jonathan.'

And he turned to leave. Towards Steven.

In the vampire's face, Steven saw no trace of desperation or plea. It was as though there was nothing there, nothing at all. Shaking, Steven pushed himself up from the wall, his hands raised, sick with anger, betrayal, hate. He knew, somehow, were he to strike, scream, do anything, the vampire would make no move to stop him.

But the vampire looked into his eyes and said, in a tone as empty as his face, 'I am sorry to lose your friendship, Steven.'

And Steven stood aside.

For a long time, nothing. They were alone.

It was John who spoke first. 'Are we just going to – to let him go?'

Too numb, Steven did not respond.

'I mean, come on. He's a… a *vampire*. Aren't we meant to…'

Steven watched Sophia, who still stared at the place where Julian had been. She began to shake, then gasp, then seemed to crumple, huddling over herself with helpless sounds, as though the air jerking into her lungs was acid and strange. John reached out a hand to her, but she flinched away.

'He hurt Sophia,' John said. 'He kills people. He killed Lucy. I mean, shouldn't we… Shouldn't we at least…'

Exhausted beyond measure, Steven leaned his head against the wall. 'Shouldn't we what at least do what, John?'

In the novels and the films it was easy. A vampire: something evil, anathema to life. Something faceless and characterless that needed to be stamped out, destroyed. Steven tried to imagine a knife in his hand, a gun. Tried to feel the recoil in his arm, the yielding as the blade pierced flesh. He tried to think of looking into that face and watching the life leave it.

'He's *evil*. He's a monster. It's…'

Steven closed his eyes. He could still hear Sophia's dry, choking, awful sobs.

John's voice went on, 'I mean, he's a murderer. *The* murderer. Shouldn't we at tell the police, or…?'

Steven felt his legs fold beneath him. 'Do you want to call the police, John? Or shall I do it? Oh, yeah – hi? This serial killer you're looking for, turns out he's a friend of ours. Oh, and he's a vampire. What? No, officer, this isn't a prank call.'

'I didn't mean…'

'Then what did you mean? It's not like we have any proof.' His voice a monotone, Steven hunched on the floor, head against his knees. 'We haven't even got any evidence; I mean, he *told* us what he'd done. Why on earth would he tell them?'

'What is wrong with you? He's been at Sophia's blood!' John's outrage was thin, high, somehow false. 'We can't just let him… I mean, you know about this stuff. Couldn't we kill him or stake him or…'

Steven had an image of the pair of them, tooled up in the way that vampire hunters were in those films that no one had ever taken seriously. A dry bark of laughter escaped him, but he pressed it down and rubbed his eyes. 'He said he wouldn't come back.'

'You trust him?'

'Do we have a choice?'

Then he dragged himself to his feet and stumbled over to where Sophia lay crying into the bedclothes. He sank down to the floor beside the bed, and put his hand on her back, to comfort her. She flinched and curled even deeper into her huddle, so he took his hand away and let her cry. Leaning his head against the mattress, he tried to sleep, knowing that it would not come. Sick with alcohol and betrayal, he waited for morning and as he waited, the words ran uninvited through his mind: *Of this, I am sure: the sun rises today on no more miserable house in all the great round of its daily course.*

22. Wisdom and Knowledge

A new life! That was what he wanted. That was what he was waiting for.
Surely he had begun it already.
– Oscar Wilde, *The Picture of Dorian Gray*

It was light before Sophia stopped crying. Every hour or so, she thought she was done and her sobbing would die down. She would feel that she had no more tears, no more energy, nothing. Then something in her mind would move and a whole new wave of wretchedness would engulf her. She had never cried like this. Even after Lucy had died it had not been like this. It was as though all the futility of her life had descended on her in a great, immovable lump and she would never be done with it, because nothing in her life would ever have meaning again.

There was nothing she could think that did not make it worse, nothing which did not remind her of it. It was impossible, illogical. Yet, all along, he had been mocking her with the truth of it, a truth she had been too closed-minded to understand.

Now she was paying the price.

Steven and John hovered around, too shaken to leave. If anything, their presence made it worse. At nine in the morning, desolation still tearing through her, Sophia collapsed from exhaustion and she fell into a restless sleep.

When she woke, she lay miserable, crying sometimes until she slept again, and when she slept, her dreams were worse than they had ever been. Time meant nothing. After too many hours, it grew dark once more. More drifting, and eventually it grew light.

The next time she woke, the sun was streaming through the windows. John moved his hand towards her face but did not touch her. His voice was tentative as he asked if she wanted to talk.

'Why aren't you at work?' she asked.

'It's a Saturday, love.'

'Right.'

She went back to sleep.

These feelings could not last forever. Still, three, maybe four, nights passed until she woke from bad dreams in the blackness of a room that was empty except for John lying next to her. She saw things, then, with a clarity that terrified her. She could not make it all stop, so instead she would finish her degree. Then she would marry John and that would be that. Children and a mortgage and no funding for an MSc.

She tried not to remember Julian's face, the hunger, the rapture there. The fingers wrapped around her wrist, the teeth in his mouth sharp. A hard, abrasive knot felt as though it were being tugged from just below her heart up the narrow passage of her windpipe, tearing through the intimacy of her chest. Never – she had never seen anyone look that intense. Even when the sex had been great and she had thought they were in love, even when he came, John had never looked that intense.

The cut on her wrist stung in time to her beating heart and she began to shake. She tried to push away the image of him, the blackness of his eyes, but the memory was barbed. It clung.

Every word he had ever spoken to her was another little dart of treachery. If, that night, he had raged at her, behaved like the heartless, murdering bastard she knew him to be, she could have borne it.

But he had stood there with the pain written on his face, meeting her eyes with a dreadful, proud plea, and had refused to say a single word in his defence. If he had only made excuses, she could have accused him of deliberate lies, cowardice, more betrayal. Instead, he had asked if she wanted him to leave.

And she had said yes.

She closed her eyes and buried herself among the bedclothes. For years, she had believed her desire to escape from the mundane was a folly; that normality was all there was for her, for anyone. But now she saw that an alternative was real.

She remembered Julian's face.

The next morning, she got up, got on, functioned. There was a thin, grey bleakness in her heart, but she could ignore it. It was possible to survive. She even managed to be quite chatty and cheerful. The girls on her course didn't notice that there was anything wrong.

She soon stopped fainting, of course. And the insomnia returned. But Sophia knuckled down and cooked and studied as if nothing had happened, as if she had never even heard the name Julian

John became very protective, especially after dark. The first time she made the opening moves to have sex with him, he seemed disturbed, concerned. 'Are you sure you're up for this, love?'

'Of course.'

'But are you not—'

'It's fine, darling. We might as well try and get back to normal, right?'

'Right,' he had agreed, and then stopped. 'Are you sure everything's okay?'

She nearly laughed. It would not have helped had she told him that nothing was okay and nothing was ever going to be okay again, but that she could live with that for as long as need be. So she did not tell him; she just said, 'Oh, I'm fine. Really. Fine.'

Who cared, after all, if lying awake at night, robbed of those delicious, yielding dreams, she heard a kind of screaming in the back of her mind? If she felt a rush of godawfulness upon waking in the morning? She could ignore it. She could get on with things the way that they were meant to be.

She made only one mistake.

One day, when she was at Steven's flat, she asked him if she could borrow *Dracula*.

'Are you sure that's healthy?'

'Who cares about healthy?' she said without thinking. 'Have you got it?'

'Why do you want it, Sophia?'

'There's just this bit I want to read.'

'Which bit?'

She did not answer him; found that she could not meet his eyes.

'Sophia, which bit?'

'Forget about it.'

He took her hand, gripped her fingers until they hurt. 'Love, I know he hurt you, but—'

'I don't want to talk about this,' she said, her voice high, verging on hysteria.

'It won't help anything if you make this—'

'I *don't* want to talk about this. Forget it. Forget I said anything.'

In the end, she went to the library to get a copy of the book. She should have gone there first.

Locked in a carrel, she searched until she found it. With Mina, she went once more through the shame, the horror, of what had been done to her – the dreadful dawning of understanding. She traced the words, trying to put her own pain on to the text, to make what she had known more bearable.

Unclean, unclean.

But she envied Mina.

Mina had not known her violator, had not loved him. Not trusted him. In anger, she tore the book between her hands, ripping it down the spine, shredding the pages until she was surrounded by scraps of paper, printed here and there with words which struck her. Vampire. Evil. Love.

Love?

She hated him. If he stood before her again, she felt that she would kill him.

And she hated herself for feeling that way.

The aftertaste of his parents' morality clung in Steven's throat. He remembered too well what it was like to live in a world where evil lurked abroad, just waiting to seduce him, entrap him, make him sin. And, yes, he disowned that philosophy with every day he lived, out and proud.

But he was still a virgin.

It was as though he had known that if the world sent him a man who embodied his every desire, then that man would be killer, a demon, a ghoul. After all, it had been so obvious. He, of all people, should have seen through it, should not have fallen for that dreadful charm.

Sometimes, in the too-empty flat, he felt the temptation of surrendering to simple faith, would feel the urge to pray, but he would close his fists and clench them until his hands began to hurt.

It would be such a relief to say that Julian was a devil, no better than a beast. It would be so comforting. It was what the stories he'd heard all his life told him to do: call it evil and cast it out.

Like they had cast him out. His own voice, broken by tears and drunkenness, '*You're a monster ...*' He could still feel the words on his tongue, and he gagged on the taste of them.

The pressure of a hand on his arm, the touch of cool, sticky lips upon his cheek. '*I am sorry to lose your friendship, Steven.*'

He thought of Lucy, cremated, her ashes scattered on the site of one of their childhood dens. He thought of Sophia, and the desperate, vapid chatterer she seemed to have become. He remembered that night. *My friendship?*

Why had he not struck? Not as some godly crusader, but as one man to another, hurt and wronged? Why had he stood aside?

I believe you know why.

Even now, he could not help dreaming of Julian, could not stop his mind from following the old habit of dwelling on that face in the quiet night when sleep would not come. Oh, he might cry and hate himself, he might pinch his arms to bruises and pace around the flat, but he could not drive them away

A long winter of enchantment lay in ugly shards about him, broken by a truth so obvious, so impossible... But he, he of all people should have known.

Of course, it was worse for Sophia. She was the one who had been attacked, who needed his comfort, his sympathy, his care. But if it had been his own bed that Julian had stood beside, if Julian had said to him, '*I believe you know why, Steven...*'?

Friend.

The thing that had killed Lucy and walked away.

My friend?

That face, those feelings.

Friend?

April dragged. Sometimes, Sophia caught the echo of her own voice whispering, *I expected better of you.*

The harder she pushed it down, the more it cracked in upon the sunny display. She would feel it brush her, the tail end of a thought just beyond the reach of her conscious mind, small and troubling as a fly banging against a window, as a headache. *Is this it? Is this everything?*

Are you happy now?

And she would shake her head and bite her tongue and smile apologetically at the person she was really talking to, letting them know that her lapse of focus had nothing to do with them. Sometimes, it felt as though a scream was starting to swell in her chest.

The worst moments were when she was alone at the library, staring out at the night and knowing that, in forty minutes, John would call and offer to come and meet her and that she would accept the offer; because then, quiet and distinct, it would whisper, *Coward.*

If she tried to ignore it, it would whisper again, *Coward.*

So she would look away from the trite smile of her reflection in the library's windows and plough on with her coursework and keep her mind busy, in the trivial hope that she might yet scrape a 2:2 in spite of all the work she had missed. And she would hear the voice in her head calling her a coward, and she would see Julian's face in her mind.

She did not sleep. There were no landmarks, no feelings, nothing for which she could muster any enthusiasm – not uni, not Steven, certainly not John. She found herself forgetting the day or the time, turning up in the wrong places with the wrong things and crying helpless tears. One day, after trying to go to a lecture, and then, too late remembering that, no, it was the Easter holidays, that today she was meeting some girls from her course for coffee, she heard it again as she apologised for her scattiness and sat down, heard it tell her, *It makes no difference.*

The girls smiled and brushed aside the excuse, hardly pausing in their chatter. Sophia stared at her chipped and broken nails and realised she already knew exactly what they were going to say. It was the same old run: chat about television shows and boyfriends, cooking and habits, worries about finals and how behind they were on their dissertations. They would have said the same things had she remained outside the lecture theatre, waiting for a talk that had never been scheduled.

She did not speak. After a while, she registered that the girls were leaving. 'Are you okay?' one of them asked as she picked up her bag. 'You've been a bit quiet, you know?'

'Yeah. No. Tired.'

'God, same!' The girl flashed her a smile and buttoned up her coat. 'Are you not coming to the library, then?'

'Uh, no. Might head home, or....' She lost her train of thought.

'You sure you're okay?'

'I'm fine. Honestly. Fine.'

In the coffee shop, she leaned into a corner and heard snatches of other people's conversations. Mature students chatted about their children and their work, the ones her age about clubs and dates. They all talked about seminars, the same phrases on a loop – 'too hard', 'bit weird', 'nothing to say'... She had heard all of this a dozen times, a hundred, hundred times. She thought of years spent waiting here, the same conversations circling endlessly. Sickness seized her, and she laid her head against the table, not caring who was watching.

Julian had never been like that.

He had his routines – they had had their routines – but she had never known what he was going to say next. That was why she had always lent forward, keen to hear what he would say. Always, except that last night, when she had asked the one question that mattered: *'Did you not think of asking my permission?'*

And he had answered: *'You would have said no.'*

Dazed, nauseated, she began to walk home. What she was doing, she knew, was not living; it was continuing for no other reason than she did not know how to stop. But when had it been more than this? The question made her shift, made her turn away, but for once she would not be deterred. For once, she would tell herself the truth. When had things ever been more than this?

On those evenings with Julian. Of course, on those evenings with Julian.

And in the dreams.

Those dreams.

My dreams.

She hugged the memory of them to her chest, of how she had felt about them when they had been hers and hers alone, when she had not understood. *Slow, the beautiful pulsing of dark water around her, the delicious bewilderment of thick, white mist.* It had hurt, it had been terrifying, and in every moment she had been more alive than she had ever been. Julian had given her that.

He had forced it upon her.

'*You would have said no.*'

'*I had a right to say no.*'

Sophia ground her teeth. *Of course I would have said no.* Had she known him for a monster, for the man who had killed her friend, she would have left, run away, turned on him and clawed his eyes out...

But the memory of that slow darkness, that warm, sexual mist....

Before that night, drunk on his attention, she had hurled herself at him. Feeling noticed, understood, truly seen, she had let him come closer and closer still. Before that night, had he propositioned her, she would not even have thought about refusing.

But to have a monster drink her blood?

She should feel nothing but disgust at the thought. She tried, desperate to make herself feel it. She tried to forget the way she had almost prayed he would be able to explain, to excuse; that even now he would seek her again and beg her forgiveness so that she could feel his teeth slip into her veins.

But he had stood, cold and dignified: *You would have said no.*

You would have said no.

When she got home she threw the keys on to the coffee table in the living room. Then she paused, and picked them up again, rubbing the key with her thumb. She took twenty minutes to get changed. She left her phone, she left no note, and she left the house before it was dark.

It was late April. The evenings were growing mellow. It seemed strange to walk the city streets in the long shadows and golden light with no jumper or coat. She had grown so used to winter, to darkness. Had anyone asked her, she would not have been able to tell them where she was going. She did not quite dare ask herself what it was she was hoping to achieve.

When she reached the house, it was deserted. Boards had been nailed over the windows, the path was wide, winter-dead plants crushed where some kind of vehicle had been parked. The padlock was wrapped once more around the gate. Something in her gave a pang, and she could not convince herself that it was relief.

Even without a boost, it was not difficult to climb the gate. When the door did not open, she remembered Steven's advice and lifted it as she pushed. Inside, the portraits were gone, the furniture shrouded. It was as though an enchantment had been broken, as though the house had died once more.

He had gone.

Like a ghost, she drifted to the room where she had whiled away so many winter evenings. It appeared as though, halfway through packing up the house, he had lost patience. Her chair still sat by the hearth, as did his. The oak beam over the fireplace had been savaged, hacked and gouged by something that looked as if it could only have been a chisel. Splinters of wood the width of human fingernails coiled over the twisted wreck of the grate where the fire once burned. She knew the red substance dusting them was not rust. She remembered the pain that had twisted in his eyes as she had raged at him, and how he had stumbled.

He's gone, he's gone, he's gone, the words circled in her mind, in time with the beating of her heart; too fast. Shards of sunlight crept around the edges of the boards. Without the fire in the hearth, the room was cold. She shivered. Whatever she had been seeking, whatever answers, whatever doom, it was too late. She was far too late.

She sat down upon the floor and waited for the sun to go down.

Early evening sunlight seeped its way around Steven's curtains, giving his bedroom a dim illumination. The stiff spring breeze stirred them, making patterns of light shift on his ceiling; he stared at them blankly. Because he was a literature student, the words 'April is the cruellest month' traipsed through his head. He could not sleep.

To be honest, it was too early to sleep. Lately, he had been finding that, when he got back from uni or the shop, his eyes were burning from the fluorescent lights or the small, close print of his course texts. In the past, he would have ignored it, ploughed on through the migraine by reading something that was friendly and familiar. But it seemed as though all his favourite books were in the box under his bed, the box he had taped shut the day that Sophia had asked to borrow *Dracula*.

It was not that he did not try; most nights, he still fished a book out of his bag but he found himself scanning the same page, over and over, taking in precisely nothing. So he would eat his dinner alone, and make himself a cup of tea, and go to bed.

And, lying there, not sleeping, his mind would wander; Julian, standing in the middle of Sophia's room, his mouth filled with sharp teeth; Lucy, broken and lifeless.

'The fifteenth year of the second Richard's reign.' The words were a dull echo, a low drumbeat in the back of his mind. 1392. Six hundred and fourteen years. And Lucy had been twenty. Then, unbidden, Van Helsing's words: *Why was it that Methuselah lived nine hundred years, and 'Old Parr' one hundred and sixty-nine, and yet that poor Lucy, with four men's blood in her poor veins, could not live even one day?*

One day.

Steven remembered that night, showing off, flirting with her killer. One day.

If he had been able to know that night, been given that one day, then what? Perhaps he could not, like the good Doctor, claim that he would have been able to save her, but could he not have said something, done something that would have meant she did not try to walk home alone?

And damn some other innocent?

As ever, Steven flinched. And as ever, he thought, *Yes. Fine. Anyone but Lucy.*

He rolled on to his stomach, trying to squirm away from that cruel word. *Anyone.* He closed his eyes and clenched his fists and wished the world would go away.

That was when the banging started on the door to the flat. It was not the tentative tap of a friend or a neighbour, nor the peremptory summons of someone who did that for a living – a postman, a gas-man, perhaps. It was loud and frantic and insistent. Steven felt his heart catch and hammer in time to the knocks on the door. *Not you,* he thought again, *not you as well.*

It was John and the first thing he said was, 'Is she here?'

'What? No. No, she's not. What's happened?'

'Has she been here?'

'Today? No, I've not seen her today.'

John's look was fierce and fearful. *Desperation.*

'What's happened?'

'Bastard. That bastard – he's... oh fuck. Fuck fuck fuck.' John started to cry, a low, desperate sobbing.

'Hang on. Hang on a moment. Are you saying that Julian...?'

'Yeah. *Julian.*' Steven had never heard a name pronounced with so much hatred. Yet, despite his anger, John looked like a child, tired and upset and struggling to keep a brave face on things. Steven wondered if he should offer some kind of comfort. 'Whatever the hell he's called. That bastard, that *fucker* has done something to Sophia and she's not at home and...'

Steven gave a decisive nod and checked his watch. It was only just past seven. 'Okay. Was there any sign of a struggle?'

John shook his head.

'Right. Just calm down for a second, John. What exactly happened?'

'I got home. And she wasn't there.'

'Right.'

'I mean... She knows I worry about her. Since... you know. But there wasn't a note. Not anything. And her phone. She knows I want to call her. Just to—'

'So, there's no reason she couldn't be at uni?'

'I didn't come straight here. I'm not an idiot.'

Steven's mouth opened of its own accord, but he caught himself. 'Alright. Where have you checked?'

'Uni. The library. Couple of places in town. I called one of her classmates, but they've not see her since... Look, she's gone, alright?'

Steven thought of level crossings, road bridges, canals. 'Okay, okay. Right. Are you sure there was no note?'

'Yeah.'

'What did she take with her?'

'Nothing.'

'*Nothing?*'

'Not her coat. Not her phone, not her bag. Not...' John stopped as though he was remembering something. 'Earrings. She... The box was gone. She kept them on the desk, by the computer and...' John's voice trailed away, as though he sensed Steven's own confusion. 'The ones you got her.'

Steven shook his head.

'For Christmas. The bats.'

'Not me.' *Earrings?* 'Sophia didn't... Sophia doesn't wear earrings.' But he recalled a memory, of little gold ear-bobs shining against Sophia's black hair – and of Lucy being evasive about them. *The party. The night that Lucy...*

No.

Why did she tell John that I'd...?

This was all irrelevant. 'But just those, then? No money? An overnight bag?'

'No.'

'John, look, are you certain that Julian took her?'

'Who else?'

Steven shook his head. 'I don't think anybody...' He swallowed hard. 'Have you thought about calling the police, about getting their help?'

'Yeah. They said they can't, not till tomorrow. And that's too late.'

Steven wondered what he'd said to them, how he had phrased it. 'So, you think it's Julian. What are you suggesting we do now? I mean, storm up there with stakes and autopsy knives and bunches of garlic flowers?'

'I'm not stupid, you know,' John said to the floor.

Steven said nothing.

'I just... You know about this stuff. You'd know how to...?'

'How to what? Look, I don't have any ancient, mystical tomes. I've got a handful of paperbacks. And...' There was something painful and breathless in his chest. 'And they're just stories, John. That's all. They're... books. Fiction. I don't know. I don't know anything about him – what he is or what can kill him or...' He stopped, the words catching on his tongue.

'He's got Sophia.'

'We don't know that, either.'

'And he killed Lucy.'

Steven flinched. 'Alright. Alright. We'll go up to the house. We'll see... If there's anything there, then we'll... I don't know. But we'll see.'

He came, as some part of her had always known he would come. His boots made no sound on the cold dust of the floors, but her spine prickled as she felt him watch her, and she looked at him.

He no longer appeared even remotely human. His hair was a limp straggle streaked with grey and white. His skin had turned the dirty yellow of old, brittle parchment and it seemed to have shrunk over those fine, pale bones. Dried out he seemed, desiccated. His lips were pale, drawn tight and thin over swollen feral teeth; teeth that belonged to a cat, not a man. His eyes were wide, the pupils tiny slits. She stood and faced the monster that she had come to seek.

There was no way, no possible way that such a hollow corpse, such a withered death's head should be able to move or speak, but he came towards her and his voice was hardly more than a whisper. 'Sophia. You must leave. Now.'

She shook her head and stared into that dreadful face. 'I'm not going anywhere.'

The muscles in his jaw bulged and knotted as he clenched his mouth shut. 'Please. Whilst I...' A dry gasp rattled down his shrivelled throat. 'Why do you not leave?'

She saw the struggle in him, the clenched fists and the grotesque bunching of the muscles beneath his skin and she laughed as she echoed him, 'Oh, I believe you know why, Julian.'

She caught a flash of something like anger cross his face and, for a moment, it seemed that he rushed towards her, but she blinked and he was standing back, across the room, opening and closing his fists, pressing those thin, dry lips together. He gave a hard, sobbing sound. His eyes were opened wide, wider than she had thought possible, and she saw the rim of white around the irises. As though he did not know what he was doing, he walked towards her.

'Sophia, I beg you. You *must* leave.' But already, he was circling her, in the way that she had heard big cats will circle their prey. She watched the teeth in his mouth swell and stretch, becoming again the long fangs she had seen in her room. Warmth flowered between her legs. 'You do not, you cannot understand the danger here.'

He looked ready to spring, the need, the hunger in him burning towards her. She could see his fists unclench, the hands curl, see his lips part as though he were waiting to tear the heart from her, to devour her with more passion that her body could ever endure, and she smiled wider than she had smiled since long before that night. A star-bright elation was burning in her, dangerous and violent as lightning.

'No. No, *you* don't understand. I know exactly what I'm doing. *And I don't care.*'

23. The Going Down of the Sun

'Kiss me again; and don't let me see your eyes! I forgive what you have done to me. I love my murderer – but yours! How can I?'
– Emily Brontë, *Wuthering Heights*

It was still light when they crossed the city – the thin, cold evening light of late spring. As they walked, John seemed unable to stop clenching his fists, muttering under his breath and swearing. For the most part, Steven went ahead to avoid the constant low murmur of, 'Bastard. That bastard.'

Sophia had not been kidnapped. They had gone to the flat first, and he had seen it – the tidiness, the signs of a quick change, the earrings taken and the note not left. There were a hundred places in the city she might have gone, and whatever she was doing, it was deliberate.

Even if she had gone to Julian, it was pointless to try and stop her. But still...

Still...

A memory surfaced from years before, from when he had still been a Christian, of the New Testament injunction to turn the other cheek. The way that, even when dying on the cross, Jesus had cried, *Father, forgive them, they know not what they do.*

To kill Julian...

But if I had been there, the night that Lucy died...

If I had been there...

He shook his head to clear away the thoughts.

And what did I do that night, in Sophia's room? Steven had no gun, no kukri knife, no communion wafer, no sacred host. He had nothing to bring to the fray. If Julian truly threatened Sophia then he would... what?

Yet he continued to walk across the city.

They reached the house as the sun was beginning to set. The place was boarded up, closed off once more, a perfect picture of desolation, of abandonment. He leaned against the fence, waiting for John to join him, remembering how he had fixated upon the place, how he had once felt a rush of pleasure at the mere sight of it. The main gate was a dark silhouette, rusting and ornate. He had been here in his mind so many times, dressing it up in fictions.

Above him, small, sharp clouds were edged with gold against the mournful blue of dusk. A chill skimmed his skin. He exhaled.

When John approached, he turned. The chain was once more snaked around the bars, fastened with a padlock. Steven tugged at it and it did not give. Relief washed through him like the warmth of indoors after a walk in the cold. 'It's locked. I suppose he's moved away again.'

John elbowed him out of the way. 'He can't, I...' The clanking noise as he yanked on the gate was harsh and discordant in the quiet evening. When it was clear that this would not work, John gave the frame a kick. 'He's still in there. I *know* he's in there. C'mon.'

'Come on, where? It's empty, John. He's left. Sophia's not here.'

'He might still be in there. Look. We climbed these gates before, it's not...'

'John,' he said, taking his arm, 'let's go.'

'But what if he's not gone? What if he's got Sophia in there?'

If Sophia had come here, if that were her choice...

Steven pushed hard against the gate, felt it creak away from him, slump on its hinges. Lucy, he knew, would have swallowed her shame, her fear. If there had been even the slightest chance that Sophia were in there, Lucy would have climbed the gate. He could almost see her, strong and blonde as she clambered up the arches and curlicues of the wrought iron. 'Piece of cake,' she'd say. 'I'll just take a quick shufti and then we'll check out somewhere sensible.' Her voice was a ghost on the evening's breeze. The clanking of the gates – *'Shit. Ripped my sodding jeans... Lay on, MacDuff...'*

He pulled himself to standing. 'Come on, John. This place is empty. Let's try again at home.'

It was the anticipation of a touch that woke her.

She could feel it, a hairsbreadth away from brushing her lips, sense the cold of it and knew that, when it came, it would be like the kiss of a snowflake. She knew, when it came, she would catch the fingers into her mouth and then it would begin again, the ebb and flow of it, the tangling of lips and bodies, teeth and tongues. Half-dreaming as she was, she yearned towards the touch and felt expectation shiver from her bloody mouth to the raw, sated wetness between her thighs.

But the touch did not come. Sophia struggled towards it, but it was not there, so she fell back, seeking another door to that blissful oblivion, reaching for the slow confusion of compelling dreams. It was then that the pain began to spread in her shoulder, an aching, a burn of muscles that bunched and clung and were somehow wrong. She tried to flinch from it, but it moved with her, twisting her whole neck, her jaw with bolts of agony. She gave a sound halfway between a moan and a gasp and opened her eyes.

A bed. An old four-poster thing, with the drapes drawn around her. She did not remember a bed.

Then she noticed that she was cold. She was lying on top of the sheets and she was naked, or mostly so. Another few moments passed and she knew that she was awake, that she was alive.

She had not expected to be alive.

That was when the memories came back to her, and with them came all the little pains that had been swallowed up by the one in her shoulder. Her whole skin throbbing as though she had been scored and scratched with a thousand pins. Her body brutalised; her lips, her nipples, even her labia. There were bruises, too. And her shoulder...

She craned her neck to look at it, saw the open mess of black-red that oozed from it, that stiffened the sheets around her. *Blood,* she thought, *my blood.* It was then the faintness came. She closed her eyes and felt the blurred nothingness of it reach up to take her. The sensation was so familiar, so delectable that she felt herself exhale, relax into the waves of it. *Of course.*

Her breathing calm and deep, her eyes still clouded, she surrendered to bashful, gloating memory.

It was like it had been over a year ago, after a weekend of good sex, when she would lie in bed and take stock of each minor bruise, each love bite, every soreness and pulled muscle and patch of carpet burn. Like that, except her skin seemed to crackle and burn with the sharp-edged thrill of it, her nipples stood hard clenched and erect, and she knew, *knew* she was not done.

Julian, she thought, and smiled, biting sore and swollen lips. She wanted him to come back, wanted to make him come back so that she could feel those lips and those teeth and those hands and not have to think anymore. She opened her eyes.

He was not there.

Sophia sat up. The pain in her shoulder flared a dull torment through her sinews and bones. Her vision turned grey, then black. She clenched her eyes shut while the sickening buzz of it hammered through her skull, waiting until she could make sense of things again; the cold solidity of the headboard against her back, the open welts of the scratches there.

She opened her eyes.

The bed was empty.

On three sides, the drapes blocked out the room and she sat propped upon the fourth. He was not there. Cold desperation shivered its way to her core. She was alive.

'No. No, no, no.' There was no way in hell that she could be alive. No way that she could have endured that embrace, no way that either of them could have left it...

...alive. She was alive.

Even his kisses could have killed her. She remembered that, remembered clinging to him as his teeth tore and split her lips, remembered tasting her own blood on his tongue and the pleasure had pounded through her like a lightning strike, and she had struggled, drawn back because she needed to breathe. And he had held her firm. Then, in the terror and the rapture of it all, she had felt her body clench and unfurl with a liquid yielding that soaked down her thighs, through her jeans, up her spine, and she had moaned and whimpered her way through it, knowing she could come from a kiss, could die from a kiss because he did not need to breathe and he would not let her go.

Would not...

She pressed her lips together and fought tears.

He had let her go. She was free. Free to go back to university, to Steven. Even to John. If she could only pretend this had never happened, then that world would take her back without a second glance. She could continue with her life.

What life? For all that was dust and ashes now, broken friendships and lost love. It was Julian who had destroyed it, tearing through it all with the force of a nightmare, a dream.

She could blame him for that, lay it all it his door. Sophia's head slumped against the wood of the headboard.

No.

It was all still there; marriage and children and a career. It was the clear, the obvious future. It had driven her to him. Tonight, yes, seeking his fatal kisses and blissful cruelty, but in the beginning as well, when it was all social play and flirtation, when the waking world and its indifference had not been enough; when she had hungered for dreams, however deadly.

Choices, the whole thing was a matter of choices.

And like all of his kind, she thought, tasting the blood on her mouth, *he needs to be invited in.*

'Julian?' she said, and her voice trembled as she spoke.

Acknowledgements

This book would not be in your hands without the help, support and belief of a lot of people. My heartfelt thanks go to every single supporter listed here.

To my families of blood and choice, unending gratitude. To Betty and Rob Earl, for giving me M. R. James, the Medieval and Early Modern, as well as their unstinting love. To Jemma Hill (partner in crime) and Edith Earl (always and for everything). To the Sprogs for being no help at all, and loved all the more for it. And to Bill and Ann for lifelong support, inspiration, *Lost Souls, The Lady of the Shroud* and setting me on this path.

I lay laurels at the feet of those brave early readers, Michael Crouch and Michael Gordon, Delyth Warlow, Victor Sage and Betty Earl again. Such accolades also go to Die Booth and Chris Farnell for all their help, and being the talented gentlemen of letters they are. I can never repay Jane Casey for not only providing hope when all was lost, but also giving me the best advice a writer has ever had.

Please join me in raising a glass to the good people of the Norwich Waterstones Book Club, especially to Debra Chapman and Claire Wade. (I suppose it's too late to warn you about Chapter 14.)

To the good people of Twitter, especially Chris Stagg of Phoenix FM, who has proved this novel's champion and a true friend of the night. Twitter is also where I found Shawn Standfast, Kiz Bruce, Ray Plummer and Kir Maier – whose friendship, moral support and cheerleading were invaluable.

This novel could not have been written without the fine city of Norwich, Maidstone Museum, or the music of Tom Waits. *I* could not have written it without the stalwart Dracularians: Katie Dyann Nadler, Erika Haase, Alandra Hileman, Mobeena Khan, Geoffery Sperl, Anna Strauss, Carlotta, and most importantly Michael Gordon (who writes as Ben Goram) for bringing us all together under the guise of @DraculaBites. You actually get my jokes – I couldn't love you more.

To the unholy trinity of Bram, Mary and Montague, my love and reverence. But also to Angela Carter, Oscar Wilde, Poppy Z. Brite, Kim Newman, Robin Jarvis, Sheridan Le Fanu, and Shirley Jackson – it is an honour to write in the same genre as you.

A great debt is owed to the NaNoWriMo forums for support, encouragement and the answers to my increasingly specific questions on blood (all mistakes my own) as I figured out how to make it all work.

Thanks must also go to the Maryle Cat for her gracious cameo in Chapter eight, and the delightful events that inspired it.

To everyone who has let me borrow tics, traits and mannerisms, thank you, especially Mr Eoghan Laverey, who has demonstrated repeatedly how one person can nurse a single glass of wine all evening without *anyone* noticing.

Enormous kudos to everyone at Unbound, with special mention of Scott Pack, who not only helped me kick *Time's Fool* into an acceptable shape, but also took a chance on my 'slightly queer homage to Dracula' in the first place. If this novel is readable, it's due to Sue Lascelles, who also caught some truly mortifying errors. Really, thank you.

And, at the last, as well as at the very start, there has been Mattie. Your selfless encouragement, tactless criticism, skills as a sounding board and willingness to provide *so much tea,* are irreplaceable and valued beyond the riches of this world. All along, they have believed in a version of this book and this writer which are perhaps better than they could ever be in reality. My love, my life, this one is for you.

Patrons

Autumnpsyche ☽
Margaret Aldridge
Eli Allison
Steve Altman
Patricia Anabel
C. Baker
Ali Baker
Deb Bee
David A Bell
Maggie Bent
Rachel Birkbeck
Rachel Blank
Jessica Blank
Femke Bolle
Selina Bonelli
Die Booth
Lucy Brady
Elfrede Brambley-Crawshaw
Catherine Breslin
Kiera Bruce
Irene Butler
Dinah Butler
Sarah Carter
Matthew Cavanagh
Elaine Chambers
Debra Chapman
Francis Colvin
Andy Cooper
Janet Crawford
Michael Crouch
Gaudi Daamen
Rachael de Moravia

Kristen Dorcey-Joyce
Katie Dyann Nadler
Arthur Earl
Betty & Robert Earl
Edith Earl
Michael Ellis
Stevie Elsdon
Cath Evans
Pamela Evans
Jack Evans
Chris Farnell
Alice Field
Fiona Fitzsimmons
Rhiannon Flood
Nick French
Ian Giles
Susan Godfrey
Jennifer Golding
Sean Gomez
Michael "@DraculaBites" Gordon
Jon Greenaway
Eamonn Griffin
Lisa Griffin
Suz Groves
Jon Grunewald
Kate Hawes
He110Ne0 He110Ne0
Caroline Hewett
Alandra Hileman
Vic Hill
Jemma Hill
Anne Hodgson
Paul Holbrook
Matt Hood
Josephine Horne
Jordan Huby

Some Idiot
Colin Jackson
Cet Jarvis
Alison Jayne
SM Jenkin
Samir Jeraj
Marjorie Johns
Emrys Jones
Tabitha Julian Cromarty
K.T. Katzmann
Aisha Khalaf
Mobeena Khan
Dan Kieran
Patrick Kincaid
Shona Kinsella
Rob Kinsman
Julia Kruk
Karina Larsen
Naomi Last
Eoghan Lavery
Ewan Lawrie
joni lawton
Cliff & Gill Leftwich
Bill & Ann Lewis
Erika Lind
Ruth M-J
Seamus MacPherson
Kir Maier
Ruth Makoff
Jo Masterson
Graham Mawdsley
Kate Maxwell
Ellen McAteer
Nick Mellish
Katheryn Metenosky
Ali Miners

Cherry Mitchell
John Mitchinson
Simon Monaghan
Alex Morey
Dave Morris
Amy Morrison
Stephen Mosley
Edward Mynors
Lee Nair
Carlo Navato
Harri Neal
Emily Newman
Willow Nicholson
Jess Nixon
Alice Nuttall
Michael O'Connor
Karen O'Sullivan
Ozzy
Scott Pack
Edd Payne
Debbie Phillips
Jennifer Pierce
Rachel Plummer
Justin Pollard
Julia Pope
Phillip Prentice
Ann Quayle
Helen Riches
Deborah Roberts
Robotophile Robotophile
Cat Rocks
Ruby
Lauren Scott
Nina Seale
Robert Selth
Laura Shepperson-Smith

Casper Shone
Heather Smith
John P. Soto III
Geoffrey Sperl
Christopher Stagg
Shawn Standfast
Isabella Streffen
Ciaran Sundstrem
Jaz Tarrant
Mike Scott Thomson
Matthew Tucker
Ruth Tucker
Mattie Tucker
Michael Tucker
Paula Tucker
Lisa Twining Taylor
Erik Tyler
Tom van Halen
Mark Vent
Claire Wade
Claire Walker
Paul Watson
Hayley Webster
Derek Wilson
Preston Wilson